Praise for Christine Feehan's Leopard Novels

"Punctuated with plenty of danger and delicious tension. . . . A wild ride with a sizzling, passionate romance at its heart."
—BookPage

"Leopards at their steamy, captivating best." —Fresh Fiction

"The premise is raw and gritty; the romance is spirited and provocative; the characters are flawed, colorful and energetic."
—The Reading Café

"Heart-stopping action. Crazy sexy-time scenes. Tender emotions. . . . [A] little bit of something for everyone who enjoys a solid paranormal romance." —Harlequin Junkie

"With a Feehan novel you know you will get well-developed characters and an engaging plot, so when you add a dose of sizzling sexuality, you have an unbeatable mix." —RT Book Reviews

"A bloody good time." —I Smell Sheep

"Heady, passionate, seductive. . . . Ms. Feehan does a fantastic job of building up to the climax for a smashing finale that leaves you breathless and satisfied." —Smexy Books

"Readers . . . will be seduced by this erotic adventure."
—*Publishers Weekly*

"Another wild ride. . . . Enter the lair of the shapeshifters."
—Romance Reviews Today

"A passionate, jam-packed adventure." —Fallen Angel Reviews

"The passion runs high and the sex is hot!"
—The Romance Readers Connection

"A phenomenal story. . . . Christine Feehan knows how to weave a tale of action, suspense and paranormal passion that has earned her so many fans and k

The Carpathian Novels

DARK WHISPER

DARK TAROT

DARK SONG

DARK ILLUSION

DARK SENTINEL

DARK LEGACY

DARK CAROUSEL

DARK PROMISES

DARK GHOST

DARK BLOOD

DARK WOLF

DARK LYCAN

DARK STORM

DARK PREDATOR

DARK PERIL

DARK SLAYER

DARK CURSE

DARK HUNGER

DARK POSSESSION

DARK CELEBRATION

DARK DEMON

DARK SECRET

DARK DESTINY

DARK MELODY

DARK SYMPHONY

DARK GUARDIAN

DARK LEGEND

DARK FIRE

DARK CHALLENGE

DARK MAGIC

DARK GOLD

DARK DESIRE

DARK PRINCE

Anthologies

EDGE OF DARKNESS
(with Maggie Shayne and Lori Herter)

DARKEST AT DAWN
(includes Dark Hunger *and* Dark Secret*)*

SEA STORM
(includes Magic in the Wind *and* Oceans of Fire*)*

FEVER
(includes The Awakening *and* Wild Rain*)*

FANTASY
(with Emma Holly, Sabrina Jeffries, and Elda Minger)

LOVER BEWARE
(with Fiona Brand, Katherine Sutcliffe, and Eileen Wilks)

HOT BLOODED
(with Maggie Shayne, Emma Holly, and Angela Knight)

Specials

DARK CRIME

THE AWAKENING

DARK HUNGER

MAGIC IN THE WIND

RED ON THE RIVER

MURDER AT SUNRISE LAKE

LEOPARD'S SCAR

CHRISTINE FEEHAN

BERKLEY ROMANCE
New York

BERKLEY ROMANCE
Published by Berkley
An imprint of Penguin Random House LLC
penguinrandomhouse.com

ISBN: 9780593439197

First Edition: November 2022

Printed in the United States of America
1   3   5   7   9   10   8   6   4   2

For Susan

For My Readers

Be sure to go to christinefeehan.com/members/ to sign up for my private book announcement list and download the free ebook of *Dark Desserts*. Join my community and get firsthand news, enter the book discussions, ask your questions and chat with me. Please feel free to email me at christine@christinefeehan.com. I would love to hear from you.

Acknowledgments

Thank you to Diane Trudeau. I would never have been able to get this book written under such circumstances. Shylah Sparks-Diehl for taking all the work off me while I got this done. Brian Feehan for making certain he was here every day to set up the pages I needed to write in order to hit the deadline. Denise for handling all the details of every aspect of my life, which was so crazy. Thank all of you so very much!!!

When my son-in-law first met my daughter, he began calling her his lotus blossom. He's a hardworking man, but very artistic with a poet's soul. I always loved the way he looked at her when he called her lotus blossom. It was his way of expressing his love. I gave that to Gedeon because he had no other way of expressing his growing love to Meiling or admitting his feelings aloud.

LEOPARD'S
SCAR

1

MEILING Chang stared in horror at the dead bodies in the open grave, dumped as if they were so much garbage. Five women. One was her cousin, her last relative on earth. She'd been too late tracking her. By how long? By the look of her, Libby had endured far too much before her life had been ended.

Meiling crouched at the edge of the mass grave, ignoring the black swarms of flies, beetles and maggots that fed in abundance on the bodies. Ants teemed over them. Overhead, large birds circled, some already sitting in the trees, beady eyes staring at the bodies, all too ready to pick them clean. The jungle was prepared to take care of business.

She wanted to scream in outrage until her vocal cords were shredded. Inside, where no one would ever hear or know, that was exactly what she did. She remained silent and small, huddled there in the shadows where it would take extraordinary vision for anyone to see her.

Her fists clenched helplessly on her thighs. She didn't move them, even when she wanted to pound them. Feel pain. Make it real. Drive the pain deep and brand it forever in her bones the way it was in her heart and soul. She didn't dare move. She was surrounded by the enemy. There were thirty of them and one of her.

She was so silly. Stupid. Just say it. She was a misfit. She didn't belong. Not anywhere. She had heard it from birth, and this proved it. She should be in that grave, not Libby, not her beautiful cousin. Libby was a golden swan. Tall and elegant. She moved like a summer breeze. Her hair was a golden waterfall of sleek silk. She could talk to anyone and charm them instantly. How could her life end by being thrown into a pit in the middle of the jungle? It made no sense. None of this made any sense. Why hadn't Libby listened to her just one time?

Grief stabbed at her. Along with it came the deep-down need for vengeance. She burned with terrible emotion. No matter how hard she tried to push it away, grief stabbed at her like ice picks, demanding retaliation. She had one pistol. She wasn't certain the damn thing actually worked. Thirty against one. She didn't even have thirty bullets.

She couldn't just go away and leave the other women in those dirty little huts she'd discovered, not now that she knew what was happening to them. But what could she do? She waited, trying not to breathe in the smell of rotting flesh and decay until the men patrolling around the third hut went away. When they did, she eased back into the foliage. Giant green leaves resembling elephant ears covered her body. She crawled through the thick stems, wincing as the prickly stalks stuck in her skin.

The huts were a good distance from one another. The youngest girls were kept in filthy conditions in a make-shift, nearly see-through hovel that appeared to have been hastily thrown up at the last minute to shelter them. It was mostly made up of leftover boards from the other two cabins

built for the young women. One held four women. They
appeared to be in their early twenties. The second cabin,
the one Libby had most likely occupied, held five women
or girls in it. All were chained to beds and appeared to
be drugged. They were anywhere from twenty to sixteen
years old.

The huts were each about a mile apart, most likely so
the women knew nothing about the others. They were always kept isolated, drugged and chained. There was no hope
of escape from their dreadful situation. Most of them accepted their fate. A few, like Libby, fought it and eventually died or were killed by the men who had taken them.
They were a ragged lot, and no one knew where they were.
The moment someone came looking, either they were
moved, or they were killed and buried in a mass grave no
one would find. Either way, those making their money off
them would never be caught or punished.

Meiling had seen it happen so many times. In her land,
in her neighboring land, the power had always shifted to
the corrupt males, those willing to commit violence in
order to get their way. She moved to a vantage point above
the first hut, where the twenty-year-old women were kept.
If she could somehow manage to free them first and enlist
their aid, she might have a chance to free the youngest ones
in the third hut before tackling the teens.

She wiped the beads of sweat from her face. The sweat
was trickling down her throat into the valley between her
breasts, which was quite a feat since she was extremely
slender. She wanted to laugh, but she knew that was hys-
teria and she refused to give in to it. The heat, the insects
and losing Libby had created a kind of surreal effect she
was trying to stave off.

It took her a good half hour to work up the courage to
move down the slope and get close enough to the small
cabin to be able to count how many of the enemy she would
have to contend with. Eight. Eight men coming in and out,

laughing and talking in low voices. One was angry, zip-ping up his trousers and complaining to another, who seemed to be in charge. That man strode into the cabin with an attitude of resignation.

The walls were thin with large cracks in them. There was a small porch. The men smoked. Two drank and passed flasks to the others. Two others she hadn't seen before came out of the jungle with dogs and stood for a few minutes smoking with the others.

Mei ling was grateful for the large plants that grew right up to the hut. Her small body was easy to conceal in the foliage. Fortunately, with the men smoking and the wind blowing in the opposite direction, the dogs didn't catch her scent. She had sprayed her body with a special chemical that was supposed to keep her own scent from leaking out, but she didn't know how effective it really was.

Suddenly the sound of voices could be heard coming from the cabin. A man sounding angry. "What do I have to do, babe? He was upset, wanted his money back, and I had to give him a fucking refund. You give the best damn blow jobs in the world, and I have to give the man his money back?"

"But Vahn, this wasn't supposed to be real. We were playing out a fantasy, between the two of us." The wom-an's voice was low, and she sounded on the verge of tears.

"You love it, Bess, admit it. It's your fantasy come true. You love having men beg you for it. You're the best and you know it. You have them eating out of your hand. I did everything you wanted. I brought your friends here. They aren't so high and mighty and they sure as hell aren't any-where as good at this as you are."

There was a short silence. It sounded as though he was kissing her. "They aren't very nice to me."

"Who isn't nice to you, babe? I'll beat the holy hell out of her."

"I don't want you to do that. Then she can't work and the rest of us have to work more."

"That's true. How 'bout this. You tell me who's being mean to you, and when I spot a customer who is going to be an asshole, I'll give him to her. He can treat her like shit, and she'll deserve it for the way she treats you."

"Patti," Bess said instantly. "Patti is always mean."

There was a murmur of protest among the women, but they stopped abruptly when Vahn spoke.

"I can arrange for several nasty customers."

Someone—Meiling presumed it was Patti—began to weep softly.

"Okay, babe, the next time I send you a customer, you treat him good, you hear me? I owe money and you're paying that debt off for me, just like we talked about. That was the fantasy and that was what we agreed on."

"Yes, Vahn. I will. I'm sorry. I just need you to come in and see me once in a while so I remember why I'm here. Tell me you love me."

"I do, Bess. You know I love you."

There was another long silence.

More kissing, Meiling supposed. That was perfect manipulation on Vahn's part. Bess was so certain he loved her and they would live happily ever after. There wouldn't be a happy ever after. Vahn would kill her or sell her after he was finished with her. He most likely had another woman or teen in the other cabin as well.

Having a conspirator in the cabin made things even more difficult. That meant Bess would warn Vahn and even fight for him if Meiling managed to sneak into the hut to free the women from the chains. If he had someone in the second cabin, that girl would do the same. Meiling's head was beginning to pound.

The sound of an engine approaching broke up the little party of men on the porch. The guards patrolling with the dogs hurried back into the jungle to make their rounds. The men congregating together looked at one another and immediately gathered tools and tried to appear busy. A Jeep came up the narrow dirt trail fast and abruptly halted just before ramming into the building. A man wearing light-colored jungle gear leapt out from behind the wheel. He was approaching forty, his dark hair receding slightly, but he wore it cut close to his head.

"Come on, Gedeon, hurry. I gotta show this to you. Make you understand. What I owe the Orlov family is *nothing*. This makes more money in a single hour than what I owe them in a month. I can pay them back. I've got the money sitting in the Jeep." He indicated the package on the seat.

The other man took the wrapped package and hefted it twice. "It's all here, Frankie? Because if I have to come back, it won't be to talk."

A shiver slid down Meiling's back. It wasn't as if the stranger had raised his voice; he hadn't. That quiet voice was a part of him. Natural. But he was the most dangerous man there. Meiling was certain of it, just from hearing his voice. He didn't tower over Frankie, although he was taller by an inch or so. His shoulders were wider. His chest thicker. He wore a suit as if it had been made for him and wouldn't dare wrinkle even in the worst of conditions. She couldn't see his face, but he had thick dark hair that was the only thing unruly about him.

"It's all there, Gedeon. But you don't want to take the money back to Victor Orlov. Let me show you the operation. I never told anyone you were coming. No one knows you're here. This could get me killed just showing you this, but I'm willing to give you part of my shares for all the times you saved my ass. I mean it."

Frankie's voice rang with sincerity and Meiling had to believe him. She noticed that Gedeon shoved the package into the inside pocket of his jacket.

"When you owe Victor Orlov money, Frankie, you have to pay him back or someone like me shows up on your doorstep to collect it. This is the third time. He isn't a patient man. I stuck my neck on the chopping block for you. Can't do it again."

"I know you did. I know you did. That's why I'm letting you in on this moneymaker. Ground floor, I swear. You take this back to him. Tell him he can come in but he brings us the product." Frankie sounded eager.

Meiling glimpsed his face. Her heart stuttered in her chest. Gedeon looked bored, but more than that, with the angles and planes of his face, the dark shadows on his jaw, he looked invincible. He walked with a fluid grace, flowing over the ground with an easy stride that made him appear to be part of nature. Her heart began to pound, and she had to concentrate on her breathing to get it under control. Did Frankie have any idea what he was dealing with?

The other men moved out of his way, showing him respect, but she doubted they really understood they'd brought a killing machine into their midst. She knew what he was. She didn't have to see him up close. She didn't have to look into his eyes to see what he was. She recognized him just by the way he moved. She didn't know what he was, what kind of title he held, but she didn't want to know. He was too dangerous to contend with. She wasn't going to get herself killed or captured.

Meiling went motionless, locking her body in a frozen stillness that made it nearly impossible for anyone to spot her. Only her eyes moved, taking in everything around her. She heard Frankie explaining to Gedeon the business, how they kidnapped women from the clubs and brought them here to the jungle, where they were trained to serve men. They were rented out while they were in training, making good money, and when they were sold at auction, they made huge amounts of money. The supplies were endless. They could get women or teens easily from anywhere, all over the country. The money was better than drugs or arms.

"Look at them," Gedeon said softly. "These are human beings. Look at the way you're treating them. They have bruises all over them. They're chained to the beds. We don't have slaves anymore, for God's sake."

Frankie shrugged. "Why not? We can have anything we want out here. No one knows. No one cares. We can do whatever we want to them. They can be replaced like that." He snapped his fingers.

Two of his men came in, pushing past Gedeon, each going to one of the women and ruthlessly catching her by the hair to drag her into a semi-sitting position. Both began to make demands and pepper the woman with slaps and a fist in various places on her body before she could accommodate them. Two more men entered the hut and eagerly claimed two other hapless women.

"I brought you at training time. We have two other cabins. The same thing is going on in those cabins right now. We're very organized. We train the sluts exactly the same. When they're ready, we sell them and bring the next ones in. We try to make that turnover as fast as possible, and the money is unbelievable."

Meiling could hear the curt dismissal in Frankie's voice. She also heard the soft warning growl that sent a shiver of terror down her spine. Had anyone else heard it? It was so low. So deceptively quiet.

"You have three cabins here in the jungle already set up and running?" Gedeon reiterated.

"That's right," Frankie said. It was clear he believed Gedeon was on board.

"All of them have the same number of men keeping these women under control?"

"Yes."

"And no one knows anything about this operation other than the men here now and your father?"

"He doesn't know," Frankie said, contempt in his voice. "He wanted Orlov paid off immediately. He would live with that asshole's shoe on his neck for the rest of his life. I tried to tell him we could get out from under him, but there was no listening to my idea. So the hell with him. I'm getting us out. The only one who knows is my brother. He'd kill me if he knew you were here. He thinks you're flying in tomorrow morning. I told him you'd be coming in then and I arranged for your arrival. I told him I'd give you the money then and you'd pay Orlov off and the debt would be cleared."

"Those men you have patrolling, you didn't by any chance give them orders to shoot me if I didn't take this offer, did you, Frankie?" There was an edge of humor in Gedeon's voice, inviting Frankie to laugh with him.

Frankie took the bait, laughing heartily. Nervously. "You know I wouldn't do that."

Meiling heard the lie in his voice. What else could he do? He'd shown Gedeon a secret operation even his father didn't know about.

Frankie was eager to offer Gedeon a share in his new business venture for all the favors Gedeon had done him in the past. A woman cried out in pain, and that must have been the catalyst for Gedeon to act. Meiling heard Frankie shriek. Plead. Women screamed. One of them yelled at Bess not to shoot. A gun went off. Meiling saw the two guards running toward the cabin. The dogs fought the leashes, desperate to get away. Swearing, the guards released them in order to retain possession of their guns. The dogs ran off into the jungle.

There was a sudden silence in the cabin as Gedeon, his elegant suit streaked with blood, somersaulted out the window closest to Meiling. He landed in the brush and went absolutely still, his gaze focused on the two men rushing up the stairs and into the cabin.

"Who did this?" one of the men shouted.

Two of the women answered that it was a stranger, they didn't know, and the guards opened fire, their guns spouting bullets. Meiling had to cover her mouth to keep from crying out. She should have known the guards had been instructed to murder the women if there was any kind of trouble. Frankie had all but told Gedeon they were expendable. That meant the teens and younger children in the huts were as well. The men "training them" had to have heard those shots.

Meiling realized it was going to be a massacre. Gedeon realized it as well. With one incredible leap he was on the porch in the doorway, his gun blazing, and then he was running for the forest, his speed a blur. She saw him shed his jacket on the run. She was fast, but there was no way she could possibly keep up with him. She did stop to pick up his jacket, folding it over her arm as she sped after him, leaping over fallen tree trunks and avoiding tall termite hills.

She spotted his shirt in a tangle of brush off the trail. He was cutting through the jungle, well off the trail. She followed, using as much speed as possible. She was used to sprints, not steady long runs. She found his trousers on a low branch and beneath it his loafers.

She knew leopards. Shifters. They were all bad. Not just bad. She had thought they were the worst kind of evil on the planet, until she had begun tracking Frankie and his brother, Miguel. The brothers weren't shifters and knew nothing of them. They came from a family of criminals, making their money running drugs and spending it like water when all around them were incredibly poor people. They cared nothing for those living in abject poverty. They seemed to care for nothing but themselves.

The moment she saw Gedeon, she knew he was leopard.

There was no mistaking them once you'd seen one. She'd never seen one quite so fast in human form. She couldn't imagine what he would be like in leopard form. She was shocked that he'd cared enough about the women to try to save them. One man—even a shifter— against so many didn't seem good odds.

As a rule, when seen or caught in the wild, the Amur male leopard weighed between 71 and 110 pounds and the female weighed between 55 and 94. Meiling had seen shifters with leopards weighing far more than that. It didn't seem to slow their leopards down at all. Gedeon was built in the way of shifters, with roped muscles, a dense chest, narrow hips leading to muscled thighs. He was astonishingly fast. Meiling was certain he couldn't be an Amur leopard, not when he had empathy for the women being treated in such appalling ways.

She kept running, but by the time she reached the second cabin, she found only death. The leopard had come too late to save the teens from the guards. They had been murdered the moment their trainers heard gunfire and couldn't raise anyone on their phones to instruct them otherwise. Despite the trainers having the advantage of knowing someone or something was coming for them, despite them having the advantage of numbers, the leopard had torn them to shreds. All of them. Then he was gone, rushing for the next cabin, leaving no one behind to sneak up on him while he was doing his best to save the children.

Meiling stopped in the heavy brush some thirty feet away from the third cabin. One of the patrolling guards lay dying another ten feet from her. The leopard hadn't delivered the kill bite to him in his effort to get to the children. Now, Gedeon knelt on the porch, one hand covering his face, weeping. Bodies of the men the leopard had killed were scattered around him in various stages of dying.

Meiling knew the children had been murdered, just as the women and teens had been. Gedeon had found them

already dead. She found her eyes blurring as well. She had
hoped. Prayed to the universe she no longer believed in.
What was wrong with these men that they could kill so
easily? She brushed at the wetness in her eyes, and when
she did, she caught movement.

The guard. The one Gedeon's leopard hadn't finished
off. He was dying. There was no way for him to live, not
with the vicious wounds that had ripped open his body.
She could see those gashes had been inflicted on the run.
The leopard had ensured the guard couldn't walk or come
after him. He'd struck brutally and continued onward. But
the guard was up to something. He was attempting to pull
something off his belt with his very shaky hands.

Meiling had to really study what it was he was trying
to get to. She didn't know much about bombs at all, but she
had read about them once and looked at diagrams. There
was a description of remote detonators, and that looked
suspiciously like one.

Not thinking, clutching Gedeon's clothes, she raised
her voice as she turned to run. She had no idea where the
bomb was, or even if there was one. "Bomb. Run. Get out
of there. Run."

It stood to reason that, after murdering the women and
children, they'd blow up the evidence. Maybe the bomb
was a string of bombs that ran along the path of the cabins.
Meiling ran away from the path. She caught a glimpse of
Gedeon's head coming up sharply as she looked back to
see if he was heeding her warning.

For one terrible moment their eyes met. His burned a
terrible gold as he shifted on the run. *On the run.* Coming
straight toward her. He was huge. The biggest leopard she'd
ever seen in her life. His fur was thick, almost creamy
white on his belly and legs, with deep gold over the cream
on his back and head. Black rosettes were large and widely
spaced over his entire body, and those eyes burned brightly
and focused as he ran.

She didn't look back but ran for her life. She knew he was coming for her. He couldn't leave witnesses. He was Amur. Deadly. *Bratya*. They murdered their women. The world thought they were nearly extinct from loss of habitat or poaching, but she knew the shifters had murdered their own kind. Now that they were down to so few, were they horrified at what they'd done? Were they looking for their women in an effort to rectify the situation? No, they were still murdering them.

She ran as fast as she was capable of running, leaping over every obstacle in her path. She was grateful for the fifty-foot start, but she knew it wasn't nearly enough. Then the world blew up. She was picked up as if she weighed no more than a feather and thrown through the air into the relative protection of the heavier brush. She landed right in the middle of thick leaves cushioning her fall. She lay covering her eyes against the flash after flash and thundering blasts that shook the earth.

She'd been right about the string of bombs that ran beneath the ground connecting the cabins. Frankie and his crew had buried enough explosives to level the buildings and cover their operation so anyone coming to try to find evidence would have to sift through jungle and ash to find anything.

Meiling waited with her hands over her head, heart pounding, realizing she still clutched Gedeon's clothes. The material helped to shield her from falling debris. She lay very still until the ground ceased trembling and the jungle was completely quiet. There was no sound. No insects. No birds. Nothing moved or voiced an opinion. Like her, everything was too shocked to protest.

Eventually, she realized she had to make certain Gedeon's leopard wasn't creeping up on her, about to leap on her and rip her to shreds any moment. She forced herself to lift her head cautiously. When nothing happened, she shook off the leaves and small branches and sat up, taking stock of her body to make sure nothing was broken. She probably had a few bruises, but she'd been lucky. All the charges had been behind her.

Her body shook as if she had tremors that were uncontrollable. There was no fixing that, so she just accepted it, as she did anything she couldn't change, and looked around her. The cabin was gone. Flattened. No, it was a hole in the ground. The forest around it was gone, the trees lying in piles of rubble and leaves everywhere. It looked like a war zone.

She started to turn away when she caught movement under one of the stacks of leaves and branches. It was a human leg and arm moving, the arm trying to throw the branch off the leg. She heard the curse. The groan. The branch settled back over the leg. The man cursed again, and she heard the raw pain in his voice.

Gedeon. Meiling closed her eyes. Naturally he would live through it. He was a leopard and probably had more than nine lives. If she helped him, he would most certainly reward her by killing her. He was Amur. What else would he do? If she didn't help him, she would forever remember him taking on all those horrid men to free the women. She would never get the sight of him kneeling on the porch weeping from her mind. The latter two things didn't fit with him being Amur leopard. Now she was the one cursing.

She made her way back to him, picking her way through the debris. "I've got a gun, and if you make one wrong move, I'm going to shoot you right through the heart. Do you understand? If you just behave, I'll move the branch, leave you your clothes and you can go on your way." Meiling made certain she didn't speak until she could do so without the slightest tremor in her voice. She was still shaking like a leaf, but he couldn't see her—at least she hoped he couldn't.

There was a small silence and then she heard him sigh.

"Lady, get the hell out of here while you can. I'm blind. My leg is broken. The branch is too heavy for you to lift, and I can't help you with my leg like this. I'm naked, by the way. If you did manage to get me free, I got a good look at you and I weigh three times your weight. How are you going to get me out of here? On your back? That's ludicrous. No doubt there are men on their way right now to see what the hell happened to their moneymaking operation, and you don't want to be here when they get here. If by some miracle you did manage to save my life and I regained my eyesight and didn't die of infection, I'd have to hunt you down, which I'm very good at, and kill you because I don't leave witnesses. On top of everything else, my cat hates everybody and I'm pretty damned weak right now and I might not be able to hold him back. So get out of here."

"You really aren't telling me anything new other than the eye thing and broken leg. If you aren't going to be useful, less talking, please. I've got to figure this out fast." She put his clothes down and considered the branch. It was large, but it was mostly the angle that was going to give her trouble. If she dropped it on his leg a second time after she picked it up, it was going to cause considerably more damage.

She was strong, and unfortunately, the moment she showed him just how strong she actually was, he would guess she was more than she seemed. That meant the moment she could, she would have to run. She'd planned on doing so anyhow, but that knowledge would double his incentive for coming after her.

She caught ahold of the end of the branch, lifted and maneuvered it off his leg, closing her ears to the sound of his hastily cut off groan. The branch was cracked in several places and made horrid creaking and cracking noises, threatening to break into several large pieces, the offshoots shivering, throwing twigs and leaves raining down.

She didn't hesitate at all but kept the thick branch moving until it was completely away from Gedeon's body. When she dropped it to the ground, it did break into pieces.

For the first time, she allowed herself to look at the man's face to see if he was telling her the truth. His gorgeous jade-green eyes were definitely damaged in some way. Hastily, she tore a strip from his shirt, soaked it in the water from her backpack and slowly approached him.

"I'm going to tie this around your eyes. It's all I've got at the moment to help. Then I'll stabilize your leg to move you."

"Why aren't you afraid of my leopard?"

"I have a way with them. Is he acting up?"

"As a matter of fact, no."

Meiling did feel a little smug at that. He sounded shocked. She wasn't that surprised. She did have a way with large cats.

"How the hell do you think you can move me?" Now he was back to irritable.

"Does it matter? I'm getting you out of here unless you'd rather I leave you the gun and you take care of doing yourself in. Otherwise, stop whining and let me get this done. I don't want to be here with you any longer than I have to."

"I have to hand it to you, little doll, you have guts."

"Don't aggravate me with your cute little nicknames right now." She did her best not to look at his body. He might be torn up, but he was the first man she'd ever seen who looked like he did. She had no idea men were built like him.

His mouth curved, but he didn't say anything else as she firmly tied the cool cloth around his eyes and then made her way to his leg. She wasn't certain the leg was broken, but it was a hell of a nasty, deep laceration. It took several precious minutes to find the right pieces of wood to stabilize the leg by bracing it on either side. She tied it firmly in several places, more than she thought necessary so there was no chance of a break worsening while she moved him.

"My car is about a mile from here through the jungle. I didn't come in on the trail and I'm not going out that way, not that there is one any longer. I'm going to take you out in a fireman's carry. It's going to hurt and I'm sorry about that, but it's the only way. Don't give me your objections and or say one word about my height."

"I'm naked."

"I'm aware. I've got your clothes, but we can't dress you with your leg like that. I can put your jacket over my shoulder if that helps with your dignity."

Meiling didn't wait for his consent. She folded his coat over her shoulder, pressed the rest of his clothing into his hands, bent her knees, crouched low and leveraged him over her shoulder.

"Your shoes are stuffed into the pocket of your trousers. The money Frankie owed your client is in the inside pocket of your jacket where you originally put it. All your weapons are still in the places inside your jacket where you keep them. Your wallet is where you left it. Your belt is intact, and nothing has been taken. Your phone is in its case on your belt. Once we are in the car, if you have people you want me to take you to or a hotel room, I'll take you there."

"That would be suicide."

She moved through the brush much slower than she had anticipated. He was very heavy and all the while she knew every step she took was terribly painful to him. The brush tore up his exposed skin. She couldn't cover him and move quickly. She had to get out of the jungle and away from the area before Frankie's brother and his crew showed up to determine what had happened.

By the time she reached her Jeep, Gedeon was nearly unconscious. What had he said about suicide if she took him to his hotel? That didn't sound good. Where was she supposed to take him? She didn't have his kind of money. She couldn't use the money he needed to send to the Orlov family. They were Russian. Amur Leopard. *Bratya*. Those people came after you if you didn't pay them. They sent men like Gedeon to kill you. The Orlov lair were embedded in Colombia. She knew them by reputation only, but she had no wish to know them by more than that. They had ties to a family in San Antonio, Texas, of all places, and another in New Orleans, Louisiana.

It ate up more minutes getting him onto the back seat of the Jeep and covering him adequately, strapping him in and then driving like hell over the bumpy, nearly nonexistent tiny road she'd been told about by some of the locals who despised Frankie and Miguel. The road took her to the edge of a coffee plantation that was really a plantation for opiates.

She maneuvered the outer road to get to the one farm everyone left alone because they needed the food that farm provided. She knew the residents there and visited often when she was in the area, bringing them much-needed funds, so she was always welcome. She didn't stop this time but paused only long enough to hand the large manila envelope she'd brought them through her window, promising she'd be back soon. Waving, she drove toward the city, using the main road now that she had done legitimate business.

Meiling imagined that Gedeon was either a resident at one of the really nice hotels or had his own residence in the good part of the city. She didn't. She needed to make certain her money always stretched. She didn't care that much where she stayed because it was never for long. She always had her go bag prepared. She could disappear in minutes. If necessary, she could even walk out without anything, go to the nearest bus station, or airport, even the train station and she would have a go bag there.

Meiling didn't take chances anymore. "You, sir, are a

huge liability to me," she hissed as she opened the passenger door to her Jeep. He was lucky there was even a door on her Jeep. "And you're lucky it's dark." Not that anyone would look twice in the part of the city they were in. Not seeing a naked man hobbling into her little apartment. This was the part of the city where every kind of sex was paid for and most of the tiny hovels were used for just those purposes. What raised eyebrows was not having someone looking out for her. "Now, I'm going to have to go back to the old ways to get the money for your doc. Everyone's going to think you're my pimp. At least they'll be happy."

Gedeon was delirious, his fever raging. That wasn't good in a leopard. She knew that much. He needed a doctor. That was going to take all her funds for certain.

She managed to get him on the bed. It was a big bed. It took up most of the apartment. The bed and the kitchen. She had laughed at that. She thought maybe after entertaining the client in the huge bed the custom was to feed them before sending them off.

Meiling called the farmhouse, the only people she trusted, to ask about a very discreet doctor who wouldn't go to the authorities or anyone else. They promised to send someone but told her he wouldn't be cheap. She sighed and glared at Gedeon. She needed to get his clothes out of sight, especially the money, and try to make certain he didn't say anything while the doctor was there. She had to convince the doctor she and Gedeon were a couple.

She gave him a cooling sponge bath after she removed the makeshift splint. He couldn't have any evidence of the jungle on him. She removed the strip of shirt from his eyes so the doctor wouldn't see the material. If she thought she had time, she would have bought him some coarser shirts and trousers just to have in the room.

"Listen to me, Gedeon. It's imperative that you don't talk when the doctor's here. He can't know you were in the jungle. I'm going to tell him your name is Jeff and you're my man. We were with friends we can't name, political friends. And there was an accident. That's all we can say. He'll think we are with a radical group trying to overthrow the government. There's always unrest, especially with so much criminal activity on the border between Colombia and Venezuela. Do you understand? You can't talk to him."

Gedeon nodded. "I'm Jeff. Got it. Where are my clothes?"

"In the wall right behind you. One gun is to your left, the other your right. You should be able to punch through the panel easily and pull them out if necessary. Point and shoot. Safety is off."

"You're not afraid I'll shoot you?"

"You need me."

"I guess I do."

She wiped the sweat from his face with the cool cloth.

"Is he going to tell me if I'm going to be able to see?"

"I hope he can. I asked my friend to send us someone who could."

2

GEDEON wasn't certain his leg was broken now that he was out of the jungle and the supports had been removed. It should have hurt a hell of a lot worse. He couldn't see the injury, but he could feel it. He ran his hands carefully over it. Swollen. Hot to the touch. He was bruised. Maybe a crack or two, but he didn't think it was broken enough to warrant a cast.

Did he want his rescuer to have that information? He brought his hand up to his eyes. She'd replaced the original bandage with a new one. This one was made of cotton and soaked in soothing cool water.

He had to admit she had saved his life. He never could have moved the branch on his own or gotten himself out of the jungle before Miguel showed up to check on his brother. He was lucky that no one knew he had come to the city yet. He was extremely lucky that the little wildcat rescuing him had chosen to come back for him.

Why? That was the burning question. He had warned her about what kind of man he was. He'd told her the truth. He didn't leave witnesses. He didn't get attached. That was the rule he lived by, and it served him well. So why was her scent already affecting him?

"Tell me your name."

"That would be a mistake on my part. You've already said you're going to kill me the minute you're back on your feet. I'm not going to make it easy on you by telling you my name."

"Don't be ridiculous. Your fingerprints are all over this room."

"You wish I'd make it that easy for you," she said with a little sniff of disdain.

Gedeon was really beginning to like her. He didn't like too many people, but she didn't seem to be afraid of him when everyone was terrified to look at him wrong.

"Guess you're going to have to get used to me calling you all my loving endearments."

She heaved a sigh. "Fine. My name is Susan. You can call me Susie."

"You can't lie worth shit. I'm going to call you my little lotus blossom."

"You most certainly are not. You're giving me a headache just talking to you. You probably give everyone headaches when they talk to you."

She sounded very tired. Exhausted, actually.

He had to get the money sent by courier or it wouldn't much matter whether she had saved him or not. He didn't know if he trusted her with that amount of money. The package had been in his jacket, right where he put it, untouched. That didn't mean if he sent her to send it off, she'd actually follow through. More than a million dollars was a huge temptation, especially for someone living in a dump. He didn't need his sight to tell him this place was no five-star hotel.

He might as well tell her the truth. "Look, little Lotus Blossom, I appreciate that you would go to all the trouble of saving my ass, especially since it's clear that you're not wild for me, but if I don't send this money to Victor Orlov by courier before midnight, I'm as good as dead. Nothing I say or do will be considered a good enough excuse."

She sighed. "You could have led with that right away." There was movement on his left side and then directly behind him. He heard her swear under her breath in a very unladylike manner.

"What are you doing?"

"Getting the blood money for the criminals you work for, what do you think? I didn't haul you all the way here just to let them send someone to kill you."

"They'll know I wasn't the one to send them the money."

"No, they won't," she denied.

She sounded totally confident. That gave him pause. There was even a twinge of sarcasm in her tone, as if she was annoyed that he persisted in underestimating her. He was beginning to think he did, but it was impossible for her to know how he sent money owed to any of his clients.

"Okay, I'll bite, baby, how are you going to send the money to them when you don't even know where to send it, how to send it, who to use, who to send it to, or the exact wording used so they know it's clean and from me?"

"I looked in your phone."

"It's password protected."

"It was until you told me your password, along with a lot of other things you shouldn't have told me. Since you were going to kill me anyway, I just let you carry on."

She sounded smug. He wanted to strangle her because he was very afraid she was telling the truth.

"And then I read all those private messages and learned more things I shouldn't know. I figured if I was going to die, it should be for a good reason, not for something stupid like I witnessed you doing a good deed killing all those

horrible traffickers I had planned on killing or because I
saw you shifting into a leopard. Whichever one of those
two things you thought it was worth murdering me for."

She had planned on killing all those men herself? That
was laughable. She probably couldn't kill an insect without feeling remorse. Putting his hands around her neck
and strangling her was a very personal way to take her out,
and right now his fingers were itching to get the job done.
Or maybe he just wanted her to be that close to him again.

"Don't trust you with all that money, Lotus Blossom.
Put it back."

"Too bad, Freaky Man who kills for a living. I didn't
save you so your nasty employers could do you in. The
money's going out tonight."

She wasn't that far from him, and he made a lunge to
catch her arm. Normally, his leopard gave him a huge advantage, but she somehow managed to elude him.

"He's here," Meiling warned. "Remember, you're Jeff."

"You're giving me back the money. In the meantime,
what am I calling you when the doc is here?"

"Audrey," she supplied.

Her footsteps were so light, they should have been impossible to hear, but Gedeon was leopard, and he knew it
took her seven steps to get to the door. The knock was de-
cisive. When the door was opened and the man spoke, it was
obvious he towered over her. That one glimpse he'd caught
of her confirmed she was a small thing. Delicate looking,
but she'd moved that branch without any help from him.
She was a mystery.

Dr. Smythe took his temperature and wasn't happy. He
examined his leg first even though his specialty was eyes. He
didn't believe the leg was broken even though it was
swollen and the lacerations were hot and ugly.

"You were struck by something very heavy, and your
skin was cut in multiple places," the doctor said. He paused,

waiting for an explanation, but neither Meiling nor Gedeon provided him with one. Smythe sighed. "I don't know why you've gotten an infection so fast, but it's alarming." He gave him a shot of antibiotics and handed Meiling a bottle of pills. "See that he takes all of these. He should have that leg X-rayed. I'm guessing it isn't broken, but I can't be certain. It is swollen, but he's moving everything without a problem."

"That's such a relief," Meiling said. "We were so worried."

Smythe removed the makeshift bandage Meiling had placed over Gedeon's eyes. "How did this occur? That will help considerably if I know what I'm dealing with."

Gedeon didn't like the questions. "Isn't part of your enormous fee for figuring all that out?" He couldn't help sounding a little threatening. That was who he was, whether or not he was blind. His leopard, quiet since the explosion, was beginning to make himself known again. Waking up. The explosion must have knocked the ferocious cat out. He didn't like the doctor touching Gedeon and was beginning to claw for freedom. Gedeon took a firm grip on him.

"I could figure it out faster with a little more information," Smythe groused. "Most of that enormous fee is for silence. Not reporting to the government or other interested parties could get me killed. I'm known for my discretion."

If Gedeon wasn't blind, he would kill the doctor after the examination. No way would he trust this man. The doctor would sell them out the moment he was offered more money. He might leave the apartment and go immediately to the government if he thought they were insurgents. If he believed they were in any way connected to the explosion that happened in the jungle, he wouldn't hesitate to turn them over to Miguel—for a price.

"What exactly are you charging? Audrey didn't tell me,"

Gedeon asked as Smythe continued his examination. His heart jumped and then accelerated. He could tell the doctor was shining a light in his eyes. That had to be a good sign.

Smythe named an exorbitant price. His little lotus blossom made a small sound of protest. "That isn't what we negotiated."

"This injury was caused in an explosion—the kind of explosion that happens when you might be making bombs. It's all over the news that rebels seeking to overthrow the government blew up an apartment building when the bombs they were making detonated because they were unstable. There is no doubt in my mind that this injury was caused by that."

Again, Lotus Blossom made a sound of distress, further cementing in the doctor's mind that the two of them were part of the many rebels seeking to overthrow the government. That was good for them in that it wouldn't occur to Smythe that they had anything to do with the explosion that happened so far away in the jungle.

"I'm going to have to go out for a short while to get the rest of the money for you, Doc. How long will you need with Jeff?"

"As long as it takes for you to get back." Smythe's voice was clipped.

"Do you think he has a chance of regaining his eyesight?"

"A very good chance. His eyes need to rest. He shouldn't be exposed to light for a few days, and then a little at a time. Very dark glasses. I'll give you a prescription for eye drops. He'll need to put them in his eyes several times a day. That's a quick diagnosis, but I'll know a lot more when I really examine them."

The truth was, Smythe really didn't know yet. He was giving little Lotus Blossom hope. Gedeon wasn't sure how he felt about that. The glimpse he'd caught of her had been so brief, but he was certain she was striking. Delicate. Just like the lotus he called her.

Then she was in his space, leaning into him, her breasts up against his chest, her lips pressed against his ear as she smoothed one hand down the back of his head. "Remember, just a foot from your hand. Smash with your fist if needed. Under your pillow is a knife. The hilt is toward you. I'll be gone less than thirty minutes."

The way her soft lips brushed against her ear was one of the most intimate things he'd ever experienced. But then, he didn't experience intimacy. His leopard didn't allow for it. He fucked all the time, but it was "do the deed and get out fast" before the vicious creature craving blood shredded the human being it detested. What was the beast doing now? It felt as if his leopard was rolling around like a lovesick kitten, making his stomach hurt.

Gedeon's first reaction was to yank her to him, sit her right on his naked lap, the one covered only by a thin sheet that did little to hide the monster of a hard-on. The second was to shove her as far from him as possible. A vicious shove, one that would send her flying hard into the wall. If he was lucky, she'd break her damn neck. He did neither. He just sat on the bed, his fingers buried in her luxurious hair, wondering why the hell when he'd met a woman like her, she regarded him like a wounded pussycat. She was *amused* by him.

Then she was gone, taking her small, delicate, *deceiving* frame and all that amazing hair along with her enticing fragrance, leaving him alone. He wasn't afraid. He didn't have much fear in him. He'd had that stamped out as a young cub. He had those scars all over his body to prove it too.

"Beautiful woman," Smythe commented.

His head was turned, watching Lotus Blossom's departure. Gedeon could tell by the direction of his voice. For some unexplained reason Gedeon didn't want to explore, his impulse was to leap on the doctor and rip his heart out. The need to do so was so intense, he shook with it, adrenaline pouring into his body. He clenched his fist, thinking to smash into the wall to retrieve a weapon and do the job right. If the doctor thought he could get away with leering at his woman right in front of him, he had another think coming.

"I hope I reassured her enough," Smythe murmured. He had turned his head back toward Gedeon. "She was hovering over you. I think she was afraid I was going to hurt you." He laughed heartily. "I can't imagine you have too many women fussing over a big man like you."

Gedeon didn't like Smythe at all, but he didn't know how bad his eyes really were and he needed to find out. His first instinct had to be put aside, but his leopard wasn't having any of it. The cat raged at him, fighting to be let out. Declaring that the man was deceitful and would get them killed.

I am well aware he is, but we need him at the moment. You didn't act this way when the woman was here deceiving us.

His cat raged more, clawing at him, raking. Forcing him to lock the cat down with tremendous strength of will.

She was saving us.

Now you sound sulky, and that's beneath your dignity. A woman is just as lethal as a man, especially if she can make you believe she's all rounded edges and innocence. You fall for that shit and we're both going to die. Gedeon warned his leopard not to trust their savior. No one did anything for free. He'd learned that lesson very young and he'd never forgotten it. His leopard should have learned it as well.

I learned it. The cat was pragmatic. *But so far, she has proven worthy. This one has not told us anything of value. It is in his mind to sell both of you.*

I am aware. But I need him to tell me what he can about my eyes. Aloud he instructed the doctor. "Get on with it. If Audrey says she'll be back in half an hour, she will be. She's very prompt. And I want to know first if it's bad news before she gets here. I'll need time to process and decide what to do."

"What to do?" Smythe echoed.

"Yeah, Doc, what to do. A man like me doesn't stick around long blind. You have to know that if you're at all who I think you are."

"Tip your head back."

The light went on again. The glare hurt. Gedeon thought it was a good kind of hurt and he tolerated it even though his first instinct was to pull away.

"I'm going to put drops in your eyes."

He'd always hated drops in his eyes. He thought as an adult he'd grow out of that particular idiosyncrasy, but he hadn't. He figured it was because he needed his sight so much. His work depended on sight.

"Go for it, Doc. How did you get into your line of work?"

"Shouldn't that be my question to you?"

"Just making conversation," Gedeon lied. The more he knew about the doctor, the easier it would be to find him later.

The doctor put in the drops. They stung like hell. Gedeon's cat roared, the sound reverberating like thunder cracking up close, shaking the thin walls of the apartment. Uneasy, not understanding where the sound came from, the doc jumped up and hastily inspected outside through the window.

"What's wrong?" Gedeon did his best to sound nervous.

"They should have bars on these windows."

"Why, what's wrong?" Gedeon repeated the question.

"That sounded like a leopard. They can get into the city, and once they do, they find out they have a smorgasbord. It takes forever to catch them." He returned to the side of Gedeon's bed but didn't sit down. He began to pace.

"A couple of years ago, one got loose in the city and killed almost every night for nearly two months. It didn't have to make so many kills, but the authorities said leave the body to act as bait. The leopard never returned to the same body. It always made a fresh kill. Twice it turned back on the hunters and killed one of them."

Gedeon had heard of that leopard. It had terrorized the city for months. The city officials had hired several renowned hunters to track and kill it, but all attempts had failed. Gedeon knew eventually a man by the name of Drake Donovan had been contacted, which on the surface made no sense. He ran a security firm reputed to be the best. His men were investigators and bodyguards. They also hired on in just about any terrain to retrieve hostages or pay ransom. They brought the kidnap victim home or exacted revenge. He had a reputation for getting the job done. He had gotten the job done when the other hunters had failed— or at least the man he sent to do the job had gotten it done.

"I think we're safe enough in here," Gedeon assured the other man.

"These leopards can sneak right into a home and drag a full-sized man from his living room right out from under the noses of his family. I'm telling you, these leopards in that jungle are no joke. You're a city man. You've never encountered them."

This told Gedeon that Dr. Smythe hadn't been born in a city. He'd dug his way out of a jungle village and never wanted to go back. It also told him the man, at some point in his life, had had an encounter with a leopard and it hadn't gone well.

Eventually the doctor got down to business and he was thorough. He seemed to know what he was doing and talked to Gedeon the entire time. His eyes reacted to the light, a good sign. Nothing was torn, another good sign. In the end, it was a wait-and-see game. If his eyesight was to return, and the doctor thought there was an excellent chance, it would return slowly over the next couple of weeks, and even then, he would need to rest his eyes, stay out of bright sunlight and wear dark glasses if he had to go out. The good news was he would have his beautiful companion at his side fussing over him.

Gedeon heard the door open and close and scented the woman. She was a few minutes early. He had an internal clock, and the passage of time was ingrained in him. She had said thirty minutes and he had been going to hold her to that. She was there. The sense of relief was overwhelming.

"Your money, Dr. Smythe. How is he? What do you think now that you've thoroughly examined him?"

She came straight to the bed. To his side. He counted the steps again automatically. Taking his hand, she sat on the edge close to him and leaned in to brush his cheek with her cool, soft lips. His heart jumped.

"He needs rest and to keep his eyes covered for at least two weeks. I've given you a soaking solution you can pick up anywhere. You have the antibiotics. I'll return in three days to check on him."

"Thank you so much, Dr. Smythe."

Gedeon didn't want her to follow Smythe to the door even to see the treacherous bastard out, so he kept a firm hand circled around her wrist. To his shock, the moment the door closed she jumped up.

"We don't have much time. I got you clothes and we've got to get you dressed. Between the two of us, we can get these trousers on you. They're just drawstring cotton pants, but you'll be decent. I'm pulling a T-shirt over your head now."

He felt her tug the shirt over his head and automatically fit his arms through the openings. She let him take it and drag it over his chest. It fit snug, but it was clothing. Then she was pulling his feet through the legs of the cotton pants and dragging them up as far as she could. She was careful of his swollen leg. The lacerations the doctor had carefully closed and covered with fresh gauze and bandages were treated with extra gentleness. He helped as best he could, lifting his body when she got to his hips. She didn't even hesitate pulling the material over his groin.

"Are you going to tell me what's going on?" He didn't know whether to be amused or annoyed that she refused to see him as a man. She treated him like a small child or a patient in the hospital she had to care for. That put him at a distinct disadvantage, which tended to amuse more than annoy him.

"You know exactly what's going on. Don't pretend ignorance. I'm exhausted and I had to use up one of the biggest favors owed to me in order to get you safely out of here. That doctor is going to go straight to the authorities and tell them he's got two of the bomb-making rebels sitting in an apartment waiting for his return. He'll expect to collect a huge reward for his trouble. We have to go now."

He wanted to kiss her. She was intelligent and she acted on her instincts immediately. She didn't just decide to hash it all out endlessly and get killed when she took too much time. And what did she mean, *use up one of the biggest favors owed to her*? She traded in favors? A woman after his own heart if that was what she did. Few people thought that way. They were all about dollar signs, forgetting that people often could give so much more in return for something you did for them. The old barter system in place. He specialized in collecting favors—and money—depending on the job.

She circled around to the other side of him and pried a board loose from the wall. Catching his wrist, she placed a gun in his palm. Replacing the board, and that meant she drove the nail back into the hole, she went around to the other side and did the same, again handing him the gun she'd retrieved. Next, she took his old clothing and stuffed it into a bag she brought in. He could hear the rustling.

"I'm going to help you to the one and only chair in the room. I've covered it with a cloth we're taking with us. You were on the sheets so we're taking those as well. I have to strip the bed. Put this cap on your head and the dark glasses. Keep them on. I trust this man with my life, but not necessarily with yours. Don't threaten anyone no matter what is said. These people are my friends and they're going out of their way to help us."

"You mean to help you." He clenched his teeth as she helped him hobble over to the chair. It hurt like a son of bitch, but he kept that to himself.

"They created new identities for both of us. Those identities will be impeccable. They don't come cheap. They're allowing us to fly using one of their private jets. That doesn't come cheap either. The flight plan has been filed and we're being picked up a few blocks from here. I can't have the neighborhood seeing the vehicle we take to the airport."

"The money you took with you?"

"I delivered the money to Orlov and put the receipt in your wallet. When we board the jet, you can ask the attendant to read the contents to you. I'd like to tell you I don't steal, but that's how I got the money to pay the doctor. So I do when I need fast money."

A surge of adrenaline caught him unawares. His leopard roared with rage. She calmly stripped the bed and stuffed the sheets into a bag she'd brought. He heard movement around the bed and catching up the pillows and stripping them of the pillowcases. He thought he caught a slight groan escaping, but if he did, she hastily covered it.

"I parked the Jeep as close as possible. I'll help you walk to it and get in the back seat. Lay down in the back seat. I'll take you to the rendezvous point and then go on to ditch the Jeep . . ."

"No." He was firm. "We stay together."

"If something goes wrong, they'll take you to the States." Now she sounded impatient. He could hear the exhaustion in her voice. Before, she'd tried to spare him; now, she was just too tired to put in the effort.

"No. I mean it, Lotus Blossom. We stay together."

She didn't waste time arguing with him. He stood up and tested his weight on the swollen leg. It wasn't going to hold up. He'd have to accept her help whether he wanted to or not. She wrapped her arm around his waist without a word, and they hobbled out together. Every step had him cursing under his breath. He wasn't nearly as stoic as he wanted to be. He couldn't see where he was going or how far it was, and she didn't give him any kind of a reference. To be fair, she was struggling to keep him on his feet. He was giving her more of his weight than he had before.

"Three more steps and you're going in the back seat." She left him for few seconds to yank open the door. "All clear. I don't feel a target on my back at the moment. Do you?"

He shook his head and then wished he hadn't. "I need to lie down before I fall down. I'm beginning to think I'd welcome a target at this rate. Should have asked the doc for painkillers."

"He left you some. I think he was afraid I'd shoot him if I came back and found you high as a kite on pills."

"Would you have?" Gedeon was curious.

"Shot him because you were high?" Amusement was back in her voice, replacing the exhaustion as she helped him the last two steps to the back seat. "I might have paid him more money just to see what other secrets you had to spill. Step up, Gedeon, I'm not going to toss you onto the back seat."

Gedeon did his best to climb into the Jeep. He made it inside, but it wasn't pretty, and he really did crawl, dragging his injured leg and swearing in several languages. Sweat broke out, beading on his body. He was on the floor of the Jeep rather than the seat. He rested his head on the seat and fought for his breath.

"I think this is just fine, right here."

She must have agreed because she shut the door quickly, was gone a couple of minutes and returned with two suitcases. Stowing them in the front passenger's seat, she hopped into the driver's side and the Jeep was in motion.

"You okay back there?"

"No, I'm dying."

"What happened to the badass who single-handedly wiped out thirty murdering traffickers in a night? Where is he in the middle of all this whining?"

He caught the note of concern in the midst of her teasing. "Yeah, I think the badass got the shit kicked out of him by a little four-foot-and-some-change lotus blossom."

The Jeep swerved sharply to the left and then straightened again. He turned his head to see her better. He'd forgotten the bandages covering his eyes for just that little moment.

"Sorry, dog in the road. We're almost there. I'm sorry, but it's another change. Nicer vehicle. We have to ditch the Jeep. Once we get to the plane, I can take better care of you. There's a bed on the plane, Gedeon. You can take whatever the doctor gave you for pain and sleep. I won't let anything happen to you."

"Why? I learned a long time ago that nothing's free. Why are you helping me? You know what kind of man I am. I was up front with you. I even told you I can't leave witnesses."

"I heard you loud and clear."

"Then why?"

"I have my reasons. I don't particularly feel like sharing them. You wouldn't understand. I had three destinations I could choose from and you had a real estate transaction in New Orleans, a house you bought, so I chose that. I'll get you there and disappear."

"Let me get this straight. After rescuing me and getting a doctor to check me out, stealing money to pay him, calling in an enormous favor to get papers and fly us out of the country, you're going to dump me in a house that needs tons of work, still blind, unable to walk, and just leave me to fend for myself."

There was a telling silence. She was getting antsy to leave him. Women fell all over him. He was used to walking into a club and having his choice. He just looked, crooked his finger or nodded and the woman hurried over to him. He didn't even have to bother walking over to her. It was a unique experience to have this woman give him attitude and not even try to persuade him that he would be better off with her.

"Put like that, it doesn't sound like a good plan, but you have money. Your clothes stank of it. Use some of it to hire nurses. They'll help. Call your friends. You have more contacts in your phone than I've ever met in my lifetime."

He wiped the sweat from his face by using his sleeve. His temperature was going back up and he was hotter than hell. "It doesn't work that way in my world, and I think you know that. At the first hint of vulnerability, I'm a dead man. All the trouble you've gone to would be for nothing."

"Don't sound so cheerful about it."

He knew he'd been right to play on her sympathy. She did have too much compassion in her. She wasn't just going to dump him. She was going to look after him until she was certain he could take care of himself. That was not going to happen until he'd figured her out and why she was helping him.

"Nothing cheerful about me right now. I wish I could say there was. I'm hotter than hell and sweating like a pig. Maybe that doctor gave me something that's going to kill me."

"Do a lot of people want you dead?"

"Yes." That was an honest answer.

"Great. When we meet with my friends, let me do the talking. I don't want them to know who you are."

"Do you think they'd sell me out?"

"No. But if you're such a badass that a lot of people want you dead, they might take it in their heads to get the job done. Considering the way you keep threatening me, your reputation of leaving no witnesses might just tip them off that you plan to kill me."

"That is one possibility." He wiped his face again on his arm. "I'm a little too weak to defend myself. I'll have to rely on you once again to save my life. It would seem those favors are stacking up."

She laughed. The sound was sweet and genuine. Low. Soft little bells on the summer's breeze. He didn't have the least inclination to read poetry, but if he did, he was certain she'd be on every page. Bright as the sun. Moody as the coming storm. Yeah. She'd be there.

He became aware of the Jeep slowing and pulling into a dark, cavernous room. A parking garage? He should have been paying attention to the route. He was too miserable to care. He was as certain as the doctor that his leg wasn't broken, but it hurt every bit as badly as if it could be. Maybe worse than a broken leg.

She parked the Jeep and shut off the engine. Just sat there waiting. "Not a good idea, Lotus Blossom. They could have ten guns on you and you wouldn't know."

"They do have ten guns on me," she admitted. "They've made that plain enough. Keep your hands in sight at all times. I've got mine on the steering wheel. You keep yours on the seat. They aren't going to hesitate to shoot."

All four doors were yanked open. He heard Lotus Blossom give a grunt of pain. It sounded as if she was being dragged off the seat. He cursed his useless eyes. A man's hands caught him under his shoulders, and he started to slide out of the car as he was jerked backward. Pain came in a black wave that made his stomach heave, and beneath the bandage the world spun and tilted.

"Stop right now or I swear I'll shoot you."

That was his feisty little Lotus Blossom, putting herself

in harm's way again for him. She wasn't playing around. He could tell by the way the man behind him froze. His self-appointed guardian angel was pointing a gun at him.

"I know you had orders to treat him gently. He's hurt, in case that escaped you. If you can't do the job you were paid to do, you put him very gently down and walk away. I'll let the man who hired you deal with you."

There was steel in Lotus Blossom. She had to be surrounded, but she refused to back down. She played her role so perfectly, as if she were in charge and those helping answered to her. He would give anything to have his sight back and be able to see her.

"Sorry, ma'am," the man behind him mumbled. "I'll be very careful."

"Thank you." She waited several minutes before speaking again. "I'll just wait here with my brother until Etienne gets here. You boys seem a little antsy."

He was carried very carefully to another vehicle and laid down on the back seat. They left the door open, and he was grateful, telling himself his little lotus blossom was coming with them. Sure enough, he caught a whiff of her fragrance. Her fingers were in his hair, featherlight. She started to climb into the vehicle and had one foot in when a voice stopped her.

"Meiling. Weren't you going to say hello to me after all the trouble I went to for you?"

The voice was smooth. Polished. Very masculine and used to getting his way. The speaker was also very attracted to Lotus Blossom.

"I had no idea you were here, Etienne."

Gedeon didn't like the way her voice lit up. At least he knew her real name—unless she had lied to Etienne as well. He doubted it. They sounded close. Affectionate. There was a brief silence, as if they might be hugging—or kissing.

"You're going to allow one of my men to ditch your Jeep?"

"Yes. But he must make sure he does it properly. I don't want this to come back and bite me in the butt. No one knows I was anywhere around here."

"He'll do it properly or answer to me. Meiling, what is this man to you? I had to see his picture in order to make the necessary papers for you. Do you have any idea who he is?"

Gedeon stiffened. He told himself his reactions to his Lotus Blossom and her answers were because of his dependency on her, not because for the first time in his life he could remember being intrigued by another human being.

"Of course I know who he is."

"He's a very dangerous man."

Her laughter was dark. "Etienne, *you're* a dangerous man."

Gedeon was uncomfortable with the entire situation. His leopard continuously clawed for freedom. That didn't help. He had always been the one in control. Always. Others deferred to him. They were on edge because he was in close proximity to them. Now he felt like a little child, relegated to the back seat, told to be quiet while in the presence of adults. It was bullshit. He wasn't emotional. That was an emotional reaction and he refused to allow emotions into his life. Whoever his lotus blossom was, she had turned his life upside down in just a few short hours.

"Tell me why you're doing this."

Gedeon wanted that answer as well. He remained very still, willing her to answer.

"You know I won't. It's personal."

"A debt, then. I'll pay it. Any amount."

"Then I would owe you. I don't think so, but thank you, Etienne. This is a matter of honor. The debt is nearly paid."

"You know to come to me first if you need anything."

There was another long silence and she got in the car with Gedeon. Sliding in behind his head, her fingers in his hair. His leopard subsided, and that went a long way to calm the strange rage in him. Ordinarily, if a woman put her hands on him so intimately, he would have knocked them off and rebuked her. He found Lotus Blossom's touch soothing. He closed his eyes and drifted off on a sea of pain, fighting nightmares, images of planes, terrible jostling and her comforting voice telling him it was going to be all right.

3

MEILING became aware of unfamiliar sounds first. The creak of old wood as if the house was settling around her. Someone was breathing in and out quietly, but rhythmically. She smelled juniper and, faintly, the jungle, a feral predatory scent that was a little alarming. Three sensations registered simultaneously: a heavy leg was thrown over her thighs, pinning her down; a very heavy arm was wrapped around her waist, holding her securely to a man's body; and fingers drifted idly in her hair.

Her heart went crazy before she could control it. She didn't remember falling into bed with anyone. Certainly not with *him*. Gedeon Volkov. What in the world had possessed her to crawl in bed with him? He could have murdered her so easily. He still could. She had to extract herself out from under him before he woke up. He was leopard. She doubted that was going to happen. One could be lucky only so many times.

She shifted her weight subtly on the bed, trying to ease out from under him. He came awake instantly, the hand buried under the pillow coming up and out with a gun in it.

"I'm just getting up." She tried to be matter-of-fact, as if she slept with men every day. "It's still early, you should just sleep as much as you can. I've got quite a bit to do."

"Such as?"

Gedeon had a note of masculine amusement in his voice that made her want to hit him over the head with a flower-pot. Or the Ming vase that couldn't possibly be authentic. He hadn't moved. Not the leg or the arm, or even the fingers playing with her hair. She had spent an inordinate amount of time while on the plane researching him. The information she found about him was just a little bit terrifying. He was also a player. Big time. Way, way, way out of her league.

"Setting up care for you until you're back on your feet. Arranging for meals to be brought in. Arranging for my disappearance so it won't be easy for you to find me."

"I doubt you're going to suddenly change your mind and sell me out, so let's take that off the table. We both know I'm not going to hunt you down and kill you. I do have an idea that might interest you. I've been thinking about it since you hacked my phone."

"I didn't hack your phone," she corrected, suddenly afraid of what his proposition might be. She might collect favors, but she didn't pay debts with her body. "I coaxed your password out of you when you had an extremely high fever."

Gedeon tugged on her hair as he slid the gun under the pillow. He did it with such ease she wondered if his sight had returned. "I think you have a dirty mind, Lotus Blossom. I wasn't going to proposition you in that way. I'm beginning to think you have a thing for my body."

She heaved a sigh. "Spit it out, Leopard Boy, I intend

to find a hot tub and spend the entire day soaking in it while people I find to wait on you hand and foot do so."

"Leopard Boy?"

"Lotus Blossom?"

He burst out laughing. Meiling couldn't help but like that she'd made him laugh. It was a real laugh too. She had the feeling that with Gedeon, laughter was a very rare thing.

"Fair enough. I want you to work for me." When she frowned and didn't answer, he hastily corrected himself. "*With* me. Partners. I need a woman with me quite often. You're intelligent, witty, you can charm the socks off a man. I can't see you, but no doubt you dress up nice for a dinner party. You remember things."

"Yes," she admitted, her mind racing. All of that was true and he'd said it in a voice that didn't lie. She heard lies.

"My line of work is dangerous. I need eyes and ears on every conversation. I can't be everywhere at once. You got me out of Venezuela with few people seeing me. No one can identify me other than that doctor or the cameras at the airport when I flew in."

"That was taken care of." She pushed at his leg. "You're heavy."

"You won't run away, and you'll listen to me?"

She pretended to heave a sigh, but, really, she was very intrigued. "Go on."

Gedeon shifted his leg off her thigh, and she rubbed at the spot where he'd lain the weight over her. He caught her wrist and felt down her hand to her thigh where he laid his palm. His hand felt very warm on her skin. Too intimate.

"Are you hurt? Tell me the truth. I won't like it if you lie to me. You know I can hear lies."

"Let's finish this other conversation first. I promise we'll go back to my health."

He was silent a moment and she willed him to continue. The last thing she wanted to do was talk about herself.

"We are circling back to this, though." He kept his hand on her thigh and it burned like a brand. "What do you mean, 'it's taken care of'?"

"The security cameras at the airport. Your flight tickets. All of it was wiped out. You never flew to Venezuela. You never got on that airplane. As for the doctor, I have no idea what happened to him, but he is well-known to Etienne. He agreed with me that it was best for us to leave immediately."

"That must have been quite a favor your Etienne owed you to do all that."

"Huge. And I used it on you. Be grateful and stop being so annoying."

"You have to get used to my annoying personality because you're going to work for me. Don't pretend you don't like danger, adventure and being with me."

"I like danger and adventure. Being with you is a real problem. And I wouldn't work *for* you. With you maybe, but definitely not for you."

He ignored the last just like she knew he would. "How many languages do you speak?"

"Five."

"That's good. I don't want anyone to know what you can or can't do up front. Or how smart you are. You need to be able to fade into the background and collect information for me. The more information we have, the more power we have. And that means . . ."

"We don't get killed."

"Exactly."

"I wouldn't really leave you until I knew your eyesight was back to normal, Gedeon," she had to admit. She didn't want him making a job offer because he thought she'd take off at the first chance she got. She might consider it. Think about it. Even fantasize about it. But she wouldn't leave him while he was so helpless. He probably knew that about her, the bastard.

"I know you wouldn't. What I do know is we'd be good together. Partnering up makes sense. You'll make more money and you'll be safer. I'll watch your back and you'll watch mine."

This was going to be difficult to admit. "I do have a gun and I know how to use it. I practice every day, but Gedeon, I've never killed a single human being in my life. I don't know if I could."

"You would have killed the doctor if he suddenly whipped out a knife and was ready to kill me without provocation."

That was true, but he couldn't possibly know that. "It isn't the same thing. You were in a vulnerable position, and I was your only protection." That and a part of her was fairly certain Gedeon would have pulled out one of the guns, aimed true and shot the doctor if he felt threatened.

"The point I'm making is, you could use a good job and we fit."

"Why would you think that?" She was a little shocked.

"Because you're like I am. You have the same gifts. You remember everything. I need your skills. You're loyal. You're fearless."

"You can stop right there. I'm not without fear. If I was, I wouldn't be in this situation. I would have been the one to kill those men, not you." She couldn't keep the shame from her voice. She felt shame that she hadn't been the one to avenge Libby.

"So, you really are repaying an imaginary debt. You saved my life more than once. I'd say that calls us even. You sent off the money using the exact method necessary to keep me out of trouble."

"Unless I lied to you." She couldn't help giving him a hard time.

"You didn't lie." He was that sure of her.

"I'll tell you what, Gedeon, I'll hang around and see you through this, and then when you've fully recovered your vision and you're not out of your mind with fever, we'll revisit this conversation." She needed time to think things through. She didn't trust so easily. "For now, I've got a lot of work to do. Who do you call when you want to get things done quickly? You need a decent eye doctor and also someone to really look at your leg. You've got an infection raging. We've got to know where it is and how to get rid of it. Those things come first. Then I'll need to stock the fridge with healthy food for you and get in cleaners. You need a sterile environment. I'm not cleaning this entire house. If you don't want anyone in your room, I'll clean it, but the rest of the house someone else is doing. After that, I have to find my own apartment."

She began to slide off the bed, but he caught her wrist. Again, he did it so fast and so unerringly, it was difficult not to think he could see. She narrowed her eyes and studied his face, but the bandages were in place. In any case, he wasn't looking straight at her.

"I told you, I want you to stay here. It's safer until we know we made a clean getaway."

"Etienne would never put me in harm's way."

"Just what is he to you?" Gedeon demanded.

"You already asked that question. He's a good friend. I said I'd stay. I just want to see what's available once you're back on your feet." She tried to sound patient, but she wasn't the nurse type. Unfortunately, he seemed to like the fact that she snapped at him.

"Are you leopard?"

That was the question she'd been dreading. She eased off the mattress, tugging her wrist free and padding barefoot across the room to stare at her face in the antique gold-framed oval mirror. She looked worse for wear.

"You should have run screaming from the jungle when you saw me shift, but you didn't. You were as cool as a cucumber."

"I ran." She opened the door to the spacious and very

modern master bath. "I ran because your leopard had every intention of killing me."

"Actually, you're wrong. He didn't. That was the biggest shock of all to me. He hates everyone. He rages night and day. I sleep with bars on the doors and windows. I'm having them installed in this house in a few more days. That way, I can get a good night's sleep."

"You slept like a log." She had too. She didn't know why she sounded so accusing. She didn't want to answer his questions.

"That's because of you. He likes you. You keep him calm. You're the first respite we both have had in years. Has your leopard come out yet?"

"I don't have a leopard." That much was true. There was no leopard inside of her. She was certain of it. Everyone in her lair was dead. She was the only survivor—and she wasn't supposed to have lived through the massacre. If her enemies knew she was alive, they would hunt her down and kill her. They'd probably hire Gedeon to do the job.

"A lair?" he prompted. Persisted. That was so like him.

"I don't have a lair. Or a leopard. There's just me. I like big cats and they seem to like me. I don't know why, it's always been that way, since I was a small child. Right now, I'm going to take a shower and try to feel like a human being again. I won't be long." She didn't want any more questions. And she wanted to remember how she'd ended up in his bed. She was still tired, but last night she'd been beyond tired.

"Run, Lotus Blossom. I always catch anything that tries to run from me. I love the hunt."

She gave him an eye roll, mostly because she was positive he couldn't see. She firmly closed the door to the master bath loud enough for him to hear.

"Where's my phone?" he called.

Meiling sighed. It seemed she wasn't to have peace

even in the bathroom. "On the right-hand nightstand where the charging station is set up."

"Thanks."

At least he did have some manners. Would she consider his offer of work if it was a genuine offer and not made because his fever was high and he was feeling vulnerable or grateful to her? She had always moved from city to city. Sometimes she'd find a little place in the country and stay there for a few weeks, but she never settled anywhere. It was a lonely life and she'd grown tired of it. Her only real human contact had been Libby. Now she was gone.

Meiling sat on the little bench made of stone tile and let herself cry for Libby. For all those lost women. For the entire previous day and all the lives lost so pointlessly. She drew her knees up and put her head down, making herself into a small ball of total misery. She was always strict with herself. She could be emotional, but emotions were a bad thing to have. She knew that. It was one of the many rules she'd been taught young, and one didn't break rules. She broke all the rules often, making her a complete and utter failure. She carried the shame of those reminders on her body.

"Lotus." The voice was a whisper of velvet over her skin. "Baby, you have to tell me what's wrong so I can help."

She raised her head, and that was a huge mistake. Gedeon was crouched in front of her without a stitch on. He might have his eyes bandaged, but she didn't. He had roped muscles everywhere. His body seemed as if it was made of nothing but muscles. Well, there were his incredible male parts, which matched the rest of him. Just as intimidating. Just as enticing. It was no wonder Gedeon Volkov was lethal. He didn't need the added advantage of his leopard. He was too rugged and tough looking to be called gorgeous, but he was definitely captivating.

Blinking back the flood of tears, she pushed at the wet

strands of black hair hanging around her face. "Gedeon, what are you doing in here? I'm taking a shower."

"Technically you're crying, and you have to stop." He reached up with one long arm and got the handheld spray. "Turn around and let me get your hair for you." With his free hand, he found the bench and easily transferred his weight to it. "Sit here." He pointed between his thighs.

If he could be casual about his nudity, so could she. Meiling tried not to think about what that meant. He certainly didn't view her as a potential partner. More like a pet he had to groom. In a way, she supposed that was a good thing. She didn't want him interested in her as a potential bed partner. That would definitely mess up any chance of working together. On the other hand, it was a blow to her ego. She was always *that* girl. The unwanted one. The third wheel. Libby had told her more than once that she needed to be more modern. To loosen up a little and have some fun.

Meiling faced away from him, grateful she didn't have to stare at his rather intimidating male anatomy. He began to massage shampoo into her hair.

"I know it was a shit day yesterday, Lotus Blossom. I didn't help much with all the snarling I did. I'm not used to relying on anyone."

"You did more yesterday for me than anyone's done in my life. My cousin was thrown in a mass grave near that camp in Venezuela like a piece of garbage by those men," she said in a low voice. "I found her too late. I'd been tracking her for two months. I knew she was in Colombia. She'd texted me that she was visiting some friends of ours there. She wanted me to join her."

Meiling pressed the heels of her hands to her eyes. "I should have dropped everything I was doing and just gone right then. I know how she is when she doesn't get her way. I was in the middle of doing some work I had promised for someone. I didn't want to go clubbing in Colombia. I told her to be cautious, to check her drinks. To watch out for who she picked up, all the standard warnings. I told her I'd fly out in a few days, but she was angry with me for not coming right away. Then she went silent. That wasn't entirely unusual with her when she was angry with me, but it persisted long past the time she normally would have answered. I have contacts in Colombia, friends who know those scenes, and they tried to help me track her, but it was like she just vanished. There wasn't even evidence of her at the hotel she'd been staying in. That told me she was in real trouble. Whoever took her had real clout."

All the while she spilled the details of her last failure with her cousin, Gedeon continued to rinse out her hair and then massaged conditioner into it.

"You do know your cousin chose her own path, Lotus. You can't take what happened to her on your shoulders. She had choices, many of them, and she went down that road all on her own. Even had you been the catalyst because she was angry with you, that was still a choice. I very much doubt you were the reason she went out that night. She was going whether she had the conversation with you or not."

Meiling knelt on the floor of the shower, staring down at the gray and blue stone tiles, watching as the water hit like teardrops and ran toward the drain. She didn't even know how she came to be in this place with this man. These were her choices, her path she'd taken. This was a man who killed easily and often. He might solve problems, but his solutions were more often than not permanent.

"Would you have killed me because I saw you shift, or because I witnessed you killing all those men?"

He rinsed the conditioner from her hair, his hands shielding her face from the water. "I'm not going to kill you. I told you that."

"I'm aware. That wasn't the question."

He began combing out tangles, careful to prevent pulling on her scalp. "Both. I can't leave witnesses to anything I've done. It's a law in the shifter world, to protect all shifters, that no outsider can know of us. I suspect you've known of us long before you witnessed me shifting."

She nodded. "That's true."

His hand came down on her shoulder, his fingers lingering on her skin. One long finger found the deep groove that slid down her back. She stiffened. Before he could tighten his grip on her to keep her in place, she scrambled away from him on all fours. Her heart went into overdrive. She didn't care if he heard.

"Thanks for talking to me and doing my hair. I can take it from here. If you need the shower, it's all yours. I don't know how you managed to stay so quiet with your leg in such bad shape." She was babbling, talking too fast, one word stumbling against the next, but she was out of his reach. Safe.

She caught up a towel and wrapped it around her hair like a turban. All the while she dried herself off, she watched him leerily as he slowly shampooed his hair, staying right where he was.

"I called Rene Guidry. He'll arrange for groceries. Text him whatever you want to add to the list. I'll give you his number. He's calling the eye doc and also arranging for a doctor to come in and X-ray my leg. Not that I think the doctor who gave me the once-over wasn't competent; he was. I just want to heal as fast as possible and would feel better with a second opinion. Rene takes care of things for me when I need them done quickly."

She shrugged. "I think that's a great idea." She folded her arms across the towel to hold it in place and walked back into the master bathroom. The cupboards yielded a jar of her favorite face cream, and it had never been used. "How many women do you let stay here?"

There was a small silence. She glanced over her shoulder

to see him draped casually against the wall just inside the room. It was disconcerting that even blind, he could walk so silently. She heard everything. Everyone. Just not, apparently, him. She made herself laugh softly, acting like it didn't matter. It shouldn't. She wasn't holding on to any girlish fantasies about Gedeon Volkov. He was leopard. Right there that meant he was ruthless and dangerous, and that was without knowing who he was. Then there was the high sex drive. Gedeon's reputation for one-night stands and casual sex was legendary. She wasn't about to be one of his many conquests.

"There's a jar of my favorite moisturizer in the cabinet. It's never been used, but you certainly don't wear it." She laughed again. "Or maybe you do. It's a really good product."

"One of the companies here, a renowned perfume company, went into skin care. At the time, they needed me to do some work for them. I was given a supply of their products and they've continued to send me various upgrades as they work on them."

"I do exchanges like that in my work, and I've never gotten a moisturizer that is this amazing." She turned back to apply it to her face.

"Just private jets and security escorts along with perfect legal documents when you need them."

She couldn't help laughing. "That's cool and all but not as kick-ass as a moisturizer that works."

"The company has a store in New Orleans, but their main operation is just outside of the city. They have a large acreage of land where they grow most of their flowers for their perfumes. The skin care line was developed in their lab there. I could arrange a tour. One of the owners, Charisse Mercier, is a little shy but very gracious when it comes to showing off her laboratory."

Meiling had no idea why she hesitated. She had a built-in radar when it came to leopards. She had been to New Orleans a couple of times, but she hadn't stayed. The place seemed overrun with leopards, and she hadn't known Gedeon had his home base there. "Is she leopard?"

He didn't speak for so long, she almost turned around again, but instead, she concentrated on combing out her hair. There was a blow dryer under the sink.

"Yes. Do you have a problem with leopards, Meiling? Nearly every one of the families I do the most business with are leopard families."

"So you do know my name." She had known all along she wouldn't be able to hide her name from him for very long.

"Your friend Etienne called you Meiling."

"He did, didn't he?" She was stalling, trying to think of a reasonable answer. She finished drying off and reached for fresh clothes. "You and I both know Amur leopards are brutal, Gedeon. The males hunt and kill females. Amur leopards are nearly extinct thanks to the brutality of male shifters. Even you admitted to me that you would hunt and kill me because I had witnessed you shifting."

He was silent so long, she couldn't help but sneak a quick look at him. He couldn't deny a single word she said no matter how much he might want to.

"In the forest, when you lifted the branch off my leg and then hauled me out of there on your own, you exhibited tremendous strength. I thought then you had to be leopard. You've said you don't have a leopard."

"I do come from a leopard background, but my leopard has never shown herself."

"Lotus, you must know that doesn't mean she isn't there. That's why you're so fast and strong. You have amazing gifts that many other leopards don't have."

She knew that was true, but she avoided leopards whenever possible. "Most of the leopard males can be quite cruel, Gedeon, you included. Don't bother to deny it. I've had plenty of time to investigate you. Your reputation with women is disgusting. That doesn't begin to touch on the reputation you have with very dangerous families from Russia. I am extremely aware of why the Amur leopard has been brought to the brink of extinction. The terrible rulers of these lairs murdered their women in order to prove their loyalty to the *bratya*. That's insane."

"I was born into just such a lair," he admitted.

She knew Gedeon Volkov was considered extremely dangerous, even by the Russian *bratya* families. What did it say about him if they feared him?

She made her way into the master bedroom. The room was quite large. There were two wide steps leading to a sitting area in front of a fireplace. Two wide, comfortable chairs faced the fireplace with a small table between them. She sank into one of the chairs and stared at the iron grate.

"I'm serious about wanting you to work with me, Lotus," he said.

She didn't turn around. "If you aren't wearing clothes, go away. I can't have a real conversation with you if you're going to insist on being naked."

"I'm sorry, Meiling. I'm always alone in my home and I don't bother with clothes. Give me a minute."

She heard the closet door slide open. She needed to think about the pros and cons of working with him. He worked mainly with the Russian *bratya*. That meant leopards. The really cruel, dangerous leopards who would watch her like a hawk. Every moment in their company she would be in jeopardy. She sighed. It would be wonderful to have a place to stay and feel safe. If she were under Gedeon Volkov's protection, she would definitely feel safer than she had since she was a child, but could she trust him? He was leopard. Admittedly Amur leopard and from a vicious lair. She'd be a fool to even consider staying. Better just see this through, wait until he had his eyesight back and then move on.

"Lotus Blossom."

The way he said her name made her stomach do a slow

roll. He had come up behind her in that silent way he had. Blind or not, he knew his way around the room. There was no stumbling on the two stairs. He found the chair unerringly and sat down, his legs sprawling out in front of him, reminding her one was still very much infected and had to hurt.

"Leopard Boy."

"You aren't going to give us a chance. I can feel the way you're determined to leave. You've got one foot out the door, just as you've had since you first met me."

That made her smile. "You can't exactly blame me, with all your threats and your reputation. You're a very dangerous man."

"That should reassure you. In any case, I would venture to say you're a very dangerous woman when you have to be. You're also very intelligent. It would be seriously remiss to turn down a business offer without thoroughly going over it."

"It's an intriguing offer, Gedeon, there's no doubt about it. I've been sitting here trying to figure out what the advantages would be for me, and given your clientele, I don't see that there would be very many. In fact, if anything, working with you could put me in some very bad situations."

"Do you want me to believe your mind doesn't insist on dangerous situations? Intrigue? You have a body built for fast reflexes. You're stronger than most men. In fact, I'd go as far as saying you're as fast and as strong as many of the male leopards. You're like me, Meiling. You think faster. Your brain demands more knowledge all the time. I know it does. You might excel more in other areas than I do, but that would be all to the good for us as partners."

She didn't want to hear what he was saying because it was all true. Every stinking word. She felt exposed. Very vulnerable. Libby hadn't even seen those traits in her and Libby had known her all her life. At the same time, someone saw her. Gedeon actually saw the real woman. That seemed a miracle.

"Everything you say could be the truth, but that doesn't negate what I said about the people you work for. One wrong move and it could all go to hell. I could put your life in jeopardy."

"You have no idea the power I wield, and the fear I inspire," he countered. "If you're my partner, no one would dare think to touch you. Unless your leopard decided to rise. Then every unmated leopard would vie for your leopard's attention, especially if you were in your first cycle."

He was coming at her from every angle, certain she had a leopard. Maybe she did, but she'd given up on believing she did when she turned eighteen and there was no sign of her.

"I thought we were going to put this conversation off until you got your eyesight back."

"You would be gone, and I'd have to chase you down. It's much better to hash it all out now. You would be a huge asset to me, Lotus. Not to mention, you calm my leopard. Having a respite from his constant fighting me for supremacy is an unbelievable miracle."

She took a deep breath and let it out. "You have a really bad reputation with women. I don't want any part of that."

"I'm not going to lie about having a sex drive that won't quit. On the other hand, I don't have women hanging around for a reason. My leopard won't tolerate them. We use each other and they're gone. I don't have relationships. No one spends the night. I wouldn't trust anyone that far anyway."

"You trusted me."

"Because my leopard did."

She banged her head against the back of the chair. "You're making it hard to say no. I don't know if I can help you with everything you do. I have a code."

"Believe it or not, so do I."

The image of him kneeling on the porch, his head in

his hands, weeping, came to her. She would never get that out of her mind. He had a code. Others may not be aware of it, but she saw it firsthand. "I know you do," she murmured. "You're making it difficult for me to say no to you. I have a good sense of self-preservation. If I decided to stay on as your partner, there would be things I would have to disclose to you. Just as there would be things you would need to tell me."

"Ultimately, Meiling, our lives would depend on each other. That means we have to trust each other. I'm willing to take a chance with you. You would have to decide whether or not you're willing to take a chance with me."

It was so tempting to have a home. A refuge. A man like Gedeon Volkov would be fiercely loyal once he gave his word. "Anything I disclosed to you would only be to you. You wouldn't share the information with your man Rene Guidry, would you?"

"No. I wouldn't expect you to share anything I tell you about me, so I would afford you the same courtesy."

Meiling rubbed her upper thigh gently with her palm while she thought over what she was going to say. "The idea of working with you has some appeal," she conceded. "But the rules would have to be very clear. We'd have to go over everything ahead of time so you know what I'm willing to do for your clients and what cases I won't work on. I'm good with computers, so I could help behind the scenes."

"You said leopards react much like mine does around you. If you're in a room with male leopards, will they be raging at you, or just ignoring you as if you don't exist?"

"They ignore me." She forced herself to look at him.

Gedeon had pulled on a black tee, stretching it over his thick chest and letting his dark hair fall free. Of course he looked tough and gorgeous. Staying in the same house with him was out of the question.

"Taking you with me when I go to a party will be such

an asset. You're so tiny. If you slide into the shadows, my shy little companion, eventually, the leopards will forget you're there. They'll be watching me. Worried about what I'm doing there. What I want. Who I'm after. The more nervous I make them, the more freedom you'll have. You'll be wandering around the room, listening to the conversations and collecting data on everything and everyone."

"I have a price on my head." She blurted it out.

He might as well know the worst. She might as well know if he was going to turn on her. She watched his reaction carefully. It was impossible to read his expression. He didn't respond right away. He sat in silence contemplating her disclosure. In the end, he steepled his fingers.

"Who put the price on your head and how much are they offering?"

"I have no idea what the answer is to either question. I lived with Libby's family since I was a small child. They were attacked on several occasions. Eventually, her father was killed. I think I was ten. Then her mother. I was thirteen. Libby and I were taken in by a neighbor, as we had no other relatives. A year later, they were attacked and killed. Libby and I escaped and ran to a friend's house. We were taken in and lived with them until we turned eighteen."

"It could have been both of you girls. Or just Libby."

"Libby isn't really my blood relative. We just always called each other cousins. Her father worked for my father and apparently just showed up with me one day. They never talked about the how and why of it. According to Libby, he planned on telling me everything about my family when I was old enough, but then he died."

"Did Libby know?"

"She would have told me. She couldn't keep a secret to save her life," Meiling explained. She spread her hands out in front of her. "I started separating myself from her for a few weeks at a time to draw the killers away from her just to be certain they were after me. I watched over her. I wanted to make certain she was safe. They followed me and left her alone."

"Were they *bratya*? Did you ever see them?"

She shook her head. "I never got close enough. I had to make money to support us. Libby is . . ." Her stomach dropped. "*Was* a spender. She liked nice hotels and pretty clothes. I would get the money to pay for those things for her."

"She didn't work?"

Meiling sighed. Libby shone like the brightest star. It didn't bother Meiling to work for both of them. Libby's family had taken care of her for most of her life. She could support Libby. "No, she didn't work. She was never attacked, not until Colombia, and I didn't get the sense that it was the same people involved. If they had been looking for me, they would have tortured her to get the information on where to find me."

"Would she have given them what they wanted to know?"

Meiling refused to cry. Libby could be selfish at times. Moody. Even temperamental. But she genuinely loved Meiling and regarded her as family. She shook her head and then reminded herself that Gedeon was blind. "She wouldn't, at least she'd hold out as long as she could. She was stubborn, and if she thought they were going to harm me, she would do her best to make them believe she didn't know where I was. Truthfully, she didn't really know. She did always have my cell number."

4

GEDEON listened carefully to every nuance of her voice. Meiling was pushing down grief as best she could. He had an unexpected urge to wrap a comforting arm around her and pull her close, just as he had in the shower. The reaction was so foreign to his nature and that of his cat that he wanted to take a little time to examine it. Was it possible she was his mate? If so, why wasn't his male pushing to claim her?

The vicious leopard, always raking and clawing to kill, had gone quiet, but he wasn't amorous. Gedeon had his own suspicions about Meiling and where she came from. It made even more sense now that he knew she had a price on her head. She had too many gifts. Amur leopards were rare, that was true. They were on the verge of extinction, and the male shifters were mostly to blame. There were only a few left in the world. Females were extremely rare. Females such as Meiling had been all but wiped off the face of the earth—deliberately.

"I'm sorry about Libby, Meiling. I couldn't save a single one of those women or children. Not one. I despise the people involved in those kinds of operations. I don't take any case involving human trafficking and all clients I work with know it."

"That wasn't your fault, Gedeon. They had a plan to murder everyone the moment anything went wrong. You couldn't have known that."

"I should have known it. That's what these kinds of people do. They have no regard for human life at all. I grew up in one of the most vicious lairs there was. My mother's legs were beaten so badly she couldn't walk so she wouldn't resist anything they did to her."

He heard her hastily cover a gasp. She was intelligent. Very intelligent. She didn't think in terms of who or what she had to be. Or even why there was a price on her head— but no doubt she had considered why he was faster and deadlier than other leopards. Why he could absorb languages so quickly and his mind worked at such a rapid rate.

The Amur leopards had three elite leopard families with unbelievable skills. The *bratya* wanted them stamped out in Russia. The rulers in China wanted them gone. The lairs in North Korea wanted them dead. Gedeon's father had been murdered along with his older brother and sister. His mother had been enslaved. He had been taken by the ruling *pakhan*. He had been so young, the *pakhan* thought he would be able to shape him into an asset.

In North Korea, the family of elites had been wiped out entirely, parents and children murdered in the dead of night. Like Gedeon's family, a friend had betrayed them and opened the doors to their home to the frenzied mob. Those genetics, whatever they had been, were gone from the shifter world, and those plotting had triumphed.

The elite family in China had been set upon, the parents, two daughters and two sons all murdered. One man, loyal to the royals, snatched up the third daughter, a child of barely two, and disappeared with her. No one noticed she was gone until they were burning the bodies to ensure the leopards weren't found. No one had any idea who had saved the child or where she had been taken. From that moment on, the search had continued.

Gedeon had honed himself into the most dangerous leopard imaginable. He killed the *pakhan* and every male member of his family. He killed his lieutenants. He hunted down every single male who participated in the murder of his family. In those early days he made his reputation as frightening to every *bratya* lair and family as possible. He had done so without giving away the fact that he was the remaining child from the family they had murdered. No one knew where he had originated.

He wished he could see Meiling. He had only caught that one glimpse of her in the jungle. She was very small and slender with shiny ebony hair and dark eyes. He was absolutely certain he was right about her being the missing child from the elite family in China. Her family had been murdered. His had been too, all but his mother, and she would have preferred it. He couldn't think about that or he would become as vicious as his leopard, and he didn't want Meiling to see him that way—not when he was trying to recruit her.

"Gedeon." She whispered his name and then her fingers brushed his arm gently. "I'm so sorry. No wonder you despise men who deal in human trafficking."

"I killed them all. Every last one of them. You need to know that about me. All those things you found out when you did your research, they're true." He was rolling the dice admitting his true nature to her. "It's even worse than that."

"Do you expect me to condemn you for killing the men

who trafficked your mother? And who brutally hurt her to keep her from running?"

"You mean took a hammer to her legs?" There was no keeping the bitterness out of his voice. When that door cracked open, it was as real and as raw as when he'd witnessed it as a child. He found he was shaking and that embarrassed him. He wasn't used to feeling his emotions or putting them on display for others. That made him feel vulnerable, especially since he couldn't see a damn thing.

He lifted his hand to the bandages covering his eyes, wanting—no—*needing* to rip the damn covering from them. Her hand very gently stopped his. It was all he could do not to knock her hand away. He was grateful for the years of discipline.

He hadn't revealed one single thing about his childhood to anyone, not since he'd left the lair in complete and utter ruin with no way to repair itself. They couldn't possibly come back from their loss of power. The powerful families around them had gobbled up their territories and swallowed their businesses, leaving them with nothing at all.

Gedeon had never wanted to claim his elite status or have it known he was the sole survivor of his bloodline. As far as he was concerned, the only thing useful about it was the gifts that came with it. His abilities that made it possible to run faster, be stronger, recall in detail information heard only once. He picked up languages fast. The list went on and on. He didn't need to talk about what he was, or who he was. He didn't want others to know. When he read the shit about him on the internet, things Meiling would have found, no one had a clue where he came from. Just Russia. No one knew about shifters. That was always kept secret.

He forced himself to continue with the conversation. Forced his voice to be casual, as if imparting information to her that she needed to know. Not that he'd witnessed firsthand. Not the kind of thing that had triggered a violent monster in both him and his leopard that could never be taken back. That monster lived and breathed in him and needed attention all the time in so many ways.

"It's more common than you think. Bastards believe if the woman isn't cooperative, they should beat the hell out of her legs with a hammer to make sure she has no choice other than to do what they say. More than once, when I've gone in to stop them, I've looked at their phones and discovered text messages detailing just how to beat the woman into submission."

He heard her take a deep breath. Let it out slowly. "Do you have clients that deal in human trafficking? These people, these *bratya* families, aren't saints, Gedeon."

"Are you listening to me? If they dealt in human trafficking, they wouldn't be my clients. All of them know it. They know if they become my enemies, they haven't long for the world. I make it my life's work to go after these people. I don't care about compensation for it. It's a betrayal to me. The drug trafficking is always going to happen. It isn't right and I don't have to like it, but it's going to keep going whether I'm around or not."

"Do you run drugs for these families?"

"No. Never. I step in when something goes wrong. Someone doesn't pay a bill and war is about to start. We don't want that because now innocent civilians could get hurt in the crossfire. I'm called in to negotiate a settlement, or to collect the money owed. I have no direct interest in the product. I just make it known that there is a time limit, and we have to settle to my satisfaction. I'm the last resort."

He heard her rubbing her thigh again. That bothered him. She *had* gotten hurt. He just didn't know how.

"I'm really not good at spending a lot of time around people, especially anyone leopard." She sounded cautious. "This man, Rene, who works for you. Is he leopard? He would have to be to spend time with you. To get you the right doctors when you've been hurt."

"Yes, he's leopard, but you wouldn't be working for him. You'd work *with* me. That means when you need something, you can ask him for help, and he'll give it to you."

There was silence. He found himself smiling. "Are you rolling your eyes at me?"

"Are you certain you can't see, Leopard Boy?" she countered, in a very disrespectful, sarcastic tone no one ever used on him.

He waited for confirmation.

"As a matter of fact, I was rolling my eyes. You want to make everything sound so easy. Your man Rene works for you. I have no idea for how long, but his loyalty is all yours. I come along, a total stranger he knows nothing about. What do you think is the first thing he's going to do? The man will require a thorough background check on me regardless of your orders. I know because I'd do one. I wouldn't care how adamant you were about not doing one, I would protect you and your idiocy."

"He knows not to go against my orders."

There was the small silence again that told him she'd done another eye roll. He'd had sex with more women than he could count, but never had one dared to roll her eyes at him. He'd never had his leopard be calm and peaceful. And he'd never wanted to smile. Not one single time. If he was looking for any reasons to keep this woman around, there were three good ones right there.

"You've spent too long with the wrong people, Freaky Man. You do that with no one challenging you and you begin to believe your own hype. That's a dangerous practice."

She had such a smart mouth. He couldn't wait for his eyes to clear. She was right, though. He couldn't fault her for being right. Rene most likely would go behind his back and conduct a search on her. It would be better to give him something and forestall a deep search.

"See why I need you? You'll keep me on my toes."

She was silent again for a few seconds, rubbing her thigh.

He couldn't take it. He reached over the small table, removed her hand and laid his palm over her thigh. Her leg was very slender, but he could feel the muscles running beneath her frame. He began a slow massage.

"What happened here? And don't tell me nothing happened. You're hurt."

Meiling sighed. "It's nothing. You have that infection in your leg, and it was really bad when I put you in the car. Your fever was high, the leg very swollen. You couldn't see. I told Etienne to have his men take extra care with you. I told them you were my brother. That asshole dragged you out of the car deliberately because he was high as a kite and wanted to prove to Etienne that he could control the situation. I've had run-ins with him before."

Alarm bells went off. "Meiling, are you saying this man knew you? He knows your name and you've had problems with him?"

"He didn't know you. He didn't even get a good look at you, Gedeon. Your eyes were covered, most of your face was. I was the one fighting them deliberately. I kept their attention centered on me."

"You deliberately brought the heat down on yourself knowing you have a hit on you." He swore, once again reaching for the bandages on his eyes, needing to tear them off.

She caught his hand. "You won't be able to see even if you take those off. Wait for the new doctor's assessment. In any case, you already know the light is going to be harmful to you."

"You shouldn't have brought attention to yourself like that."

Soft laughter greeted his rebuke.

He wanted to shake her. Instead, he laid his palm over her thigh. "Is this bruised?" He would hear if she lied.

"His name is Jules and he has a brother. Jules dragged you out of the car and I went berserk, calling him out. His brother, Louis, smashed the butt of his gun on my thigh as I turned in the front seat to cover Jules with my gun. It hurt like hell and my automatic reaction was to retaliate. I might have hit Louis just a little too hard. He dropped to the ground, and I got out of the car and managed to get around the hood before anyone else decided to take me on. I think I scared them all."

She was fierce. She didn't know him and yet she had put her life on the line to save him. In his mind, there was no question who she was and where she came from. He would bet his last penny on it. But she'd fucked up royally by drawing attention to herself when she had enemies. Jules and his brother, Louis, wouldn't forget the woman who had shown them up.

"Is Etienne going to be angry enough with those two men that he'd take them out? They went against his orders, and one laid his hands on you. He hurt you."

She shifted a little under his hand, but she didn't push it away. "Louis and Jules are related to him in some way. His nephews, I think. He wouldn't do that. At least I don't think he would. In any case, they wouldn't go against Etienne. No one does."

"Lotus Blossom." He said his pet name for her as gently as possible. He wanted to lean into her and inhale her feminine fragrance. She smelled a little like he thought the gateway to heaven might. "You accused me of being arrogant and you were right. Think about what you just said. These men already went against Etienne's orders. If they have a grudge against you, it's going to eat away at them. If they can find a way to get back at you, they're going to."

"Fortunately, they don't know where I am or who I am," she said. "I made the commitment to get you out free and clear, Gedeon. I keep my word. You were my client at that point. My responsibility. You were vulnerable and easily targeted. Your face is recognizable. I covered you up as best I could, but if Jules actually took the time to look at you, he might have been able to identify you. That was unacceptable."

He found himself clenching his teeth, biting back the need to swear. He'd never had anyone protecting him, not since the night the *pakhan* and his men had come to murder his family and force his mother—and him—into service. He had mixed feelings about Meiling shielding him. She could say he was her client, but he wasn't paying her, and as far as he knew, she didn't owe him a damned thing. He didn't like her exposed—and she was. Had he not been blind and had some infection that was still raging in his body, he would have been on the first plane to France, or wherever Etienne and his crew had their home base, and he would have eliminated Jules and Louis immediately.

"Babe, you can't go around standing in front of your clients like that, not when you're being hunted. I'm not dictating. I've been in this business a long time and I know the rules of survival. Drawing attention to yourself in order to save your client isn't an acceptable practice for any reason."

"I don't make it a habit."

"That's good to know." He stroked a caress over the bruise on her thigh, wishing he could see how extensive the damage was. "Just how often have you done it?"

She sighed. "Seriously? You're going to ask me that? Is this an interview for the job? How many other applicants are there? Because I don't think too many people will be able to put up with your rather—er—intense personality."

"I like the way you avoid answering by going on the offensive. You still have to answer the question."

"I did it the one time, just to save your butt, although I'm beginning to think it might not have been worth the trouble, especially considering the favor I called in. You can be maddening. Annoying beyond reason. In fact, Leopard Boy, I want to hit you over the head with your knockoff Ming vase and hope, somehow, a miracle occurs and you suddenly lose half your arrogance."

"Knockoff?" She made him want to laugh. He had forgotten what laughter was. He swore even his leopard found her amusing. No one had protected him and no one had ever stood up to him the way she did. "What makes you think it's fake? If you're going to hit me over the head, maybe don't choose the vase."

He was rewarded with her soft laughter. He found that the sound of her laughter did something extraordinary to his mind. She brought him peace. Just as his leopard felt peaceful, so did he. To a man who hadn't known peace, she was a miracle. She was so many parts of a puzzle and he needed to know every single one of them.

It was frustrating to be blind. He wanted to see her expressions and be able to read her. He was extremely good at reading body language. He couldn't afford to lose her because he didn't have his sight and made a misstep with her. He sensed she was always on the verge of flight. In some ways it was good that he was blind and had an infection. She wouldn't leave until he was better. He hadn't been with her that long, but he already knew that about her.

"Have you made this offer to anyone else?"

"No. I've never come across anyone who had your capabilities." He was honest. "In any case, my leopard wouldn't tolerate anyone in my space for any length of time. I would most likely have a difficult time as well. I've lived my life alone when I'm not working. My home is my space and I need it that way."

"Why would you want me to move in here?"

"My leopard is calm when you're close." Again, he was honest—or was he? Did he want her to move in just for his leopard? Or was it because she challenged him? Made him laugh? Because she'd protected him when no one else ever had? He didn't have an answer, so he left it the way he'd said it to her.

She stayed silent longer than he was comfortable with. Silently cursing his eyes, he forced himself to give her time. It was reasonable to want her near him if his leopard was calm. She had to know that.

"I'm used to having my own space."

He could understand that. He was the same way. He had forgotten about walking around naked in his home because he'd done it for years. He was comfortable without clothes. He could shift easily, accommodating his leopard when the cat wanted to curl up in the window seat to bask in the sun.

"Go up to the third floor. We can change it to suit what you need for your own apartment. You can have your own entrance. It won't take much to make that happen."

"You can put a little kitchen up there for me?"

Gedeon had hoped she'd share his kitchen, but if she wanted a kitchen and that would get her to stay in the house with him, he'd get a kitchen put in for her. "I told you, anything you want up there to make the space yours. You would have the entire floor. If you go up and check it out, you could decide how best to design it. Once you do, let me know and I'll get the workers to start as soon as possible." In the meantime, he was going to find ways to keep her close to him.

She stiffened. "Someone just entered the house." She made as if to get up.

He tightened his hold on her thigh. "That's Rene. Just relax."

She wasn't relaxing. If anything, she had pulled out a gun and put it in the chair beside her where it wasn't showing.

Gedeon's leopard knew and even tolerated Rene's presence. The cat was intelligent. Rene looked out for them, seeing to their everyday needs and providing security to their home base when they were away. They needed him. Gedeon's leopard, Slayer, although increasingly vicious, had refrained from trying to break free around Rene. For some strange reason, that didn't seem to be the case now. The male had awakened with a vengeance, catching Gedeon by surprise. The big male slashed and clawed for freedom, trying to tear free as if he needed to protect Gedeon and Meiling from Rene and his male leopard.

It took a moment to fight back and show the leopard he wasn't putting up with his crap. "What's wrong with you?" he muttered aloud.

"I'm sorry?" Meiling sounded genuinely puzzled.

"My damn leopard is losing his mind. Slayer knows Rene. He tolerates him as a rule. Right now he's acting like Rene is the enemy."

"Maybe he knows something you don't. I told you, you're too complacent." She swiveled in her chair, so she was facing the door. "Slayer? You named your leopard Slayer? No wonder he's vicious. He knows you're expecting him to rip everyone apart. You need a different name for him. I'm *not* calling him Slayer."

Once again, he wished he could see her expression. "What do you have in mind?" Despite his leopard giving him hell, he couldn't keep the amusement out of his voice.

"Gedeon?" a man's voice with a decided Cajun accent called out.

Slayer reacted again, raking at him, leaping toward the surface as if he could break through and take over their form. Gedeon fought him back. It took a minute. The leopard was in a fury. He had to breathe deeply and really reprimand the cat.

We need him. What's wrong with you? Is he coming to kill us? Is he secretly turning on us? What is he doing that is causing you to act this way?

I don't trust him with her.

That brought Gedeon up short. He didn't necessarily want Rene—or anyone else—around Meiling until he had his eyesight back and he could watch over her himself.

Was he influencing his leopard to feel the same way? Or was his leopard influencing him?

"Gedeon?" Rene's voice was closer. More insistent. A trace of worry in it.

"In the bedroom," Gedeon answered.

Meiling was silent. Very still. She didn't seem to want Rene around any more than Slayer did. He smelled Rene before the door opened. Rene had the scent of the swamp. Earthy and raw. He was homegrown. The scent was very subtle, but it clung to his skin.

There was a short silence. "You have company."

"I told you I did. This is Meiling. She saved my life."

"Meiling." Rene came closer. "I didn't realize you were here."

"I wouldn't leave him alone and unprotected." She spoke very quietly, her tone strictly neutral. She didn't have her sass. But she did have just a hint of censure.

Rene wouldn't like that. He was leopard. Arrogant. And he'd been Gedeon's right-hand man for many years.

"Did you find an eye doctor?" Gedeon interrupted before Rene could respond.

"Yes, Dr. Bouet will be here in half an hour. Drake recommended him. He's been scrupulously vetted. He's a shifter and Drake's people had him checked out years ago. Doc Eloi is on his way as well to take a look at your leg."

"Thanks, Rene. That was fast. I need you to stock the house. I'll be here awhile."

"Taken care of."

"Meiling will be moving in with me."

There was silence. Rene cleared his throat. "There seems to be a bit of a disagreement about that, Gedeon. The young lady is shaking her head."

"Gedeon, I said I'd think about your offer."

"You also said you'd stay until I had my vision back. I don't have it back."

Rene laughed. "She's making a face. A cute face."

"It's *not* cute. He's annoying me. He pushes and pushes until he gets his way."

Gedeon found he didn't like the exchange between the two. He should have wanted them to get along. When Rene first entered and the tension had risen between the two, he hadn't been happy, but now he *really* wasn't happy, and he didn't know why. He put it down to not being able to see and feeling left out even though both were including him. His leopard was still raging. That also could be making him edgy.

"Usually, he intimidates to get his way," Rene said. "Don't you find him intimidating?"

"She doesn't because I don't have my eyesight and I can't chase her down," Gedeon said.

Meiling rose and his hand slipped off her thigh. "Now that your friend is here and the doctors are coming, I'll take off. I need to get a few things. I don't have much in the way of clothes for this kind of weather."

"I'm going to talk to Rene about the third floor," Gedeon said.

"She's rolling her eyes."

"She'd strangle him if she could fit her fingers around his neck. That Ming vase of yours is very much in jeopardy. Rene, I suggest you lock that thing up if you want it to survive my stay here."

Gedeon knew she walked out, not because he heard her, but because he felt her leave.

"*Mon Dieu,* Gedeon, where did she come from?"

"I told you, she saved my life. A bomb went off, blinding me and bringing a branch the size of a small tree down on my leg. She came back for me. Got the branch off my leg, hauled my ass out of the jungle and called in a favor to fly me out of Venezuela. She's good at what she does. She doesn't miss the smallest detail."

"How do you know she isn't here to collect a bounty on you?"

"She could have done it ten times over. What does your leopard say to you around her? Does he feel she's a threat?"

"No. He's actually enamored with her. That was quite shocking. I've never had my leopard react like that before. It wasn't as if he was reacting to a female in heat. I honestly couldn't tell if she was a shifter. I've heard of a few women who seem to be able to calm leopards, not that mine is prone to temper. Drake Donovan runs a tight ship. I'm in his lair and he wouldn't put up with my leopard throwing fits for a minute."

"What would he do?"

"Most likely send me to Borneo, have me looking for a mate—the right mate. I'd go too. Drake's a fair man."

Gedeon knew Drake Donovan. Rene was right, Drake Donovan was a fair man. He was one of the few men Gedeon liked.

"I want to get workmen lined up to start on the third floor. I'll need a separate entrance built. I'm going to talk Meiling into a partnership with me. I want her living here. The only way she'll do it is to have an apartment of her own. She calms my leopard down. It's the first peace I've had in years."

"You can't offer her a partnership because she calms your leopard down, Gedeon." Rene was genuinely horrified.

"That's not the reason. I've needed someone, but there was no one qualified. She is. She's so damned intelligent I think she can strengthen what I do. I need you to do a little research for me, but it won't be easy. There's a Frenchman, a man by the name of Etienne. Very wealthy. Owns a private jet. We flew on it from Venezuela. He has two nephews. I only know their first names. Jules and Louis. I know I'm not giving you much, but you've worked with less. I need you to get as much information on them as you possibly can, especially the two nephews. Once you find them, I want to know where they are. I want to know who they talk to. Who their friends are. Keep track of them. It's important, Rene."

"Do you think someone can identify you?"

"Not me. She put her life on the line for me. She let them see her face. And they have a grudge against her."

Rene sighed. "It's my obligation to point out to you that she's putting you in danger by being close to you, Gedeon."

"You've done your duty, Rene. I want this woman for a partner. Get this information for me and find a good contractor willing to work extra hours. I'll pay double time, but I want quality work."

"Is she your leopard's mate?"

"I don't know. Her leopard hasn't risen yet. It's entirely possible. I won't know until she goes into heat. In the meantime, I'm not messing up a partnership by fucking her. If something goes wrong, I've lost her, and I'm not doing that."

"Gedeon, you're not making any sense. If you think you can carry on the way you do with women right in front of her and that isn't going to impact your relationship with her in any way, you're wrong."

"Why would it if we're just partners? If we keep things on a purely platonic level?"

"Can you do that? You have no interest in her sexually?" Rene demanded.

"Someone's at the door," Gedeon said. He didn't want to answer the question. Or the next one. He already knew Rene was going to ask if it would bother him if Rene went out with her. Hell yes it would bother him. But he would get over it. He had to. Their partnership had to come first. If she had a leopard and the leopard emerged and Slayer claimed her, that was a different story. In the meantime, Gedeon wasn't taking a chance on losing the best thing he had ever been given. Sex was just sex. It meant nothing at all. But a relationship with someone like Meiling was a gift to be treasured.

Just the idea that another male leopard might lay claim to Meiling was too much for him to consider. His mind couldn't go there. The moment it did, his leopard roared for supremacy and raked viciously at him, rebelling at just the impressions in Gedeon's head.

Meiling already knew too much about him, more than anyone else. Things he didn't want anyone to know. He would have instantly killed anyone who had discovered his past, without a qualm. He was responsible for giving his childhood away. Had he done that deliberately? Shared with her because for the first time in his life he knew he could? He'd told her about his mother, a small part of him hoping she would share her past with him. He hadn't expected her to intuitively know what happened to him. His rise from the *pakhan*'s amusing toy to assassin to the vengeful destroyer of the entire *bratya* cell.

Meiling was intelligent, and he needed that in his partner. She was able to stand up to him when no one, not even Rene, dared to. She might not be the same once he got his eyesight back. That remained to be seen. Slayer was once again losing his mind, which meant Rene was close to the master bedroom with the doctor.

I need care to get my sight back, Slayer. Calm down. And it will be very interesting to see what name Lotus Blossom gives you. He conveyed his amusement to the animal.

Some of the anger faded from the animal, leaving him perplexed. *She wishes to give me another name?*

One of affection. I call her Lotus Blossom, but her given name is Meiling. When we are alone, she calls me Leopard Boy.

Slayer was quiet, trying to process what was a new concept for him. He was intelligent and could draw on Gedeon's knowledge. He liked to learn new ideas, in fact demanded it. Right now, trying to assimilate the concept of Meiling calling him something *affectionate*, something different than anyone else . . .

Secret. Just between us. In the way I call her Lotus Blossom. That is only ours, Gedeon persisted with the explanation. He wanted Slayer to grasp the meaning, but what's more, the leopard was ignoring Rene's approach with the eye doctor.

Slayer settled down completely, although, as always when there was a stranger close, he stayed alert. Mostly he was turning over and over the information that Gedeon had given him on affectionate names given to one another and doing his best to understand.

"Dr. Bouet, this is Gedeon Volkov," Rene introduced them. "I'm closing all the blinds so no light can come in. You can open them if you need to, Dr. Bouet."

Gedeon heard Rene at the windows. Meiling had closed most of the blinds before Gedeon had joined her.

"Dr. Bouet, thank you for coming on such short notice." He could hear the man setting up a tray and laying out instruments on it.

"I'll need to know how this injury occurred."

Gedeon wasn't surprised. If he wanted truth and healing, he was going to have to trust Drake Donovan's judgment. Drake was the head of one of the largest local lairs of shifters. He didn't have a treacherous bone in his body. No one was ever going to bribe Drake—including him. Drake was a straight shooter all the way and put the health and welfare of his lair first. If he trusted the eye specialist, Gedeon would do his best to extend the man the same courtesy.

"A bomb went off right in front of me. The flash was horrendous. I tried to close my eyes, but I didn't get them closed in time."

"Were you in human form or leopard form?"

"I was in leopard form. I'd just shifted back to human

form when I got the bomb warning. I leapt off the porch, shifting as I did so. The bomb caught Slayer in the third leap, throwing us into the air. He had his eyes wide open. I shifted as we were thrown about thirty feet through the brush. I didn't want him to take the brunt of the fall. Already I couldn't see a damn thing, but I thought it was all the debris in the air and in my eyes. When I hit the ground, trees were falling, and a large branch came down on top of me." He thought he was going to die, and he didn't want anyone to see his leopard and possibly skin him for his pelt.

Dr. Bouet sighed as he unwrapped the bandages from around Gedeon's eyes. "Someone worked on your eyes at the site, didn't they?" he stated as he shone a light first in the left eye and then the right. "Whoever it was saved your vision. They knew about your leopard."

Gedeon felt the need to protect Meiling. "I saw a doctor before I left the country. He gave me eye drops and told me not to let any light touch my eyes."

"It would have been better to give you a salve, but then he didn't realize it was your leopard's eyes that were damaged so severely. By shifting, you saved his vision."

"Are we going to come back from this?"

"By staying in human form and keeping the light from your eyes, you've already begun the healing process. It will take time, but your vision will be fully restored."

The doctor spent time patiently examining Gedeon's eyes from every angle, putting drops in them to dilate them and then examining them again. "You won't need bandages, but dark glasses are a must at all times. The salve in the eyes is also a must. Putting it in will be uncomfortable, but once it's in, I guarantee it will make that burning go away. You'll very quickly begin to see little blocks of light. Don't rub your eyes or try to strain to see more. Don't remove your dark glasses. Just be patient and let your eyes recover on their own."

"I can leave the house?"

"Of course, but it would be better if you left in the evening when the light isn't harsh. You will need dark glasses even at night. If for some reason you choose to go out during the day, you will have to wear more than one pair of dark glasses. You'll have to black out the sun."

Gedeon didn't like the sound of that. He couldn't see a reason for leaving the house during the day. If he left, he'd make certain to go at night. "Thanks, Doc. I appreciate you coming to my home."

"I'll stop by in a week to check on you unless you need me sooner. Have Rene call me."

As soon as the eye specialist stepped out of the room, Dr. Eloi took his place. Gedeon had known him almost since he'd first arrived in New Orleans. The leg was swollen, bruised and infected, but Eloi was extremely positive about treating the infection with the right cocktail of intravenous antibiotics when the results came back from his lab.

"Stay out of your nightclub until I give you the go-ahead. You can't put weight on that, so walk with the crutches I'll send someone over to fit you with. And no physical activities for a little while. You tend to be a bit on the vigorous side, Gedeon."

"Having a woman suck my cock isn't going to hurt my leg, Eloi," Gedeon objected.

"Follow my instructions. Someone will come to administer the IV antibiotics daily. Or twice a day. Don't scare them off."

"No sex? For how long?"

"However long it takes," Eloi said, no sympathy in his voice as he walked out. "You can manage."

5

GEDEON had never needed sex more in his life. He woke in a sweat, his cock harder than a rock. It was his own damn fault. To tame his fucking leopard, he kept Meiling with him, playing chess or reading to him until she keeled over, so exhausted that she just slept in his bed—his goal all along. He would accuse her of cheating at chess because she moved the pieces on the chess board for them both and he would change the positions deliberately when she got him something to drink.

He liked to hear her laughter. That laugh of hers put absolute steel in his cock. She always laughed when she realized he had moved the pieces when she returned with the drinks. Once she only pretended to leave the room. He called her on it because Slayer was well aware she was lurking in the doorway. Her laughter bubbled up like the finest champagne.

She was small and light, so it was easy to gently guide her to the center of the bed and position her body right next to his. Slayer liked her close. Gedeon told himself he was doing this night after night for his leopard and suffering the hardship of becoming desperate for sex, because his hands couldn't help finding their way to her soft skin. She had the softest skin he'd ever felt. His legs tangled with hers. Twice his hands cupped her breasts.

He sat up, trying to control his breathing, trying to breathe away the fierce need. He'd always been a sexual man, but the urgency was so much more severe. His cock was a monster, so out of control. He'd always imposed such strict discipline on himself, and he'd wondered if this was the result—the one place he'd been unable to tame.

What was he doing, torturing himself? Why? Why insist Meiling sleep in his bed beside him? Was he really afraid she'd slip away in the middle of the night? He was a hunter. That was what he did—he found people who ran away from their responsibilities. She couldn't run from him now if she wanted to. He knew her.

At first, she was reluctant to talk too much about herself. The more he disclosed of his past, the more she disclosed small things about herself to him. Not anything of her past, just little things. He knew she liked to cook and watched reality shows and bad movies. They made her laugh. She never watched horror films or anything where someone was bullied.

Beside him she stirred, and he made certain the log that was his burning cock was nowhere near her body. She gave a little groan and sat up next to him, scrubbing her hands down her face. He felt that gesture as one arm slid against his.

"Oh no, I did it again. I fell asleep in your bed, Gedeon. And you're awake again." Her hand touched his face. "What is it this time?"

He was tempted to lie again, but she wasn't believing

the lies he fed her. Deliberately, he took her hand and placed it over his bare, hot, swollen cock. The monster jumped and jerked the moment there was contact with that small, soft palm. "I can't go this long without sex."

He expected her to pull her hand away and leap out of the bed, but she was Meiling, and she always did the unexpected. "Poor baby. That does give you a problem, doesn't it?" There was amusement in her voice. She patted his cock a bit irreverently and lifted her hand away.

Women found his cock *amazing*. Magnificent. She just patted it like he was a schoolboy with his first-time erection. She didn't seem to understand the dire situation. "I don't suppose you would want to take care of it?"

"Nice offer, but no thanks." She was already sliding off the bed.

He couldn't lose her. She'd go sleep somewhere and he'd sit there alone, losing his mind, in pain, with a useless rock-hard cock that *she* put there.

"Lotus, give me a break."

"What do you normally do in this circumstance?"

There was laughter in her voice. He'd give anything to see her facial expression. There was something about just being close to her that got inside of him and turned him inside out.

"I go to the club and find a woman to take care of the problem."

"At least you agree it is a problem."

How could he want to laugh when he hurt like hell? More, he was relaxing, and so, damn it, was his cock. "The only thing we can agree on is that you refused to help me when I was in dire straits. I thought you were a generous person."

"Did you really believe I was just going to give you a blow job?"

"Well . . . yeah. I go to the club and there are a hundred women who vie for the honor. At least a hundred. Maybe more. I don't have to ask, Lotus, they stand in line." He was fairly certain he got an eye roll from her.

"Do you have any idea how incredibly spoiled and arrogant you are? I hope you scrub that thing clean after putting it in all those mouths. If you can't make it to the club and you're in a bad way, what do you do then?"

"I call Rene and he brings me a woman."

There was a short silence. "Sheesh, Gedeon. You turned your friend into a pimp. That's so wrong. Why can't you pick up the phone and get yourself a woman? Don't you have a little black book or something? Your contact list is full and then some, but I didn't find women listed."

"You snooped in my contacts?"

"Naturally, but you'll have to reprimand me later. I'm trying to help you here."

"How? Were you thinking of procuring a woman for me?"

"I considered it, but I think it best if you do it. It's the manly thing to do. You shouldn't wake Rene for this. You need to learn to make those calls yourself."

So much for Meiling pining away for him. That suppressed laughter in her voice was at his expense. He should be annoyed with her, not wanting to laugh with her.

"The doctor said I wasn't to have sex."

Meiling must have paused at the door. She sounded as if she was at the door, that distance away, although he hadn't heard her, not even a whisper of sound. "You sneak. He seriously told you no sex and you're trying to get me to give you a blow job behind his back."

"I wouldn't have let you."

"You are a bald-faced liar," she accused.

That was the honest truth—he was. He burst out laughing. "Do you want to go to the Café Du Monde with me? It's a nice walk. We could grab coffee and sit by river and watch the sun come up."

"We could grab coffee, sit by the river and *I* could watch

the sun come up. You would have to wear the special glasses sent to you by the doctor. You remember him. And then there's the other one, the doc who said no sex."

He took the opportunity to get up and find his clothes. He'd named a local hangout that was a favorite of his in the hopes she would want to go with him.

"You do know you're physically superb, Gedeon. It isn't any wonder those women throw themselves at you. At the same time, you seem to think the responsibility is all theirs when it comes to sex with you. They may have certain expectations."

He paused in the act of pulling up his jeans to look toward the doorway where her voice was coming from, damning the fact that his eyes were useless. "I make it very clear there is no relationship between us. *Very* clear, Meiling. I'm a shifter. I have a vicious leopard who is always eager to tear them apart should I make one mistake and let my guard down. I'm careful because of him. I don't spend time with them. I don't promise to remember them or call for a second round with them. It's a fuck and nothing more. We both understand that."

"I'm not being judgmental about your choice of lifestyle, Gedeon." Her tone was soft. Gentle. "I just want to make certain the women go into their time with you with their eyes wide open. You're physically gorgeous. You have a mesmerizing quality to your voice. I imagine your eyes would be compelling coupled with your voice."

He loved all the things she said about him. She was matter-of-fact about it, as if stating facts, not praising him, but that made her compliments all the more sincere.

"It isn't a lifestyle choice, Lotus," he objected. "I wish it was that." He pulled on his favorite pair of jeans and slid his feet into his loafers before staring sightlessly up at the shirts on hangers. "Choose a tee for me to wear."

"If it isn't your choice to have three women in a night, what is it?"

She was closer, coming up behind him, her voice sounding curious. Gedeon stepped to the side to give her room to look at the array of shirts. She reached past him to push the shirts to one side.

"I had to find a way to counter the continual need for violence not only in my leopard, but in me. At eighteen, consensual sex seemed harmless enough. In fact, it seemed an exciting alternative. I didn't realize I was teaching my body to exchange one alarming addiction for another." He didn't confess to anyone. Why he told her these things about himself when he wanted her to like and respect him, he couldn't say, but he seemed to blurt out the truth. "Slayer was just as addicted and in need as I was."

"I like this burgundy tee." The hanger rattled and then she thrust the soft T-shirt into his hands. "Do you think Mr. Bojangles is responsible for you needing violence?"

"You are *not* calling Slayer Mr. Bojangles." He was horrified at the name. Even if they were in private, he wasn't allowing her to call his very vicious leopard a street performer's name, even if that street performer was famous and a bit of an outlaw.

Her laughter bubbled up. "I thought it was better than Mr. Sparkles, or Sparky for short."

"Woman, you are skating close to being strangled." He accepted the jacket she handed him and shrugged into it. Out of all the ones hanging in his closet, she'd found his favorite.

"You're so tough, Leopard Boy. The next time you're lounging around naked, I'll call to him and see if he'll come out. If he does, I'll be able to come up with a proper name for him."

"You want me to let out my leopard in the same room with you?" They went out of the master bedroom into the main hall and walked together toward the front door.

"How else will I get to know him?" she asked. "Do you have your dark glasses? And your walking cane?"

He despised that cane. "I think waiting until I have my eyesight back would be a better idea," he hedged. "And yes on the dark glasses. No on the cane. I can hang on to your arm."

"Gedeon, you don't know how long it will take to get your sight back. You can't count on me being here every time you want to leave the house. You need to learn to walk with the cane. In any case, Decatur Street is a bit of a distance to walk from here."

"Not tonight," he said firmly. Conversation closed. If she wanted to refuse to go out with him, so be it. He wouldn't go. He could accept staying in, even though he was sick of it.

"I understand that. I'd be the same way. I'm a little worried about the stairs, but we managed them when your leg was a mess. If you could do that then, you can manage the stairs now." She said the last with confidence.

They walked to the front door together and she stepped forward to open it. It was Meiling, not Gedeon, who went out first to ensure that no one was lurking outside to harm either of them. That did set his teeth on edge. He knew the situation wasn't going to last forever. Two and half weeks had gone by and the infection in his leg was gone.

His eyes were so much better. Already there was a small slit of light beginning to show itself at the bottom of his eyes. Dr. Bouet had told him that was to be expected and to keep putting the thick salve in and wear the darkest possible glasses. Eventually that light would grow until it would be visible throughout his eye.

It was just that—he couldn't protect Meiling properly. She was always in the position of having to protect him. He didn't like that. He felt less than a man.

Slayer stirred a little lazily. *There is no danger nearby. I would let you know.*

Gedeon was moody and bad-tempered. Out of sorts. It sucked that Slayer was calm and unruffled. He couldn't even blame his bad mood on his leopard. Meiling took his arm and led him to the stairs.

"Seven stairs, Gedeon," she told him, placing his hand on the wrought-iron guardrail.

He felt for the first step. Meiling didn't leave his side, stepping down with him. She gave him room, but she stayed close, mirroring his steps. He had never been more aware that she was very small and felt delicate and fragile.

"I don't want to fall on you, Lotus. You might want to step back and wait to see if I can get to the bottom of the stairs without mishap." He didn't mean to sound snarly and growly, but he wasn't taking chances with her either.

Meiling didn't give him one of her smart-mouth replies. She stepped back, but she didn't go up the stairs or down them. She just gave him more room. He made it down the stairs without a problem. That gave him a feeling of triumph. Meiling tucked her hand in the crook of his arm as if he was walking her rather than the other way around. Together they began to make the trek to Decatur Street and the original Café Du Monde.

They weren't in a hurry. There was no one around at that time of morning and the two of them could appreciate the quiet as they made their way through the streets together. The slight wind was capricious, rushing first one way and then the next, carrying drops from the river toward them to touch their faces with refreshing dew.

Gedeon found he really enjoyed being outside after being cooped up for so long. Stars glittered in the sky. The moon glowed, casting a silvery light that managed to find the slit that lit up the tiny, minuscule area below his eye that he could make out even with his nearly blackout glasses. That gave him a sense of joy.

"There's a full moon, isn't there?"

"There is."

Her voice contained happiness. He knew it was for him.

He realized there were so many things he got from her that he'd never had from another human being. Genuine caring. Genuine giving. She rejoiced in his progress—found real happiness in it. She never seemed to take exception when he was out of sorts and yelled at her. More than anything, she became amused at those times. She found a way to make him laugh.

"I can see this little tiny white line at the bottom of each eye," he admitted. "It isn't much, but it wasn't there before." He poured satisfaction into his voice. "Don't say you're proud of me, Lotus, for enduring. I know how you are. You're going to be sweet and act like I've been a great patient."

She laughed those musical notes that told him she belonged in New Orleans. "You can get testy, but it doesn't last long. Seriously, Gedeon, you've been great about your eyes."

"Not so much when I began to see progress," he admitted, because he knew rather than being ashamed of him, she would find his reaction hilarious. He wanted her laughter. "I tried staring at every conceivable object in an effort to widen the space so I could see more. All that did was make my eyes burn to the point I had to put cool cloths on them. I called Bouet and told him it was an emergency, that he needed to come right away. I hung up so he couldn't ask me questions."

"That poor man. Leopard Boy in full-blown arrogant get-whatever-you-want mode."

He nodded, not bothering to deny it. "It gets so much worse, babe."

She groaned and rubbed her head against his arm. "Why do these people put up with you?"

"Notice I had the Ming vase put away for safety. You're beginning to rub off on Rene. But I still can intimidate Dr. Bouet. I threatened him."

"Don't sound like you're happy about it." She punched

him hard. "The last thing you need to do is scare off your doctors. You're going to get a reputation."

"I have a reputation and you've systematically been ruining it."

"Only with Rene. I cast my eyes down and look appropriately frightened when you roar in front of anyone else."

"No eye rolling?"

"Only in front of Rene. I'm going to search the house for the Ming vase. If I find it, it's a goner and so is your head."

That little note of laughter bubbling up when she threatened him made his stomach clench in all kinds of good ways.

"How did the doc take your threats?"

"He pointed out that I needed him. I had to admit he had a point. He told me to calm down and that it was normal for my eyes to begin to see that way. He said it was a good sign overall, I could look at it as an improvement. The cavalry began to arrive." There was a little snicker in his voice.

She stiffened. "What does that mean? If that doctor called in a bunch of armed men, we can find someone else to treat your eyes. And where was I?"

"Lotus, I might be blind, but I can still defend myself, especially in my own house. In Bouet's defense, I did threaten him. He must have been given a little panic button and he hit it when I growled at him. You growl back." He ruffled her hair.

She had a lot of hair. Most of their kind did. Thick and luxurious. She was born leopard whether hers would ever show itself or not. So far, the creature was elusive, in no hurry to wake up. It occurred to Gedeon that Meiling was so opposed to male shifters and she was so strong-willed that she had inadvertently suppressed her female leopard.

Gedeon's fingers lingered in her hair. She didn't protest, but then, she rarely did when he touched her. He was tactile, sometimes needing to bury his face in her hair and inhale the fragrance of her.

"Tell me what happened."

She could be a fierce little thing. He remembered her putting her life on the line in Venezuela, the guns aimed at her when she stood for him against Jules and Louis. She hadn't backed down for a second. She risked her life to warn him of the bomb, even knowing he couldn't afford to leave witnesses. Meiling was as tough as nails, and she had a protective streak a mile wide.

"Drake Donovan owns an international security company. His men are well trained and known to be the best at what they do. He sends them to the hottest spots in the world to hone their skills. A little-known fact is they're mostly shifters. He is also the head of a lair right here in New Orleans. The lair was one of the worst when he took over and it's thriving now."

He found he knew the way to Café Du Monde without anyone guiding him. He'd been so many times—straight from his home, or the club after hours, or taking a client. The historic café was open twenty-four hours a day and was right next to the river. It was a place he could be out in the open at the height of tourist season and still enjoy.

"I take it Bouet's backup was a group from Donovan's organization." Meiling made it a statement. "How many did he send?"

"A full team. Five." Pure satisfaction swamped him. He'd been more than happy when that team of badasses had arrived.

"How did they get in? The house is self-locking. Unless they snuck in when Bouet came in, and they wouldn't have had time for all of them to come through. Your phone would have alerted you."

"My phone didn't alert me. Donovan sent a couple of men to do the security on the house. I always suspected he left a back door. A way in for his men just in case he's sent to kill me."

"Why would Drake Donovan want to kill you?"

Now her voice was pitched very low. Scary low. He could well imagine what his partner looked like when she meant business. Achingly beautiful. Hauntingly gorgeous. His perfect mate. He couldn't think of her that way. She was his partner and off-limits. He would take their friendship over never seeing her again. She made it perfectly clear there wasn't going to be sex between them. He had a code of honor. She said no. It was no.

"He didn't want to kill me, Lotus. He didn't want me killing the doctor. By the time they arrived and managed to get into the house, Bouet was already just fine. He felt a little sheepish pushing his panic button when I wasn't going to snap his neck."

Her breath came out in a long rush. "You knew he had the panic button, didn't you?" Meiling accused. "Why would you want that?" she mused aloud. "I watched you put your clothes on. I put your weapons out for you. You knew you could disappear and get out of there clean by using one of the passages. You deliberately scared that man until he used the panic button. Why?" She wasn't asking him; she was trying to puzzle out his actions.

They had walked right up to the large outdoor seating area of Café Du Monde. At the time of night they arrived, few people occupied the tables, and they walked right in and sat down at a table for two. The moment he was seated, he lost all contact with Meiling. Panic crawled up his throat and he fought it back. He would not be dependent on her.

"A café au lait sounds perfect right now." Her voice accompanied the scrape of her chair as she moved close enough that her thigh brushed his. "Although I hesitate to see what this kind of coffee can do to you." The laughter was back in her voice, the tone inviting him to share her amusement.

"Slayer loves coffee, especially the coffee here."

"He would. So, I think I figured out why you wanted Bouet to press his panic button."

"Are we going to make a wager?" He liked their little bets. For the most part their bets were for silly things, never money. She liked his foot massages and usually asked for that. He liked her scalp massages or for her to stay in his bed.

"Naturally."

The waiter interrupted them. He ordered a black coffee. She ordered a café au lait. He requested one order of their signature beignets. She changed the order to two, making him laugh.

When the waiter walked away, she propped her head on her hand, elbow on the table. "What diabolical thing do I have to do if I lose?"

"Sleep in my bed every night for a week with only a nightgown or your underwear on."

"A *week*. That's a bit much."

"Are you turning down the terms of the bet before we even get started?" His voice purred with satisfaction.

"No, just saying it's over-the-top." She drummed her fingers on the table and then abruptly pulled the offending hand into her lap with her other hand.

He'd seen her do that before. He found himself fixating on the movement. Scowling, he reached for the hand she'd placed in her lap, soothing it with his strong fingers. There were so many things about her he didn't know. Little insecurities that made no sense to him.

"If I win," she said, "you have to say thank you and please to every single person you interact with for a week. No snarling or growling."

"I can't afford to lose my reputation. That could get me killed."

"Do you think being polite means you aren't tough?"

"Some people think that."

"That's such bullshit, Leopard Boy. You *like* snarling at people. It's fun for you. Admit it. Own it."

That teasing note was nearly his undoing, making him come apart inside. But he did think about what she said. "Maybe that is how I get my fun. It's been a habit for years now. It was necessary when I was young to scare the crap out of everyone. I developed the habit and I guess I just kept it up."

"Fine, then, I won't make you say *please* or *thank you* to anyone but me."

"Best guess, then. Why would I want Bouet to hit the panic button?" He really wished he could see her face and read her expression. Everything about Meiling fascinated him, especially the way her mind worked.

"You said Donovan sent a couple of his men to put in the security system at your home. You must have suspected that they left a back door, a way to slip in somehow in case of an emergency. You're a dangerous shifter and it would stand to reason that Donovan might decide it would be prudent to have a way to get to you just in case you go rogue."

She was incredible. He didn't say a word. The waiter put his coffee in front of him and Meiling's café au lait in front of her, then added the two orders of beignets to the table.

"I love these," Meiling said. "They are so incredibly good." There was silence for a moment. "Open your mouth."

Gedeon wasn't sure he could allow anyone to feed him like he was three years old, but he was getting all kinds of new experiences with Meiling and he wanted to enjoy every one of them. He opened his mouth. She was gentle, but the beignet was sticky and warm. He bit into it. It tasted like he remembered. The powdered sugar went everywhere. He felt it cascading down onto his clothing. She tried to catch it, leaning into him. Her lips touched the corner of his mouth, her tongue catching some of the sugar. She laughed, and he couldn't help laughing with her at the absurdity of chasing after beignets.

He felt for the cup of coffee, and she took his hand and wrapped it around the mug as if she'd been doing it for a lifetime.

"It's hot," she cautioned. "I got powdered sugar all over you. It's all over me too. I don't think I have the hang of eating these things."

"There isn't a right way, Lotus. You're just supposed to enjoy them."

"It would be impossible not to," she admitted, still laughing. "I *love* them. You'll have to keep me away from this place or I'll spend my entire time eating. I think I might even give up the idea of becoming partners with you and just work here."

He caught her face in his hands and leaned into her to flick his tongue along her lower lip. Sure enough, there was a coating of powdered sugar. He took a sip of hot coffee. "That does taste good," he agreed, pulling back because he was too tempted to actually kiss her. He didn't kiss women. "But it can't interfere with our partnership. Finish telling me about your theory. Dr. Bouet and his panic button."

"Oh, that. You have excellent hearing. You knew they would come to the aid of their poor helpless doctor. All you had to do was mellow him out so he'd be quiet, and you could hear wherever they got in. In this case, you said five of them came. That's a lot. You had to have figured out where they were slipping in."

"Up on the third story. The roof. I can pinpoint nearly the exact spot. I'll be able to close it off and we'll be entirely secure."

She burst into laughter again. That sound found its way inside of him and he found himself smiling. Picking up a beignet, he took aim at her mouth. He really tried to be gentle, and he had a good ear, so he was mostly able to get her to take a bite without making too big of a mess. Beignets were messy. That was part of the appeal. He ran the pads of his fingers over the full curves of her lips. "You have powder all over your lips."

"I do?" She picked up her coffee cup and took a drink. "Did you know there was a time that white lipstick was the 'in' thing? The fashion people called it the frosted look."

"Maybe they got the idea from coming to the Café Du Monde," he ventured. "It's been around long enough."

"You do have a famous perfume company here in New Orleans. Why not start a lipstick company based on beignets? You could call the lipstick Ice. It would be all the rage if you could get a really famous model to be the face of your company."

He licked his finger, swiped it across her lips and then put it in his mouth to suck the powder from it. "You taste like beignets and café au lait."

"In other words, yummy."

"I am not going to say 'yummy,' Lotus. That is asking way too much of an alpha leopard." He drank his coffee slowly, his legs sprawled lazily out in front of him, trusting her to tell him if he was getting in anyone's way.

"I did win the bet. I think using 'yummy' is a good start to making up for the all the times you snarled at me."

"Are you eating more beignets? You sound like you're eating and talking at the same time. I believe you ate your entire order already."

"Your very yummy beignets are getting cold. I can't see wasting them." She managed to sound pious.

"I shared one with you."

"You shared a bite with me. That's not the same thing. And it was a small bite. I gave you an entire beignet. I was *generous*."

"You made certain to get powdered sugar all over my

shirt. That was your goal." He took another sip of coffee. He'd missed the coffee at the Café Du Monde. He'd missed coming here in the middle of the night and listening to the Mississippi River. If he ever lost Meiling, he would forever miss her teasing and laughter.

"What do you think about taking the job, Meiling? Being my partner?"

"You're making me crazy, Gedeon. I told you we should wait until you can see before we decide. You could easily change your mind."

"I won't change my mind and you know it. We've talked about what the job entails. What kind of money you would make. The freedom it would give you. The protection you'd have. The carpenters are already working on your private suite. There are so many pluses to you taking the partnership. The only con I see is working with me. Is that the problem? You don't want to work with me but you're afraid to tell me?"

There was a long silence. He could tell she was drinking her café au lait and pushing the beignet around on the plate. Hard knots formed in his belly, but he remained silent. Silence revealed so much more if you could just survive it.

"I like you, Gedeon. Too much. I don't stay around people, especially people I like. Not that there's been very many. It's too risky. I don't know how to be with people. Even Libby. I loved her and I know she loved me, but I didn't live with her, not after we were kids. It's just better if I don't get too involved with anyone."

There was truth in her tone. Honesty. Trepidation. She was afraid of something. Maybe him. He couldn't tell. His leopard? Slayer? That was a possibility if she thought her leopard might rise.

"Do you believe you have a leopard, Meiling? Tell me the truth."

She sighed. "The probability is high. I was surrounded

by leopards. The family fostering me was leopard. So, yes, she's never showed herself, but she most likely is there."

"You have no family at all? You're certain?"

"They're all dead. I do know that much. Libby's father told her my family was murdered. It seemed too big of a coincidence that Libby's family was murdered, even though it was some years later. Then the neighbors who took us in. I told Libby it was smarter to live apart. It made it more difficult to pay for things, but I felt it was safer for her—for both of us."

"You're certain whoever is stalking you is after you and not Libby. Libby was kidnapped and taken to the jungle camp and eventually murdered."

"Yes, but I don't think she was taken by the same people. I had to track her, and the kidnappers didn't feel the same. In any case, Gedeon, my hesitation isn't because I don't like you or because I don't want to work with you, it's just the opposite. I wouldn't know what to do being around you all the time. And I honestly don't think it's safe for you or Rene."

"I'm not going to be blind forever, Meiling," he said as gently as he could. "You like to tease me and I'll admit, from you I like it, but from anyone else I wouldn't take it. I'm not a nice man and I never will be. Whoever these people are that are stalking you, they don't stand a chance if they come looking for you and you're with me. You did your homework and looked into me. I know you did. You're that kind of woman. You have to know what I'm really like. I kill and I do it without much thought if someone deserves it. I'll protect you, Meiling."

"Who will protect you, Gedeon?" She whispered the question, her voice dripping with tears.

Gedeon couldn't help himself. He touched her face with the pads of his fingers, mapping it out like a blind man for the first time. Committing every inch to memory. Feeling for tears along with her delicate bone structure. He'd always known he was broken, and that there was so much damage and trauma done to him, there was no way to fix him or his leopard. There was only one way out for a man like him. But for just a little while Meiling had managed to bring laughter and joy into his world. She'd given him a taste of what it could be like to live and share life with another being.

He realized he wasn't the only one damaged or traumatized. Just maybe Meiling was broken too. He needed her and he knew it. He acknowledged it. But it was possible she needed him just as much. She was fighting the desire to stay with him, using every excuse possible. She did have a strong protective nature.

Slayer, this is important. Is your mate with Meiling? Is that why you accept Meiling so easily? It was difficult to get the importance of the questions to his leopard in images. Even the questions. This was never something he had discussed with his leopard. Their world had always been one of violence. He had never considered that one day Slayer's mate would walk into their lives.

I cannot say. When she is close to us, I feel at peace. I do not feel the same with any other human.

The leopard fell silent and Gedeon thought the large cat wouldn't say anything else, but he stirred again. *I reach for her at times, thinking I feel her, but if she is there, she is elusive. I do not find her even when I call to her. Meiling is good for you. She is good for me. We should keep her.*

To the leopard, it was that simple. In human terms, the situation was fraught with complication.

Gedeon set down his coffee cup and reached with both hands for Meiling's hands. "You'll protect me, Lotus. I have total faith in your abilities. Being with me will only enhance your skills. Mine will grow just being with you. Once I'm better we can work out together on a regular basis. That will bring our physical skills up as well."

He rubbed his thumbs over the backs of her hands. Her

bones were small. Felt fragile for a shifter. He despised not being able to see her. But without sight, he could feel her energy so much more acutely. There was an awareness that hadn't been there before. He let himself breathe her in. She was struggling with commitment. She wanted it. She just couldn't make herself give him her word. To her that would be binding.

"Stay with me, Lotus. I've never said this to another human being, but I need you. Slayer needs you. We were drowning before you came along. I didn't want to put that on you, but it's the truth. I think you were drowning too. Maybe not in the same way, but you need us."

She let out her breath in a slow exhale. "For six months. A six-month trial."

"A year, Meiling. It will take that long to get used to each other and work smoothly. You know that."

She abruptly pulled her hands away and he thought he'd lost her.

"You always push it, Gedeon. You're never satisfied until you get your way. I'll agree to a year, but if you say one more word on the subject tonight, I'm out."

"Fortunately, it's four o'clock in the morning, so I'm safe."

She burst out laughing, just the way he knew she would.

6

Six months later, Gedeon was elated to admit he was right about their partnership. He and Meiling worked seamlessly together, as if they had been partners forever. Meiling was a shadow at times, going with him to a meeting, finding a place to sit in an obscure corner and disappearing so she was forgotten.

She was a gorgeous woman as far as he was concerned, but she had a way of downplaying her appearance. She could remain very still once she was in the shadows. She seemed to be able to absorb not only every word spoken, but body language and small nuances. Between the two of them, they accurately judged which clients to take on. They knew who would be a threat. Who would remain loyal. Both preferred to know if a client feared an outside source and wasn't revealing that to them. Meiling was adept at feeling those fears.

They stood together waiting to be let into the back entrance of Fredrick Atwater's immense, sprawling home, located in San Antonio, Texas. The two-story house was situated on twenty-two acres of real estate overlooking the lake. They had come at night as requested, telling no one. At first Atwater had balked at the idea of Gedeon bringing Meiling with him, but Gedeon had refused to discuss anything further with him. He simply put down the phone. Atwater called three times before he picked up again.

Atwater's right-hand man, Harold Brinks, let them in through the ornate door. For a back entrance, the foyer and hallway were beautifully appointed. Meiling stayed in step with Gedeon but gave him enough room to fight their way out of any situation. She was very astute that way. Both appeared relaxed, but they were on high alert. Going into an unknown location and meeting with a client for the first time was always risky. It was just the two of them and Slayer.

"Mr. Atwater is in the conservatory," Harold Brinks told them. He opened the door to a very large room made of glass windows that angled outward. The cathedral ceiling overhead was glass and that too was all angles. Lacy plants climbed the rock walls, and in one corner a waterfall, looking as if it came out of the wall, cascaded merrily over gray and blue stones. The floor was gray and blue tile. White chairs, surrounding a glass table, invited guests to sit and enjoy the peace of the large haven.

Atwater didn't seem to be at peace. He paced around the table, which held a tablet and three slim accounting books, as well as what appeared to be several photographs and albums. He stopped moving when they entered the room, his gaze jumping first to Gedeon's face, then to Meiling's. Gedeon had seen that look of fear and despair too many times.

"Mr. Atwater," he said, breaking the ice immediately. When potential clients had that particular look, they could be overwhelmed easily. It was better to get to the problem fast. "Is this room clean? Did you check it for bugs?"

Atwater looked shocked. He exchanged a look with Harold Brinks. "I don't know. This is my private home. The people who work here have done so for years."

"That would be a no," Gedeon said. He glanced at Meiling, and she pulled a small device from inside her coat and began to move around the room. Twice there was a soft pinging noise, and both Gedeon and Harold went to the spots to crouch down and discover tiny round bugs—one in a potted plant and the other on the leg of the table.

"You haven't had any workmen in recently?" Gedeon pursued.

Harold shook his head. "Absolutely not. We shut down the house when the trouble first started some time ago."

"Then you have at least one traitor in your house," Gedeon said, stomping on the bugs and then dropping them in the glass of water on the table. "I believe Harold suspected, or you wouldn't be meeting with me in the middle of the night alone with just him in the conservatory."

Harold nodded. "You were under so much stress, Fredrick, that I couldn't add to it, so I just made sure we didn't talk about calling Mr. Volkov and his partner in front of anyone."

"Fortunately, it isn't known that I have a partner. I ask my clients to keep that confidential. In fact, I demand that it is kept confidential. If you hire me, know I don't play around. The terms are your life if you double-cross me."

He pinned Atwater with his hard gaze, knowing the man could see the killer in him. He wanted Atwater to see he meant it. He had Meiling to protect now. Before, he just didn't give a fuck. Now, killing wasn't about the violence he needed, it was about keeping Meiling safe.

"My life isn't worth much if you can't help me," Atwater said.

Gedeon indicated Meiling, who had been silent the entire time. She usually was. If she had input, it was normally in the form of a question, and that would come later, when they were discussing the aspects of the case. "This is my partner, Meiling. What can we do for you?"

Atwater raked both hands through his hair. "I don't even know where to start, Volkov. I should have called you in right away. Instead, I tried to handle this on my own and I just made it worse." He shook his head. "So much worse."

"Let's sit down and start at the beginning," Gedeon suggested. "We take care of problems. You wouldn't have called us if you didn't think we could help."

"It's your reputation for doing the impossible that had me calling you." Atwater pulled out a chair and dropped into it, as if his body was far too heavy to stay on his feet. "Really, it was Harold's suggestion. I didn't know what to do. He was the one who said to call you."

Gedeon turned his gaze on Atwater's man. "Where did you hear of me?"

"I have a friend, Elijah Lospostos, here in San Antonio, and we were talking one day. I told him I had some trouble going on and wasn't certain what to do. I didn't tell him what it was. I said I didn't want to involve him or Fredrick. He saw that I was worried, and he asked me what was up. I just said I had trouble. He said if it was bad, he knew of a man who sometimes could help. He warned me that the number he was giving me was confidential and not to give it to anyone else. He said just having it could get me killed. Elijah doesn't mess around and he isn't prone to dramatics. I almost didn't make the suggestion to Fredrick, but we didn't have anywhere else to go."

Elijah Lospostos was a big name in the mafia world. He held a huge territory and ruled with an iron fist. One didn't cross Elijah and live long. He'd been born into a crime family and had the mantle passed down to him. He hadn't had much choice in the matter. Gedeon knew him to be a man of his word. He didn't deal in human trafficking as far as Gedeon was aware. He had a wife and family and was very careful with who he let into his world. Harold

Brinks wouldn't dare drop Elijah's name knowing that Elijah would carve him into little pieces if he was lying. Gedeon had to believe the man was telling the truth. He glanced at Meiling.

Her nod was nearly imperceptible. She thought the man sounded honest as well.

"What's going on, Atwater?" Gedeon asked.

Atwater just continued to shake his head. It was Harold who crossed his arms over his chest, leaned against the door and took up the narrative. "Fredrick goes over the books himself. He's very good with numbers, always has been. It doesn't matter how many businesses he's involved with; he always double-checks everything. Because some of the people he does business with are very concerned with the amount of money owed to them with each transaction, it is more important than ever that every penny is accounted for."

"I take it the numbers weren't adding up."

Harold shook his head. "At first, small amounts of money were missing. Eventually, they became larger and larger amounts. Naturally, Fredrick replaced the money when he paid his partners their share. We tried to track the losses. He began to get blackmail threats. Whoever was stealing from him would tell his partners if he didn't give them large sums of money."

"Did you rule out his partners?"

Harold frowned. "I'm out of my depth at this sort of thing. I wasn't cut out to be a spy or sleuth. I'm a good bodyguard."

"And a good friend," Atwater said, looking up for the first time. "If it was just the money and the blackmail, I would have gone to my partners. I've known them nearly forty years. When I didn't show signs of cooperating, they took my little Lilith." He picked up the top photograph with shaking hands. "Her mother died in childbirth. She's four years old and all I have left. I'd give anything for her. Twice I've paid their ransom, but they haven't returned her. I don't think they're going to. The money is still disappearing from the business transactions and the threat of blackmail continues. I know it's the same people even though they want me to believe it's not."

Gedeon's gaze met Meiling's across the room. This case suddenly jumped to priority number one. "How long has your daughter been missing?" he demanded. He wanted to ask why the man had fucked around for so long before calling him.

"Nearly a month now. I paid the ransom twice. Another demand just came in. Even if I pay it, they won't give her to me."

"How do you know she's alive?" Gedeon asked, looking to Harold. Fredrick just kept shaking his head and moaning.

"We don't. They haven't given us proof of life. I kept telling Fredrick to wait before he paid them, that we needed to have them show us she was alive, but he was so distraught that they took her that he just paid the money."

"If you want our help in getting your daughter back, Atwater, and finding these fuckers who took her, you're going to have to do everything I say. *Exactly* what I say. You have a spy in this house. A traitor working with them. Someone is reporting to them. They can't be aware you hired outside help. I want them to think you're so distraught you can't function. You're going to be in bed, in your room, with only Harold looking after you. A doctor will come to oversee your care. Harold, you have to demand proof of life. Only you can talk to these fuckers. Atwater is too ill. Someone working here in the house will be insistent on looking in on him. You have to tell them it is the doctor's orders that no one disturbs him. I'll call Elijah and have him send a couple of men to help you guard Atwater's room. You can't be up around the clock."

"But what about getting the money to Lilith's kidnappers?" Fredrick asked. "They said if I didn't bring it to them myself, they'll kill her."

"Didn't they say that exact thing before?" Gedeon demanded.

Atwater nodded, slumping in his chair.

"That's why you're too sick to cope with anything. They've driven you beyond your ability to function. Your mental health is in a terrible state. You will be living in your room, keeping it dark and staying away from the windows where they might catch a glimpse of you. You aren't eating. Harold will sneak food in to you. The doctor is giving you intravenous treatments in order to keep up your fluids and strength."

Atwater nodded. "How is this going to help?"

"If you're convincing enough, whoever the spy is will have to report to their boss. He or she will lead us up the chain to the one who has your daughter. We take your daughter back. In the meantime, we take a look at the books and see if we can do the tracing for you. There's always a trail, even if it's a faint one. You're the key to getting your daughter back, Atwater."

It was necessary to give the man a significant role so he felt he was helping to get his child back. Gedeon wanted to get the bastards who had taken a child from her safe haven and not returned her. All he knew was, she had better be alive.

"Where was Lilith last seen and with whom?" Meiling asked.

"She went to the park with her nanny, Minny Tangra. Minny walked with her to the little playhouse and two men came out of nowhere, both wearing masks. One hit Minny hard, knocking her to the ground. The other took Lilith. They ran with her to a waiting dark-colored BMW."

"Do you suspect Tangra as being part of the conspiracy to kidnap your daughter?" Gedeon asked.

Atwater shook his head. "No. Minny was hit so hard she had a major concussion. For a couple of days, we were afraid she wouldn't come out of it. She still has some issues from the injury."

Gedeon nodded, not impressed or sympathetic. That wasn't his job. "We'll need her address. We need an up-to-date list of everyone who has worked here in the past four years. That includes anyone working on the grounds. If they're single; who they're dating, if you have the information. We'll need to know who your daughter's doctor is and her dentist. Who takes her there and why she didn't have bodyguards that day. Where were they?" He made the last a question, looking between Harold and Atwater.

"As a rule, I don't use them," Atwater admitted. "I stopped after I got married. My wife didn't like the idea of having them. I got out of the habit, other than having Harold with me." He lifted his pain-filled, very guilty gaze to Gedeon's. "It was arrogance. I have a reputation among the other families. It never occurred to me anyone would dare to kidnap my daughter."

Gedeon bit back a curse and turned away from the man. Every *pakhan* he knew had bodyguards. The heads of the Italian families had bodyguards. It was arrogance beyond anything he'd heard of to think Atwater wouldn't take a hit at some point. It hadn't been him but a child who had suffered. Gedeon might come back and slit his throat if that child had been sold into a trafficking ring.

"We need to see the rest of the house. We will also send over a team to search for bugs. Someone planted two in this room. Your home, particularly your office and private apartment, is going to be lousy with them." Gedeon was already texting Rene to arrange for the team to come in immediately. He wanted them in and out before sunup, and the mansion was huge. "How many square feet?"

Harold told him. Gedeon relayed the information to Rene. Meiling and he spent another two hours familiarizing themselves with the layout of the mansion. The doctor showed up to help set up Atwater's suite to look as if he was no longer functional and had to have around-the-clock care. Drake Donovan sent a team of bodyguards. He had men stationed in San Antonio and they arrived within minutes of the call.

Gedeon and Meiling gathered up the books and photographs and left the way they had come, trusting Harold to handle his boss and lifelong friend. Either Atwater would cooperate or he wouldn't.

"Is she alive?" Gedeon asked Meiling. "What does your gut say?"

"It says that man is an idiot. He wanted to find whoever was taking money from him and make an example out of them. He's been so long at the top, always handling everything with his own set of rules, it didn't occur to him that someone could come along with a different playbook."

"Lotus Blossom. That tells me nothing. Do you think she's alive?" Gedeon needed the kid to be alive. If she wasn't—he was going to go insane and burn down the city until he found every one of the fuckers responsible for taking her. They wouldn't die easy. Slayer unsheathed his claws and raked cruelly, adding his ire and need for violence.

She nodded. "They need her alive. Atwater may be an arrogant ass, but he's powerful, and if he finds out who has her, they'll need her in order to bargain their way out of a very bad situation. He looks like a sweet man, but he didn't get into that position by being nice. I could smell the rage in him."

The relief was tremendous. That had been his assessment as well, but it felt good to have Meiling's logical conclusion match his.

Gedeon opened the passenger door for her, keeping his smirk to himself as she slid in. She had really balked at him being the driver and called him a few choice names.

He agreed with every name she'd called him and took his place behind the wheel. Now, she was so intrigued with the books Atwater had turned over to them, she paid no attention that he was the driver. He liked her smart mouth and had to suppress the childish urge to taunt her just to get her going. In the end, she always laughed. He could use the sound of her laughter after hearing Atwater's admission that he'd waited to call for help even after his daughter had been taken.

"Leopard Boy, Atwater is supposed to be this brilliant mathematician. I read all about him online. Numbers don't lie. If someone is stealing and doing it consistently, eventually there is a pattern to it. Even if they try to hide that pattern, it will come out. Harold said Atwater checked the books of every business deal weekly. He knew those books intimately. I don't see how it's possible he couldn't figure out who was stealing from him."

She ran her hands over the cover of the top book again and again as if she couldn't wait to delve into it. "Did he seem particularly brilliant to you? He could barely speak on his own. Harold did most of the talking."

"Clearly, he was on some substance. I got close enough to him. It wasn't alcohol."

"Harold was covering for him, you think? Or do you believe Harold is part of the conspiracy and that's why the bugs were in the conservatory?" she asked, leaning her head back against the seat.

Gedeon tried not to notice her silhouette as he drove toward the heart of the city. He had become just as possessive of Meiling as Slayer was. She brought him so many different emotions, all very strong. Some overwhelming. She kept Slayer under control, which gave him peace. There were times when he did wonder if she made the ferocious burn for sex even worse.

When they were in New Orleans, he went to the club every night and hooked up with a woman to see to his needs. One woman had usually been enough for the night, but it wasn't any longer. He couldn't make his cock stand down and the sex was getting rougher and more violent. Slayer protested each time he found someone else to try to take that terrible edge off, yet it was Slayer who often seemed to drive him with his sexual needs as well. The protests were ugly and frightening in that the leopard would wait until the moment Gedeon finally managed an actual release. At that moment the cat would throw himself at the man, determined to take over their form in order to kill the woman. Each time Gedeon was with a woman was dangerous, but if he tried to go too long without, he became dangerous. It was a vicious circle. The only time he got any real peace was when he tricked Meiling into sleeping in his bed. Slayer subsided, and even if Gedeon lay awake all night with his cock as hard as a rock, he was content.

"Harold Brinks is totally loyal to Fredrick Atwater. He knows the man is being drugged. Someone is slipping him something to mess him up just enough to interfere with his ability to make decisions," Gedeon said decisively. "Harold called us in. He wouldn't have chanced calling us if he was guilty. I have that reputation, babe."

She winced when he called her *babe*. He didn't do it often, but she didn't like it and sometimes it got her going. "I might die if don't get coffee, LB. Seriously. Even a very bad cup of coffee will do in a pinch."

He raised his eyebrow. "LB? You're going to shorten your nickname for me to mere letters? No. I draw the line."

"What does that mean, exactly? Where do you draw the line? There's no sand. There's no dirt. We're in a car. You don't have a pen or a pencil to draw with. You don't even have a crayon. There's no logic in that."

"I was taking you to a bakery that has amazing coffee, but you don't deserve it, so I'm heading to our hotel. They have coffee, but it's terrible."

She groaned and set the books on the console between

them. Both hands went to her hair to pull the ribbon from it. She'd left it down, tied with a ribbon at the nape of her neck, something she rarely did. She lifted the silky mass up with a little sigh of relief.

"I have an atrocious temper, Gedeon," she suddenly confessed. "Sometimes I don't think I'm a very good partner for you. You knew Atwater was under the influence of drugs and someone had most likely administered them to him. You came up with a plan to keep him safe and at the same time buy us time to find his daughter. I didn't care that someone had screwed with his so-called brilliant mind. I wanted to bash him one for being an arrogant ass and taking a chance with his daughter's life."

He shot her a grin. He did love the way she had that fiery little streak in her. "That's why my most special vases are put away."

"Because you're an arrogant ass as well," she declared, and twisted her hair into some kind of knot that only women knew how to manage. Taking a pair of sticks from her pocket, she shoved them a little viciously into her hair to hold it in place.

"Those things weapons?" He indicated the sticks with a jerk of his chin.

"Naturally. I'd find that really nice bakery with the good coffee if I were you." Meiling tried to sound menacing, but she only succeeded in sounding like she was purring.

That sounded like purring to him, and his body stirred. Gedeon set his teeth and willed his cock under control. "Fine, although you don't deserve it." If she were his, he'd spend hours making her purr for him.

The smile faded from the luscious curve of her lips. "I really am questioning Atwater's arrogance, Gedeon. Why would he risk his daughter? He already lost his wife. Maybe not to violence, but she is still gone. Every other head of a crime family has bodyguards. Most of them have far too many hanging around. What's the big deal to hire a few to keep his daughter safe? It wouldn't make him look weak, since everyone seems to have them."

Her voice was steady, but he realized that, like he was, Meiling was shaken by the kidnapping of the little girl. Neither had been expecting it. Both had suffered too many losses. He nearly pulled the car over so he could hold her. Meiling was careful of their relationship. She wouldn't welcome him getting too familiar with her.

They had a fantastic partnership, their every step in perfect sync. It hadn't taken long to get there either. Their personal relationship was good—friendly with lots of laughter. But the intimacy that had been between them in the first six weeks was no longer there. That was on him. His fault entirely, and there was no real way to fix it.

"I get it, Meiling. He should have." He kept his voice gentle.

It was all the visits to the club. That had come between them. He needed the sex. He'd held out for as long as he could. Once he went, it was as if he was more addicted than ever. He *had* to go. Meiling stopped coming to his suite. She used her private entrance in the evenings, and that left him alone with a seething leopard and nights of no sleep no matter how many women he hooked up with.

She didn't bring up the fact that he had sex with other women. He almost wished she would so they could talk about it. He had no idea what he'd say, but at least he'd know it bothered her. The way things stood between them now, she didn't seem to care. She just went her own way and treated him like a wayward sibling or best friend.

Gedeon had been to San Antonio numerous times, doing work for several of the Italian and Russian families there. They were tight-knit. Very dangerous. Connected in ways he didn't yet know or understand, but it was all the same to him. As long as they didn't violate his code, he did his job and got paid in favors or money.

"This bakery is *bratya*, Meiling. They're leopard," he

warned. "That doesn't mean I'm not right when I say the coffee is the best and the baked goods even better."

Her dark eyes flashed and met his as he parked the car. "I have never been around so many leopards in my life. I think you deliberately just drag me around them because you know it makes me uncomfortable." She gathered up the books on the seat and pushed the door open on her side of the car. She didn't get out right away. Instead, she put out one leg and fussed with one of the books as her gaze scanned the rooftops and buildings across the street.

"Two shooters, Gedeon. One directly across the street on the rooftop and the other a block away. The blue building. Woman walking her dog. Looks like a bodyguard to me. Two coming up behind us came from the alley." She spoke low and then got out of the car as she shuffled the books in close to her and closed the door.

Gedeon locked the doors as he wrapped his arm around her, and they crossed the street together, going straight to the glass door of the bakery. The Sweet Shoppe. The name of the shop was done in calligraphy and looked very elegant. The moment Gedeon opened the door, the aroma of baked goods drew Meiling inside. Gedeon stepped back to allow her in first.

His gaze swept the interior. He'd been to the bakery multiple times. This early, there was only one table with two customers he would consider legitimate. There was a second table with two men he knew immediately were leopard and definitely bodyguards. He recognized both men. The owner, Evangeline Amurov, was married to Fyodor Amurov. He held the reins over a very large territory and did so ruthlessly. He guarded his family, his wife and children with that same ruthlessness. Few would ever dare to cross him. He was surrounded by bodyguards, and his wife and children never went anywhere without them.

Both bodyguards looked up immediately, recognized him and nodded, and then their gazes swept over Meiling

with a little too much interest to suit him. He put a possessive hand on the small of her back. If they had been home
in New Orleans, going to the Café Du Monde, Meiling
would have stepped away from him. She would have done
so casually, finding some excuse, but here, she followed
his lead.

"Evangeline," he greeted. "I don't know why I didn't
expect to see you this early in the morning when I know
you're the one who does all the baking. The last time I was
here, your sister-in-law, Ashe, let me know she was not the
baker in the family. That was all you."

Evangeline laughed. "She was telling you the truth. It's
Gedeon, right?"

"Good memory. This is Meiling. I told her you have the
best coffee and pastries in San Antonio."

"Nice to meet you, Meiling," Evangeline said. "Are you
staying in San Antonio for long this time, Gedeon?"

Gedeon remembered the genuine warmth she exuded.
She gave that to Meiling, making her feel welcome. Evangeline had a gift. That was part of the charm of her shop.
He had been surprised that a man like Fyodor Amurov
would allow his woman to continue to work in an environment that could be a danger to them both.

The first time Gedeon had come to the shop, it had been
very small, but charming. Now it was much larger, with
more tables and far more display cases, although the charm
was still there. The coffee machines were set up in a wide
U with plenty of space for the women to work. There were
rooms beyond the wide, spacious counters and, of course,
the kitchen one couldn't see into. Gedeon knew Fyodor
had an office somewhere in the building to stay close
to his wife.

"I'm not certain how much time I'll be spending here."
He put in his order and waited for Meiling to give her se-
lection. "How are Fyodor and Timur?"

"Healthy," Evangeline said, without stopping the flow

of work for a moment. She was making their coffee and putting their pastries on plates for them. She made a face over her shoulder, her eyes laughing. "Bossy."

"I love everything about this bakery," Meiling said. "The colors on the walls are so soothing." She looked up at the ceiling and then around to each wall separately. "I like that your decorator used a deeper blue for an accent wall and then chose the same color for the lines in the ceiling. I never would have thought of that."

Evangeline looked pleased, a warm rose color creeping under her skin. "I'm the decorator. When I first bought this place it was very small, and I didn't have a ton of money. I did all the painting and decorating myself. I had a lot of time to think about exactly the way I wanted it to look."

Meiling did a slow turn right there at the counter, looking around the bakery. "You did a fantastic job. You have a good eye for detail. I especially like the way you detailed the darker blue lines on the ceiling. They're so faint, but they add dimension. I moved into a new apartment recently and I was told I could paint if I wanted to. I sometimes just stare at the ceiling wondering what I want to do differently, and your ceiling opens up all kinds of possibilities I hadn't thought of."

Gedeon took the plates with the pastries. "Do you have a time limit on your tables, Evangeline? We're working. We'll be happy to pay for the time."

Evangeline waved him away. "Get to it. Meiling, later I might be able to find some of the books that inspired me."

"I'd love that. Thank you."

Gedeon went straight for a table where he had a good view of the door and anyone coming through it. He put the coffee mugs and pastry dishes down and indicated for Meiling to sit to his right. She slid onto the comfortable chair and placed the stack of books on top of the table along with the tablet and photographs Atwater had given them. The photographs were placed picture-side down.

"Do you have notebooks and pens?" he asked.

"Yes, although I should be asking you that question." She flicked him a quick glance. The bakery was beginning to fill up with customers. The bodyguards weren't watching them so closely. She placed one hand over her mouth, her eyes going wide as if astonished at how good the pastry she'd barely taken a bite of was.

"Three cameras. Four o'clock. Six o'clock and twelve o'clock. Glass is thick, looks bulletproof to me. The two men sitting just to the right of the window are leopard and are clearly guarding Evangeline. They mean business too. They're armed to the teeth." She reached inside her coat and pulled out two notebooks and a package of pens, placing them on the table between them.

"Anyone coming in look suspicious to you? As if they might have followed us?" Gedeon leaned in to her on the pretense of picking up one of the pens and a notebook. It would be impossible for the cameras to pick up his lips moving.

Meiling shook her head. "We weren't followed. I really like the atmosphere here, Gedeon, although why they let you in, I have no idea." Deliberately, she allowed the bodyguards to read her lips. "I would think you might be considered trouble."

One coughed behind his hand. The other snickered and turned it into a cough. Gedeon flicked his ice-cold gaze in their direction.

"Do you know them?" Meiling asked. Her coffee cup was up to her lips, hiding anything she said.

He nodded, not liking that she was curious. Was that interest in her eyes? He realized he was becoming more possessive of her the longer he spent time with her. That wasn't a good sign. She seemed able to detach her emotions from him. The physical attraction that had been there when they first were together had slipped away, at least on her side. Now she didn't flirt with him. She might tease him, but she wasn't flirtatious. He didn't want her flirting with the guards. He didn't want her flirting with anyone but him. He also couldn't afford to fuck up their professional relationship or their friendship with irrational jealousy.

He had come to Evangeline's bakery on purpose. Fyodor Amurov was not a man you fucked with. The other men holding territories all had close ties to him. The moment the plane had touched down and Gedeon Volkov had walked off it, Fyodor would have been informed. Gedeon was bad news. He had a reputation for leaving behind dead bodies. Fyodor, like all the other heads of the families, would want to know why he was in town. It was smart to be proactive and pay his respects to Amurov first.

"Yes, the man on the right is named Kyanite Boston. The other is Rodion Galerkin. Leopards out of Russia. They work for Fyodor and are watching out for his wife." He might not like it, but he gave them their due. "They wouldn't be given that assignment if they weren't considered extremely fast, the best he has."

"That's nice," Meiling said, taking another drink of coffee. "That he would care enough to put his best men on his wife."

Gedeon knew she was thinking about the fact that Fredrick Atwater hadn't put bodyguards on his daughter and she'd been kidnapped.

"Yeah, Lotus, Fyodor puts Evangeline first always."

"Says a lot about him. And you were so right, this coffee is good. If it wasn't for the beignets at the Café Du Monde, we would have to move here." She took a bite of an apricot scone. "Seriously, Gedeon, think about it, I could learn to fly a plane."

"I have a pilot's license," he admitted.

Her head jerked up and she narrowed her eyes at him. Those dark eyes that looked like two liquid pools of water he could drown in. She had a beautiful face. He often stared at the oval delicacy of it. The way her bones appeared so fragile, the high cheekbones and aristocratic nose and that chin that drew his attention like a magnet. He wanted to shape her face with his hands, run his fingers over her petal-soft skin, trace her full lips and commit every detail to memory over and over. He was tactile with her—not with anyone else, just Meiling.

"That is withholding important information. Do you own a plane?"

"I do. It's a small plane. Nothing fancy. I bought it for fun, not for going from one country to another."

"In the grand scheme of things, Mr. Volkov, having a plane and a pilot's license would come in very handy if I were in desperate need of an apricot scone and great coffee one morning after putting up with your annoying two a.m. calls so you can get decent sleep because Mr. Sinister is acting up."

He struggled not to laugh. She was hilarious. "Mr. Sinister?"

"Well, he's not Mr. Bojangles, and you shot down Mr. Sparkles, which was a perfectly good name. I could have shortened it to Sparky." She took another bite of the apricot scone and closed her eyes as if savoring the pastry.

Her long black lashes feathered in a crescent against her skin. He found it sexy. His body stirred again, and he had to force himself to look away from her. God help him if she moaned. He wasn't the only one looking at her. Kyanite and Rodion were looking too. For one terrible moment, that murderous part of him he always kept contained rose up, threatening to take over. That didn't happen on a job. Never out in public, especially when he knew he was being observed.

Behind the counter, where Evangeline helped a customer, the double doors leading to the kitchen opened and a tall man with wide shoulders, scars on his face and cold, flat eyes emerged. Almost at the same time, Meiling rose. "I'm heading to the ladies' room and then getting more coffee before we start work. Do you want anything?"

"Order me another as well," Gedeon said. He'd chosen the right woman. She was astute. Smooth. So natural, no one could fault her. He watched her walk to the room marked for women, her hips swaying gently. Rodion and Kyanite didn't take their gazes off her either until the door closed, cutting off their view.

7

GEDEON rose as Timur Amurov came to the table. Timur was Fyodor's brother and his number-one security man. Extending his hand, he gripped Timur's and gave him a shark's smile. "Good to see you again. How are things going?"

Timur waved him to a seat and sank into the one opposite him. "That depends on what you have to say, Gedeon."

"Came here first to let you know I'm in town on business, but it has nothing to do with you or yours. If at any point it looks as if it's going in that direction, I'll inform you."

"Before or after you take out the offenders?"

"I may have to come to you for information on this one." Gedeon chose his words carefully. The Amurovs knew his reputation. He'd always treated them with respect. He treated everyone with respect—until they didn't deserve it.

Meiling emerged from the restroom and then slowly made her way over to the counter. When she did, she managed to make it seem very natural to place herself at Timur's back. First, she ordered the coffees, laughing with Evangeline. Her laughter was contagious, a beautiful sound that turned heads, including Timur's.

"She yours?" he asked.

"My partner. We keep that on the down low. It's safer for her that way and more effective for our partnership."

"She leopard?"

"Yes, although her leopard is being stubborn."

"What information do you need, Gedeon?"

Gedeon rubbed at his temple, making a determined effort to keep his hand away from the network of spiderweb scars he'd been left with around his eyes. Timur wouldn't fail to notice them, or the fact that Gedeon spent far too much time putting his sunglasses on and then removing them. The light hanging just overhead bothered him. It was just that much too bright. He didn't like wearing the darker sunglasses indoors because they drew attention. They also inhibited his vision, and in a lair like the Amurovs', he needed to be able to see everything.

"I don't know yet, Timur. We just started, but it's a clusterfuck already and we're working against the clock. I'm going to tell you in confidence that there's a child's life at stake if she's still alive."

Timur sat back in the chair staring at him. "What the hell, Gedeon? I haven't heard one whisper that a child is missing. One of ours? A leopard?"

"Timur, Meiling and I have to be able to do our thing. This is what we do, but we have to do it under the radar. I came to Fyodor to pay my respects and let him know why we're here. If any leads come back to anyone he's affiliated with, I would inform him, but if the situation calls for immediate action, I can't guarantee he'll know ahead of time before I make my move."

Timur nodded his head. "Fyodor will want to talk to you himself. He has children. This is going to weigh on him."

"I don't have time for niceties."

"You're welcome to make this your base while you work," Timur offered. "How long is your partner going to hang out at the counter?"

"As long as you're sitting at the table." Gedeon kept his stone face with effort. His little Meiling didn't look like a threat to anyone. She was so delicate. So small. Her laughter sounded genuine and inviting. Both Kyanite and Rodion were having trouble staying on task.

Timur looked disgusted. "She's deliberately placed herself in a position to threaten me if I attack you."

"Not just threaten you, Timur, she would kill you. She'd most likely take out whichever of the two bodyguards she'd deemed the biggest threat as well. She'd be willing to sacrifice her life, although I'd be pissed at her." He sighed. "Trust me, we've had the conversation numerous times and it didn't do a damn bit of good."

"Is she that good?"

Gedeon nodded. "I think she's close to being as good as me. Maybe she's my equal." He tapped the table still looking at her. "She might have an edge because no one expects her to be so fast. She might be better."

Timur laughed. "That hurt."

"I'm getting used to it. I'll call her over to meet you and then we've got to get to work. We can't waste any more time."

Timur shifted his weight in the chair while Gedeon indicated for Meiling to come back to the table. She made her way back, two mugs of coffee in hand.

"Meiling, this is Timur Amurov. He's Evangeline's brother-in-law."

She flashed her million-watt smile. "Lovely to meet you. You're so lucky to have this shop to work out of. I love everything about it."

"It's a security nightmare," Timur groused. "I won't take

up your time. Gedeon made it clear you're working against the clock on this one. If you have any trouble at all, this is my personal number." He took a card and laid it on the table. It held only a cell phone number. "Gedeon has my number. You call that number for help, and someone will come."

"I appreciate it," Meiling answered, sounding sincere.

Her gaze slid past Timur and landed on Kyanite as Timur walked back toward the kitchen. It was the briefest of looks, but it was enough to irritate Gedeon.

"You ready to get to work or do you need more time?" he asked. He might have gotten away with it, but his voice was just that little bit edgy.

Her dark eyes moved over his face, and then she smiled at him. "Gedeon, we'll get her back. The answer is in the books or the tablet. It won't take us long to see the pattern with the two of us working."

He nodded curtly, grateful he hadn't looked like a jealous kid. He took the first of the books and she took the second one. The moment he flipped it open and started familiarizing himself with the columns, the rest of the world dropped away. The business Atwater was running seemed legitimate enough at a cursory glance, but once he started delving into it, he could see the regular payments made to the various accounts.

He didn't care about the business or how much money it made. It didn't even matter that Atwater was bleeding money from hardworking families. He was two months in when the thefts began. The first time the money disappeared it was a very small amount. It could have been put down as a mistake, but there was just a little too much gone and no way to account for it.

Gedeon wrote down the date and the business and reached for the next book, putting the first one aside. Meiling was already doing the same thing. They went through the stack of books systematically, carefully writing down the dates of each time money had disappeared from one of Atwater's businesses. They recorded whether he had a partner in the business and if it was a legitimate business or not.

Several times Gedeon glanced up at the clock. Twice Evangeline refilled his coffee cup and once she brought them pastries filled with ham and cheese. He managed to look up without breaking his concentration to give her a vague smile of thanks.

"Thank you, Evangeline," Meiling murmured. "We appreciate it. We're just swamped with work and not paying attention."

"Keep at it," she said.

Gedeon registered her answer, making him think Timur had reported to Fyodor and Fyodor's wife had been informed there was a child's life at stake. He didn't look up. He had the notebooks spread out in front of him and was comparing Meiling's findings with his.

"Fredrick had to have known who was taking the money, Meiling," he muttered aloud, more to try to puzzle out the logic than for any other reason. Deliberately, he used their client's first name. Leopards had excellent hearing, and he wasn't about to tip off the Amurov family who he was working for.

"It's too obvious for him not to have known, even if he was being drugged from the start, which I doubt. Who would know he looked at the books every week besides Harold?"

Gedeon sat back in the chair and rubbed his neck. "That's a good question. We have a long list of suspects. Fredrick listed them all, with one exception. That tells us right there that he knew who was ripping him off."

Meiling didn't say the name aloud. She wrote it down and shoved the paper to him. Gedeon glanced down. Georgi

Chaban. Leopard. Related how to the Lospostos family? "Why wouldn't Fredrick call him out on the money disappearing right away, or take it to someone above him?"

It was an excellent question. Involving a man of Elijah's stature was dangerous. They would have to find out what Georgi Chaban meant to Elijah before they informed Elijah of anything they would be doing. In fact, Gedeon wasn't going to take any chances. Georgi was up to his neck in this shit. He'd taken the money, and every instinct Gedeon had screamed that he'd taken the child as well.

She tapped Lospostos's name. Then wrote several question marks after it.

This time Gedeon made certain the cameras couldn't pick up anything he did, shielding what he wrote with his hand.

"Ruthless. Rumor has it he put out a hit on his only sister so she couldn't be used against him, although I'm not certain I believe it. He has a wife and children. Not too many people would go after his family because he'd cut out their hearts while they were alive. He'd retaliate and kill every member of their family."

The moment she read the words, he blacked them out with a Sharpie and then tore the note into tiny pieces. He stuffed those pieces in his pocket.

"Was Fredrick taking the money, and Georgi found out first? Did he blackmail him? Was that how the larger amounts started to pile up?" Gedeon mused aloud.

Meiling shook her head. "No. I can't see it happening that way. Look at the books. He hired this Georgi and almost immediately the money began to be taken. Small amounts first and then much larger amounts."

She pulled one of the sticks from her hair and a mass of shiny black tresses snaked down her back. "It was Georgi from the beginning, and he started almost immediately. He was hired on as bookkeeper and I think he came to

Fredrick with the intent of stealing from him. Whether or not someone else put him up to it remains to be seen, but he had a plan in place before he ever got there."

Restless, she twisted her hair back into the knot she favored, replaced the stick to hold it and jumped up, as if forgetting they were in a coffee shop. Gedeon had seen her like this often, her brain working so fast she could barely stay still. She needed action. Sometimes when she was putting things together, she would go outside their home and pace along the sidewalk, around the block, up and down, and come back having figured out what piece of the puzzle they were missing. Or what piece they needed.

They couldn't leave the books, notebooks and tablets out in the open, so he had to let her go out by herself. The sun was coming up. They had to figure this out soon. He texted Harold, needing some answers. If Atwater and Brinks weren't more forthcoming with them, the investigation was going to take longer, and he had a bad feeling every minute was going to count. He had instructions for Harold that needed to be followed to the letter.

He stretched, glanced up at the camera and nodded. If Fyodor wanted to have a private talk with him, now was the time. He wasn't going to keep catering to the Amurov family, although if he was being truthful with himself, he liked them better than most. They seemed very loyal to one another and to their women.

Gedeon stretched his legs out in front of him and tried not to think about Meiling pacing along the sidewalk in the early morning hours with the commuters mobbing the sidewalks. Timur would have her watched over. He would feel bound. She was on his property. They were working in the bakery where Fyodor had offices, and there was no way Timur would allow a female leopard to walk the streets unprotected no matter how lethal she was.

He knew he set everyone on edge the moment he came into town. No doubt Lospostos was already aware he was in town. He didn't like that Elijah was in any way mixed up in this. Harold and Atwater should have told him right away. A man as dangerous as Elijah Lospostos had to be cleared immediately. He swore silently as he drummed his fingers on the table.

Meiling was right. Georgi had had his plan in place long before he had been hired by Atwater. Gedeon waited impatiently for Harold's reply. Who had recommended the bookkeeper? How had he come to be hired?

Timur emerged from the kitchen. Simultaneously, Kyanite and Rodion stood and moved with fluid grace to the counter. They looked casual as they approached, but they were anything but casual. Fyodor came through the double doors on some hidden signal from Timur. Fyodor went up right behind his wife, circling her waist with one arm and bending down to place a kiss behind her earlobe. She smiled, her face lighting up.

Gedeon had never seen a time when Evangeline hid her emotions, especially when it came to her husband. She loved him fiercely and it was there on her face for all to see. Only an idiot would miss the stark, raw emotion in Fyodor's eyes when he looked at his wife, brief though it might be. She was his world.

Fyodor made his way through the opening in the counter to the main floor of the coffee shop, stepping easily into the middle of the diamond his guards provided, Timur at the top point. A fourth man, younger, built strong with blond hair, stepped behind Fyodor as they walked together completely in sync to Gedeon's table. Gedeon began to rise, but Fyodor waved him back to his seat and took the chair opposite, extending his hand.

"Good to see you again, Gedeon. I wish it was under better circumstances."

Gedeon nodded his head. The security team was smooth, taking up tables on the floor around Fyodor. The way they coordinated their moves, Gedeon doubted any customers in the bakery even noticed. "Are you getting anywhere?" Fyodor indicated the accounting ledgers and notebooks scattered across the table.

Gedeon had the foresight to close them. Even if the cameras could zoom in on them, they wouldn't know what they were looking for. Nothing would make sense, particularly in relation to the kidnapping of a child.

"We're making progress, but the beginning of a search is always painfully slow. Especially when it's this kind of case. The tendency is to move fast, but then you make mistakes. We can't afford to make a mistake. My gut tells me she's alive. Meiling thinks the same thing. I want her to stay alive, so I'm not going to run off half-cocked. They don't know I'm looking for them and I don't want them to. It's imperative to fly under the radar on this one."

"Give us a way to help you."

"Keep people out of my way. I can't be stumbling over your men when I'm working. If I need information, I'll come to you, Fyodor."

Meiling returned, walking briskly, the way she did when she was onto something. Her gaze swept the tables, taking in the security team and Fyodor. That didn't slow her down in the least. She kept coming straight to them, giving Fyodor a faint smile.

"Sorry to interrupt, but I need a couple of things. I'll just work over there." She indicated a small table in the corner with her chin while she caught up several of the accounting books, the tablet and a notebook. She didn't wait for an introduction but hurried to the table and opened the tablet and one of the accounting books.

"She's a force to be reckoned with," Gedeon said. "Once she's caught the scent, I swear she's like a . . ."

Meiling's head came up. "I can hear you. Don't you call me a hound dog."

Fyodor hid a smile behind his hand. Timur coughed. The new kid openly laughed. Kyanite and Rodion snickered.

"She's a hurricane," Gedeon said. "Sweeping a clear path to where we need to go."

"Good save." Fyodor indicated Evangeline. "Took me a good year to get myself out of trouble. I used sex."

Gedeon wished he could use sex. He didn't have that available to him. "We're business partners."

Fyodor's eyebrow shot up. "Not yours? Not claimed? Hell, man, I've got a few men with leopards looking for mates. When this is over maybe she could meet a few of them, see if they get on."

Gedeon shot him a look that told him to back off. He didn't much care if he was the biggest, baddest *pakhan* around. Gedeon would be quite willing to take him out and all his single leopards as well if they decided they were going to try sniffing around Meiling. "Not a good idea."

"I can see that," Fyodor said.

Gedeon's cell vibrated. He glanced down at the text from Harold. Bookkeeper unexpectedly died of heart attack. Fredrick put word out we needed a closed-mouthed bookkeeper. Lospostos gave the recommendation.

There it was. Lospostos. The one name Gedeon didn't want to see. He sighed. If he had to kill the man, there would be hell to pay. He'd send Meiling home first. "Anything we discuss, you keep confidential? Even from someone you may have an alliance with?"

"Gedeon, you're a man of your word. You say a child has been kidnapped, then I don't say shit to anyone until you say she's safe."

"What do you know about Elijah Lospostos?"

Gedeon could tell he had shocked Fyodor. He wasn't expecting Gedeon to ask about Elijah. Fyodor's eyebrow shot up again. "Why would you ask about him? He would never, under any circumstances, harm a child. I can personally vouch for him. If you think he has anything at all to do with the kidnapping of a child, I can assure you, he didn't. He would be the first one out hunting whoever did."

"He has a reputation."

"Gedeon, I hate to point this out, but you have a worse one."

It was true. He couldn't deny it. He deserved his reputation. He'd earned it. Maybe Lospostos hadn't earned his. Gedeon had always thought the thing with his sister was a crock of bullshit. Still, no one had that big of a reputation without a good deal of it being true. The man was reputed to be hard as nails, and Gedeon believed it. Gedeon didn't need to have an enemy like that on his ass while they were working on such an extremely sensitive and very urgent case.

"Elijah has a wife he loves and three little girls. They're just babies, but he spends as much time with them as he can," Fyodor continued. "We visit with him whenever it's possible. We know our wives and children are never going to have normal lives, so we try to give them the next best possible thing. Friends that understand the life we lead. He protects his family, and he protects my family. He would never take that child."

Out of the corner of his eye, he saw Meiling texting. His phone vibrated.

Need to know if Fredrick was sleeping with anyone after wife died.

He didn't die, Lotus.

Was he always going to feel guilty because he couldn't stop the cycle of sex or violence? She wasn't the one making him feel guilty. She had backed off and given him the freedom to carry on with his lifestyle. It was just that he didn't want that lifestyle anymore. He wanted Meiling. He didn't dare take her and make a mistake. He'd lose her for certain.

Don't give me crap. It's important, especially
if it was long term.

They had decided ahead of time that only one of them
would take the lead with Atwater and Brinks. That would
be Gedeon. It was always that way on their cases. It allowed Meiling to fade into the background, where she
could do her best work. He liked that she wasn't afraid of
him. She stood up to him, especially if she was onto
something—and he was certain she was now.

Several times he caught her sneaking glances at Timur
under the fan of her long lashes. She wanted to talk to
him. She wouldn't do it without speaking with Gedeon
first. He sent the text to Harold asking about Atwater's sex
life and then sent a text to Meiling.

Do you need me to set up a meet with Timur?

She hesitated, glanced at her watch and then bit down
on her lip. She shook her head. *Not yet.* She texted back.

I have to talk this over with you. Be certain
I'm on the right track.

That meant politely ending his conversation with Fyodor, and he still wasn't certain about Lospostos. "How
loyal is he to his men? In other words, if they were involved without his knowledge, would he stand with them,
or would he let it go?"

Fyodor sat back in the chair, studying Gedeon's face.
Gedeon knew there was nothing for Fyodor to see. Gedeon
was a merciless man when he needed to be. His leopard
had learned from a very young age to be nearly impossible
to trace, if not impossible. He slipped into houses under
the noses of leopard security and their infinite number of

cameras and assassinated his targets. It wasn't that anyone caught him at it—there were only the results of his work.

"You really believe this is going to track back to Elijah's lair?"

Gedeon nodded. "We've only been working an hour or so, but there's a strong indication. More than a strong indication, and we have to follow it."

"I can set up a private meet with Elijah," Fyodor offered.

Gedeon shook his head. "Too dangerous, Fyodor. If he's involved in any way, that child is dead. If it gets out that he's meeting with me, she's dead. There're quite a few reasons not to meet him and no good reasons to meet him."

Fyodor disagreed. "You cross that man without him realizing you're trying to save a child and he could very well kill you."

"I'll have to take that chance. I'm not risking the little girl."

"Damn, you're stubborn."

"This got dumped in my lap about three or four hours ago. I came here first to pay my respects and let you know what was going on. I trust your judgment when it comes to my life, but I can't make that call for a child. You'd be the same way."

Fyodor sighed. "I'll let you get back to it. Let Timur know if you need anything."

"We'll do that. I think Meiling may be onto something. Then we'll want to talk to him."

Fyodor looked relieved. "Keep us in the loop if you can, Gedeon. We'd appreciate it." He extended his hand and Gedeon shook it.

Fyodor rose and instantly his security rose as well. Timur stepped smoothly in front of him as he started back toward the counter. Kyanite and Rodion took up their positions on either side of him and the younger leopard dropped in behind him. They walked as one unit to the counter, where only Timur, Fyodor and the younger leopard continued through the double doors leading to the kitchen and whatever lay behind them. Kyanite and Rodion returned to their table facing the door leading to the outside, but where they could easily watch the entire room, especially Evangeline at the counter.

Meiling joined Gedeon at the table. He stood up and stretched. "Getting myself another cup of coffee. Would you like one?"

She shook her head. "I'm going switch to water. I need to hydrate."

She pushed at strands of silky black hair that were falling from the upswept do she had going. The thick mass was only held by the two sticks she'd shoved into the twist she'd made, and with all her agitated pulling, it had loosened. The lights put gleaming bluish highlights in her dark hair. When she moved, with feminine grace, her hips swayed, calling attention to her slim figure, making it known she was all female regardless of what she was wearing.

Gedeon had never been drawn to a woman the way he was to Meiling. Sometimes just the sight of her overwhelmed him. It didn't seem to matter what was going on around them; he couldn't get her out of his mind. He looked forward to hearing her laugh. He admired the way her brain worked. He especially liked the lethal component to her. There was an intimacy in knowing she could take out quite a few male leopards before others even recognized the danger. He liked having that knowledge. He liked that she was that fast and that strong. He often wondered what she'd be like when her leopard emerged.

"Evangeline, I think you work too hard," he greeted, as he put his coffee cup on the counter. "You've been on your feet for too long while I've had my butt in a chair. I'll need a bottle of water for Meiling."

Evangeline poured his coffee and then retrieved a bottle of water from the case behind her. "I have the first shift and then Ashe, my sister-in-law, Timur's wife, will relieve me. She makes the most amazing coffee."

He lifted an eyebrow. "Better than this?"

She nodded. "Seriously. She can't bake and won't go near my kitchen, but her coffee is unbelievable. Some of our customers time coming in for her shift."

"Great. If Meiling finds out, she'll insist we buy a house here and go back and forth between New Orleans and San Antonio just for the coffee. She was already telling me we needed an airplane."

He picked up the coffee cup and the bottle of water, gave her a little salute and made his way back to the table. Meiling looked up at him. She had that look in her dark eyes, the one that told him she was fairly certain she was onto something.

"Did Harold get back to you about Fredrick and his love life?" She stuck the end of a pen in between her perfect white teeth and chewed on it.

Gedeon took the pen from her mouth and handed her the bottle of water. "Not yet. He will. He knows that if they don't answer us, they won't be getting cooperation. I also made it clear I'd be coming back to cut their throats."

She blinked at him. "When did you do that? Where was I?"

"Lotus Blossom."

She sat up a little straighter. "Don't you lotus blossom me, Leopard Boy," she hissed behind her hand. "If you're going to threaten our clients, especially *bratya* clients who might just decide to put out a hit on you, you'd better let me in on it *immediately*. Sometimes I really need to know where you hid that Ming vase, Gedeon."

He leaned close to her. "Do you know how much time has gone by since that child was taken? I don't give a damn if Fredrick was scared out of his mind because he thinks Lospostos is involved in this. He could have called us. He had to have known I don't give a fuck who's involved when it comes to a child."

Meiling's eyes went soft. She reached out and laid her hand over his. "Gedeon, I'm not upset with you for threatening them. You have to let me back you up. We're partners. If I did that sort of thing and didn't tell you, you'd get a little hot under the collar."

"I'd strangle you with my bare hands." He didn't bother to deny it.

She lifted her hand away from his and took a drink of water, narrowing her eyes at him.

"I'd revive you, of course. I like having you around, mostly for my leopard. He's grown fond of your quirky ways." He indicated her notebook with his coffee cup. "Show me what you've got."

"It would make more sense if Harold answered you."

"*You* make sense, Lotus. I never have trouble following your train of thought."

For just one moment, her face lit up, and then she took another sip of water, the long feathery lashes, as black as her hair, veiling the expression in her eyes. He never liked it when he couldn't read her, especially in moments when she was giving herself away. He had come to realize no one ever gave her compliments. She had been as alone as he had. She didn't know what to do with accolades, but she needed to hear them.

Meiling made him feel as if he wasn't alone. He shared his life with someone now—for the first time since his family had been destroyed. He told her things he knew he would never tell another soul. He laughed with her over silly things, and he'd never had that with another human being. He gave that to her. She had an incredible brain. She knew it, but no one in her life had ever recognized it or given her kudos for it until he'd come along. That had to count for something. She had to need that feedback from him just as desperately as he needed it from her. The world he moved in saw him as a vicious killer. She knew he was so much more. Just as he knew she was so much more than that shadow slipping in and out of homes returning items lost—the work she'd contracted to do before she was with him.

Gedeon knew, on some level, having Meiling with him made him even more dangerous than he'd ever been. He had something in his life worth keeping. Worth fighting for. He would be ferocious in his protection of her. Everything he'd learned in those years growing up in that treacherous, ugly world, when he'd been a child fighting for his survival and soaking up every martial art as if he were a sponge, he now knew why: Meiling. She had come to be the center of his world in such a short time. He had no idea why and he didn't care.

"I don't think our man Georgi is the one giving the orders, Gedeon," Meiling said softly. "I think he was brought on board to take the money. The original bookkeeper most likely didn't die of a heart attack either. Or he did, but he was helped along the way."

Gedeon had had that fleeting thought himself. The idea of the bookkeeper just dropping dead and creating an opening for Lospostos to send Georgi Chaban in as bookkeeper for Atwater seemed a little too coincidental. And why would Lospostos do it? He didn't need the money or the territory. Gedeon kept his mouth shut, letting Meiling explain her reasoning.

"Someone *inside* Fredrick's home is feeding him drugs. They aren't coming in the mail. Unless he's taking them voluntarily, he's getting them in food or drink. I'm surprised whoever is doing this hasn't taken out Harold. And that is the next logical step, especially if they can't get to Fredrick. By placing guards in front of his door and having a doctor attending to him, that's what's happened. You've cut him off from the person who orchestrated this."

"A woman," Gedeon said. "A lover."

"Someone connected in some way to Chaban. Yes. If I'm right, Fredrick and this woman were lovers for a long while. Months, maybe even years. He trusts her. But he refused to put a ring on her finger. Or he took another lover. He's leopard. He might need several lovers. I don't know the way it works with you males. You'd know better than me."

There was no accusation in her voice, only acceptance. Too much acceptance. She believed that whoever the woman was in Fredrick's life might plot to exact revenge on him, but Meiling would withhold emotions so she would never care enough to do such a thing. Which was worse? Caring too much? Having the ability to love, or not ever loving? Damn it. Why was he even feeling guilty? She wasn't his mate. He wasn't cheating on her.

"The way it works, Meiling, is this," he said, keeping his voice even and patient. "Fredrick had a mate. He's leopard. His leopard and he both were mated to one woman and her leopard. By all accounts he loved her and was devoted wholly to her. There was no cheating. He was faithful to her. When she died, he was devastated. That didn't mean as time passed, he didn't still have the needs of a man. In his case, I don't know what he was like, or what his leopard was like. I hadn't heard that his leopard was difficult. But he most likely took lovers. More than one. He would never consider that being unfaithful, because none of them were his mate. He would only be faithful to his mate."

She frowned, that adorable frown he often had the desire to lean forward and kiss off her face, especially like now, when she was tapping the pen on the notebook over and over. "Then you believe he would tell that to the woman up front. Make it clear to her that there was no relationship and no chance of ever having one."

"Certainly a man of honor would do so."

"The women in Fredrick's house aren't all leopard, but they're all young. Did you notice that? All of them. He has twelve women working there. Seven are full-time. Five are part-time."

"That place is enormous. Keeping it clean has to take an army."

"Of women? Young women? The men he employs are for security, bookkeeping, groundskeeping, that sort of thing. The women have kitchen and essentially maid duty."

"Fredrick is a dick. We've established that." His phone vibrated and he pulled it out of his pocket. Harold had written what looked to Gedeon like a page out of a novel, the text was so long.

"Harold confirms that Fredrick has a very active sex life with the women he employs. He was in a 'relationship' with Lola Morales. He put the word relationship in quotes. They were sleeping together for eighteen months when she found out he was having sex with a couple of the other women. He fired the other two, but she ended their time together. It was an amicable ending. She's never caused a problem, not even when she's walked in on one of the women servicing him." He winced when he read that to her. Put like that, it sounded bad. There was no good way to put it. He raised his gaze to her face.

Her dark eyes met his. Direct. His gut clenched. Knots formed. Yeah, she was thinking about all the women fawning over him at the club. The way they came to the booth and tore at his trousers to get at his cock. He rarely bothered to take them anywhere private. Hell, they'd line up if he let them. Did he have respect for them? No. The answer was no. Did he have respect for himself? No. The answer was no.

"Stop it, Gedeon. There's no comparison. This case isn't about you. It's about Fredrick and what he did or didn't say to set this in motion. We have to find out as much as we can about this woman. I did some research on my top three suspects. She was one of them. She has to have a tie to Georgi and we need to find it in the next half hour."

Gedeon nodded and went to work. They had a name now. Lola Morales. They had to find out where she came from and who she had working with her, if she really was the one behind the missing money and the kidnapping of Fredrick Atwater's four-year-old daughter, Lilith. He tried finding Lola Morales, then anything she might have to do with Chaban. He came up empty. And then he tried Lospostos. He scored big there.

Lola Morales was the daughter of Pedro Morales, a trusted lieutenant of Elijah Lospostos. More, she had grown up with three boys close to her: Georgi Chaban, Alan Cano and Caleb Basco. The four had been inseparable. The boys' fathers also worked for Lospostos.

"We've got a hit, Lotus. We need to call a meeting with Timur."

8

MEILING rarely spoke in meetings with clients. She left that up to Gedeon, fading into the background so those around her almost forgot she was in the room with them. It was the way they conducted business deliberately and it worked. But this was her find.

Gedeon wanted these men to see her as an equal partner. To take her seriously. And, most of all, to know that he would hold them accountable if anything happened to her. They knew him and they knew he wouldn't just have a woman talk for the two of them. If she was speaking, it was because he respected every word that came out of her mouth, and he expected they would as well.

Fyodor, Timur, Gedeon and Meiling met in Fyodor's office. It wasn't behind the double doors that led to the kitchen, but rather down the hall, past where Evangeline and Ashe made the coffee. A nursery had been set up just behind the bakery, and on the other side of that was Fyo-

dor's office. There was access to the kitchen from his office and to the nursery as well.

It was a sweet setup for Timur. He could get to the children, to the women and to his main responsibility, Fyodor,
any number of ways in under a second. He had multiple
ways of extracting the family should there be an attack on
them. Gedeon didn't know who had designed the interior
suite of rooms, but it was brilliant. He hadn't seen all of
them, and he would bet there were hidden ways to get to the
roof or to the basement. Timur wouldn't take any chances
with his family.

Meiling looked straight at Timur, not in the least intimidated, even though she was half his size. "Timur, we
need someone fast. When I say fast, he has to be fast enough
to stop a woman from sending a text in a crowded public
place. She's leopard and she'll have someone looking out
for her. It might be a woman he knows. He can't *think* he
can get to her. He has to *know* he can. If he misses, that
little girl will die. Do you have anyone that fast?"

Timur nodded slowly, keeping his gaze fixed on her
face.

"At the same time, before we can make a move on any
of them, we have to find whoever is watching out for the
woman. I believe her backup will be either of these two
men." Meiling showed Timur photographs of Alan Cano
and Caleb Basco she had on her phone. "In any case, both
men are most likely involved."

Gedeon watched Timur's face closely, and then Fyodor's
as Timur passed Meiling's phone to his brother. Both men
had to know the two shifters Meiling was all but accusing
of being in a conspiracy to abduct a small child.

"Do you have proof?" Fyodor asked.

"If I had proof, Gedeon and I would be slitting their
throats instead of sitting here talking to you," Meiling said.
"Timur offered help. He said anything. I know I can get
the evidence. We asked for proof of life. If I'm right, this

woman"—she took the phone and showed him the photograph of Lola Morales—"will be handing off instructions to Georgi Chaban." She swiped the photograph of Lola to one side and replaced it with a picture of Georgi. "It will happen this morning."

"You're aware all four of the people you suspect are a part of the Lospostos lair?" Fyodor asked, his voice mild. Gedeon instantly went on alert. So much so that he signaled to Meiling to put some distance between her and the Amurov brothers.

"Generations of their families," Fyodor continued, "have lived their entire lives in the Lospostos lair and served them with honor."

Meiling shrugged her shoulders and wandered over to the window to look out on the street. "I am certain what you say is the truth. I'm also certain I'm right that Lola Morales had a very long affair with Fredrick Atwater after he lost his wife. She believed he would marry her and take her for his mate. The woman Atwater lost was his true mate and he was never going to replace her. Lola didn't understand that because Atwater didn't bother to explain it to her, not until she realized he had several other lovers."

Fyodor held up his hand to stop her explanation. "Atwater confirmed this?"

"Harold, his right-hand man, confirmed he had an eighteen-month-long relationship with Morales and that he regularly takes advantage of the women working in his home. Morales still works there and is aware of Atwater's sexual practices and appears not to care. She was the one to end the relationship. Atwater expressed a fondness for her and would have fired the women he was having sex with, although he made it clear to her he wouldn't marry her or have children with her."

"If he was willing to get rid of all the other women for her," Timur argued, "that was saying something about the way he felt about her. She was special to him."

Meiling glanced at her watch. "She wasn't his only. She wasn't the one he would have *children* with. Build his life around. Be the center of his world. He had *cheated* on her regularly with her right there in the house. She didn't mean enough to him to stop using other women. He was everything to her, but she didn't mean the same to him. In any case, gentlemen, we asked for your help. If we're not going to get it, we have to come up with another plan. Lola is going to go to work this morning and find out that her boss has collapsed under the pressure of his child being kidnapped and money being siphoned from his businesses along with the fear of Lospostos's retaliation."

Gedeon had to suppress a groan at the use of the crime kingpin's name. Twice he'd tried to subtly insert his body between hers and Timur's. Fyodor was a ruthless man, there was no doubt about it, but he wasn't a man to kill a woman. But if Timur thought Meiling was a threat to Fyodor, he would end her in a heartbeat. Timur was the biggest threat in the room and Gedeon would kill him first, but he needed Meiling safe. She persisted in moving, pacing, but keeping her slim body between his and Timur's. He was going to strangle the woman when he got her alone. He knew damn well she was protecting him. She just couldn't seem to help herself.

"We're going to help you. I want to understand what you need from us, Meiling," Timur said. "What exactly do you plan to do?"

"When Lola gets to work, which will be any minute, she'll find Atwater in his suite, with a doctor giving him IV fluids and insisting he can't have visitors or anyone in the rooms with him. His orders will be he needs round-the-clock quiet, with lights dim and no one to upset him. Only Harold will be allowed in. Drake Donovan already had a team of shifters here and he allowed us to put them in place to guard Atwater. We believe Lola has been drugging him. By cutting him off from everyone, it will be impossible for the drugging to continue. We also had people sweeping the house for bugs last night. Anywhere Atwater would go, his office, the conservatory, his library, even Lilith's room and his private suite, had bugs. The rest of the house was clean. We left them in place so she wouldn't be tipped off. The only ones destroyed were the ones in the conservatory, and we flooded the plants where they'd been placed."

"It strikes me that if you're correct about this, the old adage of a woman scorned can be really frightening," Fyodor commented.

"You'd better think about that," Timur pointed out. "Evangeline might look as sweet as can be right now, but you mess around on her and life as you know it could get very rough."

"Touching another woman would be out of the question for me," Fyodor said, his voice gruff.

Gedeon could hear the truth in the crime lord's voice. Fyodor would never cheat on his wife. Clearly he didn't even joke about it.

"Keep going, Meiling," Fyodor encouraged.

"Once Lola realizes she can't get to Atwater to judge his reactions, she may think she's pushed him too hard. Harold will have left a communication in the established place demanding proof of life. They don't use text messaging. That's good for us. That means Lola will go out this morning and she'll deliver a message to someone asking them to get a proof-of-life photo of Lilith. I intend to follow Lola to whomever she passes that message to and then follow him back to wherever Lilith is being held. If I'm spotted, I believe they'll kill Lilith and dispose of the evidence immediately. Who would believe anyone in the Lospostos organization would have anything to do with a kidnapping of a child?" Meiling explained.

"And you figured this out in just under two hours without knowing any of these people?" Timur said. "You're sitting in a damn bakery with customers coming and going and you've already decided who's guilty."

Meiling looked at him, her long lashes veiling the expression in her dark eyes for moment, and then she nodded. "Gedeon and I often have to work fast in order to save lives. It is possible we're wrong in our summary of who is behind this horrendous crime and why, but we had to make a decision, and this is our best one."

"You believe it?" Fyodor said.

"I do," Meiling reiterated.

"Time is slipping away," Gedeon reminded. "You have to make up your minds whether or not you think you can help based on what we've given you."

"The answer is yes," Fyodor said. "I don't have to like it, but yes."

"You do see why it would be impossible to go to Elijah Lospostos with this even if we did have the time." Gedeon made it a statement. "These are members of families deeply entrenched in his organization. One man, Georgi Chaban, we know for certain Elijah gave a personal recommendation to Atwater to hire as a bookkeeper after his longtime bookkeeper died of a heart attack. We both believe it is possible Lola helped him along with that heart attack. It seems just a little too convenient."

"Tell us what you have in mind," Timur said.

"We have to spot anyone backing up Lola. Gedeon will be backing me up. This is the first time Atwater has changed things up, so I would expect them to be on edge. Gedeon tells me if it were him, he would put one of the men on Lola and the other on Georgi. It may happen that way. If I spot Lola making contact with Georgi, I'll signal Gedeon. I'll follow Georgi, hopefully back to where Lilith is being held. Your man cannot move on Lola until we know for certain her backup has been handled and so has Georgi's. I have to also be assured that whoever takes down Lola is fast enough to get to her before she can text Georgi to kill

Lilith. She will do that. A woman who would plan this elaborate of a revenge plot most likely planned to kill Lilith all along."

"Kyanite is fast enough," Timur assured. "He wouldn't move on her unless he knew he could take her down and get the phone before she gives the order."

"We know we're putting you in a bad position with Lospostos," Gedeon said. "For that, I apologize, Fyodor. I had hoped we could handle this without you."

"He'll understand a child's life was at stake," Fyodor said. "I ask that you meet with him after this is over. You'll be able to hear the truth in his voice when you speak with him."

Gedeon nodded his head but didn't speak. Before he agreed to meet with Elijah Lospostos, he was going to have a long talk with Meiling and lay down the law. If she wasn't willing to comply, there would be no meeting. They would be getting on a plane and heading back to New Orleans within an hour of taking the kid back to her parent.

GEDEON watched as Meiling weaved in and out of the marketplace, crowded with wares and fresh fish. She was graceful when she moved, dressed in dark navy denim overalls that were still very feminine on her slight figure. Under the overalls she had on a striped navy-and-red long-sleeved cotton tee. She wore a cropped denim jacket over the tee. She seemed to blend into the shadows cast by the numerous overhead umbrellas shading the long tables of vegetables, fruits, fish, meats and wares offered by so many vendors.

She was patient, looking at everything, exploring each table, picking up a tomato or a cucumber and smelling it before putting it back down. She bargained for a basket of cherry tomatoes, and when she'd settled on a price, she placed them carefully in the woven basket hanging off her arm. She left that vendor's table but backtracked, returning to purchase two cucumbers and a small basket of mushrooms.

Meiling was several feet behind the person she followed—a tall, beautiful woman wearing thick glasses with her chestnut hair tied up in a bun. She had a larger basket on her arm and was busy bargaining at various booths or tables for goods. It was clear she was known to the local vendors. They all greeted her warmly by name and pointed out their best and freshest produce.

Gedeon's job wasn't to watch Lola. It was necessary to find her backup as soon as possible. He wasn't the only one looking. His primary role was to serve as Meiling's protection. That meant he had to ensure no one was aware of Meiling trailing after Lola. He couldn't imagine it. Meiling was extremely good at tailing her quarry. She didn't look in the least interested in her. She was by turns in the same aisle or two rows over. Sometimes she was in the opposite row. She was so small, she was lost in the crowd often. Even if someone was up above the marketplace looking down on it, as he was, Gedeon doubted anyone would focus on her. She didn't look in the least like a threat.

He scanned the crowd continually and then quartered the area around him. He paid attention to the rooftops and surrounding windows and balconies. Gedeon had detested bringing Timor and Fyodor Amurov into the entire affair. There was no way of guaranteeing that friendship wouldn't override the Amurovs' compassion for the child. They might decide to let Lospostos know what was happening. If the man was involved, he could send shooters after Meiling and Gedeon. That possibility was very real. Gedeon never let any possibility of retaliation go unheeded. That was what kept him alive.

"Two o'clock," he whispered. "You see him? That's definitely Alan Cano. Meiling called it. He's watching Lola's back. You have him, Rodion?"

"I do." Rodion's tone was clipped.

Somewhere, Timur was out there watching the entire scene unfold. Gedeon knew the head of security wasn't happy that Fyodor had insisted he come along as well. Both men were upset that members of Lospostos's lair were involved and he was not informed. Wars were started over much lesser things.

Gedeon didn't trust anyone—apart from Meiling—and she'd earned his trust by saving his life on more than one occasion. He intended to have a gun trained on Elijah Lospostos if he ended up meeting with him. He wanted to have Meiling somewhere safe, out of sight. He'd lived his entire existence this way, since the moment his father's friends had come to murder them all.

Gedeon had been very young, but he remembered each of them. They'd eaten at his family's table. His parents had helped their families time and again. He'd played with their children. Still, they'd come to murder them. Their only sin had been their extraordinary gifts, which seemed to intimidate and frighten the others. And make them jealous. Never mind that his parents had used those gifts to aid the others.

From those early days he had learned that anyone could pretend friendship and end up betraying you. It had been his father's best friend who had come late in the night, knocking on the door. His father would have been prepared for an attack had it been anyone else. He had opened the door without hesitation. He had grown up with the man and thought of him like a sibling. Gedeon had called him uncle. That betrayal had hurt his father almost more than the torture and death that followed.

Gedeon was thankful his father had died. It had spared him seeing what the *pakhan* had done to Gedeon's beloved mother. Selling her to any man. Beating her at every opportunity when she resisted. What he did to Gedeon was beside the point, but it built a rage in him and his leopard that would never go away. Gedeon could push it down, but it would always be there, and sometimes the nightmares were relentless.

Gedeon was intelligent and he had waited for his opportunity, looking compliant so the *pakhan* trained him to become an assassin for him. He found his father's best friend first, and he spent days making him suffer. First by killing his family one by one in front of him. He made certain the man had no one left. Then there were days of merciless torture, every single one in retaliation for what his mother had suffered. Finally, a slow, agonizing death. Gedeon had never felt a single ounce of remorse. He was still very young and knew he should—but he hadn't. That had only been the beginning of a long, secret campaign to get the murderers of his family.

The *pakhan* had never suspected a young boy would be behind the brutal killings. How could he be? These men were experienced. They had vicious leopards to warn them. And Gedeon always had an airtight alibi.

Time was slipping away. The longer Meiling spent tailing Lola in the marketplace, the greater the risk of her being discovered. Where the hell was the man on Georgi Chaban? For that matter, where was Georgi?

"She just made contact with Georgi," Meiling whispered in his ear. Her voice was so soft he barely heard it.

Gedeon's gaze jumped to her instantly, his heart accelerating. Her head was down as she smelled a ripe apricot. Lola was to her right and behind her, talking animatedly with the vendor while Meiling purchased a few of the apricots and placed them in her small basket. She began to wind her way through aisles around the rest of the long length of tables, walking toward the exit, ignoring Lola completely. Twice she stopped to look at something one of the vendors had to offer before shaking her head and continuing on her way.

"She's coming out," Gedeon advised.

He had to work to keep from being tense. This was the moment Meiling was most at risk. Georgi had someone backing him up, and so far, no one had spotted that man. They were all leopards. Gedeon wasn't at all familiar with the terrain, and their enemies were. This was their home turf, and they regularly made their drops here. They would know every nook and cranny to wedge themselves in to watch over their charges, but like him, when their responsibilities were on the move, they would have to move.

Very carefully, but with great speed, he broke down his rifle and placed it in the small carry case. While doing so, he barely made any movements. The entire time, he scanned the rooftops and the one little open meadow just to the right of the parking lot. That meadow kept drawing his attention. His gut knotted.

"Lotus, come back inside. I don't care what your excuse is but come back inside. Make it look real."

Meiling was a pro when it came to working with him. She didn't argue, although she had to be afraid she would lose her quarry. She snapped her fingers and turned around, nearly bumping into a man who caught her by the shoulders. She laughed softly and apologized.

"Forget something?" he asked, keeping her from falling.

"Yes, what I came for in the first place. I'm always doing that."

The older man laughed with her, and then she continued into the farmer's market while he headed toward the parking lot. She hurried immediately and then purposefully turned to her left and went straight to a vendor who had a multitude of lettuce on his table. She pointed to three different types and added them to her basket, explaining how she'd forgotten the very thing she'd come for in the first place. Chatting with him a little more, she added fresh beets and a bundle of asparagus. After paying, she turned back toward the exit just as Georgi and Caleb Basco entered. Meiling smoothly rounded the vendor's table to examine the strange artichokes he was pointing out to her. She listened carefully as he explained how to cook and eat them.

"How did you know?" she whispered as she purchased two of the artichokes. They were definitely in the thistle family. Gedeon hadn't eaten them before. He hoped she didn't think he was going to start now. She'd been like a crazy woman in the kitchen lately. He was certain she might be considering poisoning him with the thistles or at least choking him with the thorns.

"I had a hunch. I've seen this kind of setup before. Keep walking to the parking lot and get into the secondary vehicle. It looks like shit, but Timur said his cousin's wife made it into a road rocket. So far, they've come through for us."

"Um, Gedeon." There was laughter in Meiling's voice. It was the kind of thing that drew him to her. In the midst of a tense situation, Meiling always had a sense of humor. "I have no idea what the secondary vehicle looks like. That wasn't part of the discussion. You were taking control of that. I had the truck."

"That little Honda with the paint peeling off. There are four cars parked between the truck and the Honda and Georgi's vehicle."

"The shiny hot-looking souped-up truck I was going to get to drive?" she challenged, but the laughter in her voice belied her ability to sound upset.

"You couldn't even climb up into the cab," he stated.

"You feel very safe, don't you, Leopard Boy? I can't retaliate when you're making your short jokes because I'm here and you're there, but it won't be long and you're going to be very sorry. Where are the keys to the rocket?"

"Reach under the right wheel."

"That's not going to be noticeable?"

"You'll figure it out, you always do."

"Who was the actor helping me out with my little performance? The older man? He was leopard. His cologne smelled yummy."

Gedeon just stopped the grin. Caleb Basco wasn't his problem. Timur had assigned someone to take him down. "Timur asked him to help us out. Don't tell me you have a thing for older men."

She dropped one of the small packages she was carrying beside the tire of the Honda. Her hand slid along the wheel well and expertly extracted the key from the little holder. "Georgi Chaban just walked right past me without looking my way. His car is the hot little Porsche a row up and three cars over. I thought you said he was parked between us."

"He changed cars."

"He thinks he's so clever. Lola handed a note off to him. He read it, tore it into tiny pieces and dropped the pieces into three garbage cans," Meiling reported. "I indicated the cans to Jeremiah but he can't move on them until everyone except Chaban is rounded up."

"You just worry about tailing Chaban. If Timur's men are as good as he said, they'll do their jobs. If not, there isn't anything we can do about it," Gedeon pointed out.

She slid behind the wheel of the Honda. The car started right up. Chaban had already pulled his Porsche out of the parking lot and turned left. A dark blue sedan pulled into traffic after him. The sound of metal hitting metal was loud as an SUV rammed into the side of the sedan and drove it over the curb and right back into the parking lot, smashing it into another parked vehicle.

"Timur's man just took Caleb Basco out of the equation, Meiling," Gedeon reported. "The cops have been called and Caleb will not make it out of this alive. A fight will break out, and Caleb, who believes he's a total badass with a knife, will attempt to blindside Timur's man. He won't succeed. The witnesses will be a couple of cops."

Gedeon followed Meiling out of the parking lot, taking the exit to their far left. He caught a glimpse of the Porsche and accelerated around the little Honda, revving the motor of the memorable shiny blue-black truck obnoxiously as it shot past her to gain several car lengths in the middle lane.

Meiling tested the speed and agility of the little Honda, weaving it through the needle of two cars in the middle lane to get into the fast lane. She passed Gedeon and kept up her speed until she glimpsed the Porsche. He was using the middle lane effectively. Driving fast, but not calling attention to himself.

"Timur's men are reporting in, Meiling. The net's being dropped on Lola's accomplices. I hope to hell he's right and Kyanite is as fast as they say he is. If he can't get to Lola before she has time to send a text to Georgi, that little girl is toast," Gedeon mused aloud.

"I don't need to hear that right now," Meiling replied very softly. "It's going off like clockwork. We don't fail, Gedeon, because we plan out every detail. She'll stay alive and we'll return her to her dad."

She murmured something under her breath he couldn't quite catch.

"Spit it out, Lotus." Gedeon accelerated and deliberately passed her and several other cars, bringing him nearly side by side with their quarry. He didn't look over but bobbed his head up and down to the beat of the music playing loudly. He wore dark sunglasses and a baseball cap backward on his head. When the car in front of him didn't move over immediately, he revved his engine impatiently.

Meiling laughed. "You don't miss much, Leopard Boy. I just said I wanted to kick her dad hard somewhere it might do him some good."

He winced, having the feeling he knew exactly where she was thinking of aiming, and his Lotus Blossom knew how to kick.

"He deserves it," she added.

"A wise man knows not to argue," he intoned, and passed the moment the car in front of him pulled into the middle lane, almost directly in front of Georgi's pretty little Porsche. The driver gave Gedeon the finger, but he ignored it, rocking out to the music, his head banging up and down.

"When did you get wise?" she asked as the beat-up Honda glided up three cars to settle behind the Porsche.

"Suggesting kicks can straighten a man right up, Lotus," he said, and let his truck slow just enough to annoy the hell out of Georgi. He wanted the man's attention on him and his kick-ass truck, not the unremarkable little Honda sliding in and out of traffic, keeping right up with the Porsche.

As expected, Georgi pulled around the truck at the first opportunity and accelerated, wanting to put distance between him and the truck—or wanting to get to his destination faster. Gedeon wasn't in the least surprised when he took the exit leading away from the city and toward Elijah Lospostos's vast estate. The gently rolling hills were covered in trees placed close enough that their branches had grown strong but twisting together as they reached upward, forming an arboreal highway. Only a shifter would recognize it for what it was: essentially a road to use when one wanted to escape quickly.

The Honda pulled over in a small turnout under the shade of weeping trees someone had planted in the hopes of staving off the relentless sun on the side of the two-lane road. Gedeon pulled the truck in tight behind her so that not one part of his flashy vehicle was showing. He leapt from the truck into the Honda.

"Stay as far back as you can without losing him. Head for the knoll I told you about," he instructed.

She glanced at him, her dark eyes soft. "Gedeon, we're close, I can feel her."

"I wish I was closer. If that note said to kill the child instead of providing proof of life, we're fucked."

Meiling drove with the same casual ease she did everything. He kept his gaze fixed on the Porsche, which was several miles ahead of them. They were slightly above Chaban and could see his car weaving in and out around a few of the circular turns. Meiling didn't push the speed, although she had to be feeling the same sense of anxiety as Gedeon was.

This was one of those cases that inevitably took him back to a childhood where he had no control. Where murderers decided the fate of children for whatever their reasons. It didn't matter that he was called in at the last minute and he had only a couple of hours to find the victim; he always felt responsible if he didn't get there in time. Finding a dead child was one of the worst failures imaginable to him.

She abruptly pulled the Honda over and both bailed. They'd chosen this spot ahead of time because it gave them the best view of the small house Georgi Chaban leased on Lospostos land. Chaban's parents had the home a mile from his, also leased from Lospostos, but they'd held that lease for years.

Chaban pulled his Porsche into the garage and was instantly swallowed, out of their sight. The moment he was in the garage, Gedeon and Meiling swept their entire surroundings for signs of guards or anyone else who might be watching over Georgi. Both had extrasensory gifts they had learned to rely on, and when neither could spot anyone and radar hadn't gone off, they crouched low and ran toward the leased property.

Chaban's land was very neat and set back from one of the well-maintained roads on the property. Everything on the Lospostos estate was very well kept, although it could appear wild to an outsider. The trees were sculpted for leopards, the branches thick and twisted to bend toward one another throughout the massive estate.

Chaban's leased property was a distance from the main house, where Elijah and his family resided. Many of the Lospostos workers were considered family and had leased portions of the land for their own families. The land around the houses was maintained by the families, but all roads and the surrounding property were kept up by Lospostos.

Meiling and Gedeon utilized the shrubbery and foliage from the trees to help hide their approach to Chaban's home. They kept away from the main road. It wouldn't do to have someone passing by unexpectedly spot them. Anyone on the Lospostos property was most likely a shifter, with a shifter's enhanced sense of smell. Meiling and Gedeon were using a special scent blocker to prevent shifters from discovering them as they made their approach.

The sound of a weeping child caught at Gedeon's heart. He hadn't recognized he had a heart until Meiling came along. She'd softened him in ways he wasn't certain were all that good. He had been numb before—closed off. Being around Meiling had changed him in unexpected ways. The more he was with her, the more he obsessed over her—and the more he found himself caring about how some of their cases could affect her. She had a much more tender heart than he did. He couldn't imagine what the sound of that crying child was doing to her.

He signaled to Meiling to move around to the other side of the house. As they did, the sound of the child's crying became louder.

"I want my daddy," she said clearly.

The window was open, and blinds fluttered with the breeze. The blinds were wooden and had been pulled open, so when Gedeon peered into the room, he could see Chaban holding a camera out in front of a very small female child. The little girl flung herself onto an unmade bed facedown so that only a tangle of dark hair showed against the white sheet.

Chaban swore at the child. "Stop being a little monster. If you want to eat, you'd better cooperate. Your father wants to see a picture of you."

The child kicked her feet and any reply she made was

muffled by the pillow and sheets she had buried her face into.

Chaban stalked across the room and dragged Lilith's head up by her hair, making her wail louder. He snapped several pictures of her and then dropped her head back onto the pillow.

"You dad doesn't want you back. That's why you're still here," he said cruelly. "You're never going home. No one wants you because you're an entitled little brat."

Chaban stalked out and kicked the door closed behind him. The sound was loud, but more important, he had kicked the thick wooden door so hard, when it hit the frame, it shook the entire house. The child jerked in fear and pressed her hands over her ears, sobbing louder.

Meiling moved up to the side of the house in stealthy silence. The blinds swayed with the wind as she examined the window for alarms. Finding none on the window, which Gedeon found quite shocking, Meiling slid through the window.

"Lilith." She whispered the child's name. "Lilith, don't stop crying or act startled. Your father sent me to bring you home. The bad man is just outside the door. He can't know I'm here yet. My partner will make sure he can't get to you again."

Lilith flipped over onto her back and sat up, her eyes wild as she looked around the room. Gedeon, watching from the window, could see the leopard staring out from the child's eyes. There was no question that Fredrick Atwater's daughter was a shifter, and she had a leopard already looking out for her.

Meiling looked soft and gentle as she slowly approached Lilith, extending one hand toward her. "Honey, you should be able to hear lies. When you listen to people, you know if they are good people or bad, right? Lola wasn't a good person, was she?"

Lilith shook her head. "I told Daddy, but he wouldn't listen. Lola said I was bad for telling him. She called me a brat too."

"You're not a brat, Lilith. You were trying to save your daddy. That makes you smart and courageous. I'm sorry she and her friends have been so mean to you."

"They said my daddy doesn't want me back."

"You know that isn't true. You could hear their lies, couldn't you?" Meiling insisted softly. She was close to the child now. Sitting on the edge of the bed with her. Not yet touching her. Not forcing acceptance from the little girl.

Gedeon could see the leopard in the child yielding to Meiling's sovereignty. There was no demand in Meiling. No impatience. She listened attentively to everything the child had to say, leaning toward her with a little half-smile on her face and nodding as though everything Lilith had to say was invaluable. It wasn't very long before the child crawled into Meiling's lap and wound her arms around his partner's neck. For some reason the sight of that caused a curious melting sensation in the region of his heart.

Meiling signaled him, a small movement of her fingers as she flung herself somersaulting backward over the side of the bed, Lilith in her arms, tucked in tight against her body to protect the child. Simultaneously, Gedeon dove through the window, his speed making him a blur as Georgi Chaban slammed open the door to the bedroom, using his fist and a boot. He had a gun out and shot into the room without actually seeing a target. The door crashed into the wall and started to bounce closed.

Gedeon went in low, beneath the gun, hitting him at the knees and taking him down, his knife sinking into his belly several times and then his groin, severing arteries while Meiling covered Lilith's eyes and murmured reassurances to her.

9

GEDEON prepared for the meeting with Elijah Lospostos and Fyodor Amurov by packing up everything in their hotel rooms and checking out. He wanted to be ready to leave at a moment's notice. They had airline tickets, but that wasn't the only way they could escape. In fact, he wasn't counting on that being their way out of San Antonio.

He didn't trust easily. Fyodor and Elijah clearly had a long-standing relationship. Lola Morales was dead. She was the daughter of Pedro Morales, a lieutenant for Elijah whose family had worked for Elijah's family for generations. No doubt he was demanding answers and wanted revenge.

Alan Cano had also died, a young man from one of Elijah Lospostos's long-standing families that had also served for generations. His people would be seeking explanations and demanding Elijah go after whoever had killed their child.

Caleb Basco was also dead. His family knew he had

had a hot temper. They also knew he had believed no one would ever notice when he drew a knife in a fight, yet he had been seen by two police officers as he pulled a knife on a witness who was telling the policemen that the *other* vehicle was at fault, not Caleb's, but for some reason, Caleb had attacked him. The witness had been faster and had killed Caleb with Caleb's own knife.

Georgi Chaban was slain in his own home, stabbed several times. There was evidence that he had been involved in a kidnapping. There had been a child living in the bedroom where he had been killed. Evidence had been left that he had been holding the child prisoner there. His parents didn't believe it and wanted Elijah to investigate and exact retribution.

Four members of Elijah Lospostos's extended family were killed without his prior knowledge. At the very least, even if he accepted that they were all guilty and deserved death, he wouldn't be happy that he hadn't been informed of what was going on in his own lair. He was a powerful man and would make a dangerous enemy.

Gedeon had run up against many of Lospostos's kind in his career. One had to walk a very fine line between fear and respect. He could never back down, and he could never fully trust anyone. Now he had Meiling to protect.

They approached the bakery, where they would meet with Lospostos as promised. It was dark and after hours, so the bakery was closed. Gedeon and Meiling had scouted carefully. Timur, as expected, had his men on rooftops and patrolling the streets in anticipation of the meeting. Gedeon wanted to know the exact position of each of them.

Timur's man Rodion let them in and indicated the empty tables. "Fyodor and Timur are running a little late but will be here any minute. Make yourselves at home." He dropped the dark privacy screens in place over the windows, blocking out views of the streets. "Nice job getting that kid back," he added.

Gedeon was fully aware that Rodion's gaze continually swept over Meiling. Had he stepped closer to her? Did he sniff the air near her? She did have an unbelievable fragrance to her. Gedeon did his best to clamp down on what he had to consider were jealous traits. He hadn't known he even had them. He went through women all the time. He made it known he wasn't looking for a relationship, that there was no hope of one. He rarely saw the same woman twice, even if he had sex more than once in an evening. He didn't kiss or share intimacies such as breakfast or coffee or "going out." There were no dates. He was very honest with the women he had sex with. He didn't do innocents. He was careful to ensure the women knew the rules up front before they had sex with him. The sex was never satisfying, and it was getting less so since he'd met Meiling. He felt as if he'd lost so much more between the two of them, yet he didn't know how to stop the endless cycle with women that had begun so many years earlier.

Meiling smiled sweetly at Rodion. "Saving the little girl was a joint effort. You and your friends certainly helped us to get her home safely. Seeing her reunited with her family was such a gift. Thank you for that."

Gedeon forced himself not to step between them when Rodion stepped closer to her, almost close enough to brush his body against hers.

"Are you hungry? Evangeline left some fruit and baked goods in the kitchen just in case," the shifter said. "I could get you something to eat."

"That's so thoughtful," Meiling said. She turned toward Gedeon. "Are you hungry? We didn't have a chance to eat dinner."

He took the opportunity to be alone with her. It might be the only one they had before the others began to arrive. "Did she leave any of her ham and cheese pastries?"

"I think she did," Rodion said. He raised an eyebrow at Meiling. "The same for you?"

She shook her head. "I was considering one of her fruit bowls. She has the best fruit and berry bowls."

"I'll be right back. Just give me a minute. I have to heat up the ham and cheese pastry in the kitchen oven."

"Would you mind grabbing me a bottle of water out of the cooler?" Meiling asked.

"No problem." He waved them toward the tables again and disappeared behind the double doors leading to the kitchen.

Gedeon came up behind Meiling. Close. Too close. Telling himself he had to in order to ensure they weren't overheard, not because he wanted to inhale her fragrance and fantasize that she was his. Maybe it wasn't a fantasy if he thought of her that way.

"I never should have agreed to this meet," Gedeon whispered, his lips against Meiling's ear. "This could be a setup. We're on their home turf. Since they've done their massive remodeling job, I don't know the layout of the building. I'm not familiar with attics or whether they have hidden passages. We have to assume they do."

"There's a vent in the ladies' room. I can slip inside the vent and take a look around that way, map out as much as I can and get it to you."

Gedeon thought it over. No doubt they were being watched through the cameras right then. If she disappeared for any length of time, Timur would send someone looking. He shook his head. "We can't trust any of them, no matter that they helped us. Lospostos is going to be pissed that he didn't know what was going on. Amurov kept his word to us. He doesn't want bad blood between him and Lospostos, so he could very well have made another deal to sell us down the river."

"I'm not all that trusting, Gedeon," she said softly.

He knew she wasn't. He didn't fully have her trust. He sometimes thought they were close, but then she pulled away from him. She became careful around him, would distance herself from him. He detested those times and would patiently build their relationship back up again, telling himself he couldn't blame her. He hadn't done anything—like save her life over and over—to show he had earned her trust.

Rodion returned from the kitchen, placing the ham and cheese pastry on the table in front of Gedeon and a fruit bowl and a water bottle in front of Meiling. Gedeon tried not to notice that the shifter crowded close to Meiling, his body brushing up against hers. She wasn't sitting down, but she still had to look up at him. She looked very small and delicate beside the man. Gedeon cursed silently, despising his reaction. He had to stay on his guard, not be worried about whether the shifter was flirting with Meiling.

Men began to file into the bakery from the kitchen, having come in from the alleyway entrance. Timur had brought more security than Gedeon had anticipated, and it made him uncomfortable. He signaled to Meiling not to slip into the chair Rodion had pulled out for her.

The table the shifter had placed the food on was in the exact center of the room. They would be surrounded. Meiling caught the consequence of that immediately. The amount of security guards filing in and spreading out around the room already seemed too significant a force and Lospostos hadn't even entered the bakery yet.

Timur stepped in from behind the kitchen doors, Fyodor right behind him. They came around the counter, Timur leading his brother straight to the table where Gedeon and Meiling were standing. At the same time, the front door opened and Kyanite strode in. Behind him came men Gedeon recognized as Joaquin and Tomas Estrada, personal bodyguards to Elijah Lospostos. Elijah was right between them, his gaze riveted to Gedeon's face, and he didn't look happy. Behind him, at least ten more shifters followed.

Gedeon instantly signaled to Meiling to leave. She was very slight, and although she was the only woman in the building, she had a way of disappearing into the shadows.

Most of the shifters were big men in terms of density. They took up space in the bakery. If Elijah wanted to bluster at him, that would only draw attention his way. He was fine with that. It would give Meiling the opportunity to slip out of the bakery and set up with a sniper rifle across the street to cover him. She didn't miss if she was needed—and she would be needed.

Elijah was about halfway across the room to him when there was a disturbance at the front door. Gedeon spun toward the sound and saw a young shifter clutching at Meiling's diminutive form, holding a gun to her temple.

Gedeon exploded into action, using gifts he rarely showed other shifters. He launched himself at Elijah with blinding speed, using Timur's taller form to go over the top of Joaquin and Elijah. He landed behind the notorious head of the crime family and had a gun to his temple.

"I'll fucking end him right now if you don't drop your gun now."

There was instant silence. Fyodor cleared his throat. "Gedeon . . ." he began cautiously.

"Don't talk to me. You know me. I'll kill Elijah, Timur next and then you if that asshole doesn't drop his weapon now. You fucking betrayed us, Fyodor. I don't take that lightly."

"This is bullshit," Meiling said. There was a flurry of movement, and the young shifter was on the floor and Meiling had the gun in his mouth.

"Wait," Elijah said. "Don't kill him. He's a kid. He's just training. Seriously, don't kill him."

"Get moving to the door, Elijah. Meiling, back out of here. I'm coming to you." Gedeon's cold blue eyes met Fyodor's. He wanted him to see he meant what he said. Fyodor would be looking over his shoulder for the rest of his days. Elijah and Timur too. They'd come after him. So many others had. He was still alive—they weren't.

"Gedeon, this wasn't a trap," Fyodor said. "I can see

that it would look that way. We brought the men who helped you to show Elijah you weren't in this alone. That's part of the reason there are so many here tonight. It wasn't for security reasons."

"Yurik is a cub, still learning the ropes," Elijah added his voice. "I don't betray my friends. Fyodor told me there was a child involved and they couldn't give me a heads-up, and I believe him." He moved toward the door with Gedeon, waving Joaquin and Tomas back. "Was I pissed that I wasn't in the know? Hell yes, but I understood."

Gedeon continued to make his way through the crowd of shifters. They reluctantly parted for him. Meiling crouched in the doorway, eyes continually moving, scanning the crowd of shifters.

"You can hear lies, Gedeon," Timur snapped. "You're starting a war."

"*You* fucking started a war. I kept my word. I always keep my word and you counted on that."

"Hear us out," Elijah said. "You can't think I came here to kill you and your partner for rescuing a kidnapped child. A favor, Gedeon. I offer you a favor for staying and just talking."

"A favor from me as well," Fyodor offered. "You deal in favors, Gedeon."

"And me," Timur added. "We don't go back on our word."

Gedeon went still inside. His eyes met Meiling's. What these men were offering was huge. *Huge.* They were some of the biggest names in the business and they'd made the offer in front of their men. If they lied, they would never save face.

Meiling's nod was imperceptible. Very slowly Gedeon lowered the gun and made a show of indicating to Meiling to do the same. She pulled the barrel from the kid's mouth and stepped back to give him room to get up.

"I don't like anyone putting their hands on me without

permission," she said in a low tone. They were all shifters and all of them could hear her, which was her intention. She smiled sweetly at the kid and waited by the open door for Gedeon to give her an indication of what he wanted her to do next.

Gedeon released Elijah from his grip. He was abnormally strong, even for a shifter, and he knew the moment he was out of their sight, Elijah, Fyodor and Timur would be discussing how he had managed to get over the tops of Joaquin and Elijah and manhandle the crime lord so easily. He hoped they would be so intrigued by his abilities they wouldn't wonder how a woman as small as Meiling was able to throw a grown male shifter to the floor and take his weapon away from him. He didn't want them thinking too much about her at all.

Fyodor indicated a table with six chairs. "Gedeon, please come to the table and allow me to explain."

Timur shifted his gaze to Meiling, who watched the young shifter, Yurik, slowly climb to his feet. Yurik glanced warily at her and then at Elijah as he worked his jaw back and forth.

"Join us, Meiling." Timur issued the invitation, completely ignoring the young shifter.

She looked to Gedeon. If both sat at the table, it would be much more difficult to fight their way out. He doubted they would have to. He gave her the signal to come join them. She flashed Timur a heart-stopping smile.

"Thank you, I think I will. It's getting rather chilly standing here in the doorway. Or it could be the three unmarked cop cars patrolling up and down the street pretending they're not really cop cars and not really interested in anything going on here."

Elijah sighed. "Seriously, Fyodor? Couldn't you have paid off that cop who's always after your wife so we don't get raided every time we have a late-night meeting?"

Fyodor groaned. "Don't even joke about him. I keep

thinking he's going to go away, but he's very persistent, even after all this time. I think he hopes someone will kill me so he can console my widow. I made Timur promise me that if I do get murdered, he kills the cop first thing. That sanctimonious son of a bitch does not get my wife."

Gedeon waited until Meiling was beside him. He loved that she came to him rather than to the other side of the table. He seated her first and then waited until Fyodor and Elijah pulled back their chairs before seating himself beside her.

"Thank you for not killing young Yurik," Elijah said to Meiling. "He's a good kid and he'll be a good bodyguard when he stops trying to show off and allows someone to actually instruct him."

"Send him to Borneo with Drake's men," Timur suggested. "We had to put up with Jeremiah for far too long before he started exhibiting any kind of sense."

"Hey," said the young man with blond hair who was part of Timur's team guarding Evangeline. He grinned good-naturedly, as did the men around him.

"He still hasn't learned to keep his mouth shut," Fyodor pointed out.

"I don't think that's going to happen with the way the women coddle him," Timur pretended to grouse.

Gedeon wasn't a man to relax and trust because those around him were acting like they were all friends. He could appear that way to others and normally would. He did this time, but catching Meiling's eyes and communicating silently, needing her to understand he wanted her on guard. She appeared to be genuinely entertained by the banter going back and forth by the men at the table. Observing her closer, he realized that as he was doing, she was assessing the best way for the two of them to fight their way free should they need to. He looked tough and gave nothing away. She looked sweet, open and friendly. That was one of her many gifts.

"I see why you brought so many of your men with you tonight, Fyodor," Elijah interjected, sitting back as he indicated the shifters, most of whom had settled around the tables, while a few were still trying to appear casual draped against walls. Yurik had been led to the counter by two others. A first-aid kit sat beside him while he was examined for injuries other than where the thin trickle of blood came from his mouth and down his chin.

Gedeon raised an eyebrow. *He* wasn't getting why there were so many shifters. He looked to Fyodor for an explanation.

"Meiling, of course," Fyodor replied, his tone calm. Very casual, as if they were discussing the weather.

Meiling's head jerked up and her sweet expression disappeared, her dark gaze flicking around the table at the men sitting with her and then around the room at all the shifters between her and the door. Gedeon could almost read her mind. She instantly went from being his partner to being that wary, on-the-verge-of-flight woman he had spent a great deal of time coaxing to work with him.

Gedeon allowed one hand to slide under the table in order to curve his palm around the top of her thigh. He didn't look at her. "I'm not certain what you mean by that, Fyodor. There's no 'of course' that I'm aware of."

"She's leopard and she's unattached. We're fairly desperate for female leopards here. Most of the shifters in this room have been all over the world looking for their mate and haven't found her yet. It's possible Meiling's leopard is in her first cycle and would respond to one of the leopards who also has been without a mate. Or her female would recognize one of the male leopards and rise enough to allow a claiming."

"You didn't think to ask her if she was willing to have these males check her out? That maybe it would make her feel uncomfortable to know you were setting her up without even consulting her?" Gedeon asked. He kept his tone reasonable. Mild. His fingers dug into Meiling's thigh, conveying his outrage on her behalf, but no other body part gave away the tension in him.

"Well, if it's any consolation, Meiling," Elijah said, leaning toward her, "my good friend Fyodor didn't mention that you were unclaimed. Notice I didn't bring a host of shifters looking for a mate. I just brought a small crew, several of whom are being trained. You see how well that worked out. Unless you think you're compatible with Yurik. If he got bossy with you, you could wipe up the floor with him."

"*Tried* to get bossy with her," Timur corrected.

Fyodor frowned, his gaze switching from Gedeon to Meiling and then back. "I thought you would consider it an honor, Meiling."

Gedeon gave a grunt of annoyance.

Fyodor shook his head. "That wasn't the right way to put it. It was an honor for my men to be introduced to you. I thought you would be looking for your mate. Don't women want to find their mates?" There was genuine curiosity in his voice.

"Is that what you found with Evangeline? Was she looking to find a mate for her leopard?" Meiling asked.

Timur flashed a quick grin at his brother. "If Evangeline hadn't been so sweet, Meiling, I think my brother would still be standing out in the back alley with his hat in his hand and that silly-hopeful-desperate-pleading look on his face."

"I have a gun, Timur," Fyodor warned. "I'm not opposed to using it on you. Someplace your wife won't get too upset with me shooting you."

Gedeon's eyebrow shot up. "She would be okay with you shooting him?"

"Ashe wants to shoot him half the time," Fyodor explained. "Don't you find him annoying?"

Meiling's laughter slipped out. "I think you're all a little bit crazy."

Heads turned toward that sound. Conversation ceased again. Meiling didn't seem to notice. Gedeon despised all those hungry male eyes on her. He rubbed at her thigh, needing the connection with her more than she needed it with him.

The men at the table looked at one another. It was Elijah who answered for all of them. "That's true. We probably are a little insane. But that's because we married women who won't do a damn thing we tell them. Before Siena, I was perfectly sane. Unhappy, but perfectly sane. She does things without consulting me first. Just does whatever the hell she feels like and damn the consequences. Think about that, Gedeon, before you ever decide happiness wins out over sanity."

"What did she do without consulting you?" Meiling asked.

Her feathery lashes covered her dark eyes and then were back up, making Gedeon's heart ache. He could fixate on her lashes if he let himself, which was odd. He never missed little details, but he didn't let them occupy his mind to the point that he was consumed recording that image in his brain perfectly—especially right in the middle of a room filled with potential enemies.

The other thing he found very odd was Slayer, his leopard. In a roomful of shifters, Slayer would normally be insane, fighting for supremacy, wanting to tear everyone apart, especially after Meiling had been threatened. Not now. His violent, dangerous, scary leopard was rolling around as if he were a kitten at playtime, nearly purring. It made no sense. *He* made no sense, and his leopard made no sense.

"Yeah, Elijah, give us one of the many things Siena dared to do without consulting you," Timur urged. There was laughter in his voice.

Gedeon glanced over at Joaquin and Tomas, the two men who probably knew more about Elijah Lospostos than anyone else. They had known him since childhood and had been his bodyguards for years. Normally, it would be impossible to tell what either man was thinking, but even they had matching ghosts of grins on their faces, even if it was just for a moment.

"She decided to have triplets. That would be three babies, Meiling. To make matters worse, all girls. Daughters. Can you imagine me with daughters? I've doubled up on the guards for now, but those girls become teens and I'll have to quadruple the bodyguards. It's a fucking nightmare. Everyone thinks it's funny, but my little girls have a way of twisting me right around their little pinkie fingers. I give them my sternest stare and they tear up and it's game over. One starts to cry and all three of them cry."

Meiling pushed at her hair and regarded Elijah with her dark, velvet-soft eyes. "She decided on having triplets all on her own, did she? And she gave you daughters on top of that very bad decision."

Elijah frowned. "I wouldn't call it a bad decision. I never said it was a bad decision, only that it makes me a little insane. Siena scares me. The pregnancy scared me. Carrying that many was tough on her body, and she wouldn't even hear of doing anything but carrying them. I tried to tell her that she was important, but that woman can be so damn stubborn. Then girls. What the fuck do I know about girls?"

"I imagine you learn fairly quickly if you want to," Meiling said, giving no quarter. Her voice was very low. Her palm dropped over Gedeon's and then the pad of one finger traced his knuckles, the only indication that she found the conversation difficult.

"It isn't a matter of reading a few books," Elijah objected. "Not if you want to be a good father. I was born into a certain position. In the business I'm in, women are used as commodities. Bargaining power."

"For what purpose?"

Elijah shrugged. "To acquire more territory. Power. Secure a truce. Any number of reasons. I know it's expected. I already have other families reaching out to me in the hopes of securing an alliance."

Meiling's hand tightened on Gedeon's beneath the table, pressing his palm deeper into her thigh. He felt her shock. She wasn't the only one. Fyodor and Timur stared at him, just as shocked as Meiling that a man they called friend would consider such a thing.

"They're just babies," Timur murmured, scowling.

Elijah nodded. "It's expected in this business. I've had very lucrative offers from families in South America and Europe."

Meiling shook her head. "How does your wife feel about these offers?"

Elijah shrugged. "I don't worry her with things like that. She doesn't need to know crap that will never touch her. No daughters of mine will ever be used for such things. Siena should never have to worry, and neither should the girls. My men know they won't be used in this manner, and they'll guard them for me as if they were guarding me."

Elijah rubbed his forehead and then pushed back the dark hair falling nearly into his eyes. "The biggest problem with having treasures is it makes you vulnerable. An enemy manages to get his hands on them—"

"You call us," Gedeon interrupted. "It's what we do."

Elijah smiled. "I guess it is. And you're damned fast. Timur said you were ready to go in two hours."

"Just under two hours," Timur corrected.

Elijah shook his head. "I detest that those guilty were from my lair and specifically from within my organization. Not the four of them. Their parents. They worked outside the organization. I didn't recommend Georgi Chaban or, for that matter, Lola Morales, to anyone. If I don't know them personally or feel they do a good job, I would never vouch for them. Georgi quit every job he's ever had since he graduated from college. His parents paid for his education and then pulled strings to get him jobs, but he never worked for more than a few weeks before he quit, disgracing his parents. They pay his lease."

"It must be difficult being the head of a massive organization and trying to know everyone in it so this type of thing doesn't happen," Meiling said.

"There's a hierarchy in place, but I like to know most of those in my employ," Elijah said. "At least the key people. As I said, these four were not employed by me and never were."

Meiling pushed at loose strands of her shiny hair escaping. "We couldn't take the chance that you were involved. The child's life was at stake. Everything pointed your way, and we only had a very short window of opportunity to rescue her. Gedeon and I believed they were going to kill her in the end rather than return her. She knew who took her and Lola was too bitter."

"You were right about that," Timur said. "Jeremiah managed to retrieve the orders Lola had given to Georgi. He tore them up and tossed them into the garbage cans, remember? You marked the cans, Meiling. The moment the okay was given, he searched the cans and was able to retrieve the scraps. We put the scraps together for evidence. Lola instructed him to take pictures, and as soon as they were sent to her father, he was to kill the girl and dispose of her body."

There was a small silence. Gedeon gripped Meiling's thigh with hard fingers. "At least she told him to make certain the photographs got to Lilith's father before Georgi was to kill her. We might have been too late."

Meiling shook her head. "We would have saved her. It would have been messier, more traumatic for her, but we would have taken her from him."

"This was supposed to be a simple case of finding who

was stealing money," Gedeon said. "We weren't told about
Lilith until we arrived late at night and were escorted into
a private meeting. We found the room bugged. Our client
had been systematically drugged. Then the case took a very
sinister turn when we discovered Lilith had been taken
and her father had paid the ransom more than once."

"Atwater must have been certain that I was involved,"
Elijah said. "I can't blame him for that. I would have thought
the same thing. Did he suspect Lola?"

"No, but Harold did," Gedeon said. "Female leopards
are just as passionate and capable of fury as males are. She
believed Atwater was exclusive with her. She believed they
were a mated couple, and he would marry her. He selfishly
didn't disabuse her of that notion, because it suited him to
have her at his beck and call, until she caught him with a
couple of his other women. The passion she felt for him
turned completely to hate. She wanted revenge and she
planned it out very carefully."

Timur looked around the room at the unmated shifters.
"We should have talks with our men, Fyodor. You're head
of the lair and they follow your lead."

"I never led a woman on in my life," Fyodor declared.
"My leopard wouldn't have allowed it even if I was that
kind of man."

"But the men don't know that. You never talked about
that with them. The only talk you ever had with them was
that you would never tolerate the abuse of women in this
lair. You never wanted what went on in our home lairs to
happen here. What happened to Atwater, or nearly happened to him, is a lesson for all of us," Timur pushed. "We
don't want any woman to suffer what Lola suffered or to
carry out a murderous plot of revenge because we didn't
want to have an uncomfortable talk with our males."

"It isn't just the males who should be talked to," Meiling
spoke up. "You're head of your lair, Fyodor. That means
you or Evangeline should speak to every female before

there is a chance her leopard goes into heat, so the female knows what to expect and no male has the opportunity to trick her." She switched her gaze to Elijah.

"Siena is sweet, but getting anything past her is nearly impossible. She has built-in radar for bullshit. And if I opt not to say anything about what is going on, she suddenly asks me. If there were a woman somewhere, she'd know in a heartbeat. I think it would be intuitive with her."

"She doesn't even bother to try to hide the way she feels about you. If you betrayed her, how would she react? She's passionate. Her leopard is passionate, what would happen if she caught you betraying her?" Timur persisted.

Elijah looked as if he paled under his olive skin. "I wouldn't want to think about that too much. She isn't the kind to plot out something like Lola did, and she wouldn't involve her friends in something illegal, but there would be consequences."

"Ashe would cut off Timur's balls," Fyodor announced. There was some satisfaction in his voice when he made the announcement.

Elijah and Timur both nodded in agreement. "No doubt she would," Timur added, real curiosity in his voice. "What about Evangeline, Fyodor? There isn't anyone sweeter. As much as I'd like to say I know her, I honestly have no idea how she would react to betrayal of that type."

Fyodor sighed and shook his head, both hands going up to rake his fingers through his hair in a continual motion, betraying agitation. "It wouldn't happen. I would never hurt her like that. I just wouldn't. My leopard would go insane if I didn't first."

"Everyone knows that," Timur persisted, waving his brother's obvious discomfort away. "This isn't about your reaction. We're talking a woman's reaction to betrayal. What would someone as sweet as Evangeline do if she caught you red-handed going at it with another woman?"

Gedeon thought about the woman he'd met multiple

times over the last few years when he'd visited San Antonio. He always made a point of making his presence known to the heads of the crime families in the area if he wasn't investigating anything to do with them. He'd stumbled across the little bakery before it had become so wildly popular. Evangeline was just getting started. There wasn't so much space back then—but she'd always been the same welcoming, warm, kind, considerate person. It was impossible not to be drawn to her. He hadn't known she was leopard when he first met her. He honestly couldn't imagine Evangeline's reaction to betrayal. He could imagine his.

Gedeon's gaze slid to the woman beside him. He would strangle her with his bare hands, but not before he tore apart the man she betrayed him with right in front of her. Could he kill her? To his shock, his heart accelerated, rejecting the idea. Every cell in his body rejected the idea.

Meiling suddenly turned her head, those dark chocolate eyes drifting over him. He swore he felt her touching him, almost like a physical caress. She rubbed her palm over the back of his hand, reminding him that he was still gripping her thigh—hanging on to her—maybe a little too tight. Still, he didn't let loose, turning his attention back to the conversation about Evangeline.

"Fyodor?" Timur prompted.

Fyodor shook his head. "I have no idea what Evangeline would do. She's a fierce protector when she feels her family is threatened, and that includes my brother and Ashe. Also my cousins." He rubbed his chin in the palm of his hand. "Her leopard is a fierce little thing. I don't know what she would do—anything to protect Evangeline, including killing me."

He raised his head to look directly at Timur. "You're right, we need to talk to the men. Being head of a lair sucks. I much prefer to be an enforcer. No talking, just cracking heads."

Everyone at the table nodded in agreement except for

Meiling. She started to laugh again. "Seriously? If you don't want to crack heads tonight, you might want to break out the decks of playing cards you have stashed somewhere under the tables. I think the cops are about to pay us a visit."

Annoyance flickered across Fyodor's face. "I know it's that damned Brice Addler hoping to catch us at something illegal."

"One of these days he's going to set you up," Timur warned.

"Even if he managed to send me to prison, Evangeline would never desert me," Fyodor assured them. "If there's one thing I can count on, it's that my wife would never leave me while I was in prison. She isn't that kind of woman."

"I didn't mean for prison," Timur said. "I think eventually he'll set you up to be killed."

Gedeon noticed that the moment Timur voiced his very real concerns, the security detail around Fyodor, Kyanite and Rodion alerted instantly. Elijah did as well. Timur was serious, Gedeon decided, and he wanted his brother to be serious, but Fyodor instantly rejected the idea.

"Addler is a straight arrow, Timur. He won't bend the rules, not even for a man he despises. He's just too perfect."

"He's obsessed with your wife," Timur snapped, out of patience. This was obviously an argument that had been going on for some time. "I'm your head of security. You should trust my judgment."

Fyodor sighed. "I do, Timur. It's just that this cop has a long history with our family, and you have every reason not to trust him."

"It's always best to trust your security man," Elijah counseled as decks of cards appeared on the tables and were dealt out to those supposedly playing.

10

MEILING opened the sliding doors to her wide, enormous deck and stepped outside. The night air was cool, which she was thankful for. More and more she seemed to be getting so hot she sometimes felt she was burning from the inside out. It didn't seem to matter what the actual temperature was; she was just a hot mess. She ached everywhere—her joints especially.

Ordinarily if she felt restless, Meiling went for a run. Now her body hurt too badly to run. Thanks to Gedeon's generosity when he was attempting to bribe her to stay and be his partner, she had the best bathroom *ever*. How he managed it when her suite was on the third floor, she didn't know, but her tub was deep and the hot water was endless. She could immerse herself in the hot water and soak her aching joints and muscles. Sometimes it helped, but the achiness was getting worse, not better, as time went on.

She and Gedeon had been back in New Orleans for three

months when she began to experience waves of heat and aching muscles and joints. Her first thought had been that she'd picked up a virus of some sort, but she'd never gotten sick in her life. Then it occurred to her that she did, in fact, have a female leopard, and the leopard was making herself known.

Meiling paced across the balcony to the wide railing and leaned against it, lifting her face to the breeze. She didn't know where she had gotten the idea that she didn't have a leopard or why she believed so strongly that she didn't have one, but it was as if it had always been that way. One of her earliest memories was of Libby's mother telling her she was useless to the leopard community because she could never provide children for them. Libby had snuck into the little closet that had been her room and consoled her when she'd cried herself to sleep. Had Libby's mother caught her crying, she would have really gotten into trouble. She wasn't supposed to cry. She broke so many rules.

Meiling had gone to her room at ten that evening, using her private entrance, so restless and unable to understand why until the terrible sexual burning had started. Only then did it hit her that there was a real chance that she was going into the emergence of her kind: the Han Vol Dan, which was when her leopard wanted to arise.

Meiling sighed and looked out over the lights of the city. The house was close to the edge of the swamp, overlooked the city and yet also provided a view of the powerful Mississippi River. Gedeon managed to purchase his property in the perfect neighborhood, especially for a leopard. They had escape routes from every outlet.

She had a major problem—more than one. She would have been ecstatic over the discovery of having a leopard, but she knew it would change her life forever. She loved being Gedeon's partner. They worked well together. In fact, they were good together nearly all the time in every aspect of their partnership.

Since the return from San Antonio, Gedeon had been even more restless than she had been, often coming up to her room at night declaring he couldn't sleep, flopping on her bed and proceeding to fall asleep. Or he would call her on the intercom and cajole and plead until she gave in and went down to his room. She'd lie on his bed, and he'd wrap himself around her and fall right to sleep. It was disturbing the way he became more and more dependent on her to fall asleep at night. But she was becoming equally dependent on him, and she knew it.

"Gedeon." She whispered his name. Because she was falling in love with him. Worse, she actually trusted him when she'd never fully trusted anyone. She didn't want to, but to love someone, she had to trust him, not just with her life, but with her heart. If she had a female leopard, that would jeopardize everything they had together. She had no idea what she was going to do.

Her breasts felt swollen and heavy, her nipples hard pinpoints of flames desperate for attention. Between her legs flared a fire so intense she feared it would never be put out. She'd tried soaking earlier and used a toy, although that only made the sensation worse. She'd even been tempted to visit Gedeon's nightclub and pick up a partner. For the first time she understood a little his constant need for sex. But she resisted. He didn't even try.

Her bathrobe felt too heavy on her skin, rubbing against her screaming nerve endings, inflaming them more. She went back inside, leaving the doors open and closing the screen against insects. Pushing the robe off her shoulders, she paced nude in the dark. Her bedroom was enormous; so was the sitting room. The suite took up the entire third floor.

She would have to take a vacation. Leave. She couldn't risk her leopard rising around Gedeon. She didn't want him to claim her because she was leopard. Or because his leopard wanted her leopard. He would make a lousy mate. The man didn't have a faithful bone in his body. After seeing what Lola Morales had done, Meiling feared, in a moment of madness, she might be equally as insane if Gedeon betrayed her—and he would. He wasn't faithful to a woman for three hours; it wasn't in his makeup.

She would have to leave right away, before they were called out of town on another case. She couldn't go anywhere near him when she was like this. It was too dangerous for both of them. His leopard would react the moment her female began to rise, if only for a few moments. All male leopards would react. She'd need to find a retreat away from all shifters, somewhere she'd be safe. Where?

Pulling out her phone, she flung herself on the bed and began to look at various islands where she might be able to go. Transportation could be a problem in her condition. That and the fact that she had no idea how long it would take before her leopard decided to make an appearance.

She knew that the female leopard emerged when her cycle matched with her human's. She just had never seen how long that took. She pulled up a calendar to check the dates of her cycle, which, unfortunately, was irregular. That wasn't going to be extremely helpful to her. She stared at the dates while she rubbed her flat belly.

She had to find a place and she needed to go right away. Two heads were better than one. Over the past year she'd gotten to know Rene Guidry very well. She respected his expertise. He was extremely good at his job. They had become friends, although she never allowed herself to forget the fact that his loyalty belonged first to Gedeon. She looked at the time. Close to midnight, but he was always up. She wasn't certain he ever slept.

Rene, sometimes I need a break. I go off alone for a couple of weeks and do a mini retreat. Feel that coming on. Place you recommend where I'd be safe, but no one would be around?

By alone you mean without Gedeon? Or your bodyguard?

Yes. I need to just be by myself with no one around. I need that time to recharge.

You know I would have to tell Gedeon.

I planned on telling him myself. I wouldn't have put you in a position of lying to him. It's no big deal. I'll find a place.

She sighed, annoyed with Rene. Annoyed with herself. Feeling edgy and moody all over when the terrible sexual burning had begun to subside. She shouldn't have asked him.

I was just clarifying, cher. I'll find you the perfect place.

Thanks, Rene.

Meiling put her head back on the pillow and whispered to her leopard. "Listen to me, little sister. I welcome you. I do. You've helped me so many times when I needed it. Your strength. Your sense of smell, the keenness of your vision, your incredible speed. I want you to have your freedom, but I have to figure out some things before we find you a good partner."

She feared finding a partner for her leopard meant permanently separating herself from Gedeon. She didn't want a man for herself. She wanted Gedeon—and yet she knew she couldn't have him. He was very careful to keep his very active sex life away from her, but she had an acute sense of smell, and as many times as he showered, he couldn't wash the stench from him. She smelled the other women and the sex whether he showered once or ten times.

"I appreciate that he's careful to keep that side of his life away from me. He really tries. It isn't his fault that I've fallen so hard for him. He shares every other part of his life with me and seems to prefer my company the way I prefer his. It's such a tragedy that he needs so many women to keep him satisfied. I don't understand it, but he's very honest about it."

She turned over onto her belly and pressed her hot face into the pillow. "At least we never ruined our relationship by having sex. He doesn't know I think about him day and night, or that it's him I want to have sex with. I've managed to keep my cravings under control, but now that you're showing yourself, that could be difficult."

There was a faint stirring in her mind. A slight pushing against the inside of her body, as if something alive stretched. The terrible burning was already slowly subsiding, but now, for the first time, she could feel the other's presence. It was a very strange feeling and she slowly sat up, clutching the pillow to her stomach while she took stock of her body, exploring the differences.

"I can feel that you're here with me. I don't feel alone anymore," she murmured softly, in wonder. The feeling was miraculous. The bonding instantaneous. She found herself smiling, knowing the little female was doing the exact same thing—trying to discover all she could about her human.

The realization of actually having a leopard of her own began to take hold and joy burst through her. Real. Euphoric. She shared with the entity inside of her. "All of my life I've been alone, apart from everyone else, until Gedeon. And even he has had to hold a part of himself away from me. I've had to hold parts of me away from him."

Tears welled up, burned behind her eyes. "But I have you. I'll always have you. No one can take you from me. Even when I lose him, and I will, I'll have you."

She could feel the other moving in her mind, reaching to try to communicate. Meiling had been using telepathic communication with leopards from the time she was very young, but this was the first time she had ever tried with a newly awakened leopard. The images she was getting were mixed and didn't make sense. The little leopard was clearly overwhelmed and struggling to understand what was happening to her. Like Meiling, she was overjoyed to discover her partner, but she didn't yet know what was expected of her.

"We'll find our way together," Meiling soothed. "You never have to worry. We can figure it out. We've got time. Do you have a name? Something you want to be called? We can start there. I'm Meiling."

She sent the images to the leopard as simply as she could make them. The leopard had been with her, waking on and off for short periods of time, before showing herself as the heat cycle took hold. Most likely she had learned a few things about Meiling. Maybe even about Gedeon and his leopard.

I am Whisper.

Meiling was elated she understood. The name Whisper wasn't easy to understand in images. "Whisper, have you been through this before? Rising to be with your mate? Is this your first life cycle?" Meiling certainly didn't remember having been through it before. She had tried to find dreams of a past life with someone, but she hadn't caught so much as a glimpse of anyone. She had decided, because she believed she had no leopard, that she had never had one.

No memory.

Meiling's heart accelerated. If it was her first cycle, was there a way the shifters in San Antonio had known? She had thought a lot about the way Fyodor and Timur had brought their unmated men to the bakery to meet her in the hopes that she might like one of them. She'd been a little outraged at the idea that they would assume she would be desperate to be paired with a man. It took a few weeks before she realized the men were the ones desperate to find a mate.

She calmed violent leopards. Gedeon had to fight with his leopard every single minute of every day. It wore on him. She knew he couldn't sleep at night. He used the gym and worked out on the heavy bags. He went to the club and had rough sex with various women. When he came home, he was still fighting his leopard and unable to lie down to rest. He paced endlessly. Knowing she was upstairs made it difficult for him not to ask her to come down to his suite when he became desperate for sleep.

If she was truthful with herself, she wanted Gedeon to call her. She wanted to be the one he turned to when he was in need. They spent so much time together, talking softly, telling each other secrets no one else knew and laughing at the silliest jokes. She gave herself permission to bury her fingers in the wild silk of his hair.

You feel so much for him. The little female was very tentative when she voiced her observation of Meiling around Gedeon.

I do. Can you feel Gedeon's leopard when I'm with him?

There was a very brief silence, as if Whisper was trying to find a way to express herself to Meiling. This was all so new for both of them, but exciting. Very, very exciting.

Yes, his leopard is very strong. Scary.

That was a shock to Meiling. She caught the edge of fear the cat tried to convey to her. She had only been afraid of Slayer initially, when she'd warned Gedeon of the bomb and he had shifted on the run coming straight at her. That had been a little terrifying. She could admit it to herself now. But since then . . . she couldn't remember a single time Gedeon's leopard had frightened her.

She thought of all the times Gedeon had told her his leopard was particularly vicious. She'd seen how fast Gedeon was. He could be brutal when he had to be. Men reputed to be dangerous, like Timur Amurov, respected and were careful around him. That had a lot to do with his leopard. Around her, Slayer had acted almost placid.

"Why would you think Slayer is scary, Whisper?" Meiling asked. The terrible burning between her legs had subsided completely, leaving her feeling exhausted, damp and needing a shower. The offending toy she'd tried using to alleviate the fire had been thrown across the room. She forced herself to her feet. She'd need to wash that thing and put it away before showering.

Her phone buzzed. She'd laid it aside on the pillow when she'd gotten up. She knew from the brief ringtone it played her that it was Gedeon.

You busy?

Her heart did that crazy melting thing it always did the moment he contacted her. She didn't seem to have any pride when it came to Gedeon. Or any sense of self-preservation. It would be so risky to be with him now that Whisper had revealed herself.

I can stay hidden, Whisper assured.

Meiling decided to be diplomatic. She needed a shower before she could face him. He would be able to smell sexual arousal if she didn't shower thoroughly.

What's up?

Come to my apartment. I need you to calm Slayer down. I haven't been able to sleep and for some reason he's gone psycho on me. I've asked him over and over to tell me what's gotten him so riled up, but he won't answer me.

She really wanted to spend a little time getting to know Whisper. She could do that and take a shower. She has-

tened into the huge master bath. She loved her bathroom
so much.

Do you think it will do any good if I try to talk to him? I've
never done that before. I mean, sometimes I do tease him,
she admitted.

Gedeon didn't respond right away, giving her the opportunity to turn the water temperature to the perfect degree she wanted.

You tease Slayer? How?

I sometimes call him Mr. Sinister. I get the
impression of him lifting his lip at me. Lucky
for me he has a sense of humor.

Yeah, try to talk to him. Anything. I need you to
come to me.

I have a few things I have to do, Gedeon. I'll
get down there, but it could take me a little
while.

Again, there was a long pause. Meiling waited, tapping
her foot on the tiles while she twisted her hair into a knot
and secured it on top of her head.

You always come right down. It's midnight. What
do you have to do at midnight?

Meiling had to smile. She shared with Whisper. "Sometimes, although he's supposed to be this big scary dangerous badass to everyone else, Gedeon to me is like a
petulant, pouty little boy who didn't get his way."

He makes you happy, Whisper responded.

"Yes, he does. Even when he's bossy or pouty. It doesn't
seem to matter." She ignored that little part of her that

insisted on reminding her that he couldn't be faithful if his life depended on it—the part that made her incredibly sad.

I said I'd come down later, and I will. I always
keep my promises to you.

Fifteen minutes?

Gedeon! An hour. Maybe an hour and a half.
I'll be there before two.

She could make it downstairs a lot faster. She had no idea why she was being so contrary. She stepped under the steady stream of water, and the moment the water touched her, it was as if a thousand tongues lapped at her sensitive skin everywhere.

The burning returned with a vengeance, bursting over her like a wildfire out of control. She gasped and wrapped her arms around her middle, pressing the button to change the spray to gentle. She felt the female leopard writhing in need, unable to control the terrible heat driving her to the surface.

Along with the sensations of being desperate for sex, Meiling felt an itch covering her entire body. Her skin lifted like a wave as something pressed hard against the inside, moving fast underneath, adding to the unfamiliar sensations. Her jaw ached. Her skull felt too tight.

I'm hurting you.

"No, this isn't hurting, exactly. I feel what you feel. The drive to mate."

You don't like it.

Meiling needed to do a better job of shielding her leopard. She was learning, but this was all a first for her as well. "It's uncomfortable, just as it is for you. We're in this together, Whisper. It's necessary so you can emerge." She kept her voice soothing. "We both want you to emerge."

She placed both hands on the wall of her shower and let the water run off her skin. "I wish I knew more about helping you. I'll talk to one of the women I met and ask her questions. She might give me advice."

There were several women she'd met in New Orleans who were shifters. All of them had been friendly. Each had been very different. She didn't have a close association with any of them just because she didn't know how to have friends. She didn't trust easily and most likely never would.

Drake and Saria Donovan owned the LaFont Inn. He also owned one of the largest international global security companies in the world. He was renowned for his business ethics and his ability to get a job done. He also was the head of one of the lairs in New Orleans.

Joshua Tregre was the head of another lair in New Orleans but was the head of a crime family. His mate, Sonia Tregre, had a reputation for restoring old homes to their past glory.

Meiling considered talking to either of the two women, asking them questions about their leopards' first emergences, but she quickly discarded the idea. She would run into those women around New Orleans. They might ask her a question in front of Gedeon or another male shifter. That wouldn't do.

Meiling sighed. She needed answers for herself and her leopard. Who else was there? She'd met Evangeline Amurov in San Antonio. They weren't exactly friends, although Evangeline had been friendly enough. She didn't seem like the type of woman to gossip either. She could ask questions as if she was asking out of curiosity. If Evangeline didn't ask her a direct question she would have to answer honestly, she might get away with not telling her she had a leopard close to emergence.

Meiling hung her head down and breathed deeply, trying to get air to her leopard. Trying to breathe through the relentless sexual demands. "This is just the start," she murmured aloud, more to herself than to Whisper.

I need my mate. I must find him soon.

Meiling closed her eyes. Could Whisper emerge without finding her mate? Could she just have sex with a leopard through her heat and then walk away because he wasn't her true mate? Was it possible to be in love with one man while your leopard was the true mate of another man's leopard? She had to get the answers to those questions immediately. No way was she going to end up like Lola Morales.

"We'll figure it out," she promised.

Sweat beaded on her forehead and the water washed it away. There was no keeping her hair dry, so she unpinned it and washed it. Everything, the most natural, familiar, everyday actions, seemed to be an erotic act. Lifting her arms over her head to rinse her hair, she became aware of her breasts shifting. She was small and had never considered that her breasts would be so sensitive. With every drop of water hitting her skin, she felt a fiery arrow darting straight to her sex.

Whisper rose close to the surface, pressing tightly against her, more for comfort than because she thought she could get out.

"It's too soon," Meiling said, more for herself than the leopard. It was too soon.

This time the disturbing sexual heat retreated quickly, leaving Meiling feeling restless and moody.

Why don't you ask Gedeon?

The leopard didn't exactly use the name Gedeon. She sent his image, making him appear very big and scary.

Your friend. You like him best.

"He's my best friend," Meiling admitted. "We talk about everything together." She was careful patting herself dry, not taking a chance on stimulating her body any more that it had been. She could tell Whisper was very sleepy and would be fading soon. She hoped so. She needed a respite.

The leopard did as well. Neither of them knew what they were doing, and the fierce sexual hunger had taken a toll on them.

"He has had his leopard a long time. He must know things."

Who knew Whisper would be the voice of reason? Meiling wasn't certain how she could make her understand when she didn't understand herself.

"I would want Gedeon for my mate if I could have him," she confessed. "But it's impossible. We talked about having a sexual relationship and both of us agreed it would ruin what we have together. He needs other women all the time. I would not want him to be with other women if we were together."

There was a long silence while Whisper struggled to understand. *I feel your absolute rejection of the idea but cannot understand why this would bother you.*

Meiling sat on the edge of the bed, the towel in her hand. She wrapped her hair in the towel to squeeze out most of the water.

"It would be the same as if when you found your mate, he would insist on mating with other female leopards."

Again, Whisper was silent while she thought about what Meiling said to her. *You stay with the same mate all the time?*

Did every leopard couple stay together after they mated through the first heat? She didn't know. "The leopards I know only stay with each other. I always thought I would have that same relationship. I will have to ask a friend to answer these questions for us."

Once again, she made her way into the master bathroom. Her hair was fine, but there was a lot of it. She had learned to comb it out as soon as possible to prevent tangles. Since moving to New Orleans and living at the house with Gedeon, she had allowed her hair to grow longer than she ever had. She'd always had very fast-growing hair and now it was nearly to her waist. Deftly braiding it, she secured it with a covered band and then chose clothes to join Gedeon.

Most times when she went down to his suite this late, she fell asleep, so she opted for a simple lounge suit. That always drove him crazy. He preferred she didn't wear much in the way of clothes. In fact, if he had his way, she wouldn't wear anything. Now, with Whisper rising, that was never going happen.

A burst of fury rushed over Meiling, shaking her.

I don't think I would like to share my mate with another female, Whisper decided suddenly. *I would want to kill her—and him.*

Meiling was afraid of that—certain she would feel the same way. She kept her distance from Gedeon, never seeing him with other women. Never allowing herself to really think about that aspect of his life. In her mind, they weren't together, and they never would be. He had made his needs clear from the very beginning of their relationship. There had been a clear line drawn and neither had ever crossed it. Now, for Meiling, everything had changed.

She held her hand out in front of her. It was trembling. Not with fear. Or trepidation. She trembled with that same underlying fury Whisper had experienced and shared with her. The edginess had started three months earlier in San Antonio, when they had worked the Atwater case together. When Lola Morales had turned so bitter, she had been willing to kidnap—and kill—a child because her love for a shifter had turned to hatred.

At first, Meiling thought the entire matter was just so disturbing that it kept her awake at night. But then she began to have heat flashes and moments of intense sexual desire. At the same time she found herself dwelling on Gedeon's late nights at the club. It took discipline not to be angry with him, or worse—stalk him by going to the club herself. Some nights when he called for her to come to his suite, she was so filled with anger toward him she couldn't allow herself to go. She spent those nights in a warm bath crying, or she'd go out to the swamp and run.

"I need answers, Whisper. I can't afford to have Gedeon be my mate, and I have this terrible feeling that he is. Or that I've fallen in love with him. The real thing. If that's the case, we have to get away from here very quickly. We can't take the chance of his leopard claiming you. That would be a disaster."

I'm going to sleep for a long while. I'm very tired. You can talk to Gedeon and ask him questions. I won't rise and disturb his leopard.

"Are you certain?" Meiling didn't want to take any chances.

I can't stay awake even to help you.

Meiling felt the regret in the leopard. She was already as bonded to Meiling as Meiling was to her. A burst of affection spread through Meiling. She wrapped her arms around her middle to give the leopard a hug. "Go to sleep. We have time to figure this out. I'll reach out to a friend in the morning and ask her questions. Maybe I'll sound out Gedeon tonight and see what he has to say. I'm so glad you're with me, Whisper."

I'm happy.

Meiling thought about whether she could share with Gideon that she did, in fact, have a leopard. She shared everything with him. There was so much joy in her, it felt as if it was overflowing. At the same time, she knew she couldn't tell Gedeon about Whisper. She would have to be very careful about the questions she asked and how she went about gathering information.

Gedeon was proprietorial over her. She had to admit she liked that trait in him—until now. Now she had to worry about how he would react if he did find out she had a leopard. Like Meiling, he had gotten used to the two of them being together.

"I'm happy too, Whisper. Go to sleep."

Meiling finished dressing and went to the mirror to make certain the evening's events hadn't taken too much of a toll on her and Gedeon wouldn't know anything different had taken place. She did look a little different. Her skin seemed to glow more. She looked almost radiant. Her eyes were darker, sultry looking. It was as if Whisper enhanced her looks in an exotic, sensual way. She wasn't wearing makeup, so it wasn't like she could wash the look away.

Meiling chose to use the stairs rather than the private elevator. Stairs gave her the opportunity to burn off a little energy, although she could feel the same exhaustion that had overtaken Whisper sneaking up on her. Maybe just lying down beside Gedeon would be enough for a while. She could save her questions for Evangeline and then figure out what to do. Her head was all over the place, just like her emotions.

The hall was lit only by the old-fashioned sconces that matched the house so perfectly. Meiling had come to love the house. It fit with the city, the swamp, and even the Mississippi River. The structure seemed to have a personality of its own. Over the years it had taken on the flavor of the city around it, so the beauty and flaws, the music and culture were absorbed into the architecture. The restoration and additions had been done very carefully so that Gedeon's home, to Meiling, was a beautiful example of New Orleans culture.

Gedeon's suite was at the very end of the hall, creating a private, separate apartment from the rest of the house. She was used to letting herself into his living quarters and going straight to the master bedroom. She didn't need the aid of lights to see through the spacious rooms. One wall faced the swamp, just as hers did. She knew that his leopard could easily cross the short distance to reach the thick grove of cypress and gum trees, where it would be extremely difficult to find him. One of the walls in his bedroom also faced the swamp, so his leopard could escape from the bedroom. Gedeon had planned for all contingencies.

He was like that in the way he approached the jobs they took. He studied every possible outcome and had a strategy in place, usually more than one, on the off chance things didn't go right. His mind was very methodical. He didn't hurry his work and skip steps in order to get his work done faster. Still, his brain did work at an incredibly fast rate of speed. There were so many things she admired about him.

Meiling was three steps into the bedroom when the scents first hit her. Cloying perfume. Overpowering male sex. The sound of flesh slapping hard against flesh. She froze. Her mind shut down for a moment. Everything shut down while her vision focused on the woman kneeling on all fours on Gedeon's bed while he was behind her, slamming his cock into her so hard he drove her forward.

"I thought your little partner would be the first one you'd call," the woman gasped out, gripping the bedcover and pushing back.

"Really? Have you seen her? Do you really think she could stand up to my rough brand of sex?" There was just the right touch of derision in Gedeon's tone. "Shut the fuck up or get out. I can call the next on my list if you'd rather talk than fuck."

He lifted his gaze and caught sight of Meiling standing there. He looked nearly as stricken as she felt. She backed out of the room and, once out of the bedroom, turned and fled his apartment.

He'd practiced that tone. They'd written those words together. Early on they'd known someone would eventually ask why he wasn't using his partner for sex. He didn't want attention on her. She didn't want the attention, not when she knew she was hunted. They'd sat together at the Café Du Monde and written the little script for him. He'd practiced saying the lines until he'd gotten that perfect derisive tone down.

Laughing together in their favorite café had been one thing; hearing him actually repeating the phrases while he was having sex with someone was another. Sex in his bedroom. *Her* room. That was their special place that was supposed to be off-limits to anyone else. Why would he bring someone to his room if he'd asked her to come to him? Did he want her to see him with someone? Had she somehow given herself away and he wanted to make it clear that he wasn't about to have a sexual relationship with her?

She let herself out the front door and ran down the steps. There was a part of her that was so devastated she couldn't think straight. Another part of her shook with fury so strong it was frightening. She had to get herself under control before she saw him again. If he had set her up, he was an idiot. She didn't believe Gedeon was that stupid, but then, men could be when it came to women.

She walked toward the Café Du Monde. It was open all night and she could get her favorite drink and sit by the river and just think. Whisper and the overload of hormones she'd brought had caused her brain to rush too fast. She had to slow everything down.

Alone, as she walked toward the café, it was acceptable to cry. She'd lost Gedeon. She'd never really had him. He'd been her fantasy. She'd always known she was going to be alone. She'd been good at being alone. Finding him and then coming to depend on him had been both a miracle and a curse. She knew what it was like to share her life with someone. She would have to go back to being alone. The idea of it was like looking into a dark abyss.

Whisper. She had her leopard. She wouldn't be entirely alone. She hugged that knowledge to herself as she dashed away the tears and straightened her shoulders. She would build her networks again and find places far away from Gedeon's territories. He worked all over, but mostly he worked for the crime families. She didn't. He worked for shifters. She didn't. And wouldn't. Now, more than ever, she would have reason to stay away from them.

There was a rowdy table of partiers and two tables of what appeared to be tourists at the café. She also recognized Remy Boudreaux, a shifter and the head detective in New Orleans. She'd met him a couple of times. He sat at a table with his wife, Bijou, a very famous singer. Surrounding them at the other tables were more shifters, presumably bodyguards for Bijou, and a couple of Remy's brothers. Bijou sang in her club at times, and this night must have been one of those nights.

She returned the wave they gave her, purchased her café au lait and left quickly before anyone engaged her in conversation. The Boudreaux family was very nice. She knew the moment they realized she was alone, they would invite her to join them, and she didn't want to talk to anyone. She needed the solitude to sort herself out. As she walked away, she could feel Remy's frown and the way his alert gaze trailed after her. He was a protective sort of man.

Meiling continued away from the café down to the river, where there was a bench off the path. In the dark, few would see it. Bushes grew close, concealing the bench during the day, so at night she would be even more difficult to spot sitting on it. She could sit and stare at the water rushing by and listen to the power of the Mississippi while she regrouped.

There was no sound to warn her, not even his scent because the wind carried it out over the river, but she knew he was there. Gedeon sank down beside her, handing her a jacket as he did so.

Meiling stared straight ahead at the churning river, taking a sip of her drink, unable to look at him. He wasn't hers anymore. He never would be again.

11

THERE may as well have been an ocean between them. Gedeon could feel the distance—not only distance, but a wall as solid as titanium separating them. He couldn't blame her. He wasn't even certain what had been happening lately, so how was he going to explain himself? Meiling wasn't a trusting woman. He'd eased her into his world, careful of every step. In one terrible blow he'd ruined everything between them.

"We have to talk about this, Meiling," he said. Because they did. He couldn't lose her. He couldn't go back to his life without her.

"No, we don't. You don't owe me an explanation."

Her voice was such a thin thread of sound. Always so soft and delicate. Just sitting beside her, Slayer was quiet. "I want to give you one. I *need* to give you. You don't have to listen to me if you don't want to, but I have to tell you what's been happening."

Meiling didn't look away from the river. She didn't turn

toward him. He didn't feel the terrible chasm between them lessen in the least.

"Slayer has been insane lately. Truly insane. Sometimes I thought he was going to tear me apart. Ever since we returned from San Antonio, his behavior has become more vicious than ever. He never sleeps. He rakes at me day and night, demanding blood. He seems to demand sex, but then wants to kill the woman I'm with, so I can't really get any relief. He keeps me in a state of constant arousal all the time. Once I found a female leopard for him and he nearly killed her."

He rubbed at his aching temples. "Unless you're with me, I can't sleep. Sometimes I go days without sleep, Meiling. That makes the situation worse. My brain starts to slow down. I'm afraid he's going to gain control. I don't know if I'll be able to save us. Sometimes I think the right thing to do is put us both down."

He wasn't making a bid for her sympathy. He really didn't know what to do. Meiling was the only way he'd gotten any respite at all. Slayer was quiet around her and gave him time to rest. If she was with him during the day, even with others close, the leopard remained fairly calm.

"The last couple of weeks, Slayer's behavior has escalated even more. I've felt out of sorts as well. I don't know if I'm affecting him, or if it's been the other way around. I do know the need for sex tonight was horrific. I tried to stop it. I went down to the gym. I called for you, hoping you could calm Slayer and me both. When you couldn't come, I thought Rene could line someone up at the club for me. You said you'd be able to come to me at two. I had plenty of time. Rene somehow mixed up the message and sent that woman to me."

No response. Gedeon didn't know how to reach her. He wanted to pull her into his arms, but he had just come to her from having sex with another woman. She wasn't going to allow that.

"I can't explain what was happening to me. I was burning up. Slayer was hotter than hell. Sweat was dripping off me. I couldn't think straight. The moment she entered the room, she was stripping and climbing onto the bed, and I was pounding into her. Nothing was taking away that fire. It was raging out of control. I'd never felt anything like that. I felt like an animal, not a thinking being. I couldn't think."

He was telling her the strict truth and it was humiliating to do so. Blood thundered and roared in his ears. His body hadn't felt like his own. Many times his sex drive had been wrapped up in his leopard's relentless drive, but Gedeon had never encountered anything close to what had occurred.

"Meiling, you have to at least hear the truth in my voice. It's important to me that you don't think I would ask you to come to my room and then deliberately have another woman there."

"I don't believe you're lying to me, Gedeon."

She still didn't look at him. The river seemed to hold her interest more than he did. He couldn't tell from her tone what she was thinking.

"I didn't mean to hurt you."

"I know you didn't. It was just unexpected. I always thought of that space as being ours." She gave a delicate little shrug. "Sometimes it's good to check things, establish boundaries. We haven't done that in a while and maybe we needed to. I don't think either of us expected to in the way it happened, but you've always been very clear about your lifestyle."

There was no tone one way or the other. Meiling could have been reciting from a cookbook.

"That space is ours," Gedeon assured her, but he knew it wasn't ever going to be again. She had no intention of coming to his bedroom for their intimate late-night chats. She had put a wide chasm between them, and she meant to keep it there.

She didn't reply to that.

"Come back to the house. We have a meeting with a client tomorrow and you need sleep."

"You go ahead. I'm not sleepy. I'm going to watch the sun come up," she said.

He didn't move. He might not be able to sleep with her in the same bed, but he could sit with her on a bench in front of the river. His damn leopard would at least stay quiet and give him a reprieve.

"I've been thinking quite a bit about Lola Morales and Atwater," Meiling said. "Do many leopards just have sex with one another during their heats and then walk away? Is that common?"

Gedeon had excellent night vision and he examined her profile very carefully. There had been no difference in her tone at all. She didn't sound unduly interested in the answer, but given that he and his cat had been burning so sexually out of control and the condition was worsening each week since returning from San Antonio, there was a chance Meiling was asking the question for a reason.

"It is possible Lola's leopard went into her first heat and that's how she started the affair with Atwater. That would make him an even worse shifter morally than I think he is. When a female goes into heat and emerges for the first time, hopefully she finds her true mate. They recognize each other. He claims her and they only are with each other. They remain faithful to each other. Lola wasn't Atwater's mate. He never should have led her on like that."

"I see."

It was clear she didn't see.

"Once in a great while, a female is on her first life cycle. When that happens, a shifter who has never found a true mate can claim her if they are compatible. If Lola's leopard was on her first life cycle, she wouldn't have known Atwater had a mate."

"Why do you say 'once in a great while'?"

Gedeon thought about how best to answer that. "It's

rare to find female shifters who have not been claimed in a previous lifetime. Females will not accept a mate who is not her own."

"But what you're saying is that if Lola was in her first life cycle, she would have accepted anyone?"

"Not necessarily anyone, but someone her human companion was also attracted to."

"Most likely neither of them had good sense because they were experiencing an actual heat for the first time," Meiling said. "That doesn't seem very fair to Lola or her leopard."

"It wasn't. As I said, Atwater doesn't seem to have any kind of moral code."

For the first time, her gaze cut from the river to slide over him. He couldn't read her, but she chose that moment to look at him. The moment when he was talking about another man's moral code.

"I look bad with all the sex I have, Meiling. But those women want to have sex. They initiate with me, and they would come back for more if I let them. I don't. I'm careful to make it clear I don't have relationships. I don't have sex with shifters. The sex is with women who frequent various clubs. Women Rene knows. I don't like it any more than you do, but I don't know what else to do when Slayer drives us both so hard."

"I'm not making a judgment on your lifestyle. You were living that way long before I came along, and no doubt you'll be living that way long after I leave."

His heart nearly stopped. She said it so casually. Just sort of dropped that little bombshell as if it meant nothing. There was no living if she left. Not with his leopard accelerating its violent behavior. As disciplined as he was, he would never be able to control the cat. Eventually it would break free and kill someone. He couldn't have that. And that was if he didn't go insane from lack of sleep first.

"I should fire Rene for allowing that woman into the house," he snapped.

"You can't fire Rene."

He remained stubbornly silent. Rene should have known better.

"Has it occurred to you that Rene saw the state you were in and knew you couldn't go to the club? He brought the woman to the house to help you?"

As always, Meiling sounded peaceful and calm, driving some of the agitation from him. It didn't keep his lungs from feeling as if they were burning raw.

"I lost you."

She sighed. "I thought that at first too. It feels that way, but the truth is, sooner or later we were going to have to face reality. We couldn't keep on the way we were going."

Gedeon knew she was right. He was becoming too possessive of her. The longer they were together, the more he didn't like other males around her. The more he wanted to claim her for himself. He wasn't certain how long he would have been able to hold out. The minute he made a move on her, it would have ended their relationship in a disastrous way.

"What do you plan on doing, Meiling?" He might as well ask her outright.

"I don't know yet. We have that meeting today. I want to clear the cases we've been working. I've got to think things through. You should too. When we've both had a little time, we can talk again and figure out what we want to do."

She sounded so reasonable, he wanted to shake her. He knew her too well. She wasn't feeling at all the way she was pretending to be. She looked relaxed and indifferent. She acted and sounded that way. But she wasn't. She'd only looked at him once, that one flick of her eyes, a sideways glance. Nothing since.

They sat together on the bench and watched the sunrise

before walking together back to the house. She didn't walk close to him the way she'd always done. They didn't laugh together. She didn't hand him her coffee cup to throw into the trash container on the way; she dumped it herself. It was a small thing, but it was a sign of her declaring her independence. When they got to the house, she walked around to the back and he went up the front steps alone with his heart heavy, Slayer raging at him.

GUY Hawkins was in his late sixties with rounded shoulders and a receding hairline. He wore his wealth casually, from his canvas loafers to his sports jacket and faded jeans. Sending his secretary a vague smile as Gedeon and Meiling were ushered into his office, he waved them toward two chairs.

His office was in downtown New Orleans in one of the newer modern buildings. Hawkins was renowned as a composer, a record producer and a music executive with eighteen Grammy awards and nearly fifty more nominations. His net worth was well over a hundred million, but who was counting? Recently he had gotten involved with a young blues group that had taken the world by storm. They were playing at the very popular Blue's Club, owned by Bijou Boudreaux, in New Orleans.

"Thank you for coming." He extended his hand, first to Gedeon and then to Meiling. "I received your name, Mr. Volkov, on the highest recommendation from my friend, Carmine Brambilla. He told me you were discreet and able to get the job done very fast." He glanced at Meiling. "He said you worked alone."

"He was wrong." Gedeon didn't give Meiling's name.

"I see." Hawkins frowned and walked around his desk to stand behind it. He dropped into his chair and studied Gedeon's stony features.

"I understand completely if you wish to call the meeting off and find someone else. We can leave." Gedeon sounded bored and did his obligatory half rising.

A man with the kind of money Hawkins had would surely investigate Gedeon before he hired him. By now, it was known Gedeon had a partner. She wasn't as well-known and there were no pictures of her in the media, but Hawkins would have heard of her. Sometimes Gedeon was so sick of the dance, he really did want to leave. Slayer, normally quiet when Meiling was close, refused to settle, raking and carrying on as if he would split Gedeon open and crawl out to destroy their client.

"No, no. If you trust her, then of course it's fine. It's just that this is a very sensitive matter and must be kept very quiet."

Gedeon stared at him, knowing Slayer was watching him closely through Gedeon's eyes. He had no idea why he felt such animosity toward the man, but he did.

"How can we help you, Mr. Hawkins?" Meiling asked. Her voice was like a soft breeze blowing through the office, sending a calming effect through the red haze in Gedeon's mind.

Hawkins jumped up from his chair, paced behind the desk, turned back to them and gripped the back of his chair so hard his knuckles turned white. "My wife, Laverne, is thirty-seven years younger than me. Everyone assumed she was a gold digger and married me for my money. That wasn't the case. Laverne and I fell in love. It was that simple. I didn't think I had a chance with her, but she was genuine and sweet and liked all the same things I did."

He stopped speaking and stood quietly staring down at his desk before picking up the only framed photograph on it. He held it up to show them. His wife was beautiful. The same height as him in her heels, she looked regal with her reddish-blond hair piled high on her head with tendrils artfully falling around her face.

Gedeon recognized her immediately. Laverne Sanders

had been a singer and theater actress before she met Hawkins. A gorgeous woman, and they appeared happy together everywhere they went. She often starred in theater performances and was reputed to be quite good. Gedeon had never seen her, but when he'd been briefed on Hawkins, Rene had included the reviews of Laverne's work.

His leopard slammed against his ribs, battering at him to get free. Slayer raged, rending and tearing in an effort to break free and get at Hawkins. Clearly he despised the man with a passion. Gedeon found he felt the same way. So far he had no sympathy for their client. He stared at his mouth and perfect white teeth, wondering how much it had cost him to get those teeth. Why did it feel to him as if the office was staged? As if the desk had been arranged the way it might in a theater to appear a certain way—everything on it a prop for Hawkins to use.

As if she could sense that Gedeon and Slayer were struggling to believe Hawkins and not leap up and kill him, Meiling once again took control. She glided to her feet, a delicate flowing motion of pure femininity, drawing the attention of every male in the room—including the leopard.

She went up to the desk, inserting herself between Hawkins and Gedeon. "May I?" she asked in her soft, lilting voice. She held out her hand for the photograph.

Calm poured into the room. Peace filled Gedeon. Filled Slayer. Instantly the leopard was still, watching Hawkins but waiting to see what would happen, rather than trying to tear Gedeon apart to get his way.

Guy Hawkins handed Meiling the picture. Meiling smiled at it and then up at him. "She's really quite lovely, Mr. Hawkins. I can see you're very worried about her. Has she gone missing?"

Gedeon had the insane desire to catch Meiling by her shoulders and drag her away from Hawkins. If that man was stupid enough to lay his hands on her, Meiling could wipe up the floor with him. He wouldn't know that. She looked so delicate with her slim little figure. If Hawkins was so in love with his wife and so damned worried about her, why was he suddenly looking at Meiling with speculative interest? If there was one thing Gedeon could see—and smell—on other men, it was sexual interest in Meiling.

Meiling stepped back, holding the photograph in one hand, her sweet smile in place, but as she took that one step back, she kicked Gedeon in the shins, hard. *Pull it together, Leopard Boy. He's a client. Hear him out. We need to know what's going on. If Slayer is acting up, get across the room.*

The woman, for being so small, knew how to kick. He should have been angry, but Gedeon was elated. It was the first time Meiling had spoken telepathically to him since the "incident." More important, she called him Leopard Boy. Like it or not, that was a term of endearment between them.

He stood up, towering over Meiling, crowding her a little so that his body, for the first time in far too long, felt her soft form molded against his. Slayer retreated even more, content to be near the woman who always calmed him. Meiling, the consummate professional, didn't so much as stiffen. She stared down at the photograph and then showed it to Gedeon simply by holding it up.

"Isn't she beautiful? I saw her in New York two years ago. She opened on Broadway in the production of *Baby's Got the Blues*. She was absolutely brilliant."

"She was nominated for a Tony Award," Hawkins informed them.

"She should have won," Meiling said sincerely. She handed the photograph back to Hawkins. "She was wonderful in that role."

Gedeon moved away from Meiling, circling the room, taking in every aspect of it. No matter how much he wanted to view it differently, he still felt he was in the middle of a theater set. Why did he feel like Guy Hawkins had staged his office to appear as if he were grieving? The room was actually quite stark. Although spacious, there was very little furniture, which only called attention to the curved desk.

The walls were either sheets of glass or wooden panels. There were no pictures on the walls. Again, that placed Hawkins's desk as the center of attention and cast the spotlight directly onto the only framed photograph on the desk's surface. He studied the office setup from every angle while Meiling engaged Hawkins in conversation about Laverne's career on Broadway. As a musical theater actress, her reputation had grown fast.

The farther away Gedeon moved from Meiling, the more agitated he felt. That triggered Slayer into escalating his aggressive behavior. Or was it the other way around? Gedeon didn't know or care, only that he had a strong urge to separate Meiling from Hawkins immediately. The impression of danger was so strong that he crossed the room again to stand within striking distance of the man, deliberately allowing their client to see the killer in him.

What is wrong with you?

I don't know. I'm getting the impression that you're in danger. Slayer feels it as well.

He knew he should ask her if she felt in danger when she was near Hawkins. The closer he was to Hawkins, the more powerful the feeling became. He was convinced he wasn't being emotional because he'd had a fight earlier with Meiling. It was because their client was looking at her in an inappropriate way as he tried to convince them he adored his wife.

Meiling? What are you feeling? What are your impressions of him?

Meiling didn't answer him at once, but she did move away from the desk, sitting once more, very gracefully, in the chair. "Please tell us more, Mr. Hawkins. Why did you send for us?"

Hawkins's gaze ran over Meiling's slight figure in a hungry, greedy way Slayer just couldn't tolerate. He threw himself at Gedeon fast, the attack unexpected and strong, nearly tearing through his insides. Gedeon's skin lifted as the huge cat shoved against him in an attempt to escape to get at their enemy. It took all of Gedeon's strength to hold him back.

"My wife is bipolar. Her medical condition is not known and I don't want it to get out. That is for her to disclose when she deems it appropriate. I have a top publicity team in place, and when they think it is best to go public with that information, she will. That time, certainly, is not now."

Hawkins spread his hands in front of him and looked down in despair, shaking his head. Gedeon wanted to remind him that he wasn't an actor, he was a musician. He was too busy fighting back his leopard. He was furious with the cat. They had a truce when it came to his work. The leopard was a part of what he did. He was supposed to listen, to pay attention to every word said, take in every detail.

He makes me uneasy. He's telling half-truths, but it's difficult to catch everything with you and Slayer so reactive. Maybe you should leave the room and let me handle this alone.

The moment she made the suggestion, Gedeon's entire being rejected the idea of leaving her alone with Hawkins. What he thought Hawkins would do, he had no idea.

I'm staying. Calm Slayer down for me and I'll keep it together.

You sound and feel like the Grim Reaper.

He wanted to be the Grim Reaper. One swipe of his paw and that would put an end to Guy Hawkins and whatever his game was. On the other hand, he had many clients he didn't like and he'd worked for them. Done recovery for them. He didn't have to like them, he reminded himself and Slayer. He just had to do his job and collect his enormous fee. He nodded and kept breathing, turning his energy inward, determined to get his emotions under control. If he could do that, he could get his savage leopard under control.

"Is your wife under a doctor's care, Mr. Hawkins?"

Meiling inquired. She filled the silence smoothly, keeping the attention on her so that Hawkins didn't notice Gedeon and his smoldering, threatening silence.

"She has a doctor and takes medication, but every once in a while she goes off of it. That's disastrous when it happens. A complete disaster." Hawkins lifted his head, his expression stormy. "She can get taken advantage of very easily. I assigned her a bodyguard. I thought he was someone I could trust. He came with the highest of recommendations."

Again, there was a long silence while he began pacing behind his desk, his hands locked behind his back as if to keep from strangling someone. Neither Meiling nor Gedeon interrupted him. They simply observed him as he seemed to use up his restless, angry energy before getting to his point. Finally, he turned back to them, once more gripping the back of his chair.

"Her bodyguard ran off with her instead of doing the responsible thing, which was what he was hired for. He was to protect her from herself. The two of them have disappeared. She can be very self-destructive. Manic and then self-destructive. Once she's out of her manic phase, she becomes suicidal, realizing what she's done, and she feels hopeless. It loops in her head that she's worthless and has ruined everything. Our marriage, her career, that I would be better off with her dead. She must be found quickly. I called you as soon as I found them gone."

"Did you give us all the details we need on both individuals?" Meiling asked, standing to indicate they would be leaving.

Gedeon was relieved they were at the end of the interview. Holding Slayer back was exhausting.

Hawkins nodded his head. "I'll send the file to your business address immediately. You'll have everything you need. If anything comes up, my private number is in that file, and I gave it to Mr. Volkov when I asked to see him."

"Thank you," Meiling said as Gedeon put one hand on her shoulder to pull her back toward him.

Hawkins didn't bother to walk them to the door now that he had what he wanted. Gedeon thought his expression was rather smug. He didn't speak until they were in the car and heading back to their house.

"Give me your honest impression of Hawkins." He handled the sleek Audi through traffic easily. Now that they were alone and close to Meiling, Slayer was calm again.

Meiling pulled one of the sticks from her hair and a long thick swath of silky strands slithered down her shoulder. "He was being very dramatic on purpose. I don't know him, so I don't know if that's his personality or if he was acting for our benefit. The idea of acting doesn't fit. Why would he have to if his beloved wife is missing and he's racing the clock to get her back? I read the media coverage on him and then on the two of them. There's quite a lot. They seemed, on the surface, to be in love."

"I wasn't buying his act." His voice was gruffer than he would have liked. It wasn't Meiling's fault that he was so edgy or that Slayer was. He didn't know what it was exactly about Hawkins. He couldn't put his finger on it. The man was a legend in his field, yet Gedeon couldn't quite believe him.

"It was an act, yet quite a lot of what he said was true," Meiling stated.

He glanced at her. "You agree that he mixed lies with truth."

"He did, but I couldn't tell what was true and was the lie. I tried to follow a strand of truth, but the lie was woven through it or vice versa. He made it difficult to tell which was which."

"She's missing for certain," Gedeon said.

"Yes," Meiling agreed. "And he wants to know where she is. That much is true."

"The bipolar?" Gedeon asked.

Meiling took her time thinking it over. He could tell she was replaying the way Hawkins had told them about his wife's illness. Weighing his words. Trying to discern the truth amid his lies.

"I believe she is bipolar," Meiling finally concluded. "I'm not certain I believe everything else he said. Or that things happened the way he said. Certainly a manic cycle can drop into a suicidal one. I've tried to analyze his voice and decide whether he was telling the truth when he told us about that part of her cycle, but honestly, I couldn't."

"I know we don't have to like a client to take the work," Gedeon ventured aloud. "I just have this feeling he's up to something shady."

"I have that same feeling, Gedeon. We can find Laverne and make certain she's fine."

"I don't like being used," Gedeon objected. "He's got an ulterior motive."

"We don't have to tell Hawkins we found her. Not at first, not until we figure out what he wants."

Soft music flooded the car as they made their way back to his house. He easily drove the car into the garage. He turned off the ignition and they sat listening to the insects rather than the soft strains of instruments.

"He isn't in love with her," Gedeon announced abruptly, turning toward her in the close confines of the car. "He was all over you. A man who is desperately worried about his missing wife, the one he loves more than life itself, doesn't stare with lust at another woman."

Meiling drew little circles on top of her thigh. "Gedeon, the truth is, neither one of us knows that much about love. How do you know whether a man can love one woman and lust after another? We don't."

"That's not true, Meiling. You don't remember your family, but I do. I remember my parents. I remember my siblings. My mother. The beauty of her. The softness in her eyes when she looked at me. The softness in my heart when I looked at her. I know what love is."

Her dark eyes went liquid—that melting chocolate that turned his insides to mush. She shook her head. "Honey, that's the love for family. It isn't the same as love for your woman. You haven't experienced that. For all you know, Hawkins can love his wife and still crave other women. Look at all the men who have affairs. Do you think that none of them love their wives?"

"No, I don't think they do. I think they love themselves," Gedeon replied. "It's an ego thing, at least when I've worked cases involving cheaters. That's been the case every time whether it's been a man or a woman doing the cheating."

"Maybe they aren't cut out for a relationship," she ventured.

"Then they should have been honest and not gotten into one," he answered instantly. "No matter how you twist this, Meiling, something isn't right about this case. Hawkins wants us to find Laverne, but he's got reasons other than what he's giving us." Gedeon was certain he was right, so certain he stated it as fact.

"Sadly, I believe you're right. I don't want you to be, because that could mean Laverne is in more trouble than she appears to be." Meiling pushed the door open. "Let's go figure out where she might have gone."

"He's going to have us followed," Gedeon cautioned.

"He'll try," Meiling agreed. "I was certain he'd do that from the time we entered his office. He's that kind of man."

Gedeon's smile was a little cruel. "I should have said he'd try to have us followed."

MEILING was exhausted after spending the entire afternoon and most of the evening with Gedeon, working on uncovering a single thread to a trail to Laverne. It was very clear that she hadn't suddenly gone off her medication and taken off. She had planned for months to leave. No one could disappear without a trace the way she had without careful planning.

Laverne's disappearance had required a good deal of money to be siphoned off without her husband knowing. She had a hefty bank account, but it was clear that it was monitored. She had taken small amounts of money out over time for monthly charities, hair, nail, and clothing allowances. It was all regular spending that never deviated, but when Meiling tried to match it with actual dollar amounts spent, it didn't add up.

The bodyguard was a man with a good reputation. He didn't seem like the type of man to run off with someone's wife, yet he had also disappeared. He spent time with other bodyguards, specifically those around Blue's Club. He had once taken an assignment guarding Bijou Breaux at Blue's Club before she was married to Remy Boudreaux. That meant he knew quite a few of the shifters. Gedeon said he'd talk to them. That was a relief to Meiling, although she didn't let on. She preferred to stay away from the male shifters as much as possible.

When she was finally able to go to her suite for the night, she locked her doors, ran a hot bath and stripped. She needed answers and had decided to ask Evangeline Amurov. Hopefully she would answer.

Meiling sank into the hot bathtub and sent her query to Evangeline.

Have several questions I can't answer myself regarding first cycle leopard emergence.
Will you help? Would have to be as confidential as possible.

She didn't want to say Evangeline couldn't share with Fyodor because Evangeline would feel she was doing something wrong. This way she would think she was merely helping out.

> I'll do my best.

Meiling wrote out a series of questions and sent them to Evangeline, hoping they wouldn't point toward her. She tried to make it seem as if a client was asking and she had no answers as she didn't have a leopard. She never stated those things, just implied them.

> I've never heard of a female leopard and her human not staying with their mates. If her leopard chooses, she will only do so if her human is attracted and can love the male her leopard is with. That male must be able to love her.

Meiling thought about that as she soaked. Evangeline had never heard of a leopard and her human not staying with her mate.

> What if they choose wrong? Could that happen? Would they leave then?

She snapped her fingers in the water, popping bubbles while she waited.

> The male would be far more experienced and wouldn't allow the female to choose wrong. At least he shouldn't. I suppose there are terrible males. There were in Fyodor's home lair. Fortunately, that doesn't happen here, although there aren't too many shifters, so it's much more difficult to find mates.

Meiling tried to find a way to ask the next question without giving anything important away.

> Is it possible for the leopards to be attracted
> without the humans being? Or the humans
> without the leopards being?

When a female goes into heat every male for
miles is attracted. The men go insane as well.
Believe me, he will be attracted.

Meiling chewed on the side of her lip.

> Okay, this one is from me. How would a woman
> ever know if the male was genuinely attracted
> to her if he hadn't known her or showed inter-
> est until her leopard came along?

The answer took longer.

That is a difficult question, especially under
the circumstances you describe. If he is a
stranger, or has never showed interest, he
would have to find a way to prove to her that
his interest in her as a woman and partner
is for herself, not just for her leopard, and
I suspect it wouldn't be easy. At least, it
wouldn't be for me. No woman would want
to be wanted just for her leopard.

Meiling snapped her fingers harder at the bubbles.

> I took us off the questions. Sorry. What if the
> man is unfaithful? He wants to have multiple
> women in his life. Can the woman walk away

even if her leopard still prefers to mate with his
leopard?

They can't possibly be true mates if he needs
that in his life. Yes, she should walk away. It
might not be easy because her leopard may
think the leopard she's with is her true mate,
but he cannot possibly be.

There was her answer. She would have to find a way to
let Gedeon go.

If her leopard has just begun to show herself,
but the sexual desire is fierce and burning out
of control from the very first time, how long does
she have before she fully emerges?

There was a long silence.

I would have to ask someone else. My leopard came to me when I was a child because
I needed help. Let me ask someone else. I'll
do it casually and let you know as soon as
I can.

If the leopard is asleep but has been rising and
then going to sleep, can the woman still affect
males around her? As in put them in a height-
ened state of sexual tension or sexual need?

Yes. Absolutely.

Meiling pressed the heel of her hand to her forehead.
She was in the same house as Gedeon. She'd gone through

a massive, burning sexual fury just upstairs from him. He was already struggling with Slayer's needs.

> Would the leopard be affected sexually? And would that leopard's needs affect his male?

> Yes. Absolutely. Until the female emerges and is claimed, it will be very difficult on every male shifter near her. If her mate is close, he will suffer terribly.

Gedeon already had problems with his leopard's vicious sexual cycle. She had contributed to that terrible, ferocious sexual arousal he couldn't stop.

> Thanks for your help.

> Anytime. Take care and come see me when you're in San Antonio.

Meiling sent her a thumbs-up and set her phone aside. What a mess.

12

FROM the balcony, where he could so easily observe them, Gedeon stared sightlessly down at the writhing couples dancing to the pounding beat of music. He had created the perfect hunting ground with the same meticulous care he'd given everything else. The nightclub was wildly popular. The atmosphere was electric. Pulse-pounding. Sensual. Exciting.

Over the years, the club had saved him. Slayer had become so difficult, driving Gedeon close to the brink of insanity. He recognized that he was getting close to the time he would have to make the decision to end his life for the safety of others. He was well aware the trauma he'd experienced as a youth had colored his life and all relationships. He had trusted no one—until Meiling came into his life.

He gripped the railing of the balcony with both hands, his strength threatening to indent the wood with the impression of his fingers. Meiling. What was he going to do about her? She'd taken this last refuge from him. She hadn't done it on purpose, but he had no more desire to be with any of these women than Slayer wanted him to be with them. Still, his cock raged at him. His body hurt, every joint painful. His temperature raged through his body just as heated and as out of control as his cock. Slayer was in a bad way. He was as well.

He wiped the sweat from his face and tried to clear the chaos from his mind. He had never allowed himself to be dependent on anyone. He'd never allowed himself to love again, not after his family had been torn from him. Betrayal—and love—had shaped him into the monster he'd become. He hid the monster under a smooth veneer of civilization. Others were allowed to see the killer in him under the guise of the hit man if needed, but they never saw the relentless, merciless monster those his family had trusted had turned him into. He feared Meiling was opening that door he'd kept locked securely for so long.

Even in his state of agitation, he scented Rene, and he turned to face him. Rene looked upset, very unusual for the normally unflappable man. "We have a problem, Gedeon." He didn't wait for Gedeon to ask. "Meiling is here, on the dance floor, and she's . . ." He hesitated. Stopped and looked up at Gedeon. "I don't know how to describe her. I'd say a woman with a leopard in heat, but my leopard isn't feeling hers. He responds the way he does toward her but doesn't sense her leopard. *I'm* responding to Meiling the way I would if her leopard was in heat, and so are most of the men in the club."

Gedeon's heart skipped a beat and then began to pound. He went to the other side of the balcony, where he could look down over the railing directly onto the center of the dance floor. Instantly his gaze was riveted to the woman dancing in the dark bluish light. She might as well have had a spotlight shining right on her.

Meiling wore her long hair down, pulled back on one side, the rest falling in a sexy slide over her shoulder. Long gold earrings matched a multitude of gold bangles that went up her arm, accenting her glowing skin. Her eyes were done with smoky makeup and her lips were poutier than he could ever recall. She wore a dark navy-blue halter top and a little, sexy matching skirt that flared out when she turned or twisted.

She'd always been fluid walking or moving, but when dancing she had a natural sensuous quality there was no denying. She seemed to glow, drawing the attention of everyone. It was impossible not to watch her. Gedeon found he couldn't take his eyes off her. He knew if a man laid his hands on her, he'd kill him.

"Get her out of here, Rene."

"She's dancing, Gedeon. I don't have any reason."

"She's going to cause a scene soon. You know it. Blood will be shed." He was the one that would be doing the killing. "Is she drinking?"

It was rare for shifters to drink. Meiling didn't seem to drink. He hadn't seen her, but then she claimed she didn't have a leopard.

"I believe she has been drinking, but I don't know how much," Rene reported.

Gedeon couldn't tear his gaze away from the erotic sight of Meiling dancing on the shadowy, blue-lit floor. "Get her out of here, Rene. Tell her to go home. I'll be there as soon as I can get myself under control. She's got a leopard, whether she knows it yet or not, and her female has to be close to emerging. Her cat isn't just affecting me, my leopard and every man here, she's affecting Meiling as well."

"I'll ask her to leave," Rene agreed. "But Gedeon, if you're right, and I'm afraid you are, she's going to be moody and bad-tempered. It won't be easy to get her to cooperate."

"Just tell her I'm leaving as well. Whatever you have to say to get her out of here."

"You do remember I'm single and have my own leopard," Rene reminded.

Gedeon took a deep breath and let it out to control Slayer's vicious reaction. This was Rene, not an enemy. He nodded. "I'm sorry, Rene. If I could handle this myself, I would. I've had the feeling for some time that she was my mate, but she kept insisting that she didn't have a leopard."

Rene shook his head. "If you believed that, Gedeon, you should have acted on it, leopard or not. Now you're going to have a long, hard road ahead of you that might not work out. Meiling appears to be soft, but she has a will of iron. You hurt her. You said so yourself."

Gedeon didn't need the reminder. He knew he was already in trouble with Meiling. "The last thing I need to do is add murdering an innocent man to my list of sins. Please do this for me, Rene."

Rene nodded and abruptly walked away. From his vantage point above the dance floor, Gedeon watched Rene make his way through the crowd to Meiling. It wasn't easy. She was surrounded by men. They danced around her, but none made the mistake of putting their hands on her. It was possible she had warned them off her. Gedeon didn't know or care why they were leaving her alone; he was just thankful that they were.

Rene approached her from her right and called out softly before stepping close enough to interrupt her movements. She stopped and faced him. Even just standing still, she looked beautiful. She raised one hand to push at the thick silk of her hair falling around her face. Just that action tightened Gedeon's body so savagely he could barely breathe.

Meiling shook her head and gestured around her. Rene talked more. Meiling tilted her head back and looked directly up at Gedeon before pushing past Rene and walking through the crowd of men toward the exit. Rene trailed after her.

Gedeon swore under his breath. She was pissed. Really, really pissed. It didn't happen often, but when Meiling was angry, she could bring the claws out. He crossed to the other side of the balcony to watch as Rene went out the front door of the club. He was gone longer than Gedeon was comfortable with.

Settle down, Slayer. If we want to keep Meiling in our lives, you have to back off enough to let me go to her with the ability to be calm. He rarely asked his leopard for anything. He commanded and got results. At this stage, the cat had to realize they were both going to lose if the animal persisted in driving Gedeon past his point of endurance.

I cannot stop the burning. The need for sex. The need to fight. For blood.

I can't either, but we have to try. She's the only one who can save us. We're driving her away from us. I believe she has your mate. If we push her away, we'll lose her before you ever have the chance to know. We won't have a choice. We'll have to suicide.

Gedeon could feel the leopard's tremendous struggle to overcome the ferocious burning needs raging through their bodies. He knew the big cat was as scarred by their traumatic childhood as he was. It had been his leopard who had saved him on multiple occasions. He owed the animal his life and his sanity.

When Gedeon had spoken of knowing love to Meiling, he hadn't included Slayer or Meiling. He knew he loved both. He might not say it aloud, or even admit the truth to himself, because he was afraid both would be taken from him.

Rene came back inside and made his way upstairs. His shoulders were slumped, and he looked defeated.

"I take it she was upset."

"I put her in a cab and tried to give them your home address, but she waved me away and shut the door. I don't think she's going home, Gedeon."

"Who do you have on her?"

"Man by the name of Gray Duncan. He's human, not a shifter. He's older and wouldn't bother her even if she did catch him—which I suspect she might. She's too polite to be rude to an older man."

"By 'older'?"

"He's pushing seventy. Likes to keep busy and asked me for work whenever I had it available. He's sharp as a tack, Gedeon. I've always been able to rely on him."

Gedeon didn't know whether to be happy or angry about the fact that the man was older and not a shifter. At least he wouldn't be trying to cement a relationship with Meiling.

"Contact him and find out her destination. I'm heading out, and if she isn't on her way home, I'll need to know where to get her."

"She wasn't happy."

"I could see that."

"She knew you were the one who sent her away."

Gedeon shrugged. "I was the one. I wouldn't want her blaming you for something I did. When you were up close to her, did you get any inkling of a leopard?"

Rene shook his head. "I even asked my leopard to pay attention. He said he couldn't detect a female leopard close, but I absolutely believe there's a female about to emerge."

Gedeon believed it too. He often just knew things, and ever since they left San Antonio, he had been getting so moody and edgy for no apparent reason; it had started to dawn on him that Fyodor had brought those shifters together because he had sensed her female leopard becoming ready to rise. Gedeon was too close to her. He'd been with her for a year and took her for granted. He'd noticed her enhanced beauty, but he was used to her glowing skin and shiny hair.

Her sudden mood swings were few and far between. He was far moodier than she was, and he'd spent his time trying to calm Slayer. By the time it occurred to him that the problem wasn't Slayer or him, that it was Meiling, it was too late. She had walked into his bedroom, and he'd been having rough sex with another woman. That might as well have put an entire ocean between them.

"Got a text from Gray. Says she went to the Hot Nights Club in Algiers. She just waltzed right in. No one asked her for a cover fee, just showed her to the bar," Rene said. "Men are lining up to buy her drinks."

Gedeon slipped on his jacket. "I'll bet they are."

"I'll follow you and have some of the crew meet us there. This could get ugly."

Gedeon ignored the offer. It didn't matter if it got ugly. No one was touching Meiling tonight, not even him. If she was drinking, which she never did, she wouldn't be in control. That meant someone had to look after her. That someone was going to be him. No one would be taking advantage, especially not the man who loved her.

He made the trip to the Algiers club in record time. He'd been there a few times and knew the owner. He'd done a couple of favors for him. He didn't bother with the line or the security guards. He'd texted ahead and met the owner, a man by the name of Felix Jeansonne, at a private entrance.

Felix let him in. "I already had her surrounded by my personal guards before I got your text, Gedeon," he greeted. "I knew she was trouble the moment she walked in."

"We got into a fight," Gedeon said. "Meiling and I don't ever fight. She doesn't drink either. So this is all a first for us." Deliberately, he sounded rueful. "I had no idea she'd go out dancing alone."

"It's clear she has no idea what she looks like."

Gedeon walked down the hall with Felix. "No, that's part of her charm. She has no clue."

"You brought a crew with you?"

"I told them to hold back. I was certain you'd have everything under control. But when my woman gets pissed, she can be difficult." He laughed, sharing with Felix what it was like to have a rowdy woman. Felix would know. His woman was as sassy as hell and the man wouldn't have it any other way.

"I will say this for you, Gedeon, you chose well. She's gorgeous, but you may find yourself having to fight to the death to keep her."

Gedeon heard the warning in Felix's voice. He nodded. "I'm well aware. She's worth it. She doesn't ever do this. It's on me. I did something stupid, and I hurt her. She's got every right to be angry with me. I imagine she thought she'd just go out dancing and drinking and then come home."

Felix sighed. "It's never that easy when they have that special something no one can put their finger on." He opened the door leading to the club floor. The music was almost deafening in comparison to what it had been in the hallway.

Gedeon's gaze was immediately drawn to the dance floor and the woman commanding attention as she moved to the pounding beat of the music. Meiling was in a shadowy corner, and true to his word, Felix had appointed three of his security detail to surround her, cordoning her off from any of the males trying to get close to her. She seemed oblivious, her eyes closed, as she danced on her own.

"I'm going to come back out this way if you don't mind, Felix," Gedeon said. "She may kick up a fuss. If she does, she's going over my shoulder and I'm just walking out with her."

"I'll have my boys walk with you as far as this door and I'll lock it after you," Felix said.

"Thanks. I just want to get her home, where she's safe."

Felix nodded. "If it was anyone else, I'd be putting her in one of the rooms upstairs with one of my girls to make sure."

Gedeon knew the man was telling the truth. He was careful at his club. His bartenders watched as closely as they could for anyone putting drugs in drinks. It wasn't that he was opposed to his clients having fun at his club. He had back rooms and another entire level for adventurous patrons, but everything had to be consensual. The moment he found out there was a problem, his people took care of it instantly. Sometimes, it was rumored, permanently.

Gedeon purposefully strode straight to his woman, moving up behind her, sliding his arms around her waist, his body moving suggestively with hers. "Time to go home, Lotus," he murmured in her ear.

She reached behind her to find his neck, her eyes still closed, laying her head on his chest, finding his rhythm easily. "I want to dance."

"We'll dance at home." He purred the suggestion, one hand sliding up her rib cage and the slight rounded curve of the side of her breast. He bent his head and kissed her neck, pressing his erection tight against her bottom. She pushed back into him, a little moan escaping. Her body was as hot as sin, rubbing against his, inflaming him more.

"We've got to go before I take you right here in public."

She turned her face toward his. "I'm on fire."

Her eyes were still closed. He could smell the alcohol on her breath. Her body moved against his, demanding sex. He wasn't certain she knew who he was.

"Come with me now." He tightened his arm around her waist and caught her wrist. "Meiling. We're leaving. Going home. I'll take care of you, I promise."

If he didn't get out of there, they were in real trouble. He began walking her toward the hall exit, where Felix waited with the door open. The three security guards did their jobs, surrounding them, clearing the way. Meiling seemed dazed, stumbling a little, so he half lifted her, walking faster to get her out of club. In the hall, Meiling wrapped her arms around his neck and began to nibble on his ear.

Felix grinned at him. "Have a good night, my friend," he said as he closed the private entrance door.

Gedeon managed to get the passenger door open and Meiling onto the seat with her seatbelt fastened, although how, he later couldn't recall. He glanced at her. It was a mistake. She squirmed and moaned, rubbing her hands up and down her thighs as he put the car in gear and shot down the alley to the main street. Flinging her head back so that her hair fell around her like a dark waterfall and the gold earrings glittered with the lights from the city as they raced for their house, she looked like an erotic, sensual creature sent to tempt him into carnal sin.

She turned her body toward him, one leg sliding up onto the seat, her knee bent, the high heel with the thin gold straps wrapped around her ankle and calf adding to the sexy image she presented to him. He could barely keep the car on the road as she flung her head back and arched her back like a cat in heat.

The scent of sex and Meiling filled the car. Filled his lungs. He could taste her in his mouth. He gripped the steering wheel and prayed for discipline. "I know it's bad, we'll be home in a few minutes."

"I can't stand clothes touching my skin." Meiling's voice was husky. One hand crept up her thigh, pushed the hem of her skirt up to reveal a strip of dark navy lace. Her fingers caught at the two little cords on the left side, and she jerked to pull that side down over the curve of her hip. Then she did the same to the other side.

Gedeon couldn't think of a way to stop her. The red stoplight illuminated her as she dragged her panties down and kicked them aside. He groaned, his body so hard he was afraid he would shatter. It seemed an impossible task for his trousers to keep the monster inside. His foot hit the gas pedal the moment the light turned green.

Her fingers began sliding between her legs. "You have to do something. You have to make it stop."

He pulled the Audi into the garage and turned toward her, inhaling deeply. "I'm right here, baby. We've got this."

He stroked caresses up her thigh. She reacted instantly, trying to move her body into his hand. "I'm taking you upstairs where we have room to do this right."

"I can't wait." It was a wail.

He didn't answer her. He rushed around to her side of the car and dragged her off the seat, flung her over his shoulder and took the elevator straight to her suite. He had a code to get in and he used it. The moment he opened the door, the scent of a female leopard in heat filled his lungs. Slayer roared in triumph. There was no doubt that Meiling had a leopard. The cat had left Meiling in a terrible sexual state.

The moment he set Meiling on the rumpled bedsheets, she was up on her hands and knees, crawling toward him, hungry gaze fixed on the bulging front of his trousers. Her hands immediately opened his waistband, tore at his zipper and pulled it down to free his cock. He reached down and tugged at the little halter top, pulling it free from around her neck.

"Lose the skirt, Lotus," he commanded.

Her eyes were glazed over, and for a moment she didn't move, spellbound by the sight of his enormous cock. She stroked it with one hand while she pulled off the skirt with the other. That left her in her heels, bangles and gold earrings. He unbuttoned his shirt and flung it aside, shoved off loafers and trousers and simply flipped her onto her back.

"I see you tried this toy," he murmured, kissing her chin and then biting it with his strong teeth. "How did that work for you?"

She was writhing under him, her hands moving all over

his body. Panting. Begging him for his cock. He kissed his way to her breasts. Her nipples were sensitive beyond belief, hard little pebbles, conduits straight to her clit. She cried out each time he licked, sucked or bit at them.

"It made it worse," she gasped. "I'm on fire."

"What were you going to do at the club, Meiling? Find someone to put out the fire for you? Is that why you went there?" Just the thought of her with another man had him snarling with rage.

He nipped at her belly button and lapped at her bare pussy lips. She lifted her hips, desperate for him to help her. He caught up the toy and pressed the button on low, slowly inserting it, watching her face as he flicked her clit and then traced circles around it and over it.

"Answer me, baby, what were you going to do?"

She rode the toy, driving down on it, her moans louder. "Yes. Like you. I was going to find someone to fuck until this went away. First I thought if I danced until I wore myself out it would stop, but it didn't, so I was going to find someone at the end of the night."

But not him. She hadn't come to Gedeon for help. She was honest. He had to give her that. She'd also been drinking to give herself courage to go through with her plan. He tried not to be angry or hurt. His body was too aroused. He was worn out from fighting Slayer. He couldn't handle this wrong and have her despise him in the morning for taking advantage of her.

More than anything, he wanted to take advantage of her. He wanted to claim her for his own. Slayer raged at him, wanted to try to bring the female to the surface. He cautioned the cat over and over to be patient. They had to do this right. Meiling deserved right. He'd been careful of her all this time; he wasn't about to blow it at the last moment.

She hadn't been able to get herself off using the toy, but he was far more experienced than she was. He used his hands, his mouth and her toy until she was screaming, her body nearly convulsing, the orgasms rolling through her.

Gedeon tossed the toy aside and put her legs over his shoulders, desperate for her taste. She was fast becoming an addiction. No one had ever tasted the way she did. An aphrodisiac. He didn't know if it was because her female leopard had been so close, spilling hormones into her bloodstream, or because she was meant for him alone, but he was greedy beyond anything he'd known.

He devoured her, savored her, used his tongue and teeth like a weapon. He brought her to orgasm again and again until she yanked at his hair, desperate for him to stop and give her a chance to catch her breath. The fiery heat wasn't subsiding. It never did right away, not in him, and it refused to in her. It was hell descending on them, yet at the same time, the leopard's enthrallment was paradise. Fire and damnation. Never-ending. There was no way to be gentle, not with the terrible demand claiming both of them.

Somehow—Gedeon wasn't even aware of how it happened while he was eating her out—she managed to turn around under him. Then she had her mouth on him, eager to swallow him down, no matter how impossible the task. Lightning flashed through his entire body, struck with furious force right at his groin so that he pulsed and throbbed, his girth growing even more. He pushed at the soft tissues of her mouth. So hot. His hips matched the rhythm of his tongue stabbing deep into her pussy. His teeth scraping. His fingers flicking.

He drove her up fast, so she was riding him, but she didn't let loose of her prize. Not even when he began to take control, pushing deeper, needing a release, knowing it was going to be powerful. His entire body shuddered. Every nerve ending, every cell was centered in one hot, fiery explosion. Her shattered cry was muffled as his seed poured down her throat. His cock jerked over and over, on and on in a never-ending release that managed to finally sate him.

Gedeon collapsed over her, his head on her belly, his heart slamming against his chest, shocked that for once his cock actually relaxed. Beneath him, the tension in Meiling's body eased and her temperature finally returned to normal. She turned her head away from him and closed her eyes.

Gedeon waited until his strength returned before he cleaned Meiling up as best he could. Then he showered and got in bed beside her, curling around her protectively. They were going to have a very long talk in the morning. Right now, all he wanted to do was go to sleep.

MEILING flung her arm over her eyes so they wouldn't burn out of her head from the light escaping the blinds. Her stomach lurched the moment she moved, and her head threatened to explode. She tried hard not to think. Not to allow one single thought to enter her mind so she wouldn't have to face the repercussions of her behavior. Whisper had risen just enough to make her insane with the need for sex. Instead of locking herself in her room, she'd gone out to a club and danced and drunk and acted like a crazy woman. Worse, she'd acted like a leopard in heat.

She covered her face with her hands and rolled over. Gedeon had found her and brought her home. He knew. There was no way he didn't. He'd brought her back to her room and Whisper's scent was everywhere. She spread her fingers wide and peeked through them to look around her bedroom. He wasn't there. The relief was tremendous. She didn't have to face him when she felt like her head was falling off her body and she couldn't quite think straight.

There was a note pinned to the pillow right beside her. Very gingerly, as if it might detonate, she held it up and read it several times. There was no denying Gedeon's masculine scrawl. He'd left to track down their first real tip on the Hawkins case. They might actually have a lead on a trail to Laverne. He couldn't miss the meet with the informer, but he would be back as soon as possible so they could talk. Take the aspirin on the nightstand. Drink all the water in the bottle. The glass containing what looked like brown goo would do wonders for her headache and lurching stomach. Drink it all. Trust him, the concoction worked. Sleep in. He'd hurry and they'd get back on track when he returned.

Meiling forced herself into a sitting position. Everything hurt—even her eyelashes. Clearly she wasn't cut out to drink. "I'm sorry, Whisper. I can't imagine how you're feeling. How do people do this? And why? It isn't worth it." She downed the two pills set out for her and drank a good portion of the water while she eyed the brown liquid in the glass suspiciously.

Next to the glass was her toy. The events of the night came flooding back, crowding into her brain whether she wanted to remember or not. Hot blood crept up her neck into her face. Shame filled her. She'd *begged* Gedeon to fuck her. Pleaded with him. She'd done everything but assault him. For all she knew, she'd done that as well. Certainly she'd thrown herself at him.

Gedeon had been in a fierce state of arousal. He always wanted sex. He was ready to have sex with anyone—usually perfect strangers—just as long as they weren't her. He had used her toy to get her off. He'd used his fingers and his mouth. He'd been excellent with his mouth. But he hadn't used his cock. He hadn't touched her with his body.

Her face and entire body burned with shame. Hastily, uncaring that her head was close to exploding at every movement, she made her way to the bathroom and stood under the shower. She knew this day would come. She'd prepared for it. She just had to act normal and not tip anyone off—meaning Rene.

Very carefully, she braided her hair and dressed for the day. The three-word text she'd dreaded to send went out to a woman who owed her a favor. There was no doubt in her mind: that woman would drop everything and be there for her.

She had cash stashed and she put it in a money belt that went around her waist along with a new identity. Her hands were steady as she looked around her apartment. She would have to leave everything behind. That was one of the hardest things to do. There were always little things one would get attached to. She'd never allowed herself to get attached to people before, other than Libby. Now there was Gedeon—and maybe Rene, if she was telling the truth.

Refusing to dwell on what she couldn't change, she put on her shoes and texted Rene.

Am heading to Café Du Monde for my usual.
Want anything?

Every morning she went out and got coffee, and she always asked him if he wanted anything. Sometimes he did, but most of the time he said no. She sent up a silent prayer he would say no. That would give her more time before anyone realized she was gone. She liked to drink her coffee on the bench by the river. There might be some-one watching her. At times when Gedeon worried she wasn't safe, he had someone keeping an eye out. If there was a guard, that would be okay, because he would report she was doing all the things she normally did.

No thanks. You all right this morning?

She sent him several emojis of an exploding head.

Never drinking again.

Meiling walked out of her beautiful suite. It had been the first real home she remembered ever having. She didn't look back as she walked briskly along the sidewalk toward her favorite café. She didn't want to chance running into Rene face-to-face. She didn't want to try to say good-bye without appearing to do so. She might not be able to pull it off.

She couldn't blame this disaster on Gedeon. He'd always been straight with her about what his needs were when it came to sex. What his preferences were. She'd been the one with the fantasies.

She distinctly remembered him scolding Slayer, telling him to wait for the female to rise before he could see if they were compatible. That had been her biggest fear. She'd known all along Gedeon would want to find a mate for Slayer and he'd look to her female. Meiling calmed Slayer. It stood to reason he would expect her female, if she was on her first life cycle, to be well matched to Slayer.

If Slayer claimed her female, Meiling would be put in an untenable position with Gedeon. She couldn't allow that to happen. She had spent a lifetime being rejected. Gedeon had rejected her last night. She was tired of never being good enough. If she was ever going to be with a man, he had to look at her with absolute love, the way Fyodor Amurov looked at Evangeline. It was going to be all or nothing for her. She wasn't going to be wanted because her leopard had a mate. Whisper could just do without. She'd take her far away from any shifters and they'd both just suffer until the heat cycle was over.

She walked the exact pace she always did, lifting a hand toward the regulars she saw every day on her journey to the café. Was this how Laverne felt when she knew she would have to disappear entirely? Sorrow weighing her down? What had caused Laverne to make such a permanent decision? One that would take away her career. Force her to leave her friends. Why would she do such a thing?

And Edge Wilson, the bodyguard. Why would he ruin his very distinguished career? Had the two fallen in love? There was no hint of impropriety. Not one. There were cameras everywhere. Paparazzi. And yet never once had there been the slightest suspicion that Laverne was cheating on Guy. That couldn't be said the other way around. Guy Hawkins had a certain reputation with women. He never commented on it, but judging by the way his eyes had devoured her, she believed the rumor mill.

She was letting Laverne down, and she hated that, but Gedeon wouldn't. He was a professional. He would see the case through. He didn't care about the money, but he did care about the missing woman. If there had been foul play, he would find out. She was certain if Laverne was dead, her husband was behind her death.

The Café Du Monde was very full, and she stood in line to get her usual café au lait. Several times she glanced at her watch, and then she left the line to go to the women's restroom. Once inside, she hurried to a stall and stripped, passing her clothes to the woman waiting in the stall beside the one she'd chosen. She dressed in the clothes given to her right down to the hiking boots. Next, she wound her braid tightly around the top of her head and secured it with a net. Pulling on a chestnut wig with a ponytail and bangs, she pushed dark sunglasses onto her nose. Her earrings were next. She handed over the gold hoops and took the little crystal studs. Phones were exchanged. She was given a hot coffee.

Meiling walked briskly out of the restroom, ponytail swinging, bouncing on her heels, small pack on her back and coffee in hand as she strode out of the café and started down the street along the French Market to where a little Mini Cooper was parked. Climbing inside, she drove away.

Meanwhile, the small woman looking like the perfect replica of Meiling stood in line to get her usual café au lait. Once she had it in hand, she strolled down to her favorite spot by the river, put in her earbuds and sat back to relax.

Meiling used the Mini Cooper to get out of Louisiana. She stuck to the back roads as much as possible. Cities had traffic cameras. Gedeon had access to traffic cameras. He would look for her. His specialty was finding people. He would take her running as a challenge.

He knew her better than anyone else in the world did. She had gotten too comfortable with him and given too much of herself away. He knew most of the people who owed her favors. He was familiar with her network, the ones she could count on in a pinch to get her out of trouble fast. Any of them would give her up to Gedeon.

Etienne was the exception. He was hers and Gedeon knew it, so Etienne's communication would be monitored. She drove all day, stopping only when necessary to get gas and then finding a station where she didn't have to go inside. She filled the tank using the credit card with her new identity. She was using the name Vivienne LeClare, originally from Canada. Mainly she preferred hiking and camping to any other method of recreation. She was trying to hit most of the national parks across the country.

The Mini Cooper was stocked with camping gear and a very practical all-weather tent. She had several passes to the parks she wanted to visit. Her cover was solid. She just had to become Vivienne in her head until she believed she was. She couldn't forget for a moment that Gedeon wasn't the only one hunting her. He might be the one she feared the most, but only because he would tear out her heart. The others hunting her wanted her dead for no reason other than that she'd been born.

Linda Wu, the woman who had taken her place, had to do exactly as she told her and disappear as well. She had done a huge favor for Linda. Both had noticed Linda's eerie resemblance to Meiling, and when Linda wanted to try to make payments, Meiling had suggested she be ready to do this favor in case Meiling ever needed to disappear. They worked out the details meticulously.

Linda would sit on the bench for an hour, and then she would go to one of the tables and appear to puzzle out the work in the notebooks. Hopefully she could eke out another hour. She was to walk to the public transit. Along the way, she was to break down the phone, take out the card and destroy it, putting pieces in garbage cans, and then, when she reached the transit stop, get aboard. She was to get off at the next stop, where an Uber would be waiting to take her to the truck they had stashed. While aboard the public transit, she could get rid of the wig, change sunglasses, turn her reversible jacket inside out and take out the hoop earrings.

Once in the Uber, she would go near the location of where her truck was stashed, but without allowing the driver to see it. Once he was gone, she could use her truck to drive safely out of town, back to her farm.

13

MEILING'S eyes opened, and she was instantly on alert, her hand sliding under her pillow to retrieve her gun. Gedeon had found her. She knew it was him. She kept her breathing slow and even as she assessed the situation. Her go bag was within reach. She just had to get out of bed and make it to one of the exits before he was on her.

"I don't want to kill you, Gedeon, but you know I will."

"No, you won't, Lotus. You might shoot me, but you wouldn't kill me."

She wouldn't. He was right. She would wound him to give herself time to run. "I'm leaving. Just back off and let me go."

"You put me to a lot of trouble to find you. We still have the Hawkins case to finish."

He was closer. She should have been able to pinpoint his exact location, but she couldn't. That worried her. "Gedeon, I'm not playing games with you. I don't want to go back with you. I'm here alone because I choose to be alone. I'm asking you as politely as possible to leave me alone."

"We're shifters, Meiling. We're not human. We have to follow the rules of our society. You're very aware of that, or you wouldn't be hiding out alone on this little island."

He was definitely closer. He might be speaking softly, but her body reacted to his. Her skin was sensitive, her nerve endings coming to life. She tried to will Whisper to stay quiet and not react to Slayer's close proximity. She wasn't certain it was possible, not with the way she was reacting to Gedeon's nearness.

"This is my choice, Gedeon. I'm not ready to commit to some stranger in my life because I have a leopard. After how I behaved at the club the other night, I realized I couldn't control what was happening when she was rising, so I took myself out of the situation. All I'm asking is for you to respect my decision."

"You left without talking it over with me because you were afraid, Meiling," Gedeon challenged.

His hand clamped on her wrist, controlling the gun even as he swiftly used that arm to roll her onto her belly. Then he was on her, using his weight to pin her down. He was a big man and trying to buck him off didn't work. A number of her moves didn't work. He removed the gun from nerveless fingers while his legs wrapped hers in an unbreakable lock.

"Settle down, Lotus. You're only going to tire yourself out if you keep fighting. Lie still and let's talk this out."

His warm breath was in her ear. Her entire body shuddered in reaction. She closed her eyes, trying not to breathe him in. Even if she talked him into leaving, the scent of him would be in her lungs. In this room. Everywhere she turned. She'd never get him out. She lay quietly under him, waiting for his next move.

"That's my girl." He pushed her hair to the side and his

lips brushed across the nape of her neck. Instantly, her sex clenched in reaction.

"Don't, Gedeon." She began to struggle. It was self-preservation. If she had to, she'd fight him until there was nothing left of either of them.

"Stop, Meiling." He whispered against her ear again, using his weight to subdue her. "Do you feel him? I can feel him. His joy. He's never known joy. Never. His life has been pure hell until you came. You brought peace. Calm. But not joy for him. You did that for me."

She went still. What was he saying? She couldn't hear him out. Gedeon was seducing her with words, not his body. She couldn't have that. Sometimes he terrified her. She was just too vulnerable to him.

"I hadn't known such a thing as joy existed until you came into my life. Slayer certainly never experienced joy."

As he whispered to her, one hand began to push her racer-back crop top up to her neck. He kissed her nape again. "He feels her. He knows she's the one he's been looking for all these years. So many females and none of them were his."

Meiling froze. She twisted her fists into the sheets. "No, Gedeon. He can't have her. You know it won't work. If Slayer claims Whisper, then you're stuck with me. I won't have that. I'm not going to accept a man into my life who made it very clear from the beginning he didn't want me. Absolutely not."

She tried to push off the bed. To buck again to throw his much heavier body off her. He simply grew all the heavier, distributing even more of his weight on her. Gedeon didn't fight with her. He lay over the top of her, whispering softly. His voice, like smooth velvet, caressing her skin and inside her mind. He never once changed that low, soft tempo.

"Settle, Lotus. We'll work all that out. Give this to him. Feel him. Let yourself feel his elation. When you've never had such things in your life, you don't take them for granted." He brushed more kisses along her nape and then leaned down to start kissing at the base of her spine. "You never take the woman who gave you and your leopard the ability to live life, a real life—you never take her for granted."

Gedeon kissed his way up her bare spine. Meiling had a beautiful back. She might be slight, a delicate little flower, but she was all woman, her form wholly feminine. He pressed kisses along her shoulder, feeling the power of his leopard running beneath his frame. Meiling's temperature rose. His did. Their skin grew hot to the touch. Slayer waited, showing more control than Gedeon knew the leopard was capable of. He could feel the large cat vibrating in anticipation.

Then the little female flooded Meiling's body with hormones. Her body was hot under his. Slayer roared his triumph and pushed hard against Gedeon, determined to claim his mate. Gedeon fought him back.

You will not harm Meiling.

Never.

Gedeon heard the vow in the leopard's voice. There was near worship there.

She's frightened. Meiling may fight you, he cautioned the cat.

He was reluctant to let Slayer have his freedom when he hadn't secured Meiling's consent. Her female was rising close to the surface. Gedeon felt her presence. She might be newly awakened and in her first life cycle, but she was strong. She might not know what she was doing yet, but she was ready to protect her partner if need be.

I would not hurt her, Slayer insisted. *Her female would never accept me if I did such a thing. Meiling is part of her leopard. I would never harm her.*

Gedeon continued to rub between Meiling's shoulder blades and kiss the nape of her neck to soothe her. "Do you feel her rising to meet him, Lotus? She's right there. I'll bet she's a beautiful little thing just like you."

"Don't let him claim her." There was a sob in Meiling's voice. "Don't, Gedeon. If you care at all about me, don't let him claim her."

"I know he's very scary, but he would protect her with his life. He'll protect you. He's looked for her for years. Waited for the right mate. She's his mate, Meiling. There's no mistake."

Slayer was pushing hard against him and Gedeon couldn't take a chance that the female would retreat. "It's going to be all right. Let him make his claim and then we'll talk this out."

"It will be too late. He won't let her go." Meiling started to struggle again.

Gedeon retreated to allow Slayer to take over his form. They were fast at the shift, a smooth transition so that Meiling went still at the feel of thick fur sliding along her bare skin. Her gasp was audible. Gedeon stayed close, especially since he heard her let out a little choked sob.

The leopard was massive, all muscle and loose skin, his pelt heavy. He weighed in at two hundred pounds of sheer brute strength but was as agile and fast as any smaller leopard. The male could fold himself in half in midair, turn on a dime. His speed was legendary. Gedeon had never seen the cat display his gentle side until that moment. The cat's big sandpaper tongue came out and lapped at Meiling's back. The leopard was exquisitely careful to keep from taking skin off her. He nuzzled her nape with his shaggy head before turning his attention to her shoulder.

Slayer sank his teeth into her with a holding bite, injecting his hormones into her bloodstream, waiting for Whisper to rise to accept him. He coaxed her. There was no demand, as Gedeon expected. The male leopard was patient, holding Meiling under him, but doing so as gently as possible under the circumstances.

The female rose slowly, studying Slayer as she did so, and then abruptly made up her mind. She touched the male, accepting his claim, and retreated. Triumph surged through Slayer. Through Gedeon. Whisper belonged to Slayer. He would never again be alone. Gedeon had Meiling. She was his. *All* of her. There would be no more empty nights at the club with his leopard trying to tear him apart. He wasn't fool enough to think it would be easy. Meiling had made up her mind she didn't want him. She wasn't going to believe him that he was there for himself, not just his leopard. But he could deal with that.

Slayer licked at the wounds in Meiling's shoulder, making certain the coagulant in his saliva would stop the flow of blood that trickled down her shoulder. Gedeon shifted back to his own form and pressed kisses over the wounds.

"I've got a first-aid kit. Stay still until I can get it."

She didn't respond, but her eyes were open, and she was looking around the room. Gedeon located the gun he'd tossed aside before he eased his weight off her. He wasn't taking any chances. She might be upset enough with him to shoot him in places he considered sacred. He swept the gun up off the floor as he went past it.

Meiling sat up slowly, brushing at the tears on her face and jerking down the thin crop top. She sat in the middle of her bed, feet pulled up under her, rocking back and forth, self-soothing. Gedeon sank onto the bed behind her and opened the medical kit. It was a very small one. He used an antibiotic cream and bandaged the two puncture wounds on her shoulder.

"How did you find me?"

He didn't want to tell her. If somehow she managed to get away again, he wanted the same resource open to him. "I have to hand it to you, Lotus Blossom, it took hours of watching the same surveillance tapes over and over before I figured out how you did it. When I first realized you were gone, I started to panic. Can you imagine that? Me panicking? I've come to depend on having you with me. All of a sudden, to know you're no longer there was a shock to my entire system. I fell back on the years of discipline. I knew I would never find you if I didn't think logically. I just had to apply all the things I knew about you."

He wrapped his arms around her and pulled her onto his lap. She had hunched into herself, making herself smaller than ever. For him, seeing Meiling that way was heartbreaking. She was strong. He knew they could work things out once he could get her to talk to him openly again. She was honest about her emotions, much more so than he was. He didn't like that feeling of being vulnerable, or putting the only two people he loved, Meiling and Slayer—if he could call Slayer a person—at risk by his admission.

"I looked at those security tapes a hundred times. I knew if you made an exchange with someone else at the Café Du Monde, you had to have done it when you went to the restroom, yet you came out, stood in line, ordered your normal drink and went to the river as you always did."

Meiling shocked him by leaning against his chest. She didn't do that very often, not even when she'd come to his room when they first were together. It was a rare occasion, and only when he sensed she really needed comfort. She never asked him to hold her, but she did lean into him like she was doing now. He tightened his arms around her. Slayer moved closer to the surface, trying to give her comfort as well.

Gedeon knew better than to call attention to the fact that she was allowing him to hold her. He continued with what he'd discovered. "I watched the woman who was supposed to be you walking. Most often people change appearances, but they don't change the way they walk. She looked exactly the same as you when you walk. Unhurried. Fluid. Practiced."

He kissed the top of her head. "You're so brilliant. I found myself just staring at the surveillance tape and thinking about that word. *Practiced.* Was that woman wearing your clothes? Was she wearing your jewelry and carrying your drink? Was it really you or someone pretending to be you? It took a lot of studying those tapes before I realized a switch had been made. You even had her practice the way you walked."

There was genuine admiration in his voice. He didn't want to go any further. Let her believe he had found her by uncovering the woman Meiling had trained to be her. He knew everything there was to know about her, but she hadn't been able to help him find Meiling. He hadn't even bothered to question her.

He rocked Meiling gently, trying to comfort her when no matter what he did, the tears kept flowing. Tears were out of his scope of expertise. He didn't offer comfort. He fell silent, shifting her small body in his arms so that he cradled her fully against his chest. She buried her face against his heavy muscles. Right over his heart. He buried his fingers in her hair and began a slow scalp massage.

"You have to tell me where this is coming from, Meiling. I know you're upset with me, and you have every reason to be, but we've always worked. It's always been the two of us. My hope all along has been that your leopard would rise and accept Slayer. I thought, I hoped, that you would want the same thing."

Gedeon tried to be careful of his word choices. He didn't want to sound hurt or in any way put pressure on her. Trying to cope with her female's first rising was tough enough without Gedeon adding to the confusion and strain Meiling was experiencing. Still, he had to find a way to shut down the intense emotion so they could at least begin communication.

She gave a little shake of her head and his heart dropped. What did that mean? She didn't want her leopard to be with Slayer? That had never been a desire for her? An option? They were so close in every other way—at least until he blew it by having a woman in his room.

He remained silent, turning that small shake of her head over and over in his mind. Looking back over their relationship for signs he might have missed to indicate they weren't as close as he thought. There was a time when they had been. He hadn't gone to the club for weeks when he'd first returned blinded. It had taken weeks to heal his vision. It was at that time he had learned what happiness was. True caring. He hadn't realized he still had the capacity to love someone until he was with Meiling. His last thought before he went to sleep was Meiling. His first thought in the morning was for her. Slayer was at peace. She had turned their lives around.

During that time, Meiling seemed as happy as he had been. There was a genuine brightness to her. Her laughter was very real. She initiated the contact with him long before he did with her, just small touches on his arm or shoulder. He had begun doing the same. In the evenings, when he coaxed her to stay with him in his bed, she would lie outside the covers, and he would lie with his head in her lap. Her fingers drifted through his hair, massaging his scalp, feeling like caresses and caring when he'd never had that from anyone.

Okay. That had changed subtly—or not so subtly—when he began to frequent the club again. He'd held out as long as he could. After spending time with Meiling, he didn't want to be around other women. He'd never much liked it in the first place, but the relentless sexual drive had made it impossible to stop. He used the gym to work out as much of the fierce energy as possible, but eventually that hadn't worked.

Meiling knew. He didn't try to hide it from her. He was honest. That was a huge part of their relationship. He knew it hurt her. She withdrew a part of herself from him and that hurt him. He knew that was fair—the price he had to pay to keep from going insane. To keep those around him safe. To stay alive. He still had Meiling, even though he'd lost a part of their relationship.

But things went downhill after San Antonio. Meiling became moody when she never had been. Slayer became even more vicious and seemed to crave sex every hour of the day. It was a brutal cycle. Nothing satisfied the leopard. Gedeon got no sleep unless he could persuade Meiling to come to him in the middle of the night, and those nights were few and far between.

"It was your leopard," he said aloud with sudden insight. "In San Antonio, they knew it then. I could only see you, but the shifters could see her."

How had he not known then? He'd even asked Slayer at one point, but Slayer had simply said he couldn't detect her leopard. Her leopard had been asleep at that moment, so Slayer hadn't known she was there. But the shifters had known Meiling was close to the emergence. Gedeon didn't follow such things. He hadn't been in the rain forests looking for a mate. He didn't study shifter ways. He didn't expect to find a mate. If he came across an unmated female, which was rare, he always consulted Slayer, who instantly turned away from the leopard.

Meiling lifted her head and looked up at him with her dark eyes. "What did you say?"

"In San Antonio. The shifters could see your leopard in you, but I couldn't. I could only see you. That's been the trouble all along. I knew something was wrong when we came back. You were different. You, but not like you. Upset. Moody. I couldn't get close to you. Slayer was wild and I couldn't get him under control. He was affected by your female, but I was too wrapped up in you to even think that he might be needing sex because he felt your female's needs."

"What do you mean, you only saw me?" she asked again, her gaze fixed on his.

"Lotus." He said his name for her softly. "You know I can't see anyone else. I never have and I never will. There's you. There's only you."

"There's ten million women, Gedeon."

He smoothed back her hair. "There aren't, Meiling. I used those women to keep my cat from killing anyone. I used them to keep from going insane. I felt as long as they were satisfied, it was okay. I knew the day would come when I would have to suicide because I wouldn't be able to stomach what I was doing."

"But you didn't have sex with me," Meiling pointed out. "You didn't want to have sex with me."

Gedeon stared at her in shock. "Meiling. You're the only woman in the entire universe I protected. How could you think I wouldn't want to have sex with you? I had to use every ounce of discipline I possessed to keep my hands off you, but I wasn't going to fuck up our relationship when you made it clear that was a line you didn't want crossed."

"Because sex doesn't mean anything to you."

That was his Meiling, the woman he knew. She wasn't going to pull her punches. Did sex mean something to him? He had to think about that. She was right. It never had. He used sex to drain off energy. It wasn't used to express his feelings for another human being. Sex could be many things, but the kind of sex Meiling was alluding to he'd never even considered—until recently. And only in the back of his mind. In fantasies.

He couldn't lie to her. They were starting a life together. The communication between them had always been honest. Because this topic was uncomfortable didn't mean he should avoid talking about it or lie to her.

"I was never with a woman who meant anything to me before. I never had sex without Slayer threatening to kill the woman. There was never any feeling between us, just raw sex to assuage a burn. It was empty and mindless and rarely good."

Meiling buried her face against his chest again. "Why do you think you would ever be able to stop that behavior and be with only one woman, Gedeon? The cases you went after were much different from mine. Most of mine were wives coming to me asking me to prove whether or not their husbands were cheating on them. These women went into their marriages happy and so certain that they were loved. They didn't want to believe that their husbands would lie and cheat. Look them right in the eye and scold them for even thinking such a thing. All of them were different ages and had been married for various years. Some were wealthy, others weren't. If the woman was suspicious, no matter how much she didn't want it to be true, it was. I even tried to talk them out of hiring me."

"Where are you going with this?"

"Playboys remain playboys. They don't suddenly become devoted to one woman. They have a need for countless women to stroke their ego."

He believed what she said to be true. He had investigated his share of cheating men and women. No matter all the psychological bullshit reasons given, it came down to the cheater wanting someone to make them feel good about themselves. Home had hit a rough patch, and rather than fix it, they went with something shiny and new. If they wanted to get out, they should have simply manned up and said so. That was his belief.

"I agree with you, Meiling, but I don't believe I fall into the category of a playboy. I didn't have affairs. I didn't have relationships. I had sex because it was necessary for the health of my leopard. If it wasn't for him, I wouldn't have gone near those women. You can choose not to believe me, but I've never lied to you."

"You didn't have sex with me the other night. You used your mouth and my toy but refused to have sex with me."

He heard the hurt in her voice even though she tried to cover it. Gedeon wasn't going to let that stand. He caught her chin and tilted her face back up toward him, forcing her dark eyes to meet his.

"You were drunk. Your female had risen enough to put you in a heated state that left you desperate for sex. If I took advantage of that, I had no idea if you'd hate me forever. As it was, in trying to satisfy you, I felt you'd be angry with me, but I didn't know any other way to calm your body down enough to let you get to sleep. I did my best to protect you, even from me. Believe me, Slayer rode me hard. I was desperate for you myself. It was a long night needing you, but in the end, we both went to sleep thanks to the fact that I couldn't quite control the situation."

Her mouth on him had been a revelation. Women went down on him all the time, but he didn't remember them. He didn't even remember the feel of them surrounding his cock. That wasn't the case with Meiling. His cock craved the feel of her mouth pulling at him. That hot haven closing around him and drawing him deep. She had set up an addiction for her touch, for that dark, erotic cocksucking that set him on fire and gave him the biggest, most satisfying explosion of his life.

"You asked me if sex meant anything to me. The other night, when I was with you, what we did together meant something. It was different and I recognized that it was different. I may not know anything about relationships, Meiling. I'll freely admit that I don't, but I do know I'm better with you. I know it's you I want to be with and only you."

"You haven't considered that maybe you're feeling that way now because it's convenient for your leopard? If I cooperate, then Whisper will cooperate with Slayer."

"You're such an innocent when it comes to shifters, Meiling. You really did keep yourself away from them, didn't you?"

"Yes." Her affirmation came out tentatively. Once again she looked up at him, this time with too much innocence in her eyes.

"What happened the other night when you were burning up is nothing in comparison with what is going to happen when Whisper really rises. You are going to want the hottest, roughest sex you can imagine, and you won't give a damn where you are. That will continue to happen for the entire time her heat lasts. When she emerges, she is going to lead Slayer in a dance, enticing him, tempting him, demanding he pay attention to her. She will want to have marathon all-nighters with him for at least a week."

Meiling stared at him with her dark eyes a little horrified. She gave a little shake of her head. "That can't possibly be. I don't think I could survive anything worse than it was the other night. I was afraid I'd go home with a perfect stranger."

Gedeon pushed down the roar of animal rage. A protest. He kept the tension from showing in his body. "You can't look at it as worse, Lotus. We're in this together. I'll get you through it. Believe me, I'm not going to be just using my fingers or a toy. Shifter couples are exclusive."

She didn't reply, but there was a little involuntary shake of her head. Yeah, he had a long way to go to repair the damage. He was making a little progress. She wasn't crying. She wasn't trying to pull away or search for another weapon to kill him. She was even relaxing into him.

"What part of what I said made you shake your head?"

"Slayer claimed Whisper. I accept that they're a mated pair. While she's in heat, he'll want to be with her. I understand that."

"You know leopards mate for life, Meiling."

Gedeon knew Meiling was aware of the rules in the shifter world. That was a sacred rule. He kept his voice very even. She didn't want to know, but she had that piece of information.

Meiling rolled off his lap and smoothly got to her feet to pace across the room. It wasn't a very large room. Gedeon didn't stay on the bed. He wasn't taking any chances. Meiling had made her escape once and he'd called in a favor. He knew she would answer her phone, even a burner phone, if Atwater's daughter, Lilith, called her. She wouldn't be able to help herself. Meiling had stayed in touch with the child, allowing the little girl to call and video chat with her when she was upset. She'd never once failed to take her call.

He knew she'd gotten rid of her phone, but she hadn't gotten rid of her number because that was Lilith's lifeline. Atwater had no idea why Gedeon had asked that Lilith call Meiling, or why he insisted the little girl had to stay on the phone a prescribed length of time, but that was an easy enough request for Atwater to follow. Lilith loved talking to Meiling and she told her every single thing about her day and everyone in it. She sang new songs and showed off her clothes even though it was impossible for Meiling to see through the phone.

Meiling listened attentively and oohed and aahed in all the right places. If Lilith was upset and crying, Meiling soothed her. This time Lilith wanted to know when Meiling would come and visit her. She had drawings she wanted Meiling to see. Gedeon had listened in on the call while it was being traced.

Lilith called Meiling at least once a week. It wasn't as if it were unusual for the little girl to call her. Gedeon had just made certain he had a professional ready to trace the call. He wasn't about to leave anything to chance, not when it came to discovering Meiling's whereabouts. The moment he knew where she was, he didn't wait, afraid she would change locations immediately. She hadn't. She had found a little island retreat where there were few people and no shifters, and she was determined to ride out the emergence of her female.

"Slayer and Whisper could have it wrong, Gedeon. It's

Whisper's first life cycle. She doesn't know what she's doing. I don't know what I'm doing. We could be wrong."

Meiling leaned against the far wall, hands behind her
back, looking lost and alone. Gedeon went right to her.
Close. Towering over her.

"You've been with me a year, Meiling. In all that time,
you trusted me to have your back. We've been good partners. We never once had to look to see if the other was going to be there. We knew it with certainty. Slayer knows
Whisper is his mate. I know you're mine. I've known it all
along. You have to trust me to take care of you through
this. I swear to you on my life that I know what to do. You
can rely on me, just the way you have through this last year."

She stood looking up at him, her dark eyes filled with
liquid, breaking his heart as she gave a slight shake of her
head.

He stepped closer, a hand on either side of her head,
caging her in. "Talk to me, Lotus. You've always been able
to talk to me. I need to know what you're so afraid of."

"Don't you know, Gedeon?"

Her voice was a low whisper. So soft. The sound crept
over him like a caress. He shook his head. "No, baby, you're
going to have to spell it out for me."

She took a deep breath. Let it out. She had courage. She
didn't look away from him. She kept her gaze fixed on his.
"I'm in love with you."

She *loved* him? Meiling loved him? She looked him
right in the eye and said the words to him. She said she
was *in love* with him. His legs wanted to turn to rubber,
and his heart melted. She could turn him inside out with
her honesty.

"I don't want a little part of you. I want all of you. Watching you with other women is devastating. I can't risk you
ripping out my heart that way. I just can't. You have no
idea what you did to me that night I walked in on you with

that woman. I knew I couldn't have that part of you. Your cock. The sex. You gave that to other women, but your room? That was mine. We had that intimacy. No one else. You gave me everything else. At least I told myself I had everything else. I wanted you physically, but if all I got was what I had, I knew I had the best part of you."

Gedeon remained silent. He wanted to defend himself, but what the hell kind of defense could he mount? He told her what happened. Her female had made Slayer beyond insane. Gedeon had been just as bad, just as out of control. Rene had never seen him so far gone. It hadn't been Rene's fault that he misunderstood what Gedeon was telling him. He'd needed a woman and fast, but he'd wanted Rene to get him to the club, not bring a woman to his home.

"She was there. In *my* space. Where you belonged to me. I was so devastated I didn't know how to process. I could barely breathe. Or think. The worst of it was, I was enraged. Had I run across that woman I might have killed her. I'm not like that, and it shook me to know I was capable of such a terrible thing as murder simply because I was jealous."

He had to stop her. "Meiling. No. That wasn't you. When your female is in heat, her cycle is vicious on her. On you. I'm your mate. You witnessed me with another female. To you that was a betrayal. A female was with the man who was supposed to be with you. Had you been with another man at the club the other night, I would have killed him. I wouldn't have been able to stop myself. That's why shifters must be so careful when the woman comes into the Han Vol Dan. The emergence. Passions run so hot."

"Murder might be passion to you, Gedeon, but it's horrible and terrifying and *shameful* to think I would harm an innocent woman because she was with you consensually. You wanted to be with her. *In our room*."

Damn it. She had tears in her eyes all over again. Her

voice dripped with them. How the hell did men do this? "Lotus, don't. She was never supposed to be there. I don't bring women to our room. You know that. I never will again. There never will be other women. I swear to you, Meiling. There will never be another woman. It's only you. It's always going to be you."

"I don't like who I am, loving you. I don't want to be a woman who would kill another woman because my man cheats on me. I'd rather kill him if I'm going to kill someone."

"You aren't going to kill anyone," he assured her. "I earned your trust. You know I did. Whisper's rising caught us all off guard. I should have known that was what was happening to us. I'll admit that. If I hadn't been so wrapped up in you, I would have figured it out sooner. You know I've got a brain. When it comes to you, maybe I'm not so smart. I never had my emotions involved before. But I know now. I'm prepared for what's going to happen and I can take care of us."

"What is it you expect of me?"

She looked vulnerable. Fragile. Even scared. Meiling never appeared afraid, and she was afraid of him. He'd done that, frightened her. Made her feel as if he might turn on her at any moment, betray her just to have casual sex with another woman.

"I expect you to be my full partner just as you've been this last year. Take on cases with me. I expect that you will meet my needs in the bedroom just as I'll meet yours. And I expect that you will communicate openly with me so we don't have misunderstandings, especially during Whisper's rising."

"I'm not moving into your bedroom." Meiling tilted her chin stubbornly. "I like my own space. If I'm going back with you and we resume our partnership, I'm not giving up my suite."

He studied her mutinous expression. "Lotus, I got rid

of the bed and all the sheets, blankets, pillows and comforters. The room was completely fumigated. You won't be able to smell anything in there."

"I'll *see* her."

"Only if you persist in wanting to see her. You have to forgive mistakes, Meiling. You taught me that."

She had. She was clinging to anything she could so she could push him away, even though she knew he wasn't to blame for her being afraid of their future together. She'd convinced herself they wouldn't work.

Her long lashes fluttered, then lifted again. "I can't take you breaking my heart again, Gedeon. I can't. I was good being alone. I made myself strong and created a life for myself. You came along and changed all that. For all I know, Whisper would have stayed hidden if Slayer hadn't been constantly close by her. I knew how to handle everything by myself, but now there's you."

He framed her face with hands. "As vulnerable as you think you are, Meiling, imagine how I feel. I don't know how to function properly without you. I've been on my own and doing very well, if all the reports are true." He rubbed the pad of his thumb along her full lower lip. "Imagine my shock when along comes this beautiful woman who I cannot do without. Take the chance, Lotus. We'll set our own rules and live by them."

To his surprise, she laughed. It was very low, but it was her musical laughter. "You mean you'll set the rules and expect me to live with them. I won't, but you'll be ever the hopeful."

"Are you going to do this with me, Lotus? Or do we have to keep talking?"

"You make so much sense, Leopard Boy. You act like I have a choice, but in reality, I don't."

"You have choices. We can stay here in this little room while I talk your ear off. I'll be at my best with my persuasive charm while we wait for Whisper to rise. Or we can head back to New Orleans and try to follow up on the lead I got about Laverne's disappearance."

Meiling looked around the small, dark room and then sighed. "Fine. Let's go back to New Orleans, but if one single shifter tries to mate with Whisper, I'm pushing you into the swamp."

14

WHISPER had been very quiet—too quiet. Meiling didn't trust her, not when it came to work. She didn't want to chance being in the middle of a business meeting and having her young leopard suddenly decide now was the time to leap to the surface. Whisper smoldered with heat. Was fiery hot. Sultry. Flirtatious. She rose fast, wreaked havoc on anyone close and then retreated just as fast, leaving Meiling in a terrible state of arousal.

The swamp was alive with dark swirls of purple and light lavender creeping through cypress trees. The moon was out, illuminating the veils of moss hanging from branches to dip into the water's edge, turning the moss a pale, silvery blue. The crimson sunset mixed with blue to make up the rare purple. Splashes of deep red and blue slashed through the trees to pour into the duckweed-carpeted water below.

Gedeon guided their boat through the swamp with the

assurance of a man who knew his way, even in the waning light. Movement was all around them, in the water, above them in the air and through the trees. It wasn't quiet; the swamp had its own music at night. At times the bellow of an alligator signaled the resident male proclaiming his territory.

"Hell of a way to keep from being followed," Gedeon said, flashing her a grin.

The night was warm and humid with few clouds. Ordinarily Meiling loved coming out in the swamp and did so at every opportunity, but she felt the wild setting would only encourage Whisper to rise more often when she wasn't ready to fully emerge. It was nerve-racking. She had come to believe she didn't have a leopard, so she had never given the Han Vol Dan of her kind much thought. She wasn't prepared for the constant state of arousal. The heat of her skin. The burning between her legs. The relentless drive she found so hard to ignore. Now she was nervous around Gedeon, which was silly.

Gedeon stayed very close to Meiling, more protective than she'd ever imagined he could be, but always the same on the outside—that dangerous, stone-faced man others stepped aside for. He needed to stay close to her. She wanted him to, because she was terrified of Whisper rising without Gedeon right there to help her when she needed him the most. Or when Whisper needed Slayer.

Whisper seemed to sleep now that she'd been officially claimed. That didn't seem to bother either Gedeon or Slayer the way it did Meiling. They seemed to take it in stride that her leopard would just curl up and take a long nap, making everyone wait for her.

"Are you still upset because Whisper isn't showing herself?" Gedeon asked.

He was driving the boat slowly through the duckweed, maneuvering around a few floating logs, including two that were alligators, not logs.

"Clearly, she's a drama queen. A little diva," Meiling said with a hint of disgust.

Gedeon laughed. Meiling couldn't help but love the sound since it was so rare. Gedeon just didn't laugh. Never when around others. He kept that sound mostly for her.

She gave him a look from under her lashes. "It isn't really that funny, Gedeon," although with him laughing it was. "Slayer's going to have a little entitled brat on his hands. I don't even know how she got that way." Total exasperation.

"Lotus."

The way he said his chosen nickname for her always sent a shiver of heat down her spine. "Don't make excuses for her. She drives me right up the wall. I used to be even-tempered. Now I'm totally unpredictable. I don't know what I'm going to do or say from one minute to the next."

"I hate to be the one to let you in on reality, baby, but you've always been unpredictable."

Meiling assessed his demeanor. He didn't look or sound as if he was joking. She tilted her chin at him, daring him to be serious. "I am always the calm, reasonable one in every situation and you're the powder keg. Look at how you were at the meeting with Guy Hawkins. If I hadn't been there, you might have killed him."

"But then he most likely deserves killing. I have amazing judgment in these circumstances. Ordinarily, you're all about compassion, other than your atrocious temper, which, don't worry, Lotus, I'm more than willing to overlook."

His gaze had switched from her face to the water, as the boat chugged very slowly around the "bony knees" that were broken roots of cypress trees left in the shallow water. He took them down a channel that cut between two long strips of land before taking them out to the main flowing river.

Gedeon could make her laugh no matter if he was serious

or not. That arrogant assurance of his had always appealed to her from the moment she'd first encountered him.

"Why haven't you insisted on me moving in with you?" She blurted the question that had been bothering her the most since they'd returned to New Orleans.

Gedeon had made every effort to ensure that all details in their lives were back to normal. They took their walk to the Café Du Monde together in the morning and at night. They worked the three open cases together during the day. He didn't go to the club at night, but he did send Rene to gather information. That was when she realized how vital the nightclub was to their business. It hadn't been just a place for him to acquire women. It was also the place where he attained vast amounts of information. The one thing he didn't do was invite her to his bedroom.

She knew remodeling was going on because the workmen were there continually. She could smell paint. He came to her room at night, but he always asked. Always. He had the ability to get in. He had the code to her suite, but he didn't use it. He asked if he could come to her room, and she couldn't help herself—she said yes.

Gedeon would lie on the bed with her just as he had done in his room, talking about nothing and everything. Making her laugh when she was tense. She would find herself relaxing, her fingers massaging his scalp just as she did when they were in his room. Whisper would remain quiet, and they would drift off to sleep together. Slayer seemed satisfied, leaving Gedeon in peace.

"You have moved in with me, Meiling."

Gedeon's voice was gentle. When he spoke in that tone, he melted her heart. She couldn't look away from him, even when he was dividing his attention, maneuvering the shallow channel and avoiding the hazards in their way.

"I want you to be happy and to feel safe in your own home. More than anything, I want you to know you're always safe with me. Whisper will rise when she has no choice. Slayer is going to warn me when she's making serious progress. The little stops and starts she's making now are just her hormones waking her up and telling her she's coming into her own. You made a commitment to me, and you honor your commitments so there's no need to push you, Lotus. We know we have chemistry together. When you're ready emotionally, and you trust that your heart and soul are safe with me, we can move in together. Or if Whisper rises before we have the chance to cement our relationship fully, we'll continue as we are after her heat."

Meiling was grateful the boat swept around the tip of the strip of land and into open river water so Gedeon could accelerate. It was much harder to hear with the boat going faster, bumping over the choppy surface heading for the rendezvous point.

She was in love with Gedeon, and every time she thought she couldn't love him more, he would say something she found intensely beautiful and she fell even harder. He was the toughest man to understand. He really was. She'd spent an entire year with him. Technically, she did live with him. She witnessed him with others. Had she simply observed him, an outsider watching him, she would have thought he was a psychopath, incapable of caring for anyone. He never showed his emotions to others. His eyes, so alive with tenderness or laughter for her, were cold and hard, devoid of all emotion around others.

Meiling looked around her at the swamp as the night was closing in. The trees gave refuge to so many birds. Colors changed with the sinking of the sun. The bright crimson shooting through the trees had already given way to orange. The purple and lavender effects were gone, leaving the color spectrum quite different in just a short time. That was the swamp, ever-changing and yet the same.

The incessant drone of insects could be heard above the

engine. Looking up, she could see bats wheeling and dipping in a dance as they dove to catch flying bugs. Some skimmed the water close to the shore. She spotted nests high in the branches of a cypress tree. A raccoon family stopped moving to stare at them as they skimmed past.

Gedeon cut the lights on the boat just before choosing the left fork in the river. Once again, he slowed their speed significantly. She gave a little jump.

"We're okay, Lotus." His voice was steady.

He always knew when she was nervous. They were that connected. She pressed her palm over her heart.

"I'm good," she assured him. "Are we close?"

"We should be. The strip of land is right around the next bend. There should be a pier we can tie up to."

He turned the lights on again as they rounded the next strip of land, and there was the pier. A boat was already tied up there. Two men waited. Meiling recognized both. Drake Donovan owned the most well-known international security company in the world. He had a reputation for getting the job done. His people were well trained, the best at what they did. They worked in every country, entering stealthily when necessary, striking hard and getting out fast with whomever they had gone in after. Donovan was a shifter and head of one of the local lairs. She'd heard he'd had to clean up a huge mess when he'd taken over. The lair appeared to be thriving now.

The second man was Remy Boudreaux, the homicide detective and Drake Donovan's brother-in-law. Married to Bijou Breaux, a famous singer and owner of Blue's Club in New Orleans, Remy was an extremely intelligent man. He had an eye for details and an ear for lies. It would be difficult to get anything over on him.

Donovan had chosen the meeting location. Gedeon had been careful to explain that it was imperative they not be seen together. By giving Donovan the choice of where to meet, Gedeon had given him a huge advantage. There was no doubt in Meiling's mind there was a shooter concealed somewhere watching them just in case they wanted to harm Donovan. In some circles Drake Donovan had a price on his head. Gedeon was known to be a man who might collect that hefty price tag.

Meiling had excellent night vision and she took her time carefully studying their surroundings. The pier looked new, as did the landing leading up to the land jutting out to meet the water lapping at it. Fragrant smells mixed with the more natural scents of the swamp. Even the strange and intriguing aromas couldn't distract her from locating Donovan's sniper.

The swamp had been cut back, baring more land on the east side and giving those coming from the river to the Mercier property room to walk easily over to the west side, where there was a large section set up for picnics amid fields of wildflowers.

Meiling studied the trees in the swamp where the Spanish moss hung like long lacy bluish-gray veils. The shooter would need a clear view not only to the pier, but also to the picnic area, where they would have their discussion with Donovan. The sniper couldn't risk changing locations. That meant there were only so many trees he could be in.

Gedeon guided their boat in slowly.

I need a couple of minutes, she advised, not risking talking aloud. Both Gedeon and she could read lips. There was always the possibility the sniper could as well.

Gedeon bent down and began fiddling with something on the floor of the boat as she sat waiting, seemingly patiently. It was natural for her to look around at her surroundings. Mostly she appeared to be looking at the field of gorgeous flowers, but she'd already narrowed her suspect trees down to three. One of the three, the only real sturdy branch that would hold a sniper, would make the angle awkward—not impossible, just awkward. She dismissed it.

The second tree was dead center between the other two

and seemed the likeliest choice. She flicked it another quick glance, storing the details quickly before switching her gaze back to the field of wildflowers. In her mind, she went over the specifics of the trees, every little aspect. The tree seemed so perfect, the branches offering up the perfect crotch for a sniper to lie in and set up his weapon. Lacy moss hung down to give him plenty of cover. It would be difficult for anyone to spot him. At the same time, he had a good field of vision for the picnic area and part of the pier. What he didn't have was vision on the river itself or where the boats would be tying up, at least not that Meiling could see.

Best guess, sniper is in the tree to the left of the extremely tall cypress, second row back. A gum tree, behind the row of cypress trees.

Gedeon climbed out of the boat onto the pier and took a deliberate look around before tying up and then holding out his hand to her. *I spotted him. He's good. Looks like part of the tree. I wouldn't have seen him if you hadn't told me he was there. You wear that vest like I told you?*

She smiled at him. Even when he spoke telepathically to her, he could sound bossy. She inclined her head and stepped up to his side, walking with him to meet Drake Donovan and Remy Boudreaux. Both stood waiting at the other end of the pier. Meiling resisted smiling, knowing she was correct and the sniper hadn't been able to cover them where Gedeon was tying up his boat. Had he been able to see them, Donovan would have used his good manners and come to greet them.

"Gedeon, it's been a long time," Drake said, extending his hand. "Meiling. Finally in person. Seeing you in passing has been frustrating. We're always too busy to visit."

"Midnight rendezvous in the middle of the swamp are always so intriguing," Meiling replied. She couldn't resist laughing at Remy's expression. "You have to admit, it got you both out here. Thank you for coming. I imagine your wives weren't so happy giving you up this late. It isn't midnight but it is the dinner hour."

Gedeon put a proprietorial hand on Meiling's lower back as they followed Drake to a picnic table. Drake waved them to the bench, just as Meiling knew he would. Instead of sitting down, she went over to the very edge of the field of wildflowers. The wind was blowing gently, causing a ripple effect much like the wave of an ocean among the flowers. She knelt to tighten the cord on her high boot while still looking out over the fluttering petals and long stems with their various shades of green leaves.

It was easy enough to transfer her gun from her boot to her inside jacket pocket. She could shoot the wings off a butterfly with this gun at the required distance. It wasn't a rifle, but it didn't need to be. It just needed to be that accurate and have the range.

"These flowers not only are gorgeous, but they smell unbelievable," she said as she rose. She looked around her again. "Gedeon, have you been out here before?"

He took her arm and led her back to the picnic table. She subtly pressed toward his left so she could take the seat she needed to cover them. She was incredibly fast. She knew she could leap over the table and be in the field while getting off several shots at the sniper. At the same time, Gedeon could kill both Drake and Remy before Meiling needed to provide him with covering fire.

"Came out here a few years ago. Charisse asked me to do a little work for her."

"What can I help you with?" Drake asked.

"And why all the cloak and dagger?" Remy demanded.

Meiling couldn't help laughing again. Remy sounded a little disgruntled. "I should have brought snacks. You sound like you could have low blood sugar."

"He's always like that, Meiling," Drake said. "Ignore

his bad temper. Why is it we had to meet here rather than at the inn or the club?"

"Or the police station," Remy added.

"I would much have preferred the Café Du Monde," Meiling said. "I do love that place."

"You assured me that anything I say to you will be held in confidence," Gedeon said. "I need to know Boudreaux agrees to the same or we'll have to pass on the meet."

"I wouldn't have come if I couldn't keep my mouth shut, Gedeon," Remy said. "I'm giving you a bad time, but I know you wouldn't have dragged us out here if it wasn't important."

Meiling kept her gaze fixed on both men, although she did her best to sweep the area around them often. She wanted to take in as many of their gestures as possible or catch any subtle signs between them. She was very good at picking up small, nearly imperceptible signals others might miss.

"Guy Hawkins asked us to find his wife, Laverne, he claims has gone missing. He had hired a bodyguard to watch over her. She's bipolar, and when she goes off her medication, she apparently does all kinds of out-of-character things. He's worried about what she might do."

Gedeon relayed the information in a noncommittal tone.

"You don't believe him," Drake said.

Gedeon shook his head. "No, I think he's full of shit. Laverne is bipolar, that much is true, but she's careful to keep it under control. Hawkins hired a bodyguard. That man's name is Edge Wilson. He's been in the business over twenty-five years and has a stellar reputation. He isn't the kind of man to run off with a client on a whim believing he'd never get caught—especially when she's the famous wife of an even more famous music producer. Wilson is intelligent. Doesn't do drugs and I doubt he suddenly started. I could be wrong, but this feels more like a planned escape than a sudden bipolar episode. Oh, and incidentally, just in case you don't recognize the name, Wilson works for your security company."

Remy sank down on the tabletop. Meiling allowed her gaze to sweep along the swamp and the line of cedar and gum trees. The sniper was easing back at Remy's signal. That didn't make her less watchful, but it did give her an opportunity to take a closer look at the field of wildflowers that seemed to stretch for miles behind the picnic area. She'd never seen so many brightly colored flowers in various shades of red, yellow and orange giving way to blues, purples, pinks and greens in one place.

Gedeon continued with his explanation. "Hawkins was adamant that Laverne be found immediately. It was his bad luck to hire us. We dig deep and we don't stop until we complete the case we take on. In this instance, the moment we became concerned that Laverne had a reason for leaving and that she was afraid of her husband, we took a good look at Hawkins."

Drake sat down as well, absorbed in the conversation. "Guy has approached me on several occasions requesting security for his wife and himself around town and when they attend specific events, such as fundraisers. He's always appeared to be very much concerned over his wife's safety. He speaks with great pride about her accomplishments."

Remy nodded in agreement. "He approached Bijou and asked if she would highlight a new band he's backing. Bijou listened to them and agreed they're very good. They've opened in the club and have been a big hit. Most of the bands or singers Hawkins collaborates with or backs are amazing. Bijou thinks this band is going to go far."

"There's no doubt Hawkins has a good mind for business, and it's served him well. On the other hand, he isn't quite as astute in his relationships," Gedeon said. "He's had a string of lovers, most didn't last long and few lived with him."

"Until Laverne," Drake pointed out. "When he found

her, even though there was an age gap, everyone was very happy for him."

"No one kept track of his lovers," Gedeon said. "They weren't famous and newsworthy. He didn't take them to the openings of shows or push them into the spotlight. Once in a while the paparazzi would catch him coming out of a club with a woman on his arm. I believe that photograph appearing in a magazine saved her life."

Remy leaned into Gedeon's space. "What are you talking about? Do you think Hawkins is some kind of serial killer?"

"I think he might be, yes. Not your average hack-the-woman-to-pieces. I don't think he does the killing himself. I think he has someone who does it for him. But he orders it. It must give him some kind of smug satisfaction to know he can order these women killed and no one has a clue."

Meiling looked up at Gedeon. His voice changed subtly. There was growl in his voice, an underlying threat she knew was very real. A shiver went down her spine. He had a real problem with any man hurting women. The moment he had real proof that Guy Hawkins gave the order to murder his lovers, the man was going to die. Gedeon would see to it.

She looked at Remy, a homicide detective. A shifter. A man who obviously could hear lies. If Hawkins turned up dead, the first person he would suspect of killing him would be Gedeon. How could she cover for Gedeon? She was going to have to find a way because Remy Boudreaux wouldn't be easy to fool.

"Why do you believe Hawkins ordered his former lovers killed?" Remy prompted.

Meiling couldn't just sit there. She and Gedeon had talked this over, coming to Drake and Remy and disclosing what they knew and suspected of Hawkins. At the time she thought it was a good idea. Now she wasn't so certain.

She sent Gedeon a sign to be very cautious how he worded what he disclosed to Remy.

"It was obvious from the beginning that something wasn't right with Laverne's disappearance," Gedeon began. He appeared relaxed, but then, he always did. Meiling knew better. Gedeon was convinced Hawkins had ordered several women killed. "If she had a bipolar episode, forgetting to take her medicine, she would have just taken off, not planned carefully for months, siphoning off money and stashing clothes away from her house. Her bodyguard wouldn't have been on board unless he felt her life was at risk. When Meiling and I investigated Hawkins's past affairs over the years, we found six women who had disappeared. No one has seen or heard from them. The only common tie is their relationship with Hawkins."

"Why haven't the police questioned him?" Remy asked.

"I'm sure they have at some point, although most likely only briefly. He broke up with these women and it might have been six months later that they disappeared. Maybe less time, maybe more."

"No bodies found?" Remy pursued.

"No," Gedeon conceded. "Part of the reason I insisted on meeting you where we wouldn't be seen is that from the moment we left Hawkins's office we've been followed. Meiling circled back and got detailed photographs of the man watching us. His name is McGregor Handler."

Both Drake and Remy reacted, Remy with a swift intake of breath and narrowing of his eyes and Drake with a shake of his head.

"He's in New Orleans?" Drake asked.

Gedeon nodded. "Chasing Meiling and me all over. I wouldn't be too surprised if he's dragged some poor guide out of his dinner and is trying to figure out where we are."

"Does he have a tracking device on either one of you?" Remy asked.

"He tried to drop one on Meiling," Gedeon said, a slight

grin escaping at the memory. "Slid up next to her at the Café Du Monde and got in close. She never takes kindly to that sort of thing. When he tried to make the drop, she had already moved away from him and he nearly had his hand down some tourist's pants."

Remy laughed. "I'll bet there was quite an uproar."

"The woman was angry and quite loud in expressing her complaint. She called McGregor a pervert and told everyone he tried to grope her. He turned bright red and tried to say that he'd been pushed into her, but she wouldn't stop yelling. The waiter tried to calm her down. McGregor escaped with his little tracking device. Meiling was already sitting on her bench by the river, so he didn't have a clue she was aware of him."

"The tourist is lucky he didn't shove a knife into her," Drake said. "Or that he didn't follow her to wherever she was staying and do it later."

"I should have checked on her afterward, but I was so worried about Laverne I didn't think of it," Gedeon admitted. "I was afraid we were too late and she was already dead. I thought McGregor was put in place to watch us just in case we were too close and found her body."

"I didn't hear of a woman murdered recently," Remy assured. "Not like that."

"I received a tip recently," Gedeon continued, "which is why we're here. I believe Edge Wilson is in San Antonio working on Jake Bannaconni's ranch. It's impossible to get near that ranch without a special invitation. I can go through the Amurovs, they're friends with him, but that could take time as well. I need to talk to him. If I found him, McGregor can find him. If I'm right about all of this, it would be a death sentence for him."

"You want me to call Jake and arrange a meeting with you and Edge on his ranch."

"Yes. I want to make certain I'm right. I'd like to know

Laverne is safe. I want you to ask Wilson to talk to us. And I'd like that meeting to happen on the Bannaconni ranch."

Meiling thought it was significant that Remy and Drake exchanged a long look but neither asked Gedeon what his intentions were once he knew for certain.

"I'll arrange the meeting with Jake. I agree it would be best to hold it at his ranch. If you fly into the San Antonio airport, he can arrange for a helicopter to pick you up and take you to his ranch. Even if McGregor manages to follow you to San Antonio, he won't know where you're going. As soon as Jake replies I'll send you the thumbs-up," Drake said.

"Thanks," Gedeon said. "We won't keep you from your families any longer."

"You want to turn over any files to me so I can continue looking into the disappearances of those women?" Remy asked. "Their families must be looking for them."

"Hawkins chose them carefully. They didn't really have family who would look for them," Gedeon said. "That's the true tragedy. He essentially erased them."

When they were working, they were careful to keep a distance from each other just in case they had to leap into action or become weapons. The unspoken rule didn't stop her from wanting to fling her arms around his neck and hold him to her. He gave nothing away to the two men, but she *felt* the animosity eating at him.

Meiling had always been able to catch insights into his emotions. She knew him now after a year, and he could become very dangerous extremely fast when it came to anything to do with violence against women or children. She didn't want to take chances that Remy or Drake might "read" him.

She flashed a quick smile to everyone and started back in the direction of the pier, wrapping her arms around her middle. "I'd love to have a tour of this place when I have loads of time. Right this moment, I'm always concerned

my hussy of a leopard is going to start showing herself."
Deliberately, she shivered and turned a heated gaze on
Gedeon.

Remy and Drake rose instantly. Gedeon followed her
very closely.

"I had no idea you were contending with your leopard,
Meiling," Drake apologized. "Forgive me. I would have
sped things up."

"You're handling it with amazin' grace," Remy added.
"It isn't easy."

"That's thanks to Gedeon." Meiling poured confidence
into her voice along with absolute trust. She sent him a look
from under her lashes—one filled with love. She knew he
didn't like her to do anything personal when they were on
a job because it was distracting, but right at that moment
the love she felt for him was overwhelming and she had to
show him. She told herself it was the way he always reacted when someone harmed a woman. Who wouldn't fall
in love with a man like that?

*Knock it off, Lotus. You make me vulnerable. I can't
feel that way when we're surrounded by the enemy.*

He handed her into the boat, practically tossing her in,
except he didn't. He was gentle. He just felt as if he *wanted*
to throw her in. Not so much when he untied the boat and
stepped in himself. Lifting a hand to Drake and Remy, he
started the engine. It didn't dare give him any trouble but
fired right up the very first time he pulled the rope.

He was silent as he took them through the open water
and then cut through the shallow stream that would take
them back to the next shortcut to their own pier.

"You can't do that." His voice was very low, and he
didn't look at her.

She did her best to keep a smile from her voice. "Do
what, Gedeon?" Trying to sound innocent. Her freaking
cat made her sound sultry. The humidity in the swamp
seemed to go up a degree or two.

"You know damn well what you do to me, Lotus. One look like that from you and I can't think straight. I've told you that before. When we're conducting business, it has to stay business."

She rubbed her palm along her upper thigh. "You're right. I'm sorry. It's just that at times you say things or do things that I find irresistible."

He didn't turn his head toward her but stared out over the shallow but fast-moving channel. She found herself fascinated by the way his fingers curled around the rudder as he steered the boat around any obstacle. The lights shone across the water, illuminating the branches caught and held by larger rocks. The channels were continually changing. Gedeon knew the swamp, but he still had to take care in the ever-changing waters.

Meiling turned her face up to look at the sky. Despite it being overcast, bats dipped and wheeled, performing their nightly dance. Insects droned and owls occasionally shrieked a disappointed cry as they missed their prey. Fingers of fog drifted through the scattered cedar trees. The light from the moon turned swaying moss to blue-gray and the fog added an extra layer of silver to the lacy veils.

A lump formed in her throat and tears burned behind her eyes. She didn't know why she still was so unsure of Gedeon's feelings for her. She knew Slayer was wild about Whisper. She knew Gedeon wanted her body. She just didn't know if he was in love with her. He never said the words to her.

She told herself she didn't need the words—after all, they were just words. Nothing special. People told their spouses they loved them and then cheated or tried to kill them, like Guy Hawkins. Words didn't matter. Actions did. Gedeon had gutted his bedroom for her. She hadn't asked him to. He'd just done it. She hadn't asked him to wait to have sex with her. He'd done that too.

"Lotus, tell me what you're thinking."

"I'd rather not."

"Uh-oh. Are we going to play twenty questions? Is this about Hawkins? McGregor? Or me? You've got your moody aura surrounding you, so I'm not certain which of us is being scrutinized."

"I don't have a moody aura." She turned back to him, narrowing her eyes and trying to look intimidating.

Gedeon flashed a little grin and slowed the boat even more, so they were nearly stopped in the dark water. "Baby, you look so sweet you give me all sorts of bad ideas. Very bad. Indecent. In fact, downright dirty. That look you're giving me right now turns me on."

"Gedeon, drive the boat and stop looking at me. Do you not see those eyes staring at us? They're converging on the boat, and we're in such shallow water I think they could climb aboard and have a feast."

"There's that tone you use that makes me hard as a rock." He rubbed the front of his jeans. "Why don't you come over here and help me out?"

"I'm not coming over there. This boat is balanced just the way we are. If I'm over there with you, it throws the balance off and we could end up in the water with the alligators," she pointed out. "Take a look around, Leopard Boy. There are red eyes staring at us from the banks on either side and they look hungry. I'm not even going to count the ones swimming toward us. Get us moving now." She tried very hard not to encourage him with laughter.

Gedeon made a show of looking around them at the red eyes slowly going through the water right toward the boat. "They are getting a mite close."

"You are so ridiculous," Meiling said, covering her mouth with her fingers because it was impossible not to laugh. "Fire up the engine."

He increased the speed just a little, going around a particularly large alligator. "That one is bigger than you are."

"It wasn't," she denied. The alligator was longer than she was. Probably weighed more as well, but she wasn't conceding that to him.

"I could get out and measure."

"You would too, just to prove a point." There was no hiding her laughter from him.

He looked pleased, his eyes lighting up. "I love the sound of your laughter, Meiling. It could be my favorite sound in the world. That or the way you say my name sometimes."

There. He did it again. It wasn't just his words. It was the way he said them. His tone. Velvet soft, like a caress. He wrapped her up in his casual statement that wasn't casual at all. He could turn her inside out with the way he would suddenly, out of the blue, issue his declarations. Was that his way of telling her he was in love with her? She knew nothing of real relationships. She didn't trust herself to know one way or another. She just knew she didn't want to lose what she had with him.

She smiled at him, pretty certain her heart was in her eyes, so she looked away from him as he took the boat up the channel and back to the next fork heading home. He had such a great sense of direction in the swamp. In the dark of night, there weren't any landmarks, and yet he always seemed to know exactly where each turn was, even if he was taking a shortcut.

There were sections of the river where he drove fast and others where he went slower and more cautiously. She paid little attention to the actual direction and more to the beauty of the night and his skill. The way he looked against silvery-black water or the backdrop of an abundance of trees took her breath. Gedeon always gave off a quiet confidence.

By the time they made it back to their pier, she couldn't think of anything or anyone but Gedeon. When he tied up their boat, she noticed the smooth, fluid way his muscles rippled beneath his clothes as he crouched on the wooden pier and then stood to extend his hand to her. She stepped onto the wooden boards, and he tugged her to him easily. Meiling slid one arm around his ribs and leaned into him.

Gedeon cupped her chin and tipped her face up to his. "I want to show you the new master bedroom, Lotus. Will you come with me and at least look at it?"

There was seduction in the smooth velvet of his tone. In the glittering green of his eyes. There was no resisting, not with the way emotions were so overwhelming and the way her body reacted so physically to his. She nodded, unable to speak.

15

MEILING was Gedeon's, and she deserved to know she was loved for herself. Not for her leopard. Not because she was elite. Not to give their species female children. But for herself. He intended to show her that he truly loved her for who she was.

To say he was shocked at his emotional response to Meiling was an understatement. He hadn't believed himself capable of the kind of depth of feeling he had developed for her. Every trait she brought out in him—although most were good, some were dark and ugly—had developed at an early age and was now brought roaring back. Those dark traits were compounded by his leopard's vicious nature. Still, he found he had a gentle side with her. He found genuine humor with her. She'd given him so much. He wanted to give her as much, if not more.

Slayer had informed him Whisper was going to rise soon. The leopard would do so fast and Gedeon knew the heat would be intense. Sexual passion would be incredible between the two humans, but it wouldn't show Meiling that he wanted her for who she was. Whisper seemed unpredictable, and he needed to ensure his woman knew she was loved.

He didn't know how to say the words to her. He didn't want to say them. The words stuck in his throat. Choked him. Each time he thought to tell her how he felt, something dark and ugly would grow in his gut, stopping him. He resolved to find a way to show her.

They walked through the house together, not turning on lights. They didn't need them. Their night vision was superb. Gedeon held Meiling's hand, feeling the tension in her. She hadn't been near the master bedroom since the night she'd walked in and found him with a woman. He'd despised himself for the out-of-control, frenzied sexual behavior that night. Even now, when he knew the explanation—that her female was rising, causing Slayer to become so inflamed, both man and leopard had been so desperate for sexual release neither could think straight—he was still ashamed.

"I hope you like the changes I made, but if you don't, you tell me what you want different, and I'll have it done." He'd taken everything he knew of her and tried to make the perfect space for the two of them.

Gedeon opened the double doors to the master suite and stepped back to allow her to enter first. The master bedroom had been transformed completely. He hadn't wanted it to look the same at all. The wall facing the swamp was no longer a panel of windows. He had had the craftsmen construct a wall of glass that could be opened to include the wide, screened-in patio. The screen was dark so they could see out, but it would be difficult to see in unless lights were on.

The bed faced the bluish-gray stone fireplace. He'd had all the furniture changed. She seemed to prefer the colors purple and blue, so he'd woven those colors into the duvet on the bed as well as the chairs surrounding the fireplace. The designer he'd worked with brought in potted plants that nearly reached the high ceilings, the green leaves climbing along the walls of one side of the room, creating the look of a rain forest. There was even a water feature, albeit a small one. There were stairs and landings provided for the leopards along the same wall. The room was spacious. Two very large circular stairs down to the sitting area in front of the fireplace created the only division of space in the room. Two giant fans with paddles provided airflow overhead, or they could use the cool air pumped in when preferred.

Gedeon wanted the master bedroom to be all about Gedeon and Meiling, the humans. Her upstairs room could be transformed to be all about Whisper and Slayer, when they came together in a rush of wild passion—not to say it wouldn't happen in both bedrooms. He knew it would.

Meiling stared around the room in shock. Light came in from all directions. There were privacy screens, but he wanted her to have as much open space and as much light as he could give her, as well as different views.

"It's beautiful, Gedeon."

Her reaction was everything he could have asked for. The shock on her face. The little hitch in her voice, as if she couldn't believe he would go to all the trouble and expense for her. He wanted her to know he'd do anything for her.

Gedeon caught her hand again and guided her to the master bathroom. She might as well see that he'd incorporated changes there as well. The double sinks and the huge walk-in shower with the multitude of nozzles, choices of sprays and handheld devices along the racks were meant for two people. He wanted that clear. The side-by-side soaking tubs. The huge Jacuzzi meant for two. This was a masterpiece designed for them.

She turned her face up to his. "You want us to sleep down here together."

"Part of the time." He was honest. "The leopards can use the stairs going up the wall if need be, or they can escape out the window or off the patio into the swamp. It will be much more convenient from the suite upstairs by the time we finish renovating it."

"You're going to change my suite?"

He cupped the side of her face, his thumb brushing along her full bottom lip. "I've got the plans rolled up right there beside the fireplace." He indicated the long tube resting against the stone fireplace.

Her eyes lit up. "I'd love to see the plans."

"I have a few little rules for you to follow before we unroll the plans."

Her eyebrow shot up. "Rules? You have rules?"

"I like to boss you around. That's what you're always saying. I'm bossy and arrogant. So, rules. You want to see the plans for the upstairs suite, you have to follow my rules."

He came up behind her, crowding her body with his, sweeping her dark hair from her nape, pressing kisses along her neck and watching her shiver. Satisfaction shot through him. She couldn't hide her reaction to him. He wrapped his arms around her waist.

"Do you want to see those plans?" He brushed her hair from the side of her neck and kissed the tender skin there, right over her pulse. Then scattered more kisses up to her ear, where he bit gently on her earlobe.

"Yes." Her voice came out a whisper. "Tell me your rules, Leopard Boy."

He laughed, just as she knew he would. He moved around her to face her. Meiling was very slight, but most of the time he didn't notice unless they were working a case and her diminutive stature was to their advantage, or like now, when he towered over her. His shoulders were wide, and his body seemed to make two of hers. He looked straight into her dark eyes as his hands dropped to the little buttons on her very feminine blouse.

"I get the pleasure of removing your clothes first, before anything else." Very slowly he slipped the first button from the loop, the pads of his fingers brushing bare skin.

She didn't pull away. Her long lashes fluttered. She had those beautiful black sweeping lashes that were feminine beyond description and called attention to her dark, hypnotic eyes. He kept his fingers moving down that line of pretty little square buttons until her blouse was open, revealing her mint-green bra and the appealing bare strip of skin on her belly. Gedeon pushed the material from her shoulders and let it flutter to the floor. He paid no attention to her sudden shyness when he reached behind her, unhooked her bra with one hand and tossed that little scrap of lace aside as well.

He let his breath out. "You're so damn beautiful, Meiling." Catching her hips, he drew her closer to him and took her mouth. He'd resisted for what seemed an entire day. The moment his lips touched hers, she caught fire— or he did. They ignited. The chemistry between them was explosive. He wanted to give her tenderness. Leopards were hot as Hades when they came together. He wanted a slow burn for her, not this crazy wildfire that roared through his veins and poured steel into his cock.

"Lotus." He breathed her name, trying to slow things down, pressing his forehead to hers. He could still feel her on his skin, in his mouth, down his throat. Most importantly, he could feel her moving in his soul.

"Without you, I've got nothing at all. You know that, don't you?"

She gave a little shake of her head, her eyes alive with too much emotion, just as he knew his were. They both felt it. It was impossible not to be shaken when neither of them had been loved, Meiling even less than him. Now, knowing what they had together, Gedeon felt vulnerable, wide open. It didn't matter. She was worth it. If he lost, he would always have had this time with her.

His hands dropped to the waistband of her jeans even as he kept his forehead pressed against hers. All the while he forced air through his lungs. Breathing with need of her. With love for her. "I don't want you to ever think I want you for Slayer and Whisper. I'm a very selfish man. You found your way inside me, and I don't want to give you up. Not for any reason. Not for our leopards and not for misunderstandings."

He pushed her jeans and panties over the curve of her hips, crouching down in front of her as he did so until he could pick up her foot and slide the material free and then the other foot. Her hands went to his shoulders to steady herself. His name was a whisper between them. An entreaty. He didn't know whether she intended to pull him close or push him away when her fists knotted on his hair, but he wedged his wide shoulders between her legs, the scent of her calling to him.

He moved his palm gently up the inside of her thigh and allowed his tongue to follow the pads of his fingers. Her skin was pure satin. His took his time reaching his goal, that liquid honey that drew him like a magnet. He couldn't resist tasting her. He was already addicted, having fed hungrily on her when her leopard had driven her beyond her endurance. It wasn't the same. Now he wanted to spend time worshiping her.

Standing, Gedeon lifted her in his arms and carried her to the bed. Her eyes were half-dazed, her arms circling his neck, drawing him down with her when he placed her in the middle of the duvet. Using one hand to rid himself of his T-shirt, he stripped the rest of his clothes from his body, unable to take his gaze from hers.

She was so beautiful. His woman. He moved over her. Slow. Blanketing her. Pulling her hands above her head. Threading his fingers through hers. Staring directly into her eyes. He swore the earth moved. Time seemed to tunnel. Kissing her sent flames slow dancing through his veins. Arrowing to his heart.

He felt the heat of her entrance welcoming him with her honey. So hot. Surrounding him. So tight. Too tight. Until that silken haven gripped his steel cock and reluctantly allowed him home. It was a struggle to move through those incredibly constricting petals that were hesitant to give way to his invasion. Then he was all the way in her, sinking deep. For a long moment they were together. Sharing the same skin. The same soul.

Gedeon began to move. Slow at first. The friction was enough to send fiery streaks of lightning arrowing down his spine. Her silken muscles clenched even tighter around him, dragging over him. He felt every one of her heartbeats right through her sheath.

Her feathery lashes swept down and then back up. She made a sound in her throat and her fingers tightened around his. Her hips rose to meet his. She caught his rhythm as he increased his speed. He thrust harder and she gasped.

"White lightning. It's going to take us with it," he whispered to her. "Do you feel it, Lotus? Moving through us? We're going to burn together."

Her gaze never flinched away from his, not even when he knew raw emotion poured from him to her. Not when his eyes blazed with the absolute inner fire of his kind. With sheer possession. She didn't fear his strength. Or his brutality. She knew he was different, and yet she didn't run from him; she stood with him. She was his partner in every sense of the word.

Now, as his body took hers with exquisite care, he worshipped what was his, taking his time, never hurrying, keeping the burn building slow and steady. Making her feel what he couldn't say. Letting her see into his heart and soul. Looking into hers.

Gedeon expected resistance. She had to know there was

no going back from this. Once he took her like this, she would belong to him for all time. There would be no separating them. No getting them apart. His body moved faster in hers. Streaks of fire rushed over both of them. She gasped. He tightened his hold on her.

"That's it, Lotus. Relax. Come with me," he encouraged.

She gave that little shake of her head, but her gaze clung to his. He could see fear as they climbed higher and higher. As the flames seem to crackle around them and the white lightning arced and forked, jagged bolts that rocked them from the inside out just as he'd promised, he also saw trust in the brown eyes that never flinched away from his.

Her body followed the lead of his—moved with his in a perfect tango as the slow burn turned into a wildfire that burned hot and fierce. Gedeon held her on the edge for what seemed an eternity, whispering to her in a mix of shifter and Russian before coaxing her to let go for him. To fly with him. To let white lightning burn them together.

To his shock, she did exactly what he said. His woman. Fingers threaded through his. Dark eyes staring straight into his. She let her soul fly with his while they burned in the white-hot lightning together.

He let himself collapse over the top of her, desperate for air, trying to drag air into his lungs for both of them. He wasn't certain he had lungs. He thought the fire had, for once in his life, burned him clean. He buried his face in her neck, all too aware he couldn't stay with his full weight on her slight body. He was crushing her. It was just that in this moment, with his cock still jerking in her and the aftershocks rippling through her, he could still share her heart. He still shared her body. Even, like now, her very breath.

Very slowly, reluctantly, he eased his body from hers. He felt bereft. Her arms slid around his neck and clung for a moment. "I'll be right back, Lotus. Let me get a washcloth."

He washed the evidence of her innocence from his cock, reluctant to even do that. Then he returned and very gently cleaned between her legs. A little shiver went through her, but she didn't flinch away from him.

"Did I hurt you, Meiling?"

"No, it was beautiful."

He returned from the master bath and lay down on the bed on his belly, as close to her as he could get without crushing her. The moment he did, her fingers found his hair, just as she had done so many times before, only now it felt so much more intimate. Peace settled over him.

"How is it I knew I could have shot the sniper in the trees and gotten into the field before Drake Donovan or Remy could have stopped me when no others would have been able to do it, Gedeon?" Meiling asked suddenly.

She continued to run her fingers through his thick, unruly hair. He loved when she did that. It made him feel cared for. This was what they had always done together at night— lay close and talked.

He knew sooner or later she would ask questions. He wanted just a little more time before she did, afraid she might think he'd chosen her for yet another reason other than because he was in love with her. Still, he refused to give her less than the truth.

The pads of Meiling's fingers caressed his scalp as her soft voice persisted. "You're so fast when you want to be. Lightning fast, yet you hide it most of time. I have similar speed. And the strength I have isn't normal even for a leopard."

"I'm going to have to go back in the history of the leopard species a little bit to give you answers, Meiling." He tipped his head up just a little to nuzzle the underside of her breast. "It's the kind of history our people would like to forget. You're part of that ugly history and so am I."

Her fingers didn't stop moving in his hair, but he felt her gaze on his face. He kissed her bare skin. It was so necessary that she know how much she meant to him. She was his only. There had been no one before her and there would be no one after her if he ever lost her. He hadn't known he was capable of loving until she came along.

"Why are hesitating to tell me, Gedeon?"

He used his teeth to nip at the very sensitive underside of her breast, then soothed the sting with his tongue when her breath came out in a little rush of reaction. "I always feel as if I'm asking you to accept more and more of me on faith and trust."

She was silent for some time, her fingers continuing to move in his hair, although slower, as if she was thinking, turning things over in her mind.

"You recognized all the way back in the jungle when I moved the branch off you that I was different. It wasn't just that Slayer was quiet when I was around. I told you I didn't have a leopard, but you knew something about me then, didn't you?"

"I suspected, but I didn't know. I was blind at the time. I hadn't seen you, but the more I was around you, the more I had my suspicions that you had superior gifts, just as I do."

"Are there very many others with them?"

"I don't think any others still live, Meiling. That's part of the very shameful history I was about to tell you. I'm going to confess to you that when I tell you everything, I won't look the best to you. I already gave you a little of it."

He had told her a little bit, so hopefully she wouldn't condemn him. She remained silent, so he took a breath and launched into what he knew. "There were three families that seemed to be born with extraordinary gifts. No one knew if it was the combination of genetics, the female and male leopard getting together, but they all emerged around the same time, although in different countries."

Her hand paused in his hair. "What were the countries, Gedeon?"

"Russia. China. North Korea. Those three countries were

rumored to have families with leopards with exceptional gifts. The families were slaughtered."

Gedeon had carefully researched the information once he was able to leave the lair. Few remembered him—or if they did, they didn't speak of him. He left Russia and traveled around the world building his strength and then his network. Along the way he picked up as many allies as possible without giving anything of himself away. Once he found Rene Guidry, he had the man ferret out as much information as possible on the families that had been murdered in the three countries.

"It isn't as if any of the families claimed royalty or lived in castles. My parents worked, but because they could do so many things, they thrived and those working for them did as well. They were very loyal to the *pakhan* and did everything they could to aid him in every way, making him wealthier. The problem with being different is people become jealous and they fear you. Too many people went to my parents rather than the *pakhan*, and he feared they were growing powerful. Then there was the problem of their children. My father and mother had gifts, but it became evident that my siblings had even stronger ones than our parents at such young ages. Fear increased and the demand to rid the lair of us swelled in volume."

"This happened in each country?"

He nodded. "Yes. Later, when I was older, I found out there was a much larger, widespread conspiracy. A group from each of the countries had started the unrest. They wanted to wipe out all members of each of the families. They're still in play today. I imagine those are the ones pursuing you, Meiling."

"You believe I'm a member of one of the families."

He turned his head up to look at her. "I know you are. There's no doubt in my mind."

"Tell me everything that happened to your family before you tell me about mine and the others."

Gedeon knew Meiling was deliberately postponing what he would tell her because she knew it was going to be crushing information. He pressed a kiss into her rib cage and settled against her. Close. Tight. Wanting her to feel his much larger body wrapped around her so she knew she wasn't alone and would never be again.

"My father's best friend knocked on the door late one night. They'd known each other since they were boys. Dad had saved his family from being destitute. The *pakhan* at one point was furious with Uncle Yury and would have had him put to death, but my father spoke for him and saved him. Still, Yury betrayed him. He struck my father from behind and dragged him outside to the mob. They tortured and killed him. They killed my older brother and sister. My mother and I were taken to the *pakhan*."

Meiling's fingers clenched in his hair. "I spent so much time alone, Gedeon, mostly because I wanted to avoid shifters. When I was around them, I would get very upset because I could feel how depraved some of them were. It was easier to avoid them. Libby wanted to be around them, but when she was, I stayed away."

"You have no idea how truly depraved they can be. In the lair where I was raised, trafficking was a way of earning money. Women were bought and sold. The *pakhan* wanted my mother to cooperate with him, to still give him the advice our family had given him that enabled him to excel in his businesses. He also wanted her as his willing mistress. She refused. He sold her over and over to the men in the village, my father's so-called friends. They raped her. He made me watch. He let those same men rape me in front of her."

He told her the truth, keeping his voice devoid of all expression. He couldn't let the rage in him out, not while she was in the room with him. "It became a way of life. Rape and beatings. Whippings. The brutality."

At his admission, tension crept into her body until she was nearly as tight as a bow.

"I learned to be deceptive. Not to show resistance. Not to allow Slayer out. Not to show my mother a hint of what I felt for her."

A small sound escaped her throat. Her hands stroked caresses into his hair. *I understand so much more now. Thank you for telling me.*

She'd said nearly the same thing in the place on the island where she'd been staying when he'd told her part of his past. Her reaction allowed him to continue. "I was also careful never to let anyone see that I was faster or smarter. Eventually, the *pakhan* thought it would be a great idea to train me as his personal assassin. I thought it would be too." This might be even more difficult than admitting he'd been raped as a child. That his mother had been, and he'd had to stop telling her he loved her. He had to stop seeking her out or looking at her.

"I began hunting the men who murdered my family. I couldn't do it all at once. I had to be careful, and I had to make certain I always had an alibi that would hold up. I killed them one by one. I did it when I was a teen. I tried to establish telepathic communication with my mother so I could tell her I was getting justice for what they did, but I never could talk to her that way. I wanted to be able to tell her I loved her just one more time before he killed her."

"She knew, Gedeon." Her voice came out of the darkness with absolute confidence.

He loved her even more for that assuredness. "I killed the *pakhan*, and when I did, I made certain it took him a long time to die. I wasn't nice about it, Meiling, and I made certain to let him know that they missed one. I told him I had all those gifts and then some. That I was alive and would be for a long, long time."

He fell silent, waiting for her to condemn him, but he

should have known better. It was Meiling. He'd told her part of his story and she hadn't condemned him then. "It bothered me that I didn't feel anything. I had no emotions at all. What kind of monster had I let them shape me into? I knew my parents wouldn't be happy with me, so I left Russia and changed what and who I was to the best of my ability. I developed my own code. I'm not necessarily a good man, but I make it work. I hide my background from other shifters, and my reputation is dangerous and vicious enough that no one tests me."

"But then you took me on as a partner. Gedeon, you were off their radar. If those people are looking for me and I'm with you, they'll be taking a closer look at you."

"Fuck them, Meiling. They can come after us, but they'll be out of their league if they do. They orchestrated the murder of my entire family, yours and one other family simply because they feared them. I've left them alone until now, but since they're going after my woman, that's not going to last."

"What happened to the other family?"

"Same as mine—and yours. Their friends turned on them and murdered them. Wiped out even the children. Your father had a friend, a woodsman, loyal to him, and while the crowd was killing the other members of the family, the man took you. He was very clever and was able to hide your scent. In all the mob confusion, no one noticed you were gone at first. You were only two, from what I understand. Shifters had sworn you were dead. At first, they thought you were buried with your siblings. Then, when it was discovered you weren't buried with the others, they thought you had wandered off."

"I can imagine the uproar."

"Those scars on your shoulder? Those happened that night when the mob came for your family. From what I understand, one of the shifters clawed you and threw you aside. That was what allowed the woodsman to carry you off. They believed you were dead because the claws were deep and there was so much blood when he cast you aside. The woodsman picked you up and carried you away."

"Libby's father was such a good man."

"Because of the trafficking aspect, the *pakhan* of the Amurov lair was spoken to on more than one occasion, that's how I know the details. He had shifters looking. I was always in the room with him when any discussions were held. He often gave me as a gift to foreign travelers, especially the cruel ones. It pleased him to tell my mother. I just stored up information and put my mind elsewhere when things happened to my body. But I heard what they did to your family and eventually how they thought you managed to stay alive. They couldn't figure out who would dare to save you, though."

"Libby's father. That's why I was never really part of their family and they treated me so strangely. Her mother resented me and wanted me gone. I can totally understand why now. It must have been frightening to have me around. Libby treated me as a sibling. She might have been selfish at times, but she loved me, and I loved her. Her mother knew that, and it was the only reason she didn't throw me out onto the street."

"Her father must have moved away as soon as he could without raising suspicion."

"He was a good man and was always kind to me. I don't remember my family other than flashes from my nightmares. Terrible nightmares. I would wake up screaming when I was a child. I have those scars on my shoulder and back, those four scars made by a shifter. He was trying to drag me from my mother. There was fire everywhere and we were surrounded by a crowd of people. Their faces were contorted into masks of hatred."

Gedeon felt the shiver that went through her body. He

turned onto his side to gather her closer. Her body felt extremely warm to him. She moved, her body sliding sensuously against his. She seemed completely unaware.

"You don't need to think about that anymore, Meiling. We'll find out who they are. They can't hide from us. They think they have power. The kind of people they are always think they have power because they hide behind walls and guards. When I was that very young boy, naked and stripped of all power, I had plenty of time to observe what was really happening behind the scenes. Those in power were just as afraid as I was. It didn't take an army to go knocking at their front door. I had plenty of time to discover how to defeat them. A small force of one or two can slip in undetected and be gone before they're ever discovered. As long as we ensure we have proper alibis, we'll always be fine."

He waited a few moments and then sat up. "Let's go out onto the patio, Lotus. I feel like breathing the night air."

He didn't bother with clothes. When she looked around for a robe, he laughed. "No one is going to see us. I had the screen dipped in a reflective dark paint. You can see out, but unless we turn on bright lights to give people a show, no one can see a thing." He held out his hand.

She put her hand in his. "You tested this theory?"

"Don't you want to live dangerously?" he teased, running his fingernail gently from her collarbone over the slight swell of her breast, her nipple and down to her navel. At once goose bumps rose all over her bare skin as endorphins rushed through her in response.

He opened the thick wall so that it slid all the way back to incorporate the outside patio with the bedroom. At once the sounds of the swamp became a symphony of music. Varieties of frogs vied for attention, some singing and others croaking loudly. Insects hummed. Wings fluttered in the treetops. Even the branches contributed, leaves fluttering with the slight breeze.

Meiling pressed her hands over her ears for a moment, laughing. "They're so loud."

"Turn it down. That's your leopard's hearing."

"I always have excellent hearing. It shouldn't be this loud." She lifted her hands away from her ears and walked to the railing, forgetting her nudity, just as he knew she would.

The sultry heat of the night combined with the cloying scent of gardenias, night-blooming jasmine and Angel's trumpets called to her leopard, drawing her even closer to the surface. Gedeon's blood sang hotter than ever in his veins, rushing with a feral music now. He couldn't take his gaze from her glowing skin. He watched her with the eyes of a leopard. Focused. Unblinking. Recording every movement.

She moved across the patio restlessly, her body unconsciously provocative. Just seeing her in the beginnings of her heat threw his body out of control. His cock swelled into a fierce, needy monster. Slayer added his demands, a ferocious, prowling male too long denied a mate.

Meiling suddenly gripped the dark mesh with a sharp cry, notes of fear and desperation mingling together. Her head hung low and she began to take deep breaths, clearly struggling. "Gedeon. I can feel her rising, but she's in total chaos. I don't know what to do to help her."

He could see her body already covered in little beads of sweat. She couldn't stay still. Her hands moved over her sensitive skin, cupping her breasts, rubbing along her thighs, seeking the junction between her legs. Tears formed in her dark eyes.

"I feel like I'm going to burst into flames. You have to help me." She half turned toward him and her gaze instantly was riveted on his fully erect cock. Her gaze went hungry. Filled with lust and greed. Her tongue moistened her lips until they gleamed.

Gedeon bit back a groan. Meiling wasn't the only one

on fire. Slayer was creating a monster, rising toward Whisper, just as desperate, his appetite voracious, driving Gedeon as well. Now Meiling's reactions were testing his discipline. He knew he needed to calm the raging in his mind and stay in some kind of control.

"Meiling. Come here." Soft. A male leopard's purring command. Gedeon perched his ass on the railing and widened his legs, pointing to the spot between them.

She turned fully toward him. She lifted her long hair from her shoulders and then dropped it again. Her dark gaze, filled with lust and heavy with need, remained riveted on his heavy cock. He fisted his erection, pumping slowly, mesmerizing her. He pointed to the floor at his feet, and she went to all fours and began to crawl like the sensuous leopard she was.

Gedeon began to do a little sweating of his own. Muscle rippled beneath her glowing skin. Meiling looked sexier than he'd ever seen her, there with the silver streaks of moon bathing her in its light. Soft little moans escaped her throat as she approached him. She rubbed along his inner thigh, licked up his heavy balls, causing his entire body to shudder, and then knelt, looking hungrily up at him.

He buried both hands in her hair, too far gone to be gentle. They were half leopard, the burn on them. He dragged her head back. "Open your mouth. You're going to take me deep."

She complied immediately and he thrust his cock into that hot, wet cavern. Her mouth closed around him tight, but he just thrust deeper, using his hips and his hands in her hair, standing above her. He refused to allow her to move her head. He controlled everything because she was giving him paradise. Her liquid gaze jumped to his as he held himself there.

"Suck hard. Harder."

The leopard hormones were raging. In her. On her skin. In her mouth. Spilling onto his shaft. It felt like flames were burning him alive. It was agony and yet, at the same time, ecstasy. He pumped in and out of her mouth, raging at her to suck harder. The fire kept burning him until he was erupting in a storm of wild thrusting jets, forcing her to swallow before he pulled back, his cock still diamond hard.

He hadn't realized that his skin, his cock and his seed were coated with the male leopard's answering testosterone. His need to conquer. To claim and dominate. Now he had spread that fire to Meiling, mixing it with Whisper's. It was on her skin, in her mouth, inside her sex. Those flames that were burning him alive had to be consuming her.

She was nearly sobbing, on her hands and knees begging him to do something. Winding around him. Rubbing her body over his thighs, trying to climb onto his cock. Her hips rose and fell frantically. Gedeon thrust two fingers between her legs to test how slick she was. She was so hot he nearly burned his hand. She immediately began to ride his fingers.

"Hurry. Gedeon, hurry."

His cock was so swollen and hard from the continuous hormones she was spilling, he was afraid he would hurt her, not to mention he was so out of control and rough. Her female had risen much faster than either he or Slayer had predicted. Meiling wept continually.

Gedeon wrapped one arm around her waist. "Shh, baby. We've got this. She's rising too fast and wreaking havoc with us both." He tried to reassure her. Just touching her skin had to hurt her. He could feel the ripple as the little female pushed at Meiling from inside, creating even more sensitivity.

Meiling's frantic cries were heartbreaking. He swore under his breath and sank his fingers into her hips, jerking her to him as he drove his cock deep. She was so tight and hot. At once it was as if he were in a tunnel of pure fire. He was a big man, and he stretched her, filling her to capacity. He was rough, brutal even, but he could tell it wasn't enough. Meiling's cries filled the night, pleading, desperate, frantic.

He took her up hard and fast, over and over, trying to hold on to his last form of civility when she was stripping it from him. Not just Meiling. It was the perfect storm of the natural swamp, leopards and his woman in desperate heat all rising together. She kept begging him for harder. For more. Her voice was raw. Sexual.

Gedeon had always been borderline on being a rough, brutal sexual partner, but he loved Meiling and he didn't want to hurt her. She wasn't experienced enough for violent leopard sex. He tried to hold on to that thought, but it seemed an impossible task. His blood thundered in his ears. The roaring in his head increased as he drove into her, determined to stop the fiery pain that refused to let up for her. His breath sawing in and out of his lungs was every bit as ragged as Meiling's. Her cries began to crescendo. He kept driving between her thighs. A brutal madman, possessed. Heat and fire burned through him relentlessly. She begged. He was merciless. Pushing her to the absolute limit.

Without warning, she went rigid. Her body gripped his cock in a viselike stranglehold, squeezing and milking with terrible strength, but he could tell it wasn't enough. She continued to fight to impale herself on him in a frenzied kind of insanity. Her body shuddered and pulsed all around his.

Then she collapsed, going down on her elbows, her cries indistinct. Muffled. *My jaw. My skull is too tight. I can't do this, Gedeon. Something is wrong.*

"Don't fight it, Meiling." He pulled out of her body reluctantly and fumbled for the remote to open the screen to allow passage for the leopards to leap to the tree branch that formed a bridge over the water to the swamp. "You'll still be you. Let her have your form. Slayer will watch over her. They deserve their time together."

I'm too hot. Sick. Itch all over. Meiling panted with fear.

Her skin rippled as the leopard tried to push her way through but kept retreating.

"She doesn't know what to do, Lotus. Slayer says she's afraid of hurting you. You have to guide her, Meiling. You have to be in control. Take deep breaths and get her through her first time. I'm here. I'm not going to let anything happen to you." Gedeon used his firmest voice.

Meiling lifted her head; her dark eyes, looking like two bruised flowers, met his. Again, she humbled him with her trust. Taking a deep breath, she nodded. *Tell me what to do.*

"Reassure her. Tell her to rise. Slayer is waiting for her. You want her to run free. You'll be with her and she isn't hurting you. It's all new for both of you, but she needs to do this. Don't hesitate, just let it happen."

Once again, those dark eyes didn't waver, never stopped looking into his. Not when fur rippled over skin. Not when teeth filled her muzzle and her head fully formed. She was a beautiful Amur female, but very small. Her coat was very thick and pale with wide-spaced black rosettes. Slayer found her gorgeous. He led her out of the house and into the thick trees and brush of the swamp.

16

JAKE Bannaconni's home was entirely unexpected. Meiling didn't know what she was expecting, but an authentic, sprawling two-story ranch house wasn't it. Clearly the helicopter had taken them to a working cattle ranch.

They were escorted to Jake's office by a stocky man with thick, dark hair and watchful green eyes, clearly a shifter. He introduced himself to them as Tavin and indicated for them to follow him. He took them quickly through a back entrance. Meiling noted large floor-to-ceiling plants, creating the effect of a jungle, and a life-size bronze leopard crouched at the foot of a staircase as they moved away from the main part of the house down a wide hallway to what was obviously a private part of the house.

Faintly, from upstairs, Mciling heard the sounds of children laughing and a woman's low voice murmuring to them. She didn't try to hear what was being said, but just the fact that Jake's wife and children were in his home gave her comfort.

Sometimes it bothered her that Gedeon was treated like such a pariah. She knew he deserved his reputation and even needed it for his work, but she wished he wouldn't have to be so alone.

I'm not alone anymore, Lotus. I have you.

His voice was a caress, painting strokes of color through her mind. Their colors. Blues and purples. She couldn't stop herself from following his masculine frame moving so fluidly, flowing like water over the hardwood floor, every muscle rippling powerfully beneath his casual clothing. He hadn't dressed in a power suit. He had come in a pair of loose jeans and a tee stretched over his thick chest.

Jake Bannaconni represented power. Gedeon would never try to act as if he were as powerful. He didn't have Jake's money or move in his elite circles. He had asked a mutual friend for a favor, and Gedeon arrived at the ranch in that role—a grateful man prepared to plead his case and nothing else.

Meiling and Gedeon had pored over blueprints and what little information they could learn of the closely guarded security of the ranch. They would have no advantage there. Jake had mainly shifters on patrol, at the gate and as bodyguards for his family. If it went badly for whatever unknown reasons, the only thing Meiling and Gedeon could do would be to kill as many as possible to get a clear path out and run. They hoped it wouldn't come to that.

Gedeon had Drake disclose to Jake that Meiling's female had emerged and would continue to do so throughout the next seven days. They would have to have a place for her to run with her mate. Jake had promised to provide a safe area for the two leopards should it become necessary.

Because they were in San Antonio, Gedeon also contacted Timur to let him know they were in the area. He immediately invited them to stay on one of the family properties and indicated they could have the run of the place without interference. Meiling found herself hoping they would have time to visit with the shifters she'd met in San Antonio so she could get to know them better.

Gedeon's hand was suddenly on the small of her back, startling her. He *never* did that. Never touched her when they were on a job and in a situation where there was possible danger to them. Jake Bannaconni was a man shrouded in mystery. Rene couldn't find out much about him other than some of the most powerful men in the world were afraid of him.

Are you paying attention, Lotus?

I keep getting distracted, she admitted. *I'm not sure why.* She wasn't the kind of woman to be distracted, not while she was working. *You don't think that little hussy, Whisper, is waking up already, do you?* She didn't wail it, but she felt like it. *I'm sore and exhausted. Can't she give us twenty-four hours?*

Another thought occurred to her. *I don't want to embarrass you.* That would be so terrible. She always was professional. Always. *I could ask to wait in the car just in case.*

Gedeon's hand slid up her back to the nape of her neck. His fingers sank into her tense muscles. *We stay together. It would be impossible for you to embarrass me. Settle, Meiling. Just breathe. We'll get through this together, like we always do.*

Meiling sent him one emotion-laden look and then gazed around the enormous room Jake Bannaconni called his office. The space took up an entire wing of the house and was soundproof. The hardwood floors gleamed. Meiling was certain the very large wooden door off to her right led to an extremely spacious bathroom. As it was, the room made her feel very small. The desk in the middle of the room was even intimidating. It wasn't messy. Everything had a place. The top was wide. A variety of business tools were laid out on it.

The man sitting behind the desk stood. He looked as if his face could have been carved from granite, those lines etched deep. His eyes glowed icy gold, nearly all cat. He had wide shoulders and dark hair to contrast with his eyes that changed color to an icy green.

"Gedeon, Meiling. I'm Jake Bannaconni." He waved them away from his desk. "Just around this corner, there's much more comfortable seating."

Gedeon, keeping one hand curved around the nape of Meiling's neck, extended his hand toward Jake. "Thank you for agreeing to see us. I know time with your family must be at a premium."

"No problem. Emma understands. I explained you were worried about a woman who had disappeared. That was all it took."

Firm handshake. No games, Gedeon reported as they followed Jake around a slight corner to find a sitting area with comfortable-looking chairs grouped together and end tables set between them.

Meiling and Gedeon took the small love seat, sinking into the plush cushions. Gedeon turned his body slightly toward Meiling, one arm curving around the back of her shoulders. She snuggled under his shoulder, making herself appear even smaller. *Guard at six o'clock in the shadow. He appears to be Tavin's twin.*

Another one standing just at the opposite wall, Gedeon told her. *Shifter. Could be our man. The one we're looking for.*

Why would Guy Hawkins hire a shifter to protect his wife? That doesn't make sense.

I doubt he knew, Lotus. He went to someone and asked who the best was. They recommended Drake International and he ended up with Edge Wilson. He wanted the best, could pay for it and was sent Wilson.

Meiling turned that information over in her mind, lowering her long lashes submissively as Jake took the chair opposite them. A shifter would hear a lie each time Guy Hawkins uttered one. If the man had planned to kill his wife or was in any way mistreating her, a shifter would know. Everything that Gedeon and Meiling suspected made even more sense if the bodyguard Guy Hawkins had hired turned out to be a shifter.

"Before we get to the reason you're here," Jake began, "I want to make a couple of things very clear. In this room there are three male shifters without mates. Those men are bodyguards, and although I like to think I'm the boss, I'm not. I keep my promises and I agreed to bodyguards at all times, so I had to put them potentially in a very uncomfortable position. Gedeon, you have a reputation. These men are here to do a job. If your mate's leopard begins to rise, we will leave as fast as possible, but I want your word that you will do everything you can to protect my men."

Meiling did her best to control the wild color rising. She couldn't do anything about the alluring scent her female was throwing off, calling to every male in the vicinity. She had never considered that even after being claimed, Slayer might have to fight off other males.

This is normal in our world, Lotus. You have no reason to be embarrassed. Emma, Jake's wife, must go into heat occasionally. There are other mated women around them that must do the same. They live and work in a lair with a mated couple.

Gedeon's hand dropped to Meiling's shoulder and then curved around her neck. "Of course, Jake. We should be good, but truthfully, her little female is unpredictable."

Jake didn't smile. His eyes were glacier cold as he turned his full attention on Meiling. "I understand this is your female's first life cycle. She must be very frightened and uncertain of what is happening to her. You must be as well. The heat can be brutal and very violent."

Here it comes.

There was an edge to Gedeon's voice. Although he remained perfectly at ease on the outside, she felt the tension in him coiling like a snake ready to strike. Along with that came a tendril of something else. It felt like a stream of energy, white-hot and frightening in its intensity. That energy began to wrap itself around the ever-present rage coiling inside Gedeon, so ready to strike out at his enemies.

No one is going to take me away from you, Gedeon. We belong. Sometimes, like now, her love for him was so strong the emotion felt overwhelming.

I was born for one thing. One fucking thing, Meiling. I was born to be your man. To stand with you as a partner. In front of you as a shield. Behind you to guard your back. I feel you in my soul. I know you're there. You are the only thing that makes sense of why I'm alive. I don't care how many shifters he's got between us and freedom, he's not taking you away from me.

Meiling suddenly didn't care at all about her role as the submissive little girlfriend too frightened by the circumstances of her female leopard going into heat. She dropped her hand onto Gedeon's thigh and sat up a little straighter, tilting her chin and looking Jake right in his piercing, golden eyes. Waiting. Studying him. Woman and leopard both.

Jake looked a little startled, but he continued. "In the first life cycle, as the female emerges, there are times in the heat of the moment that she accepts a male who is not her true mate. I want to verify that you are comfortable with the man you have chosen, and your leopard is comfortable with the male she has chosen. If not, say so now and we'll help you."

There wasn't a doubt in Meiling's mind that Jake Bannaconni meant every word he said. He sat across from Gedeon, a man known to be dangerous, fast and without mercy and not only threatened to take his woman from

him but stated that he would. That took courage and re-
solve. It also earned him respect, as far as Meiling went.

"Thank you for caring enough about women to worry,
Mr. Bannaconni," she said. She always spoke in a low
voice. That was her nature. But she kept her tone very firm.
"Gedeon was my choice before I knew about my female.
He was my choice when she was rising and I was a mess.
His leopard is my female's choice absolutely. She wouldn't
want any other. I have no idea if I influenced that because
I'm so in love with Gedeon. That's a possibility. I had no
way of manipulating his leopard, but if I could have, I
would have. His choice was my female."

If Jake could hear truth, her tone had to have rung with
it, because every word she uttered was the raw, honest truth.
Gedeon was her choice. There was no other man and there
wouldn't be. She hadn't looked away from Jake's golden
eyes. Those eyes were going green. Little green flecks had
shaded the gold and were now taking over.

"I had to ask. To be sure. Someone has to protect you.
You picked a pretty tough man. Gedeon, you're a lucky man.
I don't know how men like us manage to be gifted with a
miracle, but we have been. I treasure mine, and looking at
you, I can see you feel the same way. I know I don't deserve Emma, but I do my damnedest to keep her safe and
happy."

Meiling liked that Jake had put himself in the same
category as Gedeon. "I'm very happy. Thank you for caring. We brought you a file we prepared. We didn't put anything online because Guy Hawkins has enough money to
hire the best hackers and we don't want him to have access
to anything in our investigation we don't fabricate or ap-
prove for him. He also has a very dangerous man shadowing us."

Jake cocked his head to one side as he studied both of
them with his unusual eyes.

Gedeon didn't seem to be in the least affected by that penetrating stare. He held out the folder to Jake. "This is part of what we've uncovered and our best conclusion. If you don't agree with us, we'll walk out and head into San Antonio for more footwork. If you do agree, we'll take it from there and show you what else we're contending with."

Jake took the file and then opened it. Silence filled the room. He read it thoroughly twice. Word for word. No one interrupted him. No one whispered or talked together. They waited just as Gedeon and Meiling did.

As they had pieced together everything they could find on Guy Hawkins behind the façade he'd built around himself, Meiling had begun to really worry about Laverne. Hawkins had the best PR group to handle his image in the media and they had been doing a tremendous job for years.

Laverne, on the other hand, was a sweet, giving, kind woman without the kind of money her husband had. She had no PR team to watch over her in the media. Lately small shadows had crept in, rumors of late-night partying with drugs, quickly squashed, but once the rumor started, it was there for all time. Meiling and Gedeon were certain those rumors had been carefully planted by someone Hawkins paid.

Jake looked up from the typed report. "I've met Guy Hawkins on several occasions. I thought he was a pompous ass with an ego the size of Texas, but if half of this is true, he's a serial killer."

Gedeon hitched forward. "He's a serial killer who will never be brought to justice in the normal way. He keeps his hands clean so there's no proof leading back to him. I need to speak with Edge Wilson for a couple of reasons. The first: I need to know Laverne is safe before I can take the next step. And second: his life is in danger until I can make my move."

Meiling once again found Jake Bannaconni's leopard

staring at them with focused eyes. Gedeon used terms like
"make my move" and "take the next step." She knew that
meant Gedeon would go hunting.

They gave Jake the evidence they had on Hawkins and
the women they had linked to him who had disappeared.
They'd related their evidence to Drake, but it wasn't the
same as seeing it in black and white.

"Edge, I'd like you to read this," Jake said. "If you prefer not to, that's all right. It's your choice." Jake continued
to look at them even as he called out to the bodyguard.
"Edge is working for me now. I thought it more expedient
if he was close. I won't order him to cooperate."

The bodyguard came out of the shadows and took the
report Jake gave him. He barely flicked Gedeon and Meiling a glance before retreating to the wall to read through
their findings.

"Are either of you hungry or thirsty? I should have asked
you that first," Jake said. "Emma has been trying to instill
manners in me for years, but I fail at civility quite often."

"At least you're giving it your best shot. Gedeon does a
lot of growling. Guests find it off-putting. I can't imagine why."

Meiling laughed. The instant she did, the atmosphere
in the room seemed to lighten. She felt as if someone had
flipped a switch and the room grew brighter. She also felt
as if everyone was staring at her. It was difficult not to
burrow closer to Gedeon.

"Jake, just to let you know, since I met the helicopter
and escorted them to your office, my leopard has been
quiet," Tavin said.

The bodyguard Meiling had been certain was Tavin's
brother spoke up. "My leopard is also quiet. I'm Talbert,
by the way. Thank your female for the respite. There are
only a few female leopards who can quiet others."

It isn't Whisper, Gedeon said. *It's you. With your gifts.
Talbert is correct. There are a rare few who can calm*

other leopards, but you have a universal gift, Meiling. Any leopard will respond to you. You may even have the ability to command it.

Do you have that gift? Meiling asked.

Gedeon leaned into her, pressed a kiss to the nape of her neck and then brushed another to her ear. "Yes." He whispered the affirmative aloud. *I practiced taking over for years until I was very good at it. Taking control of another man's leopard is dangerous, Meiling. To be able to do so sounds like a gift on the surface, but it can be a curse.*

She heard notes of regret, anger, fierce determination. That boy, tortured and forced to see his mother trafficked. Forced to see his family murdered. That boy whose innocence was ripped from him, questioning whether he was a monster because he had exacted revenge against those who had taken everything from him.

Even as she smiled at Jake and nodded to the bodyguards, she turned her face up to Gedeon, letting him see her love for him shining in her eyes. *You are everything to me*, she assured him. *We'll get through this and take care of the problem the way you always do. This is bringing up old memories neither of us needs to deal with right now.*

Edge came out of the shadows and took the chair to Jake's left. "I have no problem answering any of your questions," he announced as he handed Gedeon the file. "My main concern is Laverne's safety."

"Then you can confirm that she is alive," Meiling said. She didn't bother to hide her relief. There had always been that underlying fear that Hawkins had killed her and was using them to find her body, or he figured if they couldn't find her body, no one would.

"Laverne is alive. She realized Guy was getting ready to have her killed. Can you imagine how that would be? Living that lie every day? Knowing your husband was plotting your murder but still acting as if you were the greatest love of his life? She deserves an Oscar for her performance."

Meiling had never known that her family had been murdered. In her sleep, she knew, but not when she was awake. She didn't have those horrific memories. Gedeon had the memories and they were all too clear, burned into his mind, coloring his life forever. He knew exactly what Laverne had gone through. He had to pretend and give the performance of a lifetime in the *pakhan*'s house.

"I heard his lies. So subtle, trying to gaslight her all the time. Making her feel small. Like she was never good enough. He'd make fun of her when they were out with friends. Never anything big, just a little line or two, and he'd pass it off as a joke. She'd laugh, but I could see the hurt on her face. He undermined her confidence. What he was really good at was manipulating everyone around him into believing he was wonderful to be with a woman who wasn't quite up to his intellect. She wasn't quite his equal and yet he was so amazing to treat her so perfectly and love her so much."

Meiling had come across this kind of man before, but she'd not met men like Hawkins, who had the money to back up his killer tendencies.

"At first, I wasn't aware he intended to kill her," Edge continued. "She didn't share that belief with me. Later, when she did, she told me she didn't believe it at first. The realization came to her over time. She thought she was becoming paranoid or slowly going insane."

Gedeon tugged at Meiling's hair and then stroked one finger down the nape of her neck. "How did she come to understand he really was going to kill her? Did she say? Because her escape took careful planning on her part."

"Laverne said when she was asleep with him, she would wake up and he would be standing over her with a knife, whispering that she needed to die. She would scramble off the bed and huddle on the floor, terrified. A few minutes

later he would ask her what she was doing on the floor and act as if he hadn't done anything. He would tell her he'd been in bed the entire time or that he'd gone into another room to read so as not to disturb her. Eventually, she was afraid to go to sleep."

Sleep deprivation would only add to Laverne's feelings of paranoia. Hawkins would know that. Laverne would question her sanity even more.

"He had cut her off from any friends. She had no family. She had no one to talk to. I realized she was in a bad way, so I approached her very carefully. I knew I was overstepping, but I was worried, and at that point I didn't know half of what he was doing to her. When she eventually confessed the nighttime gaslighting and said she was afraid she was losing her mind, I offered to set up a camera he wouldn't know about."

Meiling could imagine how alone Laverne must have felt. Hawkins was the man she loved and trusted. Now she had to face believing either that she was losing her mind or that the man she loved was deliberately trying to drive her insane.

Lotus, I can feel you crying. You're so soft inside. Sometimes I'm so angry with myself for exposing you to more of these cases. Not all people are this way. We just see the worst of the worst.

She felt Gedeon draw her closer, surround her with his strength. It might be in her mind, but it was very real. After being so alone all her life, she knew what it was like to share a real connection with the man she loved. That made it all the worse knowing Laverne and others like her had endured such betrayals.

I chose to be your partner, Gedeon. I want to work these cases with you. It gives me satisfaction to help these women if I can.

Edge continued his story. "The camera proved to her once and for all that she wasn't losing her mind. It also

convinced me that we were going to have to act fast. There was no doubt in my mind that Guy Hawkins was setting his wife up for murder. The subtle rumors planted in the media about her going to parties and using drugs made me think he would do it that way."

Gedeon nodded his head. "He could lace a prescription drug she takes with fentanyl. It would be easy enough for him to do. Make it look as if she was doing coke with some friends. He could even invite some people over to the house while he was away, using her phone, and give them coke laced with fentanyl. He wouldn't mind killing others in the process if it served his purposes."

Edge agreed. "Just before Laverne and I left, Guy had begun calling me away from Laverne to do other tasks for him. I think he was doing that in preparation for me not being with Laverne when she was given the drug that would kill her."

"So you got away and disappeared. You knew he would look for her," Gedeon said. "I couldn't find anything to indicate that he would be better off with her dead than divorced from her. He had no real reason to kill her. That was what made me look much more closely into his past relationships—that, and I just had a bad feeling about him."

"We knew he would look. We had to have a plan in place immediately. We had to do it right the first time because there would be no second chances. Hawkins has too much money to think he wouldn't hire the best to find her. I didn't want to put Drake or anyone else we knew in jeopardy either. I did call in a favor to get her away safely, and then I asked to be assigned here on Jake's ranch. I knew even Hawkins would have a difficult time getting to me here."

"I'm not going to ask where Laverne is. As long as you know she's safe, that's good enough for me," Gedeon said. "Hawkins hired us with a sob story about how much he loved his wife. He told us she is bipolar and when she goes off her meds, she does bizarre things that could end her

career. She risks being ashamed of those things and would end her marriage to him over them because she doesn't want to embarrass him. He claimed he hired you to protect her from herself should the worst happen, and she went off her medication. He said you took advantage. We knew that wasn't true the moment we saw how long she'd planned her escape. We also became aware he had someone shadowing us."

Gedeon extracted another paper from his jacket pocket, unfolded it and passed it to Jake and Edge. "That man is McGregor Handler, and he is considered one of the most lethal hit men in the world today. Once set on a target, he doesn't stop until it's done. He will use any means necessary to kill. He will kill a man, woman or child. The elderly, an infant—or if innocents get in his way, he will annihilate them. This man is on a retainer with Hawkins. He has been following me and Meiling ever since we agreed to look for Laverne."

Jake passed the photograph to Edge.

"We believe his intention is for us to find Laverne and then he'll kill her and us," Gedeon continued. "I needed to ensure Laverne was safe. I have no actual proof against Hawkins. I've gathered circumstantial evidence, but it would never convict him. I know he's guilty of ordering those other women killed. I believe he would have had his wife murdered and ordered me and Meiling killed as well. I think, Edge, that you're on McGregor's list too, but I don't know that for a fact."

Edge shrugged. "He can make his try."

Jake frowned at him. "Emma told me more than once that my arrogance as a shifter was what was going to get me into trouble. Just because we have superior gifts doesn't mean humans well trained in combat situations can't be lethal. We let our guards down and they can exploit our carelessness."

"I hear what you're saying, boss," Edge said. "It was

difficult being in that house watching Hawkins act as if he was always so nice to everyone. He was supposedly kind and generous, which he was in front of cameras. Under the surface he was a cunning snake and his cruelty was often so subtle people had no idea they were even being shaded until everyone was laughing at them and they were forced to go along with the joke. He knew exactly what he was doing and how far he could take something."

A trace of anger had slipped into the bodyguard's voice. "I wanted to take care of that bastard, Jake, not just get Laverne out of there. I knew he'd come after her. He really thinks he's so superior to everyone. I doubt if any law enforcement agency in the world can touch him."

Meiling knew Guy Hawkins was well aware he would never be convicted of any crime. Even if he were arrested, the weight of public opinion would always be on his side. He'd been careful to cultivate his image in the media, and nothing was going to change what he'd so meticulously built.

She didn't look at Gedeon. Hawkins had made a terrible mistake when he'd hired him. He'd asked a friend who the best in the business was. He hadn't done research into Gedeon's reputation or what Gedeon was about. He should have avoided Gedeon. Jake had clearly investigated him. Drake had. Even the criminal families hiring him to do work for them knew enough to be very selective of what they asked him to do. There was a reason Gedeon had his reputation.

"I appreciate you allowing us to come here, Jake, to sort things out," Gedeon said. He took the photograph and file and slid both inside his jacket. "Edge, if you wouldn't mind making certain that Laverne stays wherever she is and doesn't try to reach out to anyone, I would appreciate it. Also, for the time being, if you could continue to stay off Hawkins's radar just a little longer, it would give me a chance to set a few things in motion."

Meiling stood at the pressure of his fingers on her nape. Gedeon stood with her, shaking hands with Jake and then Edge. "We'll take that helicopter ride you offered to Evangeline's bakery. Our rental car was delivered there. We don't want McGregor to realize we were ever here. Again, we appreciate you accommodating us."

Jake walked with them to the door of the office, where Tavin waited to walk them out to the helicopter pad. "It was a pleasure to meet you both." He handed his card to Gedeon. "My private number. You need anything at all, give me a call. Next time you're visiting our town, give me the heads-up and Emma and I will meet you for dinner. She's going to be disappointed she couldn't meet you this time around."

Meiling flashed him a smile. "We'd love that. Please let her know we come to San Antonio often and will make it a point to call."

She found herself resting her head on Gedeon's shoulder during the ride to the bakery and nearly falling asleep. Apparently there was a helipad on the roof of the bakery.

Meiling was worn out from the long night Whisper had spent with Slayer, running through the swamp together and mating every fifteen to twenty minutes. She had bruises and bite marks marring her skin, and truthfully, she was sore. Very sore. She wanted to be with Gedeon physically when she woke up, but she was grateful they had to hastily pack a bag, board the small plane Rene had rented for them and go. Now she just wanted to sleep.

Timur has a house for us to stay in tonight. You can rest this evening, as soon as we get there. It isn't very far from the bakery.

I wanted to visit Evangeline for at least a few minutes while we were at the bakery. Whisper is going to rise no matter what, Gedeon. Whether I'm tired or not.

Other women had done this, and she refused to be a complainer. She loved Gedeon and she loved Whisper. This was Whisper's time, so for the next week Meiling could handle whatever life threw at her, even if it meant she couldn't walk. She did intend to ask Evangeline if there was a special soak that helped heal her fast, so she wouldn't be quite so sore the next time she and Gedeon had wild sex together.

She must have fallen asleep, because she was jarred awake when the helicopter set down on the roof of the bakery. Gedeon guided her off the helicopter and down the stairs to the entrance, where one of Timur's men waited for them. She recognized the shifter immediately.

"Rodion. Good to see you. How have you been?" She managed to flash him a smile.

Gedeon tucked her under his shoulder, her front to his side, one arm around her possessively. She glanced up at his set features. He looked as if he'd been carved in stone. *I'm not sure that finding your mate has improved your mood, Leopard Boy. You're supposed to be friendly now.*

She felt his amusement, although it didn't show on his face. *I am?* To Rodion he gave a nod. "Things good?"

"Yeah, quiet for once. I see you two are a bonded pair. I expected that." If the shifter was upset about it, he kept it to himself. "You carrying weapons?"

"Naturally."

"Had to ask."

"Meiling?" Rodion persisted.

She nodded. "I don't go anywhere without them."

Rodion texted one-handed as he walked ahead of them down the stairs toward the door leading into the building. Meiling, out of habit, scanned rooftops and the alley, every door and alcove she could see, committing them to memory. She knew Gedeon would be doing the same. Rodion opened a door to a hallway. Instantly, the aroma of coffee and cinnamon mixed with apples and spices greeted them.

Kyanite waited at a side door in the hallway for them.

"Nice to see you two. Evangeline is serving her rush-hour customers, but if you give me your orders, I'll slip them in. We reserved a table for you."

"We don't want to cause you any trouble," Gedeon said. "We can grab the keys to the rental and head for the house. Meiling wanted to visit with Evangeline, but we'll be back soon."

Kyanite glanced at his watch. "Rush should be over soon. She'd be so disappointed if you didn't stay." He pulled open the door to the bakery.

The lines were long at the counter. Two women worked fast, moving as if they were a machine, never getting in the other's way. The one Meiling didn't know made drinks, while Evangeline served the customers the pastries and rang up the orders. Evangeline seemed to know most of the customers by name. She never failed to smile at them warmly as she greeted them.

Your choice, Lotus. You look tired. I can put you to bed, or we can stay for a short visit. Gedeon stroked a caress down her back.

I'd like to visit even for a few minutes, Gedeon. I like this place. It seems warm and welcoming, and I know that's really her gift.

Meiling wasn't certain why it was so important to her to try to establish her own connection with Evangeline, but the compulsion was there. She didn't have friends and had never thought she would need them. Or want them. She thought about Evangeline often. She didn't seem to fit with a man like Fyodor Amurov, and yet evidence pointed to them being a very happy couple. How?

They were escorted to the table held for them. It was close to an emergency exit. Gedeon took the chair with his back to the wall where he could see every door, the front, the hall and the kitchen. Kyanite took their orders and hurried up to the counter. He slid behind it and had a brief consultation with Evangeline and then the other woman.

She had thick blond hair. Her eyes were light brown, almost an amber color, but ringed with very dark feathery lashes. She had a beautiful figure that Meiling envied immediately.

"Is that Timur's wife, Ashe?" Meiling asked.

"Yes," Gedeon said.

"They work together so well. Look how fast they are."

"They're shifters," Gedeon's voice held amusement. "You're fast at anything you do."

"I suppose." She leaned her chin onto the heel of her hand. "I like her, Gedeon. Evangeline. I've met so many people in our business, but she's the first person I've ever met that I felt comfortable around. The kind of comfortable that I'd be willing to kick off my shoes and put my feet up and just talk and laugh with for an evening."

"She is rather special," Gedeon agreed.

"And she's with Fyodor Amurov."

"Because he's a smart man and he recognized right off that she was someone extraordinary. Just as I'm a smart man and I recognized that you are. Men like Fyodor and Timur, they search everywhere, all over the world, looking for that one woman, but honestly, Lotus, they don't expect to find her. It isn't just that the world is a big place and there aren't very many females left, it's that they know they aren't good men, and they don't deserve a mate, let alone someone extraordinary."

Meiling's gaze jumped to Gedeon's face. She knew he was talking about himself. He identified with Fyodor and Timur Amurov. "I love looking at you, Gedeon," she whispered. "Just looking at you. When I do, I feel safe." She studied the angles and planes of his face, feature by feature. "And happy. Looking at you makes me happy."

He cupped the side of her face with his palm, his thumb tracing her lips. "Men like Fyodor and Timur . . . men like me. When we find that one woman who rocks our world, we hold on tight to her and do everything in our power to make her happy. I know you want to be friends with Evangeline, and I think the feeling is mutual considering she asked the bodyguards to make certain you waited until rush hour was over."

"She did, didn't she?"

"She's coming this way now," Gedeon said. "And she's beaming."

Meiling looked up. Evangeline was beaming, but then, she always was when Meiling saw her.

17

GEDEON spread drawing paper on the small table he shared with Meiling in the early morning hours at the Café Du Monde. There were very few customers, but that wouldn't last long. Within the next half hour, the tables would fill, and the line would be long. They had grabbed a table close to the side exit on the open platform. Near them was a smaller table, and a single male sat there reading while he enjoyed his coffee. Three tables over were three women dressed in suits. A table over from them held four people, who all obviously worked together opening a restaurant.

Meiling pushed back hair that had escaped from the single ponytail she'd quickly pulled her hair into that morning when she'd crawled out of bed and into the shower. Gedeon looked up from the paper to examine her in the early morning light. She had dark circles under her eyes. Her lips looked bruised. There were smudges on her shoulders where skin was exposed. He could see bruising on her neck as well as teeth marks. He hated to think what her body would reveal if he had her strip right there. He should have checked her over before they started out this morning. It was only day three of Whisper's heat. He had no idea if other heats were as violent as Whisper's. Hell. He should have asked. Anyone looking at her would think she was a victim of domestic abuse.

"What?" she asked, giving him a sweet, joyful smile.

"I was just thinking the cops are going to arrest me for domestic abuse if they see you."

She brought a hand to her neck and covered one of the bite marks. "I didn't put on any concealer because we were going into the swamp. If it bothers you, I can go back to the house and put some makeup on."

"Lotus, really? I'm the one who puts those marks all over your body. When I see them on you, all I can do is remember how they got there. I didn't get to have you when we woke up so I intend to take full advantage when we go into the swamp."

She laughed. He knew she would, and he'd waited for the sound. He loved that sound and the feeling it gave him of fingers trailing down his spine in a long caress. Sometimes he felt her palm stroking his cock. Other times, it was her cheek rubbing like a cat against his chest. Always, when she laughed, there was some kind of physical reaction.

"Why am I not surprised, Leopard Boy?"

She had introduced him to the art of teasing. He was introducing her to the art of sex. All kinds of sex. She took her lessons seriously and she liked to practice. She wanted to be good at everything she did. He knew a part of her didn't like that he had had so many partners and she was determined to be his best partner in every aspect of sex. No matter how many times he reassured her that she was perfection for him, she hadn't yet built up her confidence when it came to their sex life.

He flashed a lecherous grin and tugged at her hair. They

had a show to put on, but he needed to know she was good. They could put this off for another day or so.

"You have a good visit with Evangeline?"

Meiling nodded. "Too short, but good. She's so nice, Gedeon. I liked Ashe too. She's edgier than Evangeline. I'm glad she's there, though. Next time we're in San Antonio, I'm hoping to meet the twins. She has a little nursery set up down the hall from the bakery. Her nanny watches them while she and Ashe work. She can feed them and go in and play or visit them and be close if there's a problem. That's so smart. Fyodor had a monitor system set up so she can see them anytime, whether she's behind the counter or in the kitchen."

Gedeon remained silent while he reached for her hand and pulled it across the table to his chest. "We talked about having children, but when we did, we glossed over it. You are aware during the heat cycle, birth control will not work. It will rarely work at any other time for us. It all depends on the female and the male."

She nodded, but her gaze slid from his. "I'm aware."

"And we fuck like bunny rabbits. More to the point, I'm pretty brutal, baby. I'm rough. The possibility of you getting pregnant is high."

"Maybe," she conceded.

"Look at me, Meiling. Eyes to mine. This is important to both of us, although we should have had this conversation before the fact, not after." He waited until she complied, and he was staring into her dark brown eyes. She looked at him with trepidation. Her fingers had curled into a fist against his chest. He reached with his free hand and uncurled her fingers one by one. He brought them to his mouth and sucked each one inside.

Meiling's eyes widened, and her breath hitched. She looked around and then her shocked gaze settled back on him. "Gedeon."

"Yes, Lotus, it's Gedeon. You want to have children with me, don't you?"

"Yes, but . . ." She trailed off, a delicate frown marring her face.

"I need to hear your objection, baby, or I can't fix it."

"Did you see all the bodyguards everywhere? I mean everywhere. Not just in the building, but outside of it. They were everywhere, Gedeon. If we have children, we'd have to hire bodyguards. Given our pasts, we'd have no choice. They'd have to be protected at all times."

The tension in him subsided. "That's what you're concerned about? Their safety? I'm prepared for that. Lotus, I surround you with bodyguards when I'm not with you. You object so I just have them pull back a little further, but they're required to stay on you. Naturally our children would have bodyguards."

She leaned toward him. "I'm going to kiss you."

"I'll let you if you let me lick the sugar off your lower lip," he teased, and proceeded to do just that. He framed her face with his hands and first took off the smudge of powdered sugar from the beignets and then brought his mouth down to hers.

The moment his mouth took hers, thunder rolled in his ears, lightning streaked through his body from his throat to his groin and his heart stuttered in his chest. His woman. Melting him without half trying. They were working. On a job. He couldn't get distracted, and she was one hell of a distraction.

He lifted his head. "Behave yourself, woman. We're supposed to be working here. Stay on your own side of the table."

Meiling laughed. "If I have to. Show me where you think the runaway couple is hiding. I can't believe they've pulled this off."

"They didn't get on a plane. We know they didn't take

a car. They're still here in New Orleans. They wanted Hawkins to think they left. I don't know what game they're going to run on him eventually, but my gut says they're still here. If I'm right, and I'm always right, this is the only place they could be." He smoothed out the paper and tapped the island he'd drawn out.

Meiling hitched closer. "We've gone out a couple of times, Gedeon, and we didn't find anything."

"I had their location narrowed down to three islands. We checked out the other two first because I thought it more likely they would go to the hunting cabins on one of them. The last one is more remote and has no electricity. La-verne is city all the way. I didn't think she'd last out in the swamp without fans and a few modern amenities. She's proving me wrong."

"You believe the two of them are camping out on that island?"

"Yeah, I do. Her bodyguard has ties to the Cajun com-munity. He goes way back. He can ask for help and some-one will deliver groceries. He knows how to fish and trap. They can live out there for a long time until they decide to do whatever it is they plan. We don't have to worry about that. We just need to take a few pictures to prove to Hawkins she's alive and give him a map to her location, and then it's up to him to decide whether he wants a divorce or he wants to go talk to her. We're clear. It isn't our business."

"I'm glad we aren't going at night. The swamp is a little on the scary side at night."

"Seriously, Lotus?" Gedeon raised an eyebrow. "I know my way around. We aren't going to get lost."

"The river seems to change all the time. One minute we're traveling along a channel that's so shallow we can barely make it through, when the day before it was per-fectly good to run through it with a boat. I can't keep up, and I get turned around all the time, especially at night."

"I know it feels like that. I'm careful, Meiling. Look, I'll show you which way we'll go and the channels we'll use. Once you see them, you're good at committing things to memory."

"I am. Thank you. It will make me feel a little better. I know we won't get separated, but I always like to feel as if I can make my way home if necessary."

Gedeon took out a pen and drew the course starting from their pier all the way to the island and back. Meiling studied it and then finished off her coffee. "Thanks, I've got it."

"Good, we'll get started."

As he started to rise, Meiling's phone lit up with what looked like colorful fireworks. Gedeon raised his eyebrow, expecting her to flash her smile, but she was suddenly very sober, the color slipping out from under her skin. He rested the pads of his fingers gently on her wrist in inquiry. She turned the phone over to allow him to see that the text was from Etienne.

> Jules Louis slipped away. I'm sorry. Sending you encryption. Read immediately. UR Danger. Will do whatever you need.

She looked up at Gedeon as her phone went off again with more fireworks. Gedeon indicated the bench by the river. She nodded. He stood, tore the map into six strips and tossed it into the nearest trash can along with their coffee cups. He held out his hand to her. "Let's get this done. It will take a while to get there, and I want to have good lighting to get the best pictures."

"Sounds good to me. I just want to sit by the river first and watch the sun come up like we always do."

"We have time." Gedeon took her hand and, ignoring the man reading at the table closest to them, walked out and down to the bench where they sat together nearly every morning. "What the fuck, Meiling? What does Etienne mean?"

"I'm retrieving the file now. He sends it encoded if it's important. If anyone tries to read it without the right key, it will burn immediately, first time." She pressed a hand over her heart. "Something is really wrong for him to break protocol and send me a firework and a warning in a text. He'll remove it once he sees I've read it."

Gedeon got as close to her as possible, his thigh pressed tightly against hers, one arm sliding along the back of the bench. He didn't give a fuck if they blew the entire setup they'd fabricated for McGregor Handler. He had a very bad feeling. He'd asked Rene to keep an eye on the Frenchman's two nephews, but he hadn't followed up. He should have. He knew better than to leave loose ends, especially when his gut told him not to. He told himself to take a breath; they could handle the two men if they came looking for trouble.

She pulled up the email from Etienne but didn't open it immediately. She retrieved another program and opened the email in that program. At first there were only numbers and symbols floating all over the page, but then order began to restore itself quickly and lines of text appeared.

They read the report Etienne had compiled for her. Jules and Louis had left their home in France and traveled back to Venezuela. From what Etienne could ascertain from a quiet investigation, they had heard someone was making inquiries about a woman with Meiling's description, or at least a vague or close description to hers. The people looking for her were willing to pay a great deal of money for any information that might lead to her whereabouts. Jules and Louis knew she had friends who lived on a farm in the area.

Beside him, Meiling stiffened. A single sound escaped her.

Gedeon wanted to yank the phone from her hand. Damn these relentless, cruel bastards who would never stop hunting her because she had gifts they feared. Now they really had someone to fear. They had a reason. Had they simply left her alone, everyone would have been fine, but they just wouldn't stop coming after her. Gedeon wasn't going to allow it to continue.

The phone was shaking. He removed it from her hand to steady it so they could both finish reading. The farm was burned to the ground. Those residing there were tortured. Etienne described the way the tortures had been conducted and Gedeon recognized them. They were very distinctive and had been used on his father. They had also been used to make a point on some of the women who wouldn't cooperate when they were trafficking them. Etienne's conclusion was that the men seeking Meiling now knew her name and everything her friends at the farm knew about her. He advised she move immediately and go into hiding. He had tracked down his nephews and dispensed justice to them. He owed her more than he could ever repay.

Gedeon watched as the document slowly destructed, blackening first around the edges, and then black holes appeared throughout until it was entirely gone, as if it had never been. Meiling didn't say a word. She sat staring at the river, watching the water rush past. He doubted she knew tears were on her face. He knew they weren't for her.

"Tell me about them."

She turned her face up to his. He brushed at the tracks of wet with his thumb as gently as possible. She broke his heart.

"Your friends on the farm, Lotus Blossom. Tell me about them. Give them to me."

Her tongue moistened her lower lip and her hand slipped onto his thigh. She did that sometimes when she sought comfort. He knew she was unaware of that very small gesture, but he loved it. Meiling was a woman: confident and independent. It wasn't often that she admitted to herself or anyone else she needed comfort or help.

"Bridget and her husband, Esteban, own the farm. Esteban went to school to become a better farmer and understand how to keep the soil rich and producing. Their farm has done so well, producing enough food to feed the neighboring farms and ranches. Most of those are run by the reigning crime family and harvested for drugs, not food. So Bridget and Esteban provide an enormous amount of the vegetables for the workers on those farms. They were always left alone." Her voice broke.

He caught her chin. "Tell me about *them*, Lotus. Not their farm. What they were like as people. You aren't to blame for this any more than my father was to blame for what his best friend did to our family. We can't shoulder those responsibilities, as much as our brains would like us to take them on. We make too many mistakes of our own. Tell me about Bridget, your friend, and Esteban, her husband."

Her fingers dug into the muscle of his thigh, but she turned her face up to his again and he got a genuine Meiling smile. It was a bit watery and melancholy, but he would take it.

"Bridget is the sweetest, kindest woman on planet Earth. I've never seen her without a happy smile on her face. She's kind of like the sun coming out in the morning. You can't be grumpy around her. Her laugh is contagious. All the while she's talking to you, she's working. She can't be still. She's cleaning, or cooking, or baking or gardening. She loves her garden." She fell silent abruptly as she realized she was speaking about Bridget as if she were still alive.

"And her husband? Esteban?"

"Esteban adored her. He was brilliant and he was going to provide whatever Bridget needed. If she wanted a farm that would produce enough food to feed all their neighbors, he would find a way to get that done. He developed this automatic watering system that used the minimum amount of water each type of plant needed and provided only that much. Some of the plants had cages over them. He used old wire from boxes to weave covers over plants birds and other wildlife would attempt to eat. He didn't start out with tons of money, so he got inventive with how he put things together. He'd gather old parts from junkyards or wherever they could get them and build whatever they needed."

"Now they have money?" he prompted.

"I don't honestly know," Meiling admitted. "I just assumed so because each time I saw them, they had so much more equipment, expensive equipment, like tractors. I didn't ask, that would have been rude, and frankly, I didn't care."

The tears had stopped. Meiling seemed steadier. He turned on the bench and pressed his forehead tight against hers, staring directly into her liquid-chocolate eyes. "Meiling, listen to me. I can handle this on my own. It might be better that I do it alone anyway. We'll walk on back to the house and you can go nap for the afternoon. I'll take care of McGregor and come right back to you. When we finish this, we'll go after the ones who murdered your friends."

She gave a little shake of her head. To his shock, her eyes brightened, and she lifted her hand to cup his jaw. "I can't help but fall harder and deeper every day for you, Gedeon. It doesn't matter if you're being sweet like this or bossy and arrogant to the point that I want to kick you into the river. You're always going to be the one."

"You say that shit to me and we're alone in the swamp, things are going to get intense between us," he whispered. Because they were.

"What does that mean?" There was a trace of amusement in her voice.

His thumb swept over the curve of her lower lip, and in between their bodies his other thumb swept over her left nipple. "That means you might be riding through the swamp naked or on your knees between my thighs. It means I'm going to be inspecting those bruises and bite marks you haven't shown me this morning. *All* of them."

"Let's go, Gedeon. Prepare for inspections and whatever else you have in mind because I'm going to keep saying those kinds of things to you for the rest of your life."

That was his woman, squaring her shoulders and getting on with it. They had a job, and she was going to see it through. More, if he turned things sexual between them, she was ready for him. She was always ready for him, no matter what.

WHAT are you doing?" Meiling asked, backing away from Gedeon as he stalked her across the very short distance between the cabin walls.

The island Gedeon had chosen to lure McGregor Handler to was small and covered in trees, so much so that it looked like a small jungle. This wasn't a good thing because spiders built incredible webs in those trees and all sorts of birds made their nests in the canopies. The ground was spongy, which meant there wasn't a tremendous amount of soil to support them as they walked across it. Gedeon cautioned her several times to step where he stepped.

The hunting cabin was built on stilts, as many of the cabins were, to keep the floodwaters from washing them away or, at the least, ruining them. This cabin was very small, no more than six hundred square feet. It was one room. There was a counter and a woodstove that served the dual purpose of heating the cabin and cooking. The crude cupboards held flattened plates and a few spices in jars. The drawers revealed old silverware, a roll of paper towels and a bar of soap.

Meiling held up her hand to Gedeon. "Seriously, stop right now. You look like Slayer when he's stalking Whisper."

"That's because I feel like Slayer right now. I've been too long without you."

"We're *working*. That crazy man might come anytime. He's likely to have a sniper rifle and shoot us right through the window."

"We'd go out so happy. In the throes of a climax. Take your clothes off if you don't want to ride home naked in the boat."

"Be serious, Leopard Boy," Meiling entreated, but her hands had gone to the buttons of her blouse because she was afraid he was serious. He *looked* serious. He sounded serious. He stole her breath. Already, despite her determination not to fall into his trap of temptation, her body had caught fire. Every nerve ending was on alert, aware of him, too sensitive to abide having material touching her.

She slid the buttons out of the loops and opened her blouse. His eyes darkened with lust. When he looked at her like that, her brain just seemed to short out and her body took over. It was exactly what she needed. Gedeon always seemed to know and he provided it for her.

His shirt was already off. When had he taken it off? His chest was magnificent. She loved his chest. She slipped the catch on her bra and set it aside with her blouse, her gaze dropping hungrily to the front of his body. It was so strange, a true puzzle. He was a big man, and when she was in the thrall of her leopard, she could take him deep in her mouth, but when it was just her with her man, no matter how hard she tried, she could only fit so much of him in. But she loved the taste of him. The texture of him. Most of all, she loved how it made him feel when she did her best to take him deeper and deeper.

Gedeon had carried a backpack into the cabin and now he opened it. Pulling out a blanket, he spread it over the counter. "Sit up there, Lotus."

She raised her eyebrow but did as he ordered. The counter was right in front of the sink. The water was pump action, gravity fed. She wouldn't want to try to use it after it hadn't been used for a long while. The window was a long bay window taken out of another structure and was now streaked with dirt. Still, the sun shone through, so when she sat on the counter, she knew Gedeon could see every inch of her body easily.

He came across the room dressed only in his lightweight cotton drawstring trousers. He stretched her left leg to one side as if she were doing the splits and gently placed her foot on a small ledge she hadn't noticed. He then did the same with the right.

"Is that position uncomfortable?"

It wasn't. She was very limber and made certain to keep herself that way. She shook her head.

"Good. Lean back on your elbows." He reached into the duffel bag and brought out a small pillow he slipped between her shoulder blades and neck. "Stay like that. I don't want you to move at all."

Meiling shivered at his tone. His blazing eyes held hers captive for a moment and then dropped to her neck. He pushed her hair out of the way, the pads of his fingers lingering on the bruises there. He bent his head slowly and brushed his lips over each mark. A whisper. Barely there. Back and forth. His tongue touched the marks. Licked at them soothingly—except Meiling didn't find his ministrations soothing at all.

His body was wedged between her spread legs. The material of his trousers rubbed against her bare inner thighs. Against the lips of her exposed sex. Against her inflamed clit. Each time he moved, she was more aware than ever that beneath the fabric covering his body, his cock was hard and straining, rubbing tightly against her now-slick and pulsing entrance. Her entire attention was centered on her desperately growing need. His was all about the bruising on her neck and shoulders.

She made a soft sound of distress and rocked her hips into him. At once he turned his head, his eyes meeting hers.

"Did you already forget what I asked of you? Don't move, baby."

He was asking the impossible and he knew it. Meiling needed to rub against him just a little harder and she might be able to implode. She took a deep breath and forced her body to stay still. She knew Gedeon. He was well aware of what he was doing to her. He returned to inspecting her body, this time shifting to the other side of her neck. As he did so, he pressed tightly against her wet core, causing her breath to hitch and the muscles in her thighs to jump.

Fire raced up her legs. Tension coiled tighter in her sex. She needed to grip something—anything—with her fists, so she caught at the blanket. Gedeon's head dipped lower, to her right breast, and despite her best effort, when he sucked gently, her body shuddered with pleasure, and she rocked her hips against his cock and ground down in desperation.

He moved back, a torturously minuscule movement, just enough that it was impossible for her to reach him and get any kind of relief.

"Gedeon, really, I'm all right."

"I have to see for myself. You're covered in bruises, Meiling." He sucked at her left breast and then kissed the bruises on her belly. "Bites can get infected." He suddenly crouched low. "You have these bite marks on your thighs. Clearly I got carried away." He gripped her calves, kissed his way along her outstretched left leg and then slowed to run his tongue over the bites marring her inner thigh.

She didn't feel the bites, but she felt his tongue like a lash of flame dancing over her skin. The fire in her core only blazed hotter. A whimper escaped. She did her best not to move as his mouth moved closer and closer to where she wanted it. Where she *needed* it. His hair touched her first, sliding over her inflamed clit, and her entire body shook.

He lifted his head away and was back crouching low, one hand circling her ankle.

"Honey, please. I need you."

"You need to learn patience, Meiling. Meditation. We practice breathing techniques every morning after working out and you still have trouble staying in control." His tongue moved along her right thigh and his lips kissed gently. She bit her lip in an effort to keep from squirming, but she vowed to herself she was going to show him she could make him lose his precious control sometime very soon.

He came so close. Breathing. Blowing warm air. His tongue dipping. Tasting. Driving her crazy. She really did think it was possible to go insane. Then she became aware of the slow burn. Those tiny little flames licking at her thighs. At her breasts. Arrowing through her body to her clit. Crackling over her skin so that every nerve ending leapt to life.

Gedeon's fingers settled on the tops of her thighs and gripped her there, and without warning, his tongue lapped at her bare lips, flicked her clit and then plunged deep. She heard herself cry out his name as she unraveled. Came apart. Little lights danced behind her eyes. The orgasm rolled through her and kept going because he did. He devoured her, driving her up again and again, demanding more. Always more until she was certain she was going to die of too many orgasms, or maybe it was one continuous one that never stopped.

Gedeon towered above her, lodging his cock in her hot entrance. She was helpless to do anything but accept him. He thrust deep. Hard. Driving through her tight folds. She was slick from so many orgasms, so ready for him. With the angle he had and her body so open to his, he was able to drive deep into her silken tunnel. So tight and hot. She was always so snug every time he took her. He could feel the walls of her channel surrounding him, gripping his cock and squeezing and massaging like so many fingers, stroking like so many tongues. The sensation was unlike anything he'd ever experienced.

He began to move in her, surging deep, watching the miracle of her body swallowing his. Taking his. He varied the speed and roughness and then caught her left leg and wrapped it around his hip. Did the same with her right. He lifted her off the counter, never missing a stroke, pressing her close to the wall, looking for leverage, the fierceness of the leopard gripping him. She leaned forward and bit his neck hard.

White-hot lightning forked through his body and settled in his cock. He jerked and pulsed in time to her body's squeezing and milking. He heard himself curse in Cajun French and then he wrapped his arms tight around her and rocked her hard before setting her feet on the floor and allowing his cock to slip free of her.

Before she could move away, he caught her to him and tipped up her face, needing to see if she was good. She was. Her eyes soft. Clear. Her head was in the game, not wondering if she was to blame for what happened to her friends.

They cleaned up, ate a sandwich and drank water. Just as they were returning everything to the backpack, the insects went quiet. The birds, ever in motion, suddenly ceased movement.

Gedeon signaled to Meiling and she went out the back door first. She barely opened it. The stairs were rickety and looked as if any weight would have them crumbling. She took no chances and leapt lightly to the ground below, landing in a crouch and staying low while she took a long look around. She moved to her right to make room for Gedeon.

He had the backpack strapped to his back as he dropped right beside her.

Can you tell where he is? Meiling asked. She was fairly certain McGregor hadn't yet set foot on the island. It didn't feel as if he had, but he was disturbing the wildlife, so he was close enough.

He's right next to our boat. He isn't a swamp man. I don't blame him. The terrain is spongy, and you can see the alligator slides, Gedeon said.

He's got to be rethinking killing all of us out here, Meiling pointed out.

It makes so much more sense for him to kill Laverne, Edge and the two of us, weigh our bodies down and hope no one but the alligators finds us for years, he said.

Are we going to let him come to us?

Meiling was willing to allow Gedeon to take the lead on this one. She didn't lie in wait to kill her targets. She knew McGregor had murdered countless men, women and children. She knew he had followed them into the swamp with the intention of killing Laverne and Edge and then finishing off Gedeon and Meiling. It wasn't that she was opposed to killing him. It was just that she wasn't certain how she felt about luring him out to the swamp and then essentially murdering him.

It isn't murder. He'll have his chance at me, Gedeon objected.

Her heart jumped and then accelerated. *What does that mean?*

I plan on talking to him. Unlike you, I'm not opposed to walking up behind him, sticking a gun to his head and blowing it off, but you're with me and you have a moral compass I don't have.

Now that he said he would put himself at risk, she wasn't as certain she had a moral compass. McGregor did deserve to die. *I could look at it as justice.*

The insects, rarely quiet for long, had begun to sound

off again. They grew louder and more confident as Mc-Gregor remained offshore. Birds once again flitted from tree to tree; squirrels chased one another up the tree trunks while rodents resumed scurrying under the leaves looking for seeds.

Stay here while I go have a talk with him.

Meiling gave him a sharp glance. *That wasn't the plan.*

Gedeon sighed. *No, Lotus, it wasn't the plan. But it wasn't the plan to have Etienne send news that two of your friends were tortured and murdered before we came out here to exact justice for those murdered lovers of Hawkins or to keep him from killing poor Laverne.*

I can do this, Meiling hissed at Gedeon.

You think I don't know that? Mon Dieu, Lotus, you're the strongest woman I know. Has it ever occurred to you that I want to take care of you? That there are times I need to take care of you?

Gedeon. She moved closer to him and framed his face with her hands. *Sometimes I don't know what to do with you. If I lost you now, I couldn't take it. You can't be careless the way you have been in the past. You have to know I'm waiting for you.*

He didn't tell her it was easier not to think about someone waiting. In the past he didn't care if he lived or died. That always gave him an edge. He leaned into her. *You're so beautiful, my beautiful little mate. Let me do this.* When she still looked unsure, he brushed another kiss on top of her head. *Do what you do best. Back me up.*

I can do that.

Of course she could. His woman. Meiling. She could do anything no matter how difficult. He was so damned lucky and so damned undeserving. He was also too intelligent to blow it with her. He kissed her thoroughly and then turned toward the side of the island where he had tied up their boat.

Gedeon stripped, bundled his lightweight pants into a

small roll and shoved them into a pack along with a couple of weapons. He strapped the pack around his neck and shifted as he covered ground. Slayer padded carefully through the trees to keep insects and birds from giving away his presence. He was a big leopard and had to choose where to place his paws in order not to sink into the spongy terrain. Most of the island was fairly stable but there were places where the crust was thin. Eventually, as he approached the outer edge of the thick trees, he clawed his way up a tree and used the branches to continue to make his way toward the strip of land where they'd left the boat.

McGregor stood on the shore, binoculars up to his eyes, seeking to peer through the trees. He walked closer to the trees, shoving impatiently at the veils of hanging moss. As he did, he dislodged spiders from their webs. Cursing, he slapped at them and took several steps backward. As he did, something moved in the shadows, catching his attention. He had no idea what was in the trees, but his heart began to pound alarmingly.

Both hands were clutched around the binoculars. He needed his gun. He backed up more and felt one of his loafer-clad feet fall into some kind of sinkhole. Deep. Whatever the thing watching him was emerged from the shadows in a slow stalk as he tried to pull his foot from the hole. His entire body froze as a large head came first, and then he saw part of the body.

A leopard. Not just any leopard. This one was enormous. Its golden gaze was fixed on him, wholly focused, as it began to stalk him in a freeze-frame motion that was the most terrifying vision imaginable. McGregor took an involuntary step back with his free foot and buried that one in the sinkhole as well.

He struggled and sank to his thighs. The leopard stopped, those eyes never leaving his face. Very slowly, so as not to trigger the large cat's instincts, McGregor put the binoculars down and reached into his jacket for his gun. He'd barely managed to pull it out when the leopard was on him, his teeth clamping around his arm, crunching down on his bone, sawing through skin, muscle, bone, everything, so he screamed in agony and dropped the gun. The leopard backed off, although the eyes never stopped staring at him.

McGregor watched in horror as the leopard contorted, the muscles and head shifting and moving until he was no longer looking at a leopard but at a large, very muscular man. He recognized him instantly. Gedeon Volkov casually pulled the pack from around his neck and dragged on a pair of drawstring trousers.

"You came out here to kill me, McGregor. Not only me but my woman as well. That wasn't smart. Hawkins is too arrogant to do any research into who he's hiring, but you're smarter than that. You wouldn't have your reputation and you wouldn't have stayed alive this long unless you knew what you were doing."

McGregor was too horrified at what he'd just witnessed to respond. Yeah, he'd done his research. He'd thought about walking away, but the temptation to kill Gedeon Volkov was too much to give up.

"Those women you killed for Hawkins, you want to tell me where you buried them?"

"Fuck you, Volkov," McGregor snapped, trying to think of how he was going to get out of the mess he was in.

Gedeon was a few feet away from him one minute; the next, he was so close, McGregor could smell the leopard in him. Volkov moved so fast, he was a blur. McGregor's clothes were in tatters, strips floating in the air as the leopard tore them from him in a fury. His skin was next, long rakes, deep, his chest and back, his neck, those terrible claws sinking into him and ripping through his flesh.

Gedeon was on him in a flash and gone just as fast, so at first McGregor thought he'd gone crazy, that the man hadn't morphed into a partial leopard and ripped him into pieces while the ground held him captive. Looking down, he saw that it was true. The pain was excruciating.

That wasn't even the worst. Tiny flies and other bugs found their way into the open wounds and began to feast. He felt as if he was being eaten alive. He looked down at the floor of the island. The leaves had come alive with ants. They formed bridges and crawled up his legs to find their way into the wounds. Beetles joined them. He heard the flutter of wings and found large birds with thick curved beaks and shiny eyes staring down at him from the branches above him. He was surrounded.

"Just kill me, for God's sake," he yelled at Gedeon.

"Why would I show you one ounce of mercy, McGregor? Did you show those women any mercy? Any of the victims you murdered, did you show them one moment of mercy?"

"Kill me."

"Where are they?" Gedeon persisted.

In the end, McGregor made up several locations before he told the truth. Gedeon moved fast, using his knife to make the kill, opening the jugular, not wanting Slayer to make the kill. He made his way back to Meiling, afraid she would reject the man he was. She saw him at his worst, when the monster was out, but she simply put her arms around him and held him before asking him to take her home.

HAWKINS," Gedeon greeted. "You look smug sitting there reading that text from your number-one man, McGregor. Looks like he found Laverne and took care of her and Edge for you right along with my woman, Meiling, and, of course, me. But then, if he did, how am I sitting here in your grandiose bedroom that's more for show than for reality?"

Hawkins slowly lowered his tablet and stared at Gedeon

as if he had two heads. He looked around the large room. "It is ostentatious, isn't it? I hire designers and this is what I get."

"It's always someone else's fault, never your own," Gedeon said. He held up McGregor's phone. "Your man missed this time. You should have done your homework before you sent him after me and mine. I spotted the shadow the very first night. I knew then I was going to kill him. And then I was going to kill you."

Hawkins chuckled. "I don't think that's necessary, Gedeon. I'll be the first to admit I could have made a mistake about you. There's always room for negotiation."

"We can negotiate pills or knives. Either is acceptable. There are a couple of pills on your nightstand. You can take one now and we keep talking. Or I can slice a knife across your belly, not too deep but enough that you feel it and we keep talking. Your choice."

"What's the pill?" Hawkins picked it up and looked at it.

"It's Percocet. Right out of the bottle on your nightstand." Gedeon held a knife up so the blade caught the light from the lamp on Hawkins's nightstand. "The blade is sharp. Goes in clean. You'll barely feel it at first."

Hawkins sighed, put the Percocet in his mouth and tossed it back with water from the glass on his nightstand. "Is Laverne dead? Did you wait to kill McGregor so he could do his job?"

"No, Laverne is alive and well. She'll inherit everything when you're gone. She's a good actress. I imagine she'll garner a great deal of sympathy, being such a young widow. Such a young, *wealthy* widow. It was a good thing you insisted she inherit everything if you died."

"That's just bullshit, and you know it. They'll suspect she murdered me. She's been gone for this last week with no explanation."

"She went to a women's retreat. All the women there

will testify to her being there." Gedeon watched him closely. "She's going to come home early when she's contacted by the police. They'll find you dead. Your prescription drug habit was kept under wraps. Tight. She wasn't aware of it. Only a close few knew. Sadly, your Percocet was laced with fentanyl. You should have been more careful, Hawkins."

For the first time, the smug smirk was wiped from Guy Hawkins's face. He looked from his nightstand to Gedeon and then touched a hand to his throat, or tried to. His head lolled back on his neck against his pillow.

Gedeon stood up and walked across the room, shoving his knife back into the scabbard at his belt. "Your reputation will suffer just enough in the media to start the rumor mill gossiping, and your widow will defend you. This way to die is far too easy for you, Hawkins. If I had my choice, I would have made it a hard one. You would have paid for every single woman you had killed. As it is, you can die knowing Laverne will have your money. The gossipmongers will chew on your reputation. A really shrewd homicide detective is unraveling the deaths of those women you had murdered by McGregor, all of whom he can tie back to you. McGregor gave up the location of their bodies so the police can recover them. You'll be dead, but your music legacy will be marred by your image."

Hawkins couldn't speak clearly. His words were slurred. Gedeon smiled at him. "Don't worry about me, Guy. No one saw me come in and they won't see me slip out. I've got an alibi even if they thought they saw me. I won't leave behind any trace of me. It will look as if you were completely alone in your room. There will be no evidence of the last message between you and McGregor, but I find it nice you would have concerns."

He waited for Hawkins to stop breathing, confirmed it by taking his pulse and then took his time hiding Hawkins's prescription drugs all over the suite. He had the prescriptions filled from all different pharmacies from various counties and states. All were opiates. Some were obtained from unknown sources. Once Gedeon had placed evidence of Hawkins's drug use throughout the suite, he left the music mogul slumped over in his bed, dead, to be found by his staff in the morning.

Slipping out into the night was easy enough. Meiling waited for him, sliding down from the rooftop of the mansion across the way after breaking down a sniper rifle and placing it in her case. He took her hand and walked around the block to their car, avoiding the street cameras and the door cameras that seemed to be on every door nowadays. Laverne and Edge were safe. Hawkins and McGregor were dead, and the women Hawkins would have marked for death would be safe. It was the best they could do. The job was finished and there was satisfaction in that.

18

A VERY small female leopard darted swiftly across the open meadow, where streaks of early morning light illuminated her thick, pale coat with its startling black rosettes. She was a gorgeous female, perfectly proportioned, her body sleek and balanced. When she ran, the muscles beneath her fur rippled and flowed, accentuating her beautifully marked pelt. Even with the meadow being open, the spotted coat of the leopard in the shadows and light managed to camouflage her, so she seemed to be more illusion than reality.

Moments after she disappeared into the trees, a male leopard's large head pushed out of the brush. He was much more cautious, testing the air before he stepped fully into the open. He was a huge male for his kind. He had to weigh in at over two hundred pounds of solid muscle. When he moved, he was fluid, agile, clearly as flexible and supple as any cat weighing less. His thick fur was marred with scars in a few places, showing he had experience fighting. He walked with confidence, a male in his prime. When he crossed the meadow after the female, he did so staying within streaks of shadows, making it nearly impossible to follow his progress.

Gedeon had allowed Slayer to have his time with Whisper after they'd inspected the area where the cabins had been in the Venezuelan jungle. Gedeon wanted to be certain Miguel hadn't started up his human trafficking enterprise again. He also wanted the cat to smell around the mass graves he knew were there. He wanted to know how many graves there were. The jungle had been quick to reclaim the territory the humans had taken from it. Already the brush had grown thick and wild. Trees were coming up as well. If Gedeon hadn't known crude roads and cabins had once been there, he wouldn't have detected the evidence.

The leopards had been out all night together. Whisper was playful and very vocal. She flirted and rubbed along tree trunks, scent marking, being alluring and tempting Slayer to follow her. She raced over downed trunks and around tall termite mounds. She splashed through shallow creek beds and rolled in crackling piles of leaves. Slayer followed her patiently.

Every fifteen to twenty minutes she crouched down, and he was on her, his teeth sinking into her shoulder to hold her in place while he mounted her. After, he stood close while she rested, and then she would be up again, exploring while he followed her. Slayer took in all the coordinates of the jungle. Every road cut into it. The wild, unexplored interior. If they approached the outer edges, he urged Whisper back under cover, even as he gathered data to pass to Gedeon and Meiling.

Dawn broke when Gedeon instructed Slayer to herd

Whisper back to the utility vehicle they had brought and parked on a nearly nonexistent trail in the jungle. Slayer had to get Whisper to her feet several times. She was exhausted and kept lying down and curling up into a little ball, falling asleep instantly. By the time the male leopard got her to the vehicle, she was stumbling on her velvet paws. Gedeon shifted immediately and called to Meiling. Whisper had curled up on the front seat.

He shook the leopard. She protested with a snarl. He kept it up, commanding her to shift. Meiling finally made the ultimate effort and did so. She didn't bother to sit up and put on her seat belt. She simply laid her head in his lap and went back to sleep. He caught up a blanket, yanked it over her and took them to the house he'd rented. He'd gotten the information they needed about the former human trafficking site. It was possible Miguel had started up somewhere else, but if he had, Rene hadn't found evidence of him doing business with anyone. Gedeon had a good idea of the routes in the jungle, and Slayer and Whisper had had their time together and were sated for the time being. It had been a productive night.

GEDEON crouched down beside the bed and pushed back the tangle of silky black hair spilling across the pillow so he could see Meiling's face. She was out. Deep sleep. So exhausted after Whisper's night in the jungle with Slayer. Meiling looked so young and innocent in her sleep—so completely not meant to be with a man like him.

He hated waking her. He'd let her sleep as long as possible. "You're going to have to join the land of the living, Lotus Blossom," he whispered, tracing her cheekbone with the pad of his finger. Memorizing her the way he did every day. She was already imprinted in his bones. It didn't matter. He still needed to map out her features with his hands, feel her bones and skin under his. The moment was always intense. Overwhelming. In some ways shocking to him. He would never fully believe that the universe had decreed that this woman would walk beside him through life. "We've got a meeting with Lubin and Miguel Diaz in an hour."

Her long lashes fluttered, and his gut tightened. His cock hardened. It didn't take much around her. He waited and the feathery lashes lifted. He found himself falling right into her dark chocolate eyes. That was another moment he looked forward to. There were so many and none he'd ever get tired of. Then she smiled and his heart contracted. Was squeezed liked a vise. He compared the feeling to having his cock strangled by her tight sheath. Agony and ecstasy. It hurt like hell, but in a good way he never wanted to end.

"There you are." He leaned in and brushed the corner of her eye with a kiss. "Sit up, Lotus, I brought coffee."

She blinked several times, the long lashes feathering up and down, and then her face lit up. She allowed him to help her into a sitting position. The sheet fell away from her body, pooling around her slender waist. She didn't seem to notice. She was too busy reaching for the coffee mug he held out to her. He noticed.

She thought her breasts too small. He thought she was perfect. Her skin was the softest thing he'd ever felt in his life. Right now, no matter how gentle he tried to be, the moment Whisper began to rise and the heat hit, control went out the window. The evidence was there like a proprietary label, all over her. He used to want to see his marks on her. Now he winced at seeing them there. The bruising and the bite marks were worrisome to him. She didn't complain because Meiling didn't complain.

"You're frowning, Leopard Boy." Meiling rubbed at the frown with her finger. "What's wrong? What did I miss?"

He caught her finger with his lips and drew it into the heat of his mouth. *You haven't missed a thing. Just waking my woman up with her coffee.* He sucked on her finger for a moment, watching desire creep into the dark chocolate in her eyes. She was so beautiful, she stole his breath.

She never flinched away from the hard things. Never. This was hard. Coming back to Venezuela, where Libby had been kidnapped, trafficked and murdered. Where her friends had been tortured and murdered. She refused to stay back and let him come alone. Before, he had always wanted her with him. Now, he wanted to shield her. Meiling just smiled sweetly and refused to stay behind.

Gedeon nipped at her fingertip before releasing it, so she could drink her coffee. "I've met Lubin Diaz several times and done work for him. He's never gone back on his word, not to me, and as far as I could tell, not with anyone else. That hasn't been as true with his sons. Frankie was a mess. He was the most likable family member. He meant well. He always had ideas and they were always shit ideas. Miguel didn't have a lot of patience with him, but Lubin, as much as he would act annoyed in public, doted on him."

"Do you know why Miguel and Frankie were so different? Did they have different mothers?"

Gedeon shook his head. "No. When Frankie was born, he was deprived of oxygen. He nearly died. His mother did. He was all Lubin and Miguel had left of her. As much as Miguel would get pissed at him, he loved him too. Anyone who made fun of Frankie got the crap beat out of them, or worse. Miguel didn't let anyone mess with his brother. He did. All the time. He thought he would toughen him up."

She sipped at the coffee, sometimes closing her eyes as if savoring it, as if it were the nectar of the gods. He ran his finger from her collarbone over the swell of her breast to her nipple. Instantly he got a reaction. Her nipple hardened into a tight bud. He dipped his head, sliding his arm around her back to steady her while he licked, suckled and then drew her breast into the heat of his mouth. He flattened her nipple against the roof of his mouth with his tongue and pressed it there while he sucked.

Meiling cradled his head with one arm, holding him close to her, her breath coming in ragged little pants. He took the coffee cup out of her hand and set it aside before the dark liquid spilled everywhere, all the while his mouth stayed busy. He dragged the sheet from her body and took her hand, guiding it between her legs. Using his fingers, he curled hers and inserted two into her already wet entrance. She was like that for him. Hot. Ready. Never turning him away. This was not about their leopards. This was about Meiling wanting to be with Gedeon.

She loved pleasing him. She worked at taking his length and girth in her mouth. She gave him that without thought for her own pleasure. Now she gave her body to him, whatever he wanted. When they were out and he kissed her, no matter where they were, she kissed him back without reservation.

He curled their fingers into her and stroked, pressing against that little bundle of nerves that could drive her wild. "Right there, baby. Keep that up. Don't stop." He whispered the command against her breast and brought up his hand to cup her left breast while he worked her right with his mouth.

She did what he said. He watched her fingers moving and her hips rocking, pushing up to meet her fingers. The sight was sensual. Erotic. He tugged on her nipple. Pinched down. Bit gently. She moaned. The sound went through his body like a spear of pure fire, arrowing straight to his cock. He kissed her breasts and dropped his hands to his jeans, opening them, releasing his erection. He was so full and aching.

Catching her easily by her thighs, he lifted her as he dropped to his back. "Ride me, Lotus." His voice was hoarse.

Husky. He positioned her body right over his straining cock and began to lower her, holding her thighs apart. "Pinch your nipples the way I was doing. Arch your back for me."

Meiling never disappointed him. It couldn't be easy balancing while he held her by her legs, but she did it. Her hands slid up her body to cup her breasts, fingers tugging and pinching her nipples, head thrown back so that her long hair cascaded down like a shiny waterfall. She shuddered with pleasure, moaning a little, arching her back, her legs trembling.

Gedeon lodged the broad head of his cock in her entrance, and fire streaked up his spine at the roiling heat. He let her weight settle over him, so that she sheathed him slowly, her tight silken tunnel a vise gripping him with a ring of fire.

"Slow, Lotus. Ride slow."

Slow might kill him, but the way she moved, the sight of her, was not only erotic but mesmerizing. Taking him apart inside. He slid his hands over her satin thighs, watching the two of them come together as he had so many other times. Like those other times, it seemed a miracle.

His eyelids felt heavy, hooded, dropping partway down as he took her in, realizing the jolting streaks of lightning arrowing up his body and settling in his groin weren't the best because her pussy was the best—although he'd forever believe it was. It was the emotions welling up in him when he was like this. Choking him. Pure lust mixed with feelings so deep for her, he knew he'd never feel them for any other being on earth.

"Gedeon." She whispered his name. Touched his face with gentle fingers. Reading him. Undoing him.

She loved him. She showed him that love in more ways than he could count. He showed her with his body. With his touch. When he was vulnerable to her—broken open and spilling out so she could see who he was. Good. Bad. Ugly. All of him loved her. He just couldn't voice his emotions the way she did. He needed the words from her. Wished she would say them more often. It wasn't fair because he never gave that to her. He gave her this . . .

Intensity. Surging into her with slow strokes. Watching the pleasure on her face. In her eyes. Hearing her breathing turn ragged. Panting. Picking up the pace with infinite care. Making them both wait, knowing the end would be so worth it. Reaching for her hands, threading their fingers together and looking into her eyes. Losing himself in her soul. In the helpless building desire and passion that crept into all that dark brown looking back at him. In the way she couldn't keep focus no matter how hard she tried, when she ground down on him and whispered his name in her little breathy moans.

Her body clamped down hard on his, taking him with her the way she did, the friction burning over his cock like a white-hot lightning storm, cleansing him of sins and throwing him out into the universe, where he floated in the serenity of absolute peace for a time. Meiling collapsed over him, her body folding over his so she lay on his chest, his cock still in her while they just breathed together.

Gedeon loved their morning sex. This might be in the afternoon, but it was still wake-up sex. He buried his hands in her hair and breathed their combined scents in. "You good, Lotus? I'm still ready to go another round."

"I'm good. Another round would make me too sore to accommodate you when Whisper starts to rise again."

He stroked his hand down her hair. She was always honest with him. She needed to be. Leopard heat was brutal, there was no doubt about it. His cock refused to relax all the way, not without the rougher sex or more frequent times per day.

She lifted her head to look at him, her eyes soft. "Take a shower with me. I can take care of you."

That was his woman. Knowing. Generous. Always thinking of him, not herself.

* * *

THE drive leading to the Diaz estate was lined with sweeping trees. The road was paved and very well maintained. Guards patrolled the grounds with dogs. The guards were armed, and they regarded the little utility vehicle Gedeon drove with suspicion, but no one made a move to intercept or stop them once they had passed the initial inspection at the front gate.

Lubin and Miguel were expecting them. They were "guests," and when Lubin Diaz declared someone his guest, no one dared to say otherwise. There was a roundabout at the front door of the sprawling two-story mansion. A long balcony overlooked the first story, providing shade for the wide verandah wrapping around the lower story. The massive front door was a good sixteen feet tall, made of thick oak and framed with black rounds of oak. The walls were thick and the glass inside the windows was thick.

Set up for war, I see, Meiling observed.

Most of these estates are. The moment the words were out, he wished he could take them back. Her friend's farm hadn't been. The farm had been an open, friendly place. Gedeon knew that Lubin's kitchen staff had purchased vegetables from the farm in order to feed Lubin and Miguel fresh food.

Meiling didn't reply. He couldn't give her comfort because there were too many eyes on them. The door opened and a servant in a crisp white uniform ushered them inside and quickly closed the door against the heat, humidity and insects. The hallway was wide and cool. The floor was hardwood. Gedeon had been there on many occasions, and he always thought it was a mixture of class and a bit over-the-top.

They were shown into the study, Lubin's favorite place. His bodyguards were placed in their most discreet positions. They could fade into the background, and no one would notice them. Lubin could conduct business or visit with his friends and yet still be safe should someone have an unexpected desire to attack him.

"Gedeon." Lubin stood, both hands extended in greeting. The lines in his face revealed strain. His eyes showed real tension, but his grip as he took both of Gedeon's hands was strong. "It's good of you to come. Thank you."

"Of course, Lubin. This is my partner, Lotus." Gedeon had no idea if Meiling's name had been compromised. He wasn't taking any chances.

Few things shocked Lubin Diaz, but it was clear Gedeon Volkov having a partner did. Lubin nodded to her. She flashed one of her demure smiles but kept her eyes lowered. Miguel greeted Gedeon as well. Gedeon assessed his reaction to their arrival. He seemed just as happy to see them as Lubin did, which was odd.

Once they were settled and the servant had brought in refreshments, Lubin got right to the point. He wanted to hire Gedeon immediately. He explained that, without his consent, his sons had dabbled in human trafficking. The implication was that it was Frankie more than Miguel who had set the operation up, although Lubin had to know Gedeon wasn't a fool. Frankie wouldn't have had the first clue how to do such a thing. He let that pass.

Miguel took up the story. "There was a woman. A blonde. She was staying at the Regent, you know, where all the tourists with money stay." Miguel glanced at his father and then down at his hands. "I wasn't told about this until afterward. Frankie found out that these men were hunting her. They offered a steep reward for her. She liked to go out to the clubs and dance, so Frankie thought it would be easy enough to snatch her up. Apparently he was right. His thought was to grab her and negotiate a higher price for her."

Gedeon had perfected the art of looking bored. He

didn't look at Meiling. Miguel was talking about Libby. Libby had been hunted by the same group of men who were hunting Meiling. He willed Meiling not to interrupt, not to ask questions or say anything at all.

"Frankie and his crew drugged the girl and took her out to our cabins in the forest. The boys had a go at her. They usually start training right away. She was a fighter. She didn't look like one, but she put up a fight like you wouldn't believe. I was out there briefly, and that's when he told me these other men had been looking for her. I thought she was more trouble than she was worth. I told Frankie to sell her to them and I left."

"Did you know who they were?" Gedeon asked. "The ones who wanted her?"

Miguel shook his head. "I didn't find out until recently. Had I known, I would have personally delivered her to them and hoped they would have been satisfied. No, I didn't know. I left and thought Frankie would take care of it. Instead, his men thought they could tame her. They ended up killing her. That brought hell down on us."

"So you know who they are now."

It was Lubin who nodded. "That's why I called you, Gedeon. We have trouble here. Frankie got us into big trouble. He didn't mean to, but you knew him. He always acted the big shot. He thought he could take on the world. He always went behind my back starting new projects that were going to make us big money. This girl, this Libby. The men who wanted her are members of Dragon Throne Justice." He whispered the name.

Gedeon studied Lubin's pale face beneath his olive complexion. It would be difficult to feign that level of fear. It made a kind of sense. The Chinese had their Dragon Throne. In Siberia there were rumors of Dragon Justice. If shifters decided not to allow anyone more gifted than those in the Dragon families to live, what could be more natural than to band together and murder the unsuspecting families of those with more talents?

"How many serve on Dragon Throne Justice?" Gedeon asked. He slipped a small amount of compulsion into his voice so that Lubin would want to answer.

"Five, although Longwei Lis, from China, has a son, Kang, chomping at the bit to take over or be added to the board. Frankie thought he might want to keep this woman, this Libby, for himself if she had talents, but it seems he was wrong. They wanted her to lead them to another woman." Lubin looked from Gedeon to Meiling and then back to Gedeon. "Her cousin."

"You want me to find this Libby's cousin?" Gedeon guessed. He was grateful Meiling had her silky black hair and dark chocolate eyes, where Libby had been tall and blond. They hadn't been cousins by blood, but the two of them hadn't ever made a big deal of it.

Lubin nodded but looked mournful. "You do the impossible, Gedeon. This is the impossible. These people have threatened to kill my only remaining son. Miguel had nothing to do with Libby's death. He ordered her taken to them, but Frankie didn't comply with that order. You knew him. He changed his mind or forgot. Still, the order is there. These people don't play games. We must deliver something to them, or Miguel is dead."

Lubin and Miguel didn't give a damn that Libby had been kidnapped and murdered. Neither gave a second thought to her. They were concerned that the men making up the powerful Dragon Throne Justice would order them killed. They wanted Gedeon to fix it for them by finding Libby's cousin and delivering her into the board's hands. They didn't care what the board wanted with her, or even if they killed her. They simply wanted to be left alone.

"Do you have anything to go on, Miguel? Frankie must have cleaned out the hotel room when he took her. Did you save her things? Personal items? Cell phone? Anything at all I can use as a starting point?"

Miguel nodded. "I have all of that bagged for you. I knew you'd need it. It's already loaded in your vehicle."

"I'll pay your regular rate," Lubin stated.

"Frankie was my friend," Gedeon said, waving away the idea of taking money. "I'll see what I can do. Miguel, lie low. Stay close to the house and watch over your father." He stood up. He didn't know how much more he could stomach, or how much longer Meiling could be in their company without telling them what she thought of them.

He kept his body very close to hers as they followed the servant down the hall to the heavy front door. He let the servant open the door. It was a habit not to touch more than he had to anywhere he was. He didn't like to leave evidence behind that he'd been there. Meiling didn't look at him as they made their way to the car. She didn't say one word as they got inside, closed the doors and he started the vehicle up.

Once they were back on the road headed toward the airport, Gedeon glanced at her. She stared out the window, her soft features set.

"Are you okay?"

She shook her head. "I don't think I can talk yet. The two of them, talking like that. They're evil, Gedeon. You know that, don't you? They didn't give Libby a second thought. Miguel saw her. He raped her. He didn't give a damn about her. She was too much trouble, so he wanted her sold to the other men who had been looking for her. He didn't mind that she was dead, that they'd killed her, only that that got their family in trouble."

Her voice hadn't risen. Her tone remained the same. Soft. Too calm. On the outside she appeared stoic. Strong. But inside, where no one could see, he felt tears dripping down her heart. He felt them in her soul.

She didn't take her gaze from the window, but she continued speaking. "Do you know why I called out to you about the bomb when I despised shifters? When I knew you might even kill me for witnessing you killing all those men who trafficked those women? I watched you come out of those cabins and your grief and rage were genuine. You can't fake something like that." Her tone was still strictly neutral.

Gedeon nearly pulled the little utility vehicle over, but they couldn't afford to miss their flight. They'd chartered a plane for home. Why was it he never seemed in a position where he could comfort her?

"Lotus," he murmured gently.

"That last cabin, you came out of it, and you put one knee to the porch and covered your face with your hand and wept. I'll never get the sight of you like that out of my mind. You cared about those women. You cared enough to kill for them. No other shifter that I'd ever come across would have taken risks like that, or even thought twice about the women. I thought you were magnificent." Her voice lowered to a whisper. "Being with you all this time, nothing has changed my mind. If anything, I think it even more."

A lump crawled up his throat and lodged there. His woman. His Lotus Blossom. He glanced at her. She looked very small and fragile, as only Meiling could look. He reached out and took her hand, uncaring that she had huddled as far from him as possible. He didn't say anything, just ran his thumb over the back of her hand. What was there to say?

"When this is over and we've managed to find these Dragon Justice people, I want to make certain we revisit those two smug bastards."

She'd never once asked him for anything. Not one time.

"Consider it done, Lotus," he assured. He'd been planning on it anyway. He'd almost instructed Meiling to go to the car and wait for him. He would have done it right then, but there were too many guards and servants who could identify them.

Once at the airport, he'd text Rene to find out where the members of Dragon Throne Justice were and who they were. He wanted to have that information by the time they landed in New Orleans. He wanted to have as much information on each member as possible.

THANKFULLY Whisper's heat was over, giving them a respite. Rene had gathered as much information as he thought possible on the board members calling themselves Dragon Throne Justice. As Lubin had said, five made up the board. They were older now, much older, which to Gedeon meant they were the original members calling for the deaths of his family and Meiling's. Three members were from a lair in southeastern Russia, the other two from China near the Russian border.

It was rumored the three men from Russia were members of the *bratya* and, like most of the lairs in that area, refused to mate with the woman who would be their true mate. This drove their leopard insane. No male heirs had the same gifts their fathers had. Gedeon thought it was most likely due to the fact that the men hadn't mated with the right females. The same was true of those men in China. They had also chosen not to mate with their true mates. That seemed to weaken their genetics, and no heir was born with the gifts their father had. The one son insisting he wanted on the board was a shifter, but had no special talents that anyone had ever seen.

Meiling and Gedeon built a replica of the very large palace, which was really a fortress the Dragon Justices retreated to with their army of soldiers. The structure was built on the border between the two countries and was heavily guarded.

They studied every entrance and exit, the roof, the outside walls, the gates and the guard shacks. They memorized the changing of the guards, every routine from the kitchen to scraping ice from the walkways. The palace, with its extensive grounds, had been built to withstand an army. The Dragon Justices expected to have to fight off soldiers attempting to take over their territory. They wouldn't consider that two motivated assassins might slip inside their domain, kill them where they found them and leave without ever being seen.

Meiling and Gedeon packed to board the plane that would take them to Russia. They crawled into bed, Gedeon wrapping his arms around her. As Meiling placed her cell phone on the nightstand, sudden fireworks seemed to explode.

Startled, she lifted the phone so both could read the screen.

Email now. Urgent. E.

Meiling's eyes met Gedeon's and there was open fear in hers. Both could feel the urgency in Etienne's text. Meiling opened her email and then the program with the key so she could insert his email into it.

Jules and Louis betrayed me as well as you. They told these people you were close with Cosette. That you talk with her several times a week. She must have told them. They're her cousins. Why would they betray her? She's been taken again. She was at her music class. I had three bodyguards on her. They were killed. The note said only you can get her back. If you don't come for her, she will live but wish she is dead. My poor Cosette. Again. I know they are saying you must trade your life for hers. I cannot ask you to do this, but I don't even know who they are.

Gedeon cursed under his breath. "Cosette is his daughter?" He had done his research into Etienne. The daughter was around eighteen or nineteen.

Meiling nodded.

Etienne was asking Meiling to trade her life for Cosette's. The Frenchman knew that was what he was doing. He might not feel he had any other choice, but he should just own it. Not pretend he wasn't putting Meiling's life on the line. Already the program was eating the message, the black holes appearing in it.

"Tell me about this girl and your relationship with her," Gedeon commanded.

"That was how I first met Etienne. Cosette could be considered one of those poor little rich girls. Her parents loved her, but they didn't spend any time with her. Etienne was always working and her mother, Manon, had too many society events to attend to really bother noticing what her daughter was up to. Cosette craved attention, so she tended to seek it in negative ways. She would do all sorts of outrageous things to get herself kicked out of school. She'd attend parties that she had no business going to. Eventually, Manon left. She ran off with another man and she didn't want anything to do with Cosette because the new man didn't. That just made things worse."

Meiling sat up, pulling her knees to her chest and wrapping her arms tight around them. "Cosette spent a great deal of time online and eventually met someone she shouldn't have. You know how that story goes. She snuck off one night to meet him. Etienne called me when she didn't come home. He didn't think anything of it other than she was being outrageous again, looking for attention."

Gedeon sat up as well, reaching for Meiling. He wasn't going to allow her to ride this one out alone. He lifted her easily and settled her onto his lap. Wrapping his arms around her, he pulled her in tight against his chest. "You didn't believe that was the case."

She shook her head. "I read her diary. I went through her computer. She was only fifteen, and I found myself furious at her father. He had this beautiful daughter who wanted to be a part of his life and he was too busy to give her the time of day. If I was right about my suspicions, he might never be able to give her attention again. I found myself invading his office and giving him a piece of my mind.

"He told me she had tried to talk to him about some friend she met online, but he didn't let her into his office. He was on a conference call. He didn't remember what she'd said. I told him he'd be damned lucky if he ever got to talk to his daughter again, and I hoped the money he made was worth his daughter's life. Then I stormed out."

Gedeon felt her heart beating beneath his palm. He had Meiling wrapped up as tight as he dared without hurting her. All the while he rocked her gently, subtly, offering her comfort. She'd gotten the girl back from a very bad situation. Meiling had tracked her, finding the much older man from his online profile. He had taken Etienne's innocent fifteen-year-old daughter to a house out in the country to share with his four friends. She was kept nude, chained and available to the five men, who did whatever they wanted to her any time of the day or night.

Meiling brought her home and stayed in her room with her to make certain the nightmares didn't consume her. She stayed even when Cosette began counseling, because the girl clung to her. Meiling refused the money Etienne offered, but she wasn't opposed to accepting favors in return. Eventually, Cosette was able to allow Meiling out of her sight for longer and longer periods of time, but they still talked three times a week. Evidently, Cosette had confided that little piece of news to her cousins, Jules and Louis, not realizing they despised Meiling.

"You know even if you tried to exchange yourself for Cosette, they would either kill her in front of you or traffic her. They won't keep their word and release her." Gedeon was compelled to tell her the truth. He didn't want to. He felt as if she'd been struck by one body blow after another.

"I'm well aware, Gedeon." She turned her head, her eyes glowing with green and gold flecks, indicating Whisper was close. "I'm counting on you. On Slayer and Whisper. We'll do this. We just have to stick to the plan."

Gedeon bent his head to her shoulder and pressed a kiss to her bare skin. "Exactly. It's a good plan. They expect you to come for her, Meiling. But they expect you to bring an army with you. Soldiers you've acquired over time. It won't occur to them that you would ever dare penetrate their lair with just your partner."

"My mate," she corrected.

His heart nearly seized in his chest. "Say again?" His throat had constricted to the point he could barely get the words out. They sounded hoarse.

"My mate," she repeated. "You're my partner, but going into their fortress, you're my mate. My man."

"I am," he agreed. "That's exactly who I am."

19

THE fence surrounding the front of the fortress was very high, a good twenty-five feet of twisted metal, with each anchor ending in a sharp spear. The anchors were close together; some pointed straight up toward the sky, while others on either side of them pointed outward or inward. This was clearly to keep leopards from scaling the fence and getting in.

Outside the fence was heavily patrolled by four teams of two shifters each, with AK-47s hanging easily on their shoulders. Trees had been cleared right up to the fence, leaving the ground bare. The road leading to the fortress was paved and kept in good shape with no potholes. The ground sloped in gentle swells for miles, with little or no brush or trees thanks to the continual clearing being done.

Gedeon timed the patrols. The shifters were fairly consistent in their routes and how long it took each of them to make the circuit back to the front gate. Gedeon tracked them one by one. Meiling had infiltrated the grove of fruit trees that stood outside the tall fence. The grove had its own fence but wasn't within the much more protected fortress. When they had checked out the fruit trees, Gedeon could understand why. In the winter, the fruit trees had to be protected from the biting cold. Whoever had originally planted the fruit trees had chosen the best possible location for them, out of the wind, protected on three sides. They could be covered, and if the temperature dropped too low, they could use machines to keep the trees alive.

He had an appointment to see Bolin Wang and Makar Turgenev, two of the Dragon Justices, in a short period of time. It was an opening ploy. Meiling would be inside, covering him. She had to go in first. Phase one was to make certain their information was correct. They had to know they could count on their exit and entrance routes. This was where they had to be shadows. Ghosts. No one could know they were there. Not even Cosette. Meiling could take a few minutes and locate her, but she couldn't reassure her. They couldn't chance it.

As far as Gedeon knew, all five Dragon Justices still resided in the fortress. The lair seemed to be packed with their soldiers and the servants needed to feed and entertain them. The fortress housed a village as well as the palace. The smaller dwellings were on either side of the palace and behind it in a large semicircle. Those homes would only be a problem if Gedeon and Meiling were forced to run in that direction and couldn't hide themselves. They didn't foresee that happening, but they had a plan just in case.

He checked the time and waited for the guards to pass out of sight before he eased out of the depression he was in and began to belly crawl to the next strip of grass. He did it slowly. There were cameras everywhere. That didn't mean anyone was paying close attention. Those watching had been doing so for months, perhaps even years, and had to be bored out of their minds. Still, it paid to be cautious. Gedeon was a cautious man.

They bring girls here all the time, Gedeon, Meiling said. *For the soldiers to use. These men traffic them from the other lairs.*

It didn't surprise him. That was the reason Fyodor, his brothers and cousins had gotten out. They couldn't stomach what was happening to the women in the lairs. They could see the devastation it caused. They could even see the Amur leopard was on the verge of extinction, but still, to prove loyalty, the men continued using and killing the women.

They abuse their own leopards as well. These are sick lairs, Meiling. Those in charge have to know they're destroying the lair and the shifters from within, but they don't want to admit they're wrong, so they continue to make the same mistakes instead of trying to fix what they've done.

I'm listening to the kitchen staff gossip as they harvest from the garden. They know just about everything going on inside the palace.

She wasn't supposed to be inside the gates yet. Not without him. He reminded her of their timeline.

I saw the opportunity, Gedeon, and had to take it. For as many people working inside, they do know one another. If I'm spotted, I'll stand out like a sore thumb.

Who are those working in the palace? Can you tell? Are they trafficked women? Would they help you get to Cosette?

These women are all married. I think their husbands are soldiers for the various lairs. I don't know if they're true mates of those soldiers or they were bought and given to the soldier, but they're definitely married.

You can't trust them to help you, he concluded.

No, I wouldn't dare. I'll find her.

That palace is a fucking big place. I can only stall them so long before they become suspicious.

I'll find her. I have a . . . Meiling broke off.

Gedeon waited. He knew she had gifts. Important ones. He had them too, but he didn't have Meiling's personal radar that included finding a lost person in a giant maze where someone had hidden her. She was not only a miracle but a treasure.

Gedeon, they don't expect that anyone is looking for her. They know you're coming because you made an appointment with them. You were even respectful and told them what it was in regard to. If they check up on you, they'll find you were just in Venezuela a few days ago and you did visit Lubin Diaz and then flew to New Orleans. You have a reputation, Gedeon. Best guess, they'll try to hire you themselves.

That would be fucking funny if they did. *Should I accept the offer to hunt you down, little Lotus Blossom? Take their money from them? We can have a hell of a time looking for you.* He knew there was a time she had feared he might turn on her and take money to turn her over to those looking for her. That was before she knew and trusted him. Before she knew his past. He would never betray her. Never give her up. He could tease her.

Do you think they pay their debts?

Not to someone like me. They would consider me a rogue. Someone without a lair. An easy target. He sent her one of his cruel smiles—the ones he reserved for their crap clients. He let her hold that image in her mind. *I like that they'll think that. You stay out of sight, Meiling. Don't show yourself even for a moment, no matter what the temptation is. There isn't a good enough reason to show yourself.*

Her silence made him uneasy. She'd agreed that if she

gave up her weapon, it would only make it that much easier for their enemies to kill her and Cosette, if that was their intention.

I think it is very important for you to understand that I do have a brain. Not only do I have a brain, but it also happens to be an above-average one.

There was that little bite to her voice. He *loved* that edge she got sometimes. *Lotus, we're working. How many times have I told you not to talk to me like that when we're working? You sound like that, I get hard. Not just hard. I get hard as a fuckin' rock. I can't move. I'm stuck right here in this meadow waiting for the guards to come back around and find me just lying here.*

You're always hard.

Not so hard I can't walk, he denied.

You're so dramatic. You'd better not wait there in the open for the guards. I'm going to take a look around inside and see if can find Cosette. The teasing note disappeared from her voice. *This place is insane. It looks like a palace in China. The real deal, all themed around dragons. Gold edging on the chairs. There's a huge chessboard and I kid you not, Gedeon, it's gilded in gold. The pieces are all trimmed in gold.*

Gedeon didn't like the mixture of awe and repugnance in her voice. It took concentration not to be seen. Yes, remaining hidden in plain sight was a gift, but it also was one that required the wielder to be aware at all times of his or her surroundings and utilize every bit of the energy close to shield her.

Lotus, baby, stay focused. He had to stay focused as well. Losing her wasn't an option. He hadn't told her that. He should have. Doing so in the middle of their mission was just plain ludicrous.

Gedeon, I'm solid. No worries here. You filled me in on what to expect. The greed and the true hatred against women. I was expecting both, but when you come into this place and see the fortune they've acquired and realize it isn't enough for them, I think it will shock even you.

He knew it wouldn't. He'd seen it over and over again.

These men have trafficked men, women and children for decades, amassing fortunes, Gedeon, ordering the murders of villages, of families, while they lived here doing whatever they wanted, and still, it was never enough for them. When is it enough?

He didn't have an answer for her. He hadn't ever found that answer.

Why do they see themselves as superior? Or entitled? What makes them believe they are? The circumstances of their birth? What gifts were they born with that made them believe they could put themselves before any other shifter?

I told you, they have the ability to produce fire.

Just those original five.

To my knowledge. I have never heard that any of their children were able to do so, including Longwei Lis's son, Kang Lis, who lives at the palace with them now and is eager to sit on the board.

Is Kang the only child any of them have?

The only living child that Rene and I could ascertain. It was common practice to murder any female child when they were born, along with the woman who gave birth to the female child. No sons were born with the ability to produce fire.

They murdered infant babies simply because they were female?

The bite in her voice became even more pronounced, worrying Gedeon even further. He was out of the open meadow and heading back to his vehicle. He'd told her of the practice. She knew that in some remote villages in other countries in modern times the practice still held true. Male children were prized, for whatever reasons. Females were always less than . . .

His woman could get riled. She did have a temper. It took a lot to get her there, but when she went off, she went nuclear. They needed her calm, able to move freely around and know exactly where she was going. The palace was a labyrinth of secret passages, apartments, and secret entrances and exits. It was not simply the front rooms they presented to visitors. It was a mini city. In one night, they would need to navigate that city without being caught. They had the added burden of finding Cosette and bringing her out with them.

Getting worried, baby. This is a difficult one. You have to keep your head in the game.

There was a short silence, and then she flowed into his mind. Meiling. The way she did. Filling him. Her strength. Delicate, but so fucking strong. She'd taught him that women could be like that. Gentle, able to bend when the wind came at them with the force of a hurricane, but they didn't break. They were that strong. *She* was that strong. Meiling would stand with him no matter the cost to her. Together they wouldn't allow these men to continue their reign of terror.

My head is totally in this game, Gedeon. I would never risk your life by losing sight of what's important. I'll be in that room with you to back you up. I'm being cognizant of the time. After, I can do more exploring. The kitchens are hotbeds of gossip. There are three kitchens.

It occurred to me that if each of the five has his own home within the palace, Cosette would most likely have been taken by one of the Russian lairs. The men looking for her were made up of Russians from the Amurov lairs. They were bratya. *Shifters. If you come across any of the three lairs, those are the ones I would check first.*

You're right, Gedeon. I was looking at the palace as a whole and making it into a grid pattern in my mind to section it. We would have been here for months looking for her.

He would have taken one of the mighty Dragon Justices prisoner and tortured him to get the information, but he wasn't going to admit that to her. She probably read that shit in his mind, but if she did, she wouldn't condemn him for it. She never did, not even when he expected her to.

Gedeon returned to his vehicle and boldly drove right up the road toward the gates.

Making my way up their drive now. Half their army is on me. If I were an ordinary man, I might be intimidated.

I'm so thankful you're anything but ordinary.

He drove the Jeep right up to the fence. Up close it was even more impressive than in all the photographs they had of it. For one thing, the iron was far thicker than it appeared in pictures. There were barbs, metal hooks, woven into the anchors, so if anyone dared to try to climb the fence, those barbs would tear into their flesh and eventually hold them in place. It was a wicked but very effective way to prevent an army from getting to those inside the palace.

Gedeon, after close inspection, was brought up the wide marble steps—steps he thought ostentatious and useless when trying to escape or fight in winter or during a rainstorm; they would be as slick as hell. Marble might show off wealth, but it was a mistake if one wanted to be certain they could fight off an army. The five Dragon Justices counted on the fence to keep out their enemies.

He entered through the highly decorated double doors. Thick with gold inlay. Real gold. The enormous wings of a dragon made up the two doors while the body and head were carved in the center. When the doors were opened simultaneously, the dragon appeared to move. Gedeon thought the artwork was incredible, breathtaking. Reds and blacks made up the dragon, but the scales were all gold. He would have liked to take his time studying it. Rene would have loved it. Rene was a huge fan of art.

He was ushered into a very large room meant to impress

visitors. The ceilings were high. The walls shimmered with ivory. A long table of black enamel was surrounded by high-backed chairs all edged in gold. The chess set Meiling had told him about dominated the center of the room, with two ornate chairs on either side of the playing board. The chairs represented the chess pieces, one a red dragon, the other a black dragon.

Everywhere Gedeon looked, from the tall vases in various places on the floor to the paintings on the walls, the room held tremendous artwork. He could have spent weeks there, just in that one room, and never be able to see all of the priceless art.

"Mr. Volkov." The voice was smooth. A hint of arrogance. Of amusement. The man knew the impression that room would make on anyone. He found Gedeon's reaction particularly amusing and let him see.

Gedeon turned his gaze from one of the paintings depicting two dragons falling from the skies, talons locked together as they spun toward the ground, wings out. The artist had been so good Gedeon could almost feel the combat, the way the two males were fighting for supremacy, both refusing to give in even when death was so close. He turned cold eyes on the men who had orchestrated the murders of his family members.

He had been certain, when he had asked to see them, they would have him investigated. He knew they wouldn't ever find a connection to his family, long dead now. No one ever thought or remembered that the *pakhan* had kept his mother and the youngest boy alive. There had been no one left alive to remember.

He had the kind of reputation that would intrigue these men. He had never failed to get a job done—unless he had made his client disappear. One didn't ever double-cross him. He could track and find anyone, given enough time. He negotiated deals between lairs that despised one another and made them stick. He had become legendary. He knew he would be facing all five of the board members, not just two. That suited his plans. It also meant he had to be much more careful.

"Please take a seat, Mr. Volkov, and let us know how we can be of service to you," said Bolin Wang, the appointed spokesman. From everything Rene could dig up on them, Bolin Wang was often the front man. He was soft-spoken and very slow to rile. "I'm Bolin Wang. These are my colleagues, Longwei Lis." He indicated the shorter man with gray hair worn pulled back in a ponytail. Lis wore traditional robes almost as ornate as the dragon chair he sat in. His son, Kang, sat behind him looking annoyed, bored and petulant. He wore a suit, as did the three Russian *bratya*. Each of those men was introduced, and Gedeon marked them for death. Makar Turgenev. Ilari Morozov. Klim Zima. These were men from the same region Gedeon's family had originated from. One of these men had gone to the others out of jealousy and conceived his plan of ridding the world of anyone who might be smarter, or faster, or better at anything than they were.

Gedeon had been a toddler, but he had a good memory. Once an event took place in his presence, it was imprinted on his brain. What's more, it was there in Slayer's memories as well. He called up his leopard. They simply needed a trigger. One small word or gesture, the way the man turned his head or gestured with his hands, would bring the memory to the forefront.

Gedeon seated himself in the ornate high-backed, gold-edged dragon chair facing the five men. He was well versed in appearing confident because he was. He had already assessed the situation. Each of these men had bodyguards, but they were arrogant and had ordered their guards to stay to the other side of the room. The room was enormous. Not one of the bodyguards, even though they were shifters, could get to their primary target before Gedeon could kill them.

He knew he could kill at least three of them before the others could react. Meiling would take out the other two and possibly Kang. Then it would be a fight to make it out of the palace without the soldiers getting to them before they could escape the country. Without their leaders, the lairs would collapse into chaos for a time. Gedeon doubted new leaders would want to seek revenge, but if they were that reckless, he would cope with the fallout when he had to.

He studied the faces watching him so intently as he explained that he had taken the job of finding an unknown woman for Lubin and Miguel Diaz. He understood these men wanted the woman delivered to them. Since they wanted her, perhaps they had more information on her that would aid him in his work. Lubin and Miguel had no information whatsoever on her. It had been Frankie who had kidnapped her cousin, Libby, and ultimately killed her. Gedeon sounded bored, as if he were repeating facts, data he'd acquired.

"This is the hotshot investigator, coming to us for information because he can't do his job," Kang sneered.

Gedeon didn't deign to look at Lis's son. "If you can't—or won't—help me, no worries, I can run her down, but I thought it would be faster if you had more data on her. It seemed as if you were in a hurry to find her. I can leave," he offered.

"You are an arrogant son of a bitch," Kang snapped. "Do you think you can just walk out of here without our permission too?"

"Kang," Longwei cautioned as Gedeon slowly raised his gaze from the five Dragon Justices to the younger man sitting behind them.

His gaze had gone from blazing green to warning amber and gold. Killer eyes. Flat. Ice-cold. "I will say this one time. In agreeing to see me, all of you agreed to the terms of my coming here. I will not be disrespected any

more than I would disrespect you. If this man wants to
challenge me to a fight to the death, as he seems to be doing, he will need to do so in an open, clear way for everyone to hear. When he is dead, I do not want anyone to say
there was no challenge. I don't want interference when he
is losing the battle. I don't want hard feelings when he lies
lifeless, staring up at you."

Deliberately Gedeon dismissed Kang as inconsequen-
tial, knowing each word he said would be a blow to the
young man. After sending him one chilling look, he turned
his focused leopard's stare back on the five Dragon Justices. Watching them closely. Waiting for the reactions.
Kang was predictable and did exactly what Gedeon was
certain he would. The young man leapt up, the heavy chair
scraping along the marble floor. He tried to draw his sword,
but it got caught up in the heavy drapery on the back of the
chair.

Kang was seated behind his father and Ilari Morozov.
The moment Kang sprang up, Ilari Morozov jumped up as
well, half turning as if facing a threat, one hand going
inside his jacket and emerging with a gun.

Does he seem at all familiar to you, Slayer? Gedeon
asked.

He felt the leopard studying the Russian crime lord
closely just as he was doing. *No. This man is a stranger
to me.*

Ilari was going to die anyway, but he wasn't the man
Gedeon was looking for. He knew Meiling was fully aware.
He could feel her, their connection strong.

"I do challenge you," Kang shouted, finally managing
to pull his sword from the scabbard hanging on the back
of his chair.

"Kang," Longwei said, with a long-suffering sigh. "Sit
down. We have business to discuss with this gentleman."

"For God's sake, Kang," Makar Turgenev snapped, a
sneer in his voice. "I'm sick to death of your needing con-

stant attention. Longwei, send him to his room. Have a couple of the soldiers escort him there. He can play with his latest acquisition and make himself feel like a man."

It took every ounce of discipline Gedeon had to maintain his bored expression and relaxed body at recognizing the Russian kingpin's voice. The body language betraying his attitude that he felt he was so superior to Kang. He waved his hand dismissively and even pointed toward the far exit and made a shooing motion with his fingers, as if Kang were an unruly child, not a full-grown adult.

Longwei didn't take offense on his son's behalf. Instead, he jerked his chin toward the door across the room. "Go now, Kang. When you challenge an enemy to a fight, you first must know you can defeat him. You could not defeat this man."

Kang cursed all of them, but he stormed off without challenging Gedeon further, crossing the marble floor in his very expensive Italian leather shoes, tossing the sword irreverently onto the chair. The sword slid from the seat to the floor with a clatter. Kang didn't look back but continued to the exit, where he disappeared, slamming the heavy door as best he could.

Klim Zima laughed. "That girl you gave him to entertain himself with is in for a long night. He'll take his frustrations out on her."

The others laughed as if this was the funniest thing in the world. Gedeon didn't crack a smile. He portrayed a bored expression.

The new acquisition very well could be Cosette, Meiling. Follow him.

We are returning this evening. We have the layout of the five lairs. We'll find her. I am your backup, Gedeon, and we don't deviate from the plan.

Those were his rules. He couldn't very well object when she threw his own rules at him. She was right too. The biggest danger they faced at the moment was right there in

that room. All eyes were on him, and he couldn't give away
the fact that he was smarter or faster than any of them.

"The woman, Libby Chang, the Diaz family kidnapped
when we were offering a reward was not really a blood
relationship of the woman we are seeking." Again, it was
Bolin Wang who spoke, his voice calm and gentle. "The
woman we seek is called Meiling. She was raised with
Libby. Libby's father, Jian Chang, stole her from her family and took her to be raised by his wife. Meiling is unaware of this. We wanted only to talk to Libby, to ask her
questions about how we could find Meiling. The Diaz family run a human trafficking ring and are not experts in training the woman they acquire. They were brutal in their
methods, and they killed Libby before we had a chance to
speak with her."

Bolin sounded reasonable with his mixture of truth and
lies, as if they had no intention of harming Meiling.

"Why would you care about this Meiling?" Again,
Gedeon was careful to sound offhand, as if it didn't matter
one way or the other if Bolin even answered him.

"Her father was my closet friend. When he was brutally murdered, I promised myself I would take care of his
family or what was left of it."

He is lying, Meiling announced.

Gedeon's gut knotted. *Yes, I can hear the lies. When
Makar Turgenev came to him with his murderous plan
formed from pure jealousy, he was eager enough to hear it.*

*And act on it. I should remember. I remember every-
thing, but not that. Only glimpses. Dark memories saved
for my nightmares.*

I don't want you to remember, Gedeon told her. *You
deserve to live a happy life, Lotus, free of all this continual ugliness. It's bad enough that I insist you accompany
me on these cases we take together, but now we're delving
into your childhood. I knew this was going to be a shit
show.*

Instantly he was flooded with all things Meiling. Her kindness. Her sweetness. Most of all her love for him. How did he exist without her?

"You have her name. Surely one woman can't be that difficult to find," Gedeon said.

"She lives off the grid. I believe her foster father must have taught her to do that, and she's very good at not being found," Bolin continued. For the first time, the merest hint of admiration crept into his voice. "If you were to find this woman, we would be very grateful, Mr. Volkov."

"I'm working for Lubin Diaz and his son," Gedeon reminded. "According to them, Miguel's life is forfeit if I can't find this woman. Frankie is dead and Miguel is Lubin's only remaining son. I came here in good faith to gather information in order to better find this woman for them to turn her over to you. Or at least let you know where she is."

"You could give us that information directly, or bring her to us," Makar snapped impatiently.

Gedeon allowed his ice-cold gaze to sweep over the Russian, a touch of disdain in the gold and green flecks. "No, I could not. My word is my bond. I don't screw my clients. Not ever. I told them I would find this woman and I will. What they do with the information is up to them. What you do when they give it to you is up to you." Gedeon made a movement as if to rise.

Longwei waved him to his seat. "It has occurred to me that we may have been too hasty blaming Lubin and Miguel for what Frankie did." He looked at the others, one gray eyebrow raised. "We should call them and tell them to call off their deal with Volkov. Once they do, he would be free to work for us without a conflict of interest."

The other justices nodded solemnly, as if just by one stating Gedeon would work for them, it was a done deal and Gedeon would agree to it. Makar snapped his fingers and immediately a servant ran forward and placed a phone in his hand.

"Just like that, you're going to call Lubin and let them off the hook."

"Yes, we'll see that you're compensated," Bolin said. "And let them know that you came to us in good faith for them."

It was all Gedeon could do not to allow his leopard to appear to smirk like a wolf.

GEDEON and Meiling studied the tall fence. It had been built with the specific idea of keeping shifters out. If any of the *bratya* families made a move against them, they would be hard pressed to get past the fence to get inside before the soldiers would be ready to deal with them. Gedeon and Meiling didn't need to climb the fence; they could simply jump over it.

You certain you can clear it? Gedeon wanted reassurance. Meiling was small but she was a powerhouse. He really didn't have doubts, but he knew exactly what she would do.

She punched his arm. Hard. He grinned at her. She grinned back at him. They could be walking into a nightmare, but she didn't flinch. She wasn't an assassin, but she still stood solidly with him.

When we get inside, you go directly to Kang's room. Hopefully we're right and Cosette is there. No matter what shape she's in, she'll have to be on her feet so we can bring her out. That's your job, Meiling. Get her on her feet. Keep her mouth shut and keep her moving. Rene has a car waiting at the west gate. If we can get her there, we can get her to the airport and be out of here before anyone has any idea they're all dead.

She'll do what I tell her, Meiling assured, confidence pouring into him.

He believed in Meiling. He didn't believe in Etienne's daughter. Kang was an asshole and he had wanted to take his frustrations out on someone. If Cosette was the woman in his room, she was going to be a mess.

They waited for the break in the patrolling of the guards, and both crouching low, they went up and over the fence, clearing the height easily. Neither could be detected by the shifters with their enhanced sense of smell due to the spray and the pills ingested. This product was not offered on the market to just anyone. It was only because Rene had a very special relationship with Charisse Mercier that Charisse allowed Rene to even know of its existence.

The two of them went right up the stairs to the front entrance. They didn't have to wait long. The soldiers were leaving to go home, and new soldiers were arriving to take over. They walked right in with the new guards. It was a matter of staying to the shadows and willing those around not to see them. It took intense concentration, but it could be done.

Once inside, Gedeon took the left corridor that led to the Russian lairs. Meiling went right. *Stay connected to me.* Meiling didn't respond, but he didn't expect her to. He moved fast, utilizing Slayer's stealth as he bypassed the first two abrupt turns that would take him to the sections that would lead to the other lairs. He wanted to start with the leader farthest out—Ilari Morozov.

Morozov's luxury apartments were located all the way at the very back of the palace. His soldiers and their families had homes directly behind the palace. It made sense that they stayed close to him to protect him. Soldiers patrolled the hallway leading to the corner directly before the corridor to Morozov's double dragon doors. Just like the front doors, those dragons were red and black with scales blazing gold.

Two guards stood on either side of the doors, and they didn't look as if they intended to go anywhere soon. That could be a problem. The soldiers didn't come all the way to the apartment, but rather stayed on the other side of the corner. That still made it risky to take out the guards. The chances of discovery before he and Meiling were finished with killing all of the justices and were clear of the palace doubled. Still, he had no choice.

Meiling, we may have to change up our plans. They have guards on the doors.

I'm already on my way back to you.

That was his partner. Already one step ahead. Gedeon moved along the wall, part of it, keeping his energy low so it couldn't be felt by the shifters. As he approached the guard on the left, he could tell the shifter's leopard was leery. The guard grew restless to the point that he broke his position and walked down the corridor to the corner to peer down it for a moment. His partner joined him. They held a brief discussion, giving him just enough time to slide into the apartment, not through the large double doors that would tempt anyone to enter but would also trigger alarms throughout the palace. He entered through the slim door hidden in the panel behind the guard's position, which was used by the Russian for his own private entrance.

Gedeon hurried through the sets of spacious rooms toward the very back of the apartment, where Slayer indicated Ilari Morozov was. The Russian was still in his immaculate suit, although he wore no shoes and paced up and down in front of a long basin. The basin took up most of one wall, which was constructed out of ceramic. Morozov paused every now and then and would throw his hands at the wall. Gedeon could see the wall had charred spots that appeared to be old. There were no new ones and hadn't been for some time.

"It seems you've lost your ability to throw fire," Gedeon said. "That's such a shame. Do the others know?"

Morozov spun around, his eyes wild, shock on his face. "How did you get in here? Who are you?"

Gedeon had been across the room when he spoke. Now

in one single leap he was in front of Morozov. "I'm the boy you missed when you had my family murdered. Just as you missed Meiling when you had her family murdered. I hunted them down one by one and killed them. Tonight, all of you will die." He didn't wait. He used Slayer's speed and was on the older Russian, snapping his neck and dropping him onto the floor, grateful he didn't have time to do the things he would have liked to—things that would have reinforced that these people had shaped him into a monster.

It's done, Lotus. Get the guards to look the other way. They are. Get out of there.

Gedeon exited the apartment and hurried down the hallway to the corner where the guards were conferring once more. Their leopards were already calming due to Meiling's influence. He joined her and they made their way to Klim Zima's luxury suite. Zima's apartment was on the northern end of the palace and had a similar entrance to the one Ilari Morozov had, although his patrolling soldiers seemed far laxer.

Meiling distracted the guards at the double doors, allowing Gedeon to slip inside the apartment. Klim was in nightclothes, dozing in front of his massive television screen in his media room. Gedeon slipped up beside him.

"Klim. I just wanted you to know, before you die, that you lived your life stupidly. You should have found a mate for your leopard and someone to love you. Nothing you have is worth being alone and rotten inside."

Klim opened his eyes. His leopard stared at Gedeon with sick, crazed eyes. He nodded. "I know, but it was too late to turn back."

Gedeon broke his neck. *It's done.*

Come out now.

Meiling was like a breath of fresh air in his mind. He wanted to cling to her. There was no malice in her. No need for revenge or an eye for an eye. She wanted evil stamped out, but she didn't think in terms of making them pay. Because she was able to be so calm and think that way, she allowed him to be the same.

Gedeon was grateful for Meiling's calming effect as he entered Makar Turgenev's apartment. This was the man who had initiated the murders of his family. He was responsible for the murders of the family in North Korea as well as Meiling's family. The hatred and fear had originally begun with this man. Gedeon didn't want to feel that same hatred. He didn't want any part of Makar Turgenev's legacy in him.

As he walked silently through the man's living quarters, Gedeon was struck by how lavish and decadent each room was. Unlike the other apartments, Turgenev hadn't collected art or spent his fortune so much as hoarded it. There were gold bars stacked in several rooms. Other than enormous plants and a variety of beautiful water features in each room, the apartment's décor was mainly about the life of its occupant. On the walls were photographs of Turgenev duplicating the poses in portraits of powerful men from the past. He had them on the walls in every room. Some were paintings. The portraits were all of him. There were mirrors everywhere.

This was a man who appeared, on the surface, to be self-absorbed and vain. One might accuse of him of feeling superior to everyone else. Looking around the apartment, Gedeon got the impression it was just the opposite. He believed Makar Turgenev had no self-esteem and was doing everything in his power to build it.

There on the shelves in his library was an entire section of self-help books on building self-confidence. Self-image. This man had crushed the other families out of real fear. He had been afraid of them, so much so that he had devised a plan to wipe them all out so their children wouldn't have gifts that could allow them to slip past his guards, enter his home and confront him, just as Gedeon was doing.

"Turgenev. I think you know why I'm here and who I am."

Makar Turgenev stopped in the middle of doing a kata. He wore nothing but a loincloth as he performed his evening ritual before going to bed. He kept fit, practicing mind and body fitness regimens in order to be in as good shape as possible at all times.

"Volkov? I wondered about you. You were too confident. No one has ever been confronted by all of us and handled it the way you did. You impressed the others, but you made me suspicious."

"And yet it was still easy for me to get to you." Gedeon allowed amusement to creep into this voice.

"Why are you here?"

"You call yourself justice," Gedeon said. "But I seek justice. You plotted the murder of my family and Meiling's family. I'm here to see that justice finds you."

Makar glided closer, drying the sweat from his hands and face with a small towel. "That may be rather difficult if I don't agree to it."

"Then agree," Gedeon said and moved into Makar's attack.

The older Russian sprinted toward him, teeth bared in a vicious snarl. Saliva drooled in two long strings from the corners of his mouth as he snapped at Gedeon. His hands came up and he pushed a wall of flames at Gedeon.

Gedeon was prepared for whichever dragon move the Russian would choose to use. He had pulled every drop of water from the air in the apartment as he'd moved through it. Knowing he'd need it, he called on the water features Makar had incorporated into his décor. The rain clouds were already heavy, and the moment the flames rose seeking him, Gedeon countered the dragon fire with a leap into the air. His soaring move took him over the wall of flames as he dropped the deluge of water on the fiery blaze.

As he leapt over Makar, Gedeon delivered an extremely

strong front kick that snapped the Russian's head back and
sent him flying across the room. Makar landed on his back
and Gedeon was on him, knee to the chest, hand around
his throat, eyes blazing gold and green.

"You missed a boy as well as Meiling when you sent a
mob to murder innocent families, Turgenev. Yes, we have
gifts and we're fast and capable, but unlike you with your
petty jealousy and fear, Meiling is all about compassion
and kindness. She makes the world a better place. You
make me ashamed to be a shifter. She makes me proud to
be one. Your kind feel superior to the women because you
think you're so much stronger than they are. You're killing
our people, stamping them out of existence, and you're too
stupid to see it. Women like Meiling would have saved us."

As he spoke the truth as he saw it, his fingers bit into
Makar's throat and his knee pressed into his chest. He was
enormously strong. He was leopard. He had gifts. He didn't
have Meiling's compassion in these situations, although he
was desperately trying to be a better man for her. He stared
right into Makar's eyes as the life went out of him, looking
to see if the shifter had any regret or realization of the
crimes he'd committed. He saw nothing but hatred. There
was no remorse. What was wrong with these men that they
would trade hundreds of lives, maybe thousands, for wealth
that did nothing for them? It made no sense to him.

*It is done, my love. Come back to me. We have more
work to do before we go home.*

Gedeon left Makar on the floor with his oiled body and
his loincloth that no longer covered his flabby genitals.
The Russian's eyes were wide open, staring up at him without life. Makar lived no life, and it occurred to Gedeon
that he hadn't been living until Meiling entered his life.

Stop. Come back to me, Leopard Boy.

Love flooded his mind. "Fuck you, Turgenev. You don't
get any more of me. Not ever again." He turned and left
the apartment, not once looking back.

Bolin Wang sat in his hot tub, bubbles churning all around him. The room was dark, but the tub had ever-changing colors glowing on the walls and ceiling. The man's head rested on a pillow, and he was staring at the ceiling watching the colors change. Classical music played low but matched the rhythm of the changing colors.

"I knew you would come tonight, Gedeon," Bolin said, without turning his head. "The moment you walked into the room, I knew you were the one to bring retribution for what we've done to our people. So many mistakes. So many deaths on our heads. Once a path is chosen and we start down it, leaving it seems impossible."

"And the women you traffic? The women bought and sold? Brought into this place to pleasure your soldiers and then killed when you no longer wanted them around? What of them, Wang? Many of these women are really young girls. Is that one of these paths you started down and then couldn't get off of? Did you use these women and girls for pleasure and cast them aside as well?"

Gedeon saw the golden knife Bolin wielded beneath the water. The blade sliced into skin and a scarlet ribbon snaked through the crystal water.

"I did. So many women. Selfish pleasure. The only plea-sure I had in my life." The knife shifted from one hand to the other. The blade sank again as if thirsty for more. "Women are put here for our pleasure, Gedeon. To serve us." More crimson leaking into the water. "I'm surprised you haven't learned that lesson."

"I learned there are women who enjoy sex and will freely and mutually consent to any kind of sex I want. I don't take."

"Taking is part of the fun." Bolan smiled up at the ceiling.

Gedeon didn't have to pull Wang's head back. It was already back, lying on the pillow as he stared up at the colors. Gedeon reached for the hand still holding the knife under the water. Wrapping his fist around Bolan Wang's, he brought the blade up to Wang's throat and drove it deep, cutting into it, creating a smile. Let him smile while thinking about women whose lives he had destroyed.

Coming out, Lotus. I feel a little sick.

We're almost done.

Gedeon wanted to take her somewhere clean. Home. The swamp. Where people were not like this. Humans or shifters.

Gedeon entered Longwei Lis's apartment and it was empty. There was no sign of him. He had been there at one point. The robe he'd been wearing when Gedeon had seen him was laid out on the bed, but the man was gone. Gedeon checked every room carefully. That gave him a bad feeling in the pit of his stomach.

Not here. Let's check his son's room.

Kang had gone to his room in a shit mood because he had a woman there. He had planned to take out his frustrations on her. If Longwei had joined him, the woman could be in far more trouble than she could handle. He knew Meiling caught his thoughts.

I'm going in with you, Gedeon.

That might not be a good idea, Meiling. Let me check it out. We don't even know for sure if the woman is Cosette.

I know. I feel it. I have to go in with you.

Gedeon didn't argue with her. They slipped past the guards together and entered Kang's apartment. It was very quiet. Too quiet. The scent of blood was overpowering. Meiling reached out to him and Gedeon took her hand, just for a moment, to reassure her. He moved ahead of her to go into the bedroom.

Kang lay on the floor, blood congealed around his head. There were stab wounds on his chest. He'd been dead for hours. Longwei Lis, Kang's father, lay near the bed, completely naked, his tongue hanging out, blue, his eyes bugging out of his head, a wire around his neck pulled tight, cutting into the flesh.

On the bed, Cosette sat, fully dressed, her hands folded together in her lap. One foot tapped nervously, the only movement she made as she tracked Gedeon coming into the room. She looked like a young predator sizing him up.

"Cosette?" Meiling stepped out from behind him.

Cosette blinked several times, her gaze flicking back and forth from Gedeon to Meiling and finally settling on Meiling. Her lips trembled. She pressed her fingers to her mouth. "Meiling? I knew you would come. I knew you would. I did what you taught me and I was waiting for you."

Gedeon looked at the two dead men on the floor. His sweet, kind, compassionate woman had taught this little woman how to do *that*? He looked from one woman to the other.

Meiling gathered Cosette into her arms. "You did what you needed to do. I'm so proud of you. Let's get you home. We still have to get past the guards and make it through the lines of soldiers." She turned to Gedeon. "Did you bring that pill and the spray with you?"

He nodded and fished out the little bag, handing it over. Meiling gave the pill to Cosette to take. The girl did everything Meiling said without hesitation. She stripped, allowed Meiling to spray her body without asking questions and took the thin, rolled pants and long-sleeved tee that matched the ground outside in the dark. She tucked her hair into the dark cap and allowed Meiling to stripe her face with darker colors.

"Don't move or speak unless Gedeon or I direct you to. This is going to be very difficult," Meiling instructed.

Gedeon took one last look at the two dead men Cosette had killed in self-defense. He had no doubt that she would do exactly as they instructed.

They had planned for bringing out a prisoner once they knew Cosette had been taken. They took her out the side exit, careful to keep from triggering an alarm. That was the most difficult task. Gedeon had studied the palace's security system with meticulous attention to detail and then had Rene go over it with him just to be certain. Even a slight disturbance would be detected, but if the cameras or alarms went back online immediately, security would put it down to a glitch. Those did happen when the palace was so remote.

In the end, Gedeon was shocked by how easy it was to get Cosette out of the palace and through the line of soldiers to the car Rene had waiting for them. They went directly to the airport, where Etienne's private plane waited to fly them out of the country. Cosette waited until they were safely away until she had a much-earned breakdown.

As Gedeon watched his woman comforting the younger woman, he found himself fighting anger at the shifters who were so callous. Maybe they shouldn't survive as a species. Then Meiling looked up at him and smiled.

You spend too much time in the wrong world, Leopard Boy. We need to connect with some of the good ones.

Good men?

You're a good man. There are more. That was firm. His woman. Meiling.

20

GEDEON lay on the bed in his favorite place, his head on Meiling's belly while her fingers drifted through his hair. The sounds of the swamp played through their bedroom. Alligators bellowed at each other—two bulls bent on establishing dominion over territory and the females in it. A youngster had been foolish enough to challenge the resident male. Big Boy, as Meiling called him, wasn't taking any nonsense from the upstart.

Insects droned in relentless pursuit of musical talent when they had none, although Gedeon had come to love the sounds. All the different whistles and hums. The louder piercings and softer brushings, all coming together to make a background that was a ceaseless cacophony of noise. Snakes plopped into the water from the overhanging branches occasionally, emphasizing the rasping of the bullfrogs. The small tree frogs had a lot to say as they called out in an effort to attract mates. Gedeon wasn't impressed with their voices, and Meiling wanted to know where the Disney frogs were hiding so she could hear them sing.

There was the continual flurry of feet and fur pushing through the vegetation, the leaves and twigs that covered the floor of the swamp. Rats, voles, and numerous other rodents foraging for food and trying to stay under cover as they did so. To Gedeon, the sounds were loud and added to the symphony he heard playing.

"Love this, Lotus. Just lying in bed with you like this, listening to the swamp. Slayer's never been happier. I've never been happier. We're in a good place, aren't we? Tell me you're good."

Because after what he'd gotten himself into—not himself. This was no longer about Gedeon. This was Gedeon and Meiling together.

There was silence. A long one. Ordinarily, he would have raised his gaze to meet hers to get the lay of the land, so to speak. She wasn't the best at hiding her expressions from him. He thought it more prudent to just lie still and feel her fingers moving through his hair as long he could.

"Does that question have anything to do with the strange text I received from Evangeline a few minutes ago?"

His heart stuttered. He hadn't given his answer. He hadn't had time to broach the subject with Meiling. He didn't know how he felt about the things Drake Donovan had spoken to him about.

"What strange text?"

"All of sudden you want to share?"

Her tone was mild. Sweet even. But he winced all the same. They weren't prone to fighting. Meiling didn't throw tantrums. She wasn't moody unless Whisper was in heat. She was accommodating, usually following his lead or telling him what she'd like to do decisively. She wasn't the kind of woman to pick a fight for no reason.

Her fingers were still moving in his hair. Gentle. The

way she did when she was loving on him. "Do you have something you want to tell me, Gedeon?"

"If I wanted to tell you, Lotus, I would have shared already. I'm still working out in my head how to say it." He blurted it out. Yeah. That was him being a dumbass. He kept telling himself he was evolving, but when push came to shove and he did something he knew she wasn't going to like, he fell back on the old ways and acted like a complete idiot.

Her fingers stopped moving in his hair—a really bad sign. He turned over to lie on his side, propping up his head with his hand so he could look at her expression when they talked. He would need to know what she was thinking. She wasn't good at hiding her emotions from him.

"We talked about getting out of the business numerous times," he opened with. They had. Meiling often initiated the conversation.

Her eyelashes fluttered. That lower lip of hers drew his instant attention when she sucked it into the side of her mouth and bit down with her small white teeth. He couldn't help cupping the side of her face. Looking at Meiling meant touching her. That was just the way it was. He ran his thumb over the full curve of her lower lip, gliding over the spot where she had bit down for that one little moment.

"You seemed opposed to the idea, Gedeon," she reminded.

He had been opposed. She knew he wasn't someone to sit around idle. He needed to be busy. He wasn't the kind of man to take orders from someone else either.

"I'm not good at sitting around twiddling my thumbs, baby, you know that about me." He watched her carefully. As he did, he thought about what Bolin Wang had said about once taking a path and then not being able to get off it. Was it time to get off what he'd started? He'd accomplished a lot of good working the jobs he'd done, but he'd seen a lot of really bad shit. "I'm not stuck specifically on continuing with what I've been doing."

As for prepping her for the talk of what their future might hold, he didn't think he was doing a very good job. She must not have either, not with the look on her face. He didn't like that look. He'd never seen it before and couldn't interpret it.

"I know Drake Donovan has dropped by several times and spoken to you privately. You always tell me what's said in any private meeting, but you didn't after he talked with you. That's unusual. I waited. I was patient. Now I assume he was offering you a job with his company."

Gedeon cursed under his breath. Meiling. Too damn smart for her own good. They'd promised to have open communication. Tell each other everything. He sighed.

"It's a lot more complicated than that, Meiling, or I would have told you about it right away. I don't know exactly how I even feel about it." He sat up and ran both hands through his hair, the beginnings of a headache touching both temples.

"Maybe sharing, I could have helped you sort it out," she pointed out. "This way, you're carrying that burden alone. Since Donovan wanted to talk alone to you and you allowed that not just once, but *twice*, I would presume whatever job he's offering you, I'm not a part of and I'm not needed."

His chest constricted. Her tone was soft but there was an edge to it. Something different he hadn't heard before, just like the expression on her face. He started to open his mouth, give an immediate rebuttal, but he needed to listen to her. This had cut deep. He could see that it had. He hadn't meant it to hurt her. Damn it, when he didn't know what to do, he fell back on old habits.

Meiling sat up and scooted away from him, up toward the headboard. She settled there, pulling the sheet up to her waist, taking that from him. In the moonlight spilling from the open porch, she looked almost ethereal. She also looked sad.

"Donovan is offering me a job. I don't know if I even understand what he wants from me. It doesn't make sense. Well." He sat on the edge of the bed and then stood so he could pace, suddenly restless. "Maybe it does. I would never do the job without you. I just needed time to process what he was saying to me because, like I said, it didn't make sense."

"He's offering *you* the job. Not *us*," she qualified. Her gaze didn't leave his face. "Did you think about that, Gedeon?"

He had. He'd thought about that and how she wouldn't be in danger the way she was every damn time they took a job, although he wasn't sure what Donovan was offering would make things better. "What I thought about was keeping you safe. Knowing you'd have the friends you've always wanted. I didn't think in terms of who was doing the actual job because, like I said, I wasn't certain what it actually entailed."

"It sounded, from the text I received from Evangeline, like you had taken the job."

"I said I'd think about it. I would never take a job without talking it over with you first." He had told Donovan he was willing to learn more about the job.

Meiling remained silent and just looked at him. It was impossible to keep anything from her. She knew he wasn't telling her the entire truth. He didn't want to share. She wouldn't like it. Why was he even considering it? Because he needed the adrenaline rush.

"Tell me, Gedeon. All of it."

He turned back to her. "I've lived too long being a fixer, Lotus. I can't just retire. I know myself. I need the rush. The physical and mental activity." He made the admission reluctantly. With the admission came the reality of being who he was. What he was. Fixing problems didn't just mean negotiating. Calling in favors or trading them. Sometimes—often—it meant killing someone.

She didn't move or take her gaze from his face. She simply listened to him. He couldn't find judgment in her expression or in her mind.

"Donovan came to me and said he had a proposition. He noticed the way we were able to move so fast. He has been slowly taking out the heads of crime families and replacing them with men who will keep the crime from spilling beyond a certain level. I'm not explaining this very well." He pushed a hand through his hair. "There's always going to be an underworld, with criminals exploiting good people. The goal is to minimize the damage to those people, by controlling the underworld."

Her dark eyes stayed on his green ones. Focused. No blinking.

"They have people in place to stop human trafficking, but at the same time, they have to appear to be criminals. They work with other criminals. That way they always know what's happening in that world."

"What does Donovan want you to do?"

"He's setting up another one of his men to take over a territory. It's a particular brutal one that needs cleaning out. His man needs someone to head up his security detail. He'd like me to be that man. I thought if we liked the idea, we could take the job together. At least until you know if you're pregnant or not."

Her dark, feathery lashes fluttered. "Is that what this is all about? You're worried I'm pregnant? You're concerned I can't back you up properly anymore?"

He sank down onto the side of the bed. Close. "No, I'm not afraid of you. Just for you. I can't live without you, Meiling. As in I wouldn't want to be alive. I know you think I'm strong and I can do anything, but I couldn't do that. I wouldn't want to. So best answer, find a profession where I keep you at a distance from it. I put babies in you and hope like hell you want to stay home and raise them."

He blurted out the fucking truth. She could take it or leave it.

"I've loved you for so long, I don't even know when it started. I don't love anyone else. You're it, Lotus. I know I make you crazy with the way I do things sometimes, but I do them because I can't lose you. I won't lose you. You can get angry with me. You can give me that stare down you like to think is going to burn me but I think is cute. It doesn't matter. I'm keeping you alive any way I can. While we're at it and I'm laying this shit out for you, we're getting married too. No more stalling."

He was losing it. He *did* lose it. He'd just blurted out everything that was in his mind, in his gut, pressed deep into his chest, and had unfurled all at once and burst out of him before he could censor it.

Meiling stared at him without moving. Without blinking. Just stared at him as if he'd grown two heads. Hell. Maybe he had. He felt as if he'd run a mile. He pressed his hand over his chest. She turned him inside out.

"You said you love me. Out loud." Meiling whispered it, her dark eyes going liquid.

Gedeon forgot everything he was going to say. "Lotus, I tell you I love you. You have to know I do." She had to know.

"I know. You show me all the time, but you don't say it. This was the first time. It just caught me off guard is all." She looked up at him again, her eyes filled with love. "So, do you think you're going to take this job?"

"Only if Donovan offers us a good salary. By that I mean equal pay for you. I don't anticipate you working long because I think you're pregnant, so we'll need to negotiate money immediately."

"I'm not showing any symptoms." Meiling was indignant.

"Honey, in the last four days, you've cried a total of sixteen times. Three of those times were over shoes and how cute you thought they were. Two were because we were out of your favorite berries. Once was because the bed wasn't made properly, and you were too tired to make it. I pointed out that we were going to get in it, and that brought another flood of tears because you were so relieved. I'm just saying you aren't a waterworks kind of girl as a rule."

Meiling made a face at him. "Has it occurred to you that the raging hormones are leaving my body, and now I'm just trying to lead a normal life?"

"No, that didn't occur to me."

"It could be happening." She glared at him and then burst out laughing. "At least I'm not puking everywhere. That's a plus. If I were pregnant, I'd be puking. And I could be crying all the time, which I'm not, because I wanted to be pregnant and I'm not. Did you think about that? No, you didn't."

She wasn't making the least bit of sense. Meiling always made sense. And they had veered far off topic. He studied his woman carefully, trying to hear what she actually meant, the underlying subtleties that he might be missing. The truth was he didn't know shit about women or relationships. He only knew he loved her and he wanted her safe.

She looked especially beautiful to him, even with tears tracking down her face. Her skin had that glow to it that should have meant her leopard was coming close to a heat, but he knew she'd just gotten out of one.

Slayer, is it possible for Whisper to be going into another heat so soon?

Everything about Whisper's heat had been different than what he'd been told by other shifters. She'd risen too fast, almost without warning, and when she did, the results were nearly uncontrollable. It was almost as if she had too many hormones spilling from her body. She was such a small thing, but Gedeon suddenly remembered that, like Meiling,

Whisper would also carry the genetics for the special gifts. That might be the answer for the raging chemicals that had been dumped into Meiling's body just as Slayer dumped them into his.

She cannot go into heat again for a long while.

There was smug satisfaction in Slayer's tone, sending up all kinds of warning flags. Gedeon moved closer to Meiling, her shield now. Her dark knight. She blinked up at him with those feathery lashes that he always felt in his groin.

Gedeon framed her face with his hands, thumbs moving over her impossibly soft skin while he looked into her eyes. "I should have been telling you all this time how much I love you, Meiling. I showed you with my body, but I should have given you the words."

Slayer, why do you say it like that? Is Whisper already pregnant? Is Meiling pregnant?

Of course, they are pregnant. We are very virile. We will have strong children. Again, there was that smug, almost arrogant tone.

He bent his head to brush kisses from her left eye to the corner of her mouth. "I was a coward, afraid if I said the words out loud, let them out into the universe, you would be taken from me."

"I'm not going anywhere, Gedeon. I love you. We'll work out this job thing. I know you need action. I need to be with you. We'll work it out."

"You're pregnant." He announced it without preamble, sitting back, but still holding her eyes. "I hope you meant it when you said you wanted my children. I asked Slayer and he confirmed it. You should confirm with Whisper. I want children with you, Meiling. I want a family." Right then, he wanted the opportunity to have her again, drag her down on the bed and put his mouth between her legs, devour all the sweetness that was his Lotus Blossom.

More flutters of those eyelashes as she spoke with Whisper. A shocked look on her face. She flung out a hand toward

him. He caught it. He would always be there for her. Her
face lit up. The knots in his belly unraveled and he did exactly what he wanted to do. He caught the sheet and dragged
it off her before catching her ankles and pulling her down
to the center of the bed. She was Meiling, meaning she
didn't protest.

"Got to have you right now, Lotus. Celebration in order. Then we talk getting married immediately. Rene can
arrange it if you don't want to."

He heard her murmur something, but he had already
slid her legs over his shoulders and put his mouth exactly
where he needed it, tongue and teeth busy and the roaring
beginning in his ears. In other words, he couldn't hear a
thing. He could only feel his love for her welling up to mix
with the desire and lust that rose at the same time. His
Meiling. His woman. Bringing him to life.

Keep reading for an excerpt from
the next novel in the Torpedo Ink series
by Christine Feehan . . .

RECOVERY ROAD

Available soon from Berkley Romance!

EVERYONE had a breaking point. Everyone. Kir "Master" Vasiliev was aware he had been well past that point when he agreed to take the assignment. He never should have done it. Burning out when behind bars with no backup was a bad idea, especially if he didn't give a fuck whether he lived or died—which he didn't.

The only reason he didn't kill the two guards and the four prisoners right then and there was because he had a job to do, and he never let a job go unfinished. That was drilled into him. His club, Torpedo Ink, needed the intelligence, and he had been given the assignment to get the information and then kill the four men who had threatened their president and his family. That meant the two dirty guards who were involved with them had to die as well.

The eighteen charter members of Torpedo Ink had grown up together in a place loosely called a school in Russia.

Their parents had been murdered by a powerful man named Kostya Sorbacov. He took the children of his political enemies and placed them in one of four schools, supposedly to become assets for their country. That was true of three of the four schools, although all of them were brutal.

The fourth school was located far from the city, where the prison for the criminally insane—the ones the government refused to acknowledge existed—was housed. Pedophiles. Rapists. Serial killers. These were the men and women Sorbacov utilized as instructors for the children in the fourth school. Supposedly the children were to become assassins—assets for their country. What they really were, were playthings—toys for Sorbacov and his friends. Over twenty years, two hundred and eighty-nine children entered that school. Only nineteen survived.

Destroyer, the nineteenth survivor, had recently found his way to them and joined Torpedo Ink. Like Master, Destroyer knew his way around prisons, but Master had been trained to take these missions from a young age, and Torpedo Ink relied on him. Of all the members, he was the only one with a record in their new country. They all had impeccable paperwork, thanks to Code. Even Master's prison records were mostly manufactured. Still, the fact that he was officially dirty, when the rest of his club was officially clean, set him apart. Only Destroyer would understand that concept.

Torpedo Ink now spent a good deal of their time hunting pedophiles and those running human trafficking rings. None of them could ever live normal lives after what had been done to them as children, teens and young men and women. To survive, they had turned their bodies into weapons and developed what others might refer to as psychic talents. Czar had explained that he believed everyone had talents; they just didn't have to use them, so they never worked at making them strong. The members of Torpedo Ink had started as young children to practice through those long, endless days and nights in the basement of their hideous torture school.

Master was positive the cameras in the laundry room where the guards had brought him had been turned off. After all, the guards wouldn't want to be caught on film if the four prisoners about to beat the shit out of him accidentally killed him. Still, that didn't stop him from making certain the cameras weren't working. He wasn't about to take any chances. He never did. That was what kept him from ever getting caught.

Master had been sure to offend these specific prisoners several times in the yard that afternoon, even after he'd been warned. He'd done it out of anyone's hearing so that when the prisoners and the guards were found dead in the morning, and he was back in his cell, no one would think to connect him with the bodies. That was always key in this kind of mission. As the primary assassin, you were never caught with the target, not by anyone. There was nothing to connect you to the death. If you had to draw attention to yourself to get put into solitary, you picked a fight with some other prisoner, not the target.

It had taken time and expert maneuvering to get locked up near these four men so they would share the same yard and floor. Torpedo Ink had to be certain the intelligence was right about them. Once they'd locked onto them, Master had been put in place. Then it was a matter of finding out who was aiding them—passing on messages to them and allowing them out into the world when they were needed.

Master had grown up in Russia. He knew every classic way to hide an assassination team. Master had been placed in several prisons, hidden there, to be used when Sorbacov deemed it necessary. These four men were protected in that prison. They came and went, and they had special perks. Women were brought to them when they asked for them. They had whatever kinds of meals they wanted.

Cushy rooms. Master recognized it all, because he'd lived that life from the time he was a teen and could pass for an adult. It was a shit life to live. He spent a lot of time fighting, killing, getting beaten by guards, pacing in small cages, trying to stay sane.

Master stood against the wall, where the guards had thrown him. Just waiting. This was such a common scenario. He couldn't count the times he'd been in it, the new prisoner, stupid enough to cross those older ones who ran the prison and bribed the guards. It was always the laundry room or some smaller, concrete room with a hose to wash down the blood. Sometimes there were small windows where guards watched and bet on the action. He knew this wasn't going to be one of those times because it was probable the intention was to kill him. As if he gave a fuck. He didn't. And that was bad. For him. For them. Mostly for them.

The guards hadn't bothered with cuffs. Why would they? Four big Russians about to beat the fuck out of him for his "indiscretion." The guards locked the laundry room doors and sat back to watch the show. They parked themselves on the long table that prisoners used to fold the laundry, grinning from ear to ear. This certainly wasn't the first time they'd brought someone for the four Russian assassins to teach a lesson to.

"He's a big fucker, Boris," Shorty, one of the guards, said. "Strong as an ox."

Boris didn't bother to answer the guard or even look at him. "You got something to say to me now, freak?" he hissed.

Master raised an eyebrow. Answering in Russian, he called him several names, including degenerate, a brainless obnoxious pig who could only hang with monkeys. He indicated the other three men with him. He was fluent in several languages, but like Boris and the other four prisoners, he had been born and raised in Russia.

He might look all brawn, but he had a brain. He was born with the odd talent of seeing in numbers. He could compute numbers almost faster than any computer. His brain just worked out any problem and spit out the answer. He had instincts for investments, and when Code, their resident genius hacker, stole money from criminals, he knew how to utilize that money to the fullest. As the treasurer of the club, he oversaw the money and made the investments. He also played several instruments, and his main job was construction. He had an affinity for wood. Now, looking passively at Boris, he taunted him in his bored voice, getting creative with his insults, because he was a creative kind of man.

Boris roared and came at Master, his arms spread wide. Master stayed with his back against the wall, on the balls of his feet, shoulders loose, and as the other man came in, he snapped out his hand like a knife, driving it straight into the exposed throat. Boris choked, coughed. His eyes rolled back in his head and he went down to his knees, both hands going up to wrap around his throat. Master followed up with a strike to the back of his skull, driving him hard toward the cement floor. Boris face-planted so hard the sound seemed to reverberate through the entire laundry room.

"Damn!" Shorty laughed. "That was fast. Should have been taking bets on the new guy."

"Too late now," Longfellow, the other guard, said mournfully. He moved a little closer to survey the damage Master had done to Boris.

The Russian assassin was vomiting, but not lifting his head, so he was by turns choking and getting the mess all over his face. He lay gasping for breath, desperate to breathe around the endless retching.

The three other Russians fanned out, coming at Master from three sides. They were silent as they tried to surround him, their faces masks they'd learned from their teachers in the schools they'd attended, but they couldn't hide the fury—or slight trepidation—in their eyes. In their experience, no one had ever bested Boris in the prison. Most likely they had never dealt with anyone as fast or as calm as Master.

Master didn't move, keeping the wall at his back and Boris on his left. That meant he only had to deal with two of them immediately and the guards. The third had to get around the body of his fallen friend before he could actually be of some help to his friends.

Kir "Master" Vasiliev had been in this scenario too many times. He knew their moves before they made them. They might be faster than any who had come before, but Sorbacov's sick trainers had forced him to learn these tactics in very brutal ways. That fourth school, the one he'd attended, had been right there with its own prison on the grounds. The instructors had plenty of opportunities to teach a young boy how the prison system worked. How corrupt the guards could be. How complicit. How the inmates could be beaten, raped or killed by other stronger, more powerful prisoners in just such setups as this one. He'd learned all of the various setups because he'd lived through them all.

His training hadn't been simulated. Unlike other children who had been sent into the prison to be "trained," he hadn't died. He'd survived. He'd become a warped, scarred, dead soul of a man with a hefty criminal record. He was the only member of Torpedo Ink who still had that record, and it was ongoing. Absinthe could get rid of the charges eventually, but they were still out there, looking as if he had been freed on technicalities.

He waited, knowing what was coming, and there it was, without warning, the familiar adrenaline rushing through his veins like a drug. The need for violence. The only time he felt alive. He wasn't like Reaper and Savage, or even Maestro. He didn't need or want to take an opponent apart.

That wasn't his thing and never would be. No, he needed the actual war, the fight, the pounding of fists, the slash of the knife, the precise blow of the foot sending so much power and energy through a human body that the shock shattered internal organs.

He had spent a good portion of his life behind the walls of some kind of prison. That had been his specialty, what Sorbacov had him trained for. He was the chameleon, able to, even as a teen, get into the right block, assassinate the right prisoner and never have an ounce of suspicion directed his way.

In order to gain those skills and accomplish the mission, again and again, he'd been beaten and raped repeatedly from the time he was a toddler. He'd learned to kill. To make weapons out of nothing. To make himself into a weapon. To endure pain and put it to use. Pain kept him sharp when he was completely on his own in those hell-holes. Pain fed the anger and craving for violence so that it raged in him and made him stronger mentally and physically. Now that his companion was here, racing through his veins, he moved with blurring speed.

Master kicked Avgust, the largest of the four assassins hiding in prison, so hard in the kneecap they all heard the sickening crunch. Adrenaline-laced joy rushed through his veins. These were the only moments left to him now to actually feel, as disgusting as it might be. The edge of his boot caught the assassin in the side of the head deliberately as he swung around in a flowing motion toward Edik, one of Avgust's partners. The blow snapped Avgust's neck, killing him. He wasn't important to the interrogation anyway.

Master spun away from Edik's homemade knife, catching his wrist as he did so, completely controlling his arm with his superior strength and the momentum of both their bodies. He plunged the razor-sharp blade into Edik's throat, dropping him and then going straight for Longfellow, who stood just one scant foot away, his mouth gaping open.

Slashing the blade across the guard's throat, Master kept moving with blurring speed, having gone over and over the moves in his mind, knowing what he had to do to survive. He slammed his fist into Shorty's throat, putting his body weight behind the blow, going in for the kill.

There was one prisoner left standing, and two alive. Boris was still on the floor, unable to stand. Still coughing. Master had killed four men in under a minute.

The remaining assassin, Ludis, faced him with disbelieving eyes. "Who the fuck are you?" he demanded. He was the acknowledged leader of the group, the one Master needed to answer the questions he'd been sent in to ask.

Master calmly walked over to Boris and snapped a front kick to his left temple with the toe of his boot, again putting his body weight behind it. The angle allowed him to slam Boris's head into the concrete wall so hard they heard the fracturing, as if the skull were an eggshell. Boris tipped over, his breath coming in ragged pants, his eyes wide open in shock.

"Need you to answer a couple of questions for me," Master stated calmly. "You had a nice setup. Hiding in plain sight. Must have been paid a great deal of money to sit in prison though. Fuckin' hate these places."

Ludis was calm. He lit a cigarette and leaned a hip against the long table where the guards had been sitting. "You're the one we've heard rumors about all our lives. You slip in and out of prisons, no matter how high the security. You assassinate your target right under the noses of the guards and no one ever figures out who you are or how you do it. You've been at it for years. Makes sense that you're Russian. One of us."

Master nodded. Ludis was thinking hard, speculating, trying to figure out how he was going to kill Master and get out of the situation alive. That wasn't happening.

"The four of you were sent out by your little mistress

to wipe out a man's family in Sea Haven. Viktor Prakenskii's family. She wanted all of them dead."

Ludis's face went very still. Master walked over to Boris and slammed his boot into his ribs, deliberately crushing them, right over his left lung. Ludis straightened, but when Master turned toward him, he put his hands up and once again rested his hip on the table.

"We couldn't get near them. We were lucky to get out of there with our lives. Our intel wasn't good. You taking over the job?"

Master shrugged. "Did she pull you back or did you make the call?"

"I made the call. We don't take suicide missions. She was pissed as hell."

"Her name."

Ludis shook his head. "I can't tell you that. You know the code."

Master turned and stomped Boris's left lung. Boris gurgled and little red bubbles appeared around his mouth.

"What the fuck?" Ludis shouted, losing his feigned cool.

"Isn't that what you had in mind for me?" Master asked.

Ludis settled with obvious effort. "I still have it in mind."

"Her name. I've got all night, remember. The guards arranged to have the room so you could take your time with me."

Ludis swore in Russian.

Master delivered another kick, this time to Boris's groin, smashing through his balls and crushing his penis. "You know when he's gone, I'm going to have to start on you. You aren't giving me much choice."

"She goes by Helena now. She wasn't Helena when she was a child, but that's what she calls herself now."

"Helena what? Where is she?" Master asked patiently.

"Helena Smirnov. No one ever knows where she is. When she wants to see you, she comes to you."

"How many teams does she run?"

"Ours and at least one other. She has access to more, but we were hers exclusively and so is the other team. She does all the recruiting."

"For the Russian and his Ghost assassins."

"If you know everything already, why the fuck did you come here to kill everyone?" Ludis demanded.

Master could see the man was working himself up to make his play. Ludis shifted to the balls of his feet, and then sudden comprehension slid into his eyes. He swore again in his native language.

"You're one of them. From the fourth school. Sorbacov's killers. You're one of them. No one has ever seen one of you. No one believed any of you actually survived, but you're one of them, aren't you? I was just making shit up when I implied you were the chameleon, no one ever believed there was such a person. But there is. You're from that school. You are the chameleon."

Master didn't react. Didn't blink. Just stared at him with a blank expression.

"Damn you, at least give me that much. You're going to kill me. You killed my team."

"You didn't recognize the name? Viktor Prakenskii? Think about that name. Where have you heard it before?"

Ludis shook his head. "She wouldn't. Not after him. I never connected the name with him. Not once, because he had to be dead. He was a legend. Not real. Not real, like you're not real. And she wouldn't send us after him."

"She sent you after him," Master confirmed. "Viktor sent me after you. And she's going to die for what she did. He'll wipe out every one of the Ghosts if they come after his family. No one fucks with him." Master shrugged again, watching Ludis carefully.

Master rarely talked. He saw no point in conversation once he was through with them, once he was going to kill his opponents, but it was possible Ludis would give him more information simply because he was shaken or angry. Master had come to this prison to get as much information as possible and to kill the assassination team sent after Czar's family. No one tried to kill the president of Torpedo Ink's family and got away with it. No one. Master wouldn't have considered going back to prison for any other reason than this one.

Czar's wife, Blythe, was the heart of their club. Without her, none of them would have a clue about humanity. Czar had been their moral compass growing up. He'd given them a code to live by, but they were killers, they had to be in order to survive. He'd brought them home with him to Blythe. She'd taken the club members in and taught them what unconditional love was. Not a single one of them had believed Czar when he'd told them about her—what she was like. Now they believed she could walk on water.

Nothing, no one, would have ever persuaded Master to enter a prison willingly again, with this one exception. Blythe. Czar's children. All of them were adopted. Blythe had taken in the three girls they'd rescued from a trafficking ring. At least two of the girls, the third, their little sister, they'd gotten from the foster home so they could all be together. Then Kenny, a teenage boy the club had rescued on one of their missions. Lastly, little Jimmy, a boy being auctioned off to the highest bidder. She'd welcomed all of the children. Every last one of them.

"I was part of the second school." Ludis gestured toward the others. "We all were. We didn't want to be part of the Ghosts. We stuck together and went out on our own. Helena approached us and ended up hiring us for a few of her own jobs separate from what the Russian wanted. She works for him, but she wanted her own teams, loyal only to her."

"Who is the Russian?"

Ludis shook his head. "Only Helena knows. At least she's the only one who talks directly to him. Seriously, I never thought it was possible to meet one of you. I never would have gone after Prakenskii's family had I known it was him. You have to believe me."

Master waited for the attack. It was coming. Ludis was definitely working up his courage. "Why would Helena send you after them?"

"I have no idea. She started acting strange a few weeks ago. Secretive. She always talked to us. All of us sudden, she went very closed-mouth. She began going to a kink club in San Francisco regularly and wanted a couple of us with her to have her back. It isn't all that easy disappearing out of here weekend after weekend like she wanted us to."

Ludis made his play, coming at Master with a smooth number of fast-snapping front kicks to drive him back and into the position he wanted him. Master simply stood still, on the balls of his feet, legs shoulder-width apart, blocking every kick with a smooth bat of his palm. He moved with blurring speed, suddenly gliding on the floor with his body, catching his legs between his opponent's and rolling, taking him down in a scissor move.

Ludis hit the cement floor belly first, Master coming down hard on top of him, his fist hammering hard several times in his kidneys. He planted his knee on Ludis's spine and trapped his head in his hands, snapping the neck with a hard jerk.

Kir Vasiliev would leave this prison very soon. The charges against him would be dropped. All evidence would be proved false. He would go back to his club and be their numbers man, bury himself in his music and working with wood, in the things that kept him sane—he hoped. Absinthe would come for him.

It wasn't like he had the information the club had hoped for, but they were a step closer—and he'd gotten this assassination team. Helena might think twice before she sent her second team after Czar's family. Could she afford to lose more of her men? She'd have to weigh that price tag.

Consider what it would mean to pit her people against Torpedo Ink. She'd lose her teams, one man after another. She had to know who they were and where they came from.

Master made certain there wasn't a trace of blood on him. He'd been careful of his clothes and boots. He hadn't wanted to use a knife. Often, when one stabbed or sliced into flesh, you cut your own skin, leaving behind traces. He hadn't. He was too professional for that shit. Still, he was meticulous, going over every inch of what would become a crime scene in the morning when the bodies were discovered.

He had to make certain the guards' phones didn't contain any evidence that he had been the prisoner they were bringing to Ludis and his crew. He took his time, not hurrying, not letting nerves get to him. When he made his way back to his cell, he was just as careful, not touching anything, not allowing a camera to pick him up. He also made doubly certain he followed the exact route the guards had taken him, back through the narrow hallway only the privileged used, so no prisoner spotted him as he let himself once again into his solitary confinement cell.

It was only a matter of allowing time to pass without losing his mind or letting anything get to him before Absinthe came to get him out. Absinthe was their club attorney, and he could work magic on paper or off, get anyone to do what he wanted. He could compel truth from just about anyone. They wanted Absinthe to get his hands on the Russian woman and find out just why she was after Czar. No one knew, not even Czar.

Master paced back and forth like an animal for the next few days in that small cell. Push-ups. Pull-ups. Sit-ups. Pacing again. Anything physical to keep his body as exhausted as possible. He didn't sleep much. He hadn't for years, which left time for a lot of physical activity as well as reading, music and his investments.

Just as expected, all hell had broken loose in the morning

when the guards and four longtime prisoners were found dead in the laundry room. The laundry room appeared to be locked from the inside by the guards. It was a mystery that the detectives and prison authorities were frantic to solve. The public—and the politicians—tended to demand answers when murders happened inside a prison.

The glitches in the security cameras were later attributed to the guards. There was money in their accounts going back several years that seemed to be unaccounted for. The rumors were rampant in the prison—as they always were. Evidence was piling up that something shady had been going on with those prisoners and the guards. Who had killed them and why?

It was a classic assassination meant to rock the system and be very public. Evidence was fed to the investigators in just the right places. Bank accounts. Tips. Other prisoners coming forward to tell of the privileges given to the dead men—how everyone feared crossing them because they were protected. It was even rumored from prisoners that women were brought in for them or they were taken out often when those four prisoners wanted to leave to party.

Master wasn't even part of the investigation. He had no interaction that anyone really saw with the prisoners or guards in question. He hadn't been in that prison for very long. He simply waited, counting the days and nights, sliding back into that well of darkness that had been his home for far too much of his life.

He was quiet and he functioned, giving the club what they needed. He played in the band, practiced with the other band members often. He worked with his hands with the wood, building whatever was needed. He was good at it; the wood revealed so much of history to him. And there were always the numbers. He lost himself in numbers and that was what kept him sane—if he was sane. He questioned that often. Too often, lately. Especially when he did pull-ups in that small little cell.

What was he going back to? A life where no one saw him. He really was what others had whispered about him—the chameleon. He became what Sorbacov needed. And then his country. And now the club. It didn't matter that no one saw him because if they did, they would see the killer in him. The man who couldn't feel anything but that hot rage flowing through his veins. Or hot need.

The others didn't understand that either. What happened to him when he came out of the small little cell. What Sorbacov and his friends had programmed his body to need. He could already feel that building inside. That dark lust. One more terrible difference to set him apart from the others in his chosen family.

#1 *NEW YORK TIMES* BESTSELLING AUTHOR

CHRISTINE FEEHAN

"The queen of paranormal romance...
I love everything she does."

—J. R. Ward

For a complete list of titles,
please visit prh.com/christinefeehan